BOUND F

Inca Empire

COLUMBIA
ECUADOR
Quito
Tomebamba (Cuenca)
Tumbes
BRAZIL
Cajamarca
PERU
(Lima)
Machu Picchu
Cusco
(La Paz)
Pocona
CHILE
Empire Boundary
Stone-paved Road
ARGENTINA
Tucuman
500 miles
500 km
(Santiago)

Bound for Inca Snows

K.L. Smith

North Star Press of St. Cloud, Inc.

Cover art: Cynthia Kath

Illustrations: Corinne A. Dwyer

ISBN: 0-87839-216-5

First Edition, July 2005

www.incatales.com

Library of Congress Number:

Cataloging Data:
1. Inca 2. Machu Picchu 3. Peru 4. Andes 5. Ecuador

Printed in the United States of America by Versa Press, Inc., East Peoria, Illinois.

Published by
North Star Press of St. Cloud, Inc.
P.O. Box 451
St. Cloud, Minnesota 56302
nspress@cloudnet.com

Acknowledgements

It is said that hindsight is 20/20. Nonsense. Distinguishing fact from fiction is remarkably difficult; ask any jury or politician. Within our own lives, we are all revisionists. We remember only fragments of our lives and modify our memories over time. As a result, our personal histories are biased and often contradict the memories of our family and friends. In a similar fashion, the accounts of the early Spaniards in South America are also incomplete and conflicting. As a result, I have relied on the work of contemporary scholars whenever possible. These professionals return to archeological evidence to draw conclusions about the pre-Hispanic cultures of South America, and dovetail those findings with the early writings.

Although fiction, this book could not exist without the excellent work of these professionals. Of particular importance were: David Dearborn, Michael Moseley, Suasan Niles, Rusty Russell and Vick Funk of the Smithsonian Institution, William Sillivan, and Gary Urton. Any errors in interpreting or extrapolating the work of these scholars are entirely my own. See the website for a complete bibliography.

For their invaluable expertise in transforming a manuscript into a book, Corinne Dwyer, Seal Dwyer, and Cynthia Kath deserve a standing ovation.

On a personal note, I am grateful for the support I received from my writing colleagues and friends. Without Jane Sarno's encouragement and guidance, I doubt I would have found the courage to write. The 42nd Street Irregulars, my writing group, offered excellent help. Dan, Candy, Rick, Kit, Don, Jean, Renee, and Marydel each provided expertise from their fields of writing, weaving, spiritualism, copy editing, and reading. Finally and most important, I can never adequately thank Dan Smith, my spouse, who applauded my efforts and lovingly buoyed my spirits.

While this book includes many aspects of the known history, it is a work of fiction that is colored by my travels, intuition, and dreams. I hope to portray my profound respect for today's indigenous people of the Andes and their ancestors and to honor their trials and accomplishments. Yusulipayki!

Contents

Genealogy of the Incas

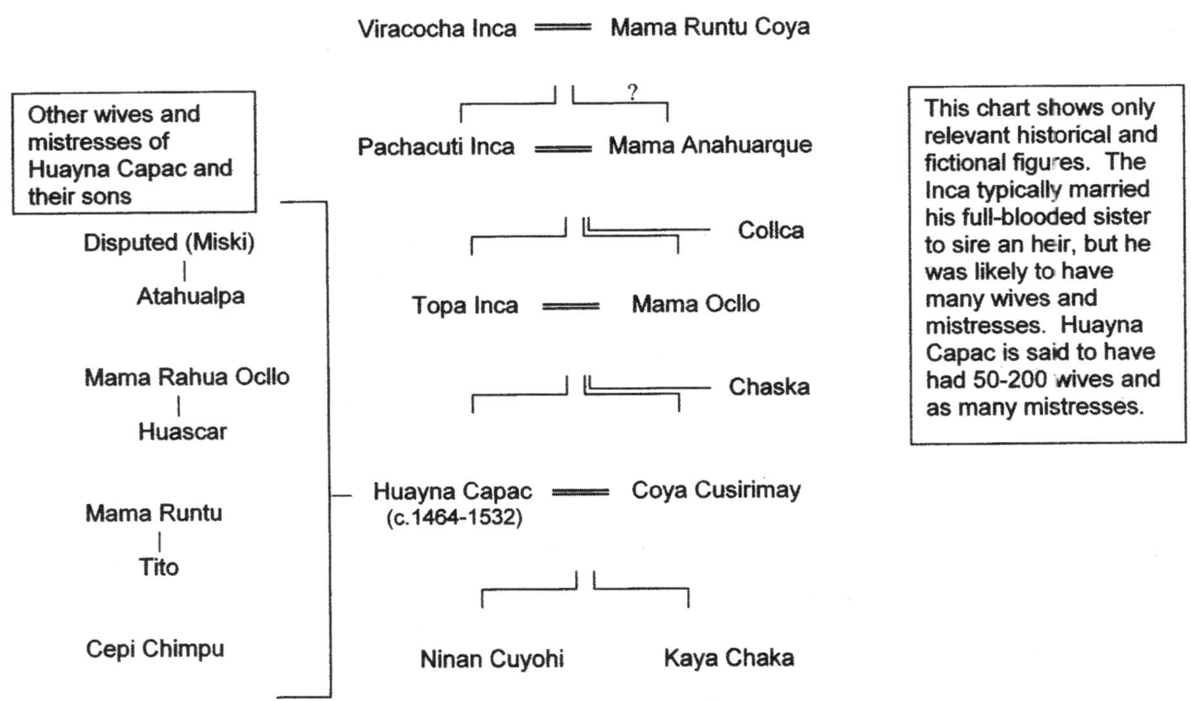

Bound for Inca Snows

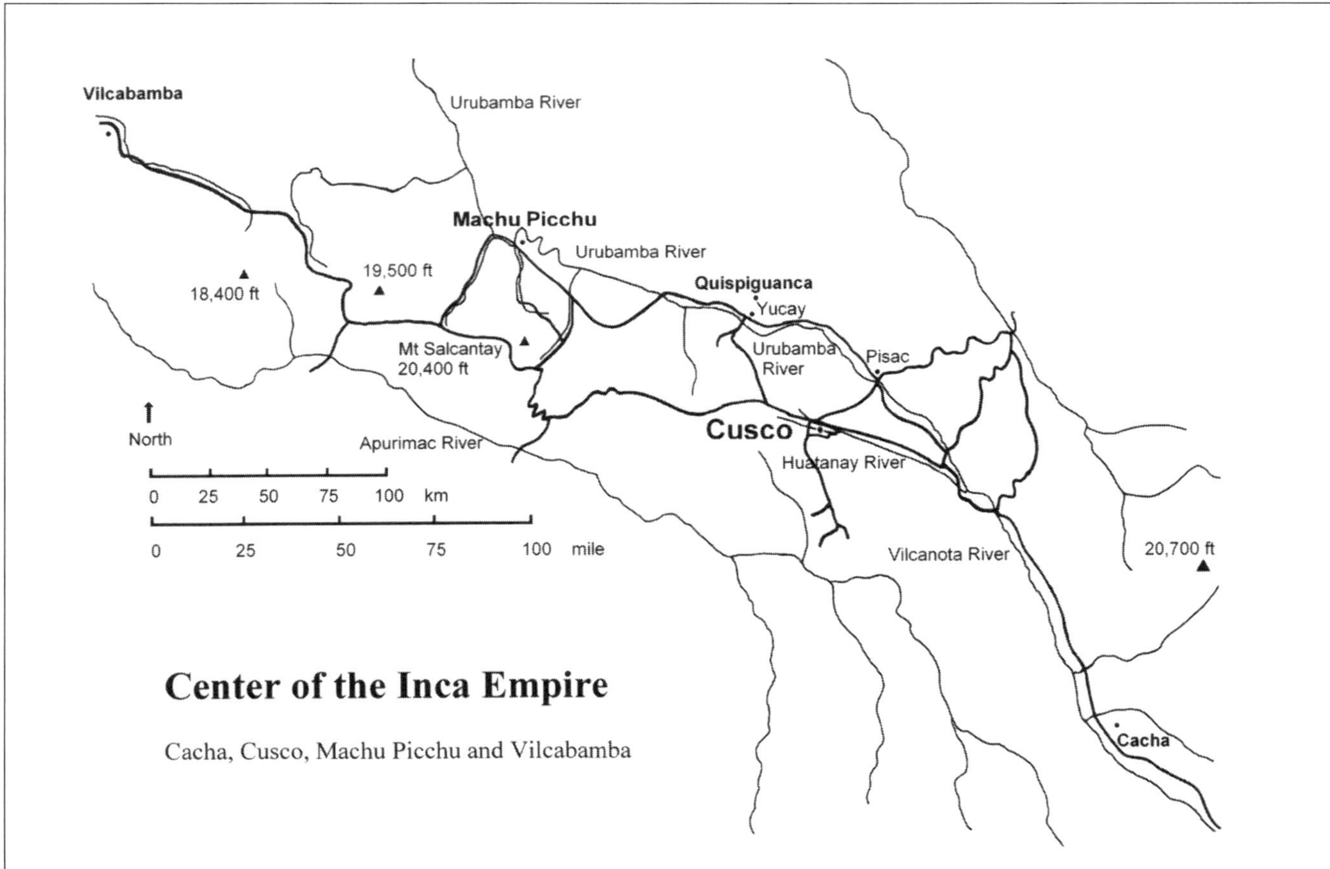

Center of the Inca Empire

Cacha, Cusco, Machu Picchu and Vilcabamba

Cusco

Ninan

My father strode past me into the courtyard, while my mother chased after him. "This is ridiculous. Just tell Umu Pilaca you canceled the ceremony," she demanded.

"I can't," he replied.

"Or you won't. What's the matter with you? Have you no decency?"

"All right, I won't. I have a duty to perform, and I intend to do it." He walked away, adding with a dismissive wave, "Besides, you've always known this day would come."

"Have you no feelings for your only daughter?"

"Of course I do, perhaps even greater than you. Judging from your carelessness, it's your affection that's questionable." He tipped his head toward me, but locked in a mutual stare, neither parent looked my way.

"That was an accident. Ninan is an active boy," she rightly defended herself. While I had been running along the top of a stone wall, I had turned to see how close Pacas was following me. The wall curved and I had run off the edge and landed on my ankle in the street below.

"You can't seem to care for one child. He could have been killed." The corners of his mouth turned up slightly as he crossed his arms. "He's still a bit young, but I think it's time he was in my care."

Being with the men before going through the rites of manhood was an exciting honor, and I smiled broadly, although neither noticed.

"Absolutely not! He's my son," she erupted. "He's too young. You can't have him." She paused and added, "Besides, you're too busy with your women to care for Ninan."

His smirk disappeared. "Other women know how to care for my needs." He nodded as he thought for a moment. "I could make time for the boy."

"He's not ready to be with the men!" my mother screamed.

"Then take care of him. Surely you can raise one child."

"I can raise two. Now cancel the ceremony!"

"No! We leave for Coricancha at noon."

Without noticing me, my father stormed out, and my mother, red with fury, retreated in the opposite direction. Ignored by both parents, I sat alone on a courtyard bench wondering what ceremony could cause such an argument. There was no festival today, at least none of the standard ones. Inti Raymi, the new year's festival, was still a week away. I'd never heard my parents fight before, or in the many years since. I probably wouldn't have heard this argument if I hadn't hurt my ankle. Normally I'd be playing with Pacas, but instead I was confined to the family courtyard. My swollen ankle still throbbed whenever I tried to move it, so I sat quietly and played with my soldiers. The cool, sunny morning passed slowly as their fight gnawed at me.

At noon my father returned wearing his regular clothes: a *cumbi** tunic stopping just above his knees, a red cloak hanging to mid-calf and sandals on his feet. Since he carried his scepter and wore his gold helmet with a red wool fringe on his forehead, I knew he was ready to leave Casana, the official name of our palace. Tall, muscular and proud, he was a handsome man. His dark eyes found me sitting on the same bench. "Where's your mother?" he asked in a deep, resonant voice.

"I don't know. She hasn't come back."

Surrounded by fitted-stone buildings with thatched roofs, the courtyard was rather small for such a tall man. He crossed it with ten paces, stopped and returned. Next he followed the circumference, inspecting the small fountain directly opposite me as he passed. Irritated to be kept waiting, he charged off toward his private quarters as he threw a comment over his shoulder. "Tell your mother to wait."

A short while later I heard shuffling sandals and a quiet conversation in the corridor leading to my mother's dwelling. Still out of sight, my mother said softly, "Well, at least our secret is safe." A fight and a secret. At the time, I understood neither but I knew something important was happening.

With my sister cradled in her arms, my mother rounded the corner with Cepi, my father's second wife. Cepi, walking beside my mother, smiled and cooed to the baby. They were in the middle of the courtyard before either looked up to realize that I, not my father, waited for them. "Where's

* See glossary at the back for words specific to the Inca era.

your father?" my mother asked. Her puffy eyes accentuated her usual gaunt appearance.

"He was here, and then he left again. He said you should wait."

"Humph," was her only reply. She tightly clutched my sister who was half-hidden by my mother's royal blue shawl. Made of the finest vicuna wool, the shawl hung from her shoulders to her calves and nearly covered her ankle-length, rather ordinary white dress. As usual, her luxurious black hair was tightly pulled off her face but drifted down her back almost to her waist. Cepi's similar dress showed occasional stains and one obvious place where she had hurriedly darned a tear. Together they settled on the bench close to the bubbling fountain, but they didn't have to wait long.

My father's confident gait carried him to the courtyard where he noted my presence and the others across the courtyard with a single sweep of his head. Still wearing the gold headpiece of the Inca and carrying his scepter, he glittered as brightly as the noonday sun. "Let's go. Cepi, you carry Ninan."

"Me? I'm not dressed for such an important occasion," Cepi replied, astonished by his command.

He waved his empty hand. "It doesn't matter. Bring the boy. He must witness the event." He impatiently watched as she helped my mother rise with my sister and walked to me.

I had no idea I was to go to the ceremony, but I was bored and was happy to be included, whatever the reason. Protecting my ankle, I stood on the bench, and Cepi hoisted me to her ample hip. With my injured foot dangling in front, I hung on her shoulder while she supported my bottom with her interlocking hands.

My father, the Inca Huayna Capac, and my mother, Coya Cusirimay, walked side-by-side across the courtyard and down the open-air corridors while Cepi and I followed at a respectful distance. We wound through the palace and finally reached the main courtyard beside the front entrance. Much larger than the family courtyard, this was my favorite place in the palace because the walls were painted white and decorated with brightly colored wall hangings. Fashioned entirely of feathers, their geometric designs came to life in the ripples of the reflecting pool before them.

We crossed the courtyard without stopping, passed through the enormous wood door and emerged on Haucaypata, the main plaza of Cusco. Now in public, my father slowed his pace to a stately strut and held his scepter across his chest. Never lifting her head to see the plaza, my mother walked beside the emperor with my sister in her arms. As usual, small groups of people were scattered about, and the Inca greeted the men by name as we passed. For the first time in days, I was out of Casana, and I relished the wide open expanse of the plaza and the magnificent palaces of the former Incas that surrounded it. The home of my grandfather proudly stood across the plaza from ours. The palace of his father, the great Pachacuti, towered to our left, and beside it laid the mansion of the first great ruler. Over the walls, the peaks of thatched roofs suggested the arrangement of the buildings and courtyards beyond. Pacas and I were regular visitors to all of them, but secretly we agreed that Casana was the best because it had more buildings to hide in and more open space to play.

Cepi followed my parents along the stone channel of the Huatanay River, leaving the Hanan section of the city behind us. The wide stone road we followed was lined with homes of prominent citizens and led into the Hurin section, the religious area of the city. Eager to see everything, I wiggled about while Cepi panted to keep pace.

We were halfway to the temple when the curved walls of the platform beneath the sacred buildings came into view. At the base of the platform a grassy garden stretched across the floodplain to the river. Along the river, pepper trees provided a shady retreat from the summer sun and rows of mature, carefully tended nut trees and acacia shrubs lined the other sides of the plaza. The gardens were nice, but dominating the platform above us, the Coricancha Temple inspired every visitor with its unforgettable splendor. Covered with gold and silver sheets, every exterior wall shone with the brilliance of the sun. Occasionally, someone moving among the temple buildings accidentally reflected a beam of sunlight that radiated a momentary sparkle. I watched for sudden bright spots in the shady corners around the entire valley and even up the mountain slope behind the temples.

My father still walked beside my mother as they ascended the stairs to the temple. Still carrying me, Cepi struggled to climb the stairs. We had only just removed our sandals, as was the custom, when Umu Pilaca arrived with an unfamiliar priest. My father spoke first, as usual. "Good afternoon, Umu Pilaca and Umu Riku."

"Good afternoon and welcome," Umu Pilaca responded for both priests. "We're ready to begin in the Temple of Inti."

The first time I saw Umu Pilaca I was frightened by his wrinkled face and white hair, but my father explained he was just very old. He stood with his head bent forward, so I thought he was angry, until I learned he was just very stern and insisted on perfect behavior in the temples. Leading the way, Umu Pilaca shuffled across the dense white sand of the central courtyard. My mother walked with us, while my father placed his hand on Umu Riku's shoulder and greeted him informally, "Riku, how are you? I trust your journey from Machu Picchu was satisfactory."

"Yes, thank you. I was a bit slower than usual since I traveled with Iska, but the weather was fine and the road is in good repair. We'll return immediately after the ceremony."

"Excellent. Is everything prepared for Kaya?"

Riku nodded, and my father stated his approval as they stepped into the open air Temple of Inti.

Cepi scanned the temple, and a friendly woman pointed to the bench near the altar where Cepi quickly unloaded me. "You should be able to see from here, but if you want to move, let me know," she said.

I nodded, having no idea what I was to see or what the best vantage point might be.

Umu Riku followed us to the bench and stood beside the woman who directed us there. "You must be Ninan. It is a pleasure to finally meet you."

Feeling uneasy, I stared up at the strangers while Cepi joined my mother near the entrance. With eyes lost behind her pudgy cheeks, the round woman watched Umu Riku, who stood silent for a moment, his large head resting on his slightly rounded shoulders. Not as old as Umu Pilaca, he showed his years with only a few white streaks in his hair, making him the second person I'd seen with white hair. "I am Umu Riku, a priest, and this is Iskanikin Mama, a Mamacona. Most people call us Riku and Iska. We're both from Machu Picchu and have come for the ceremony." Riku studied me as he spoke; I felt as transparent as clear water under his inspection.

"How did you hurt your foot?" he asked, and I was forced to explain that I fell when I was running. He knelt in front of me and gently pressed the bandage as he moved my foot back and forth. "It will hurt for a while, but you've done no permanent damage. That's very good because then you can visit me at Machu Picchu when you get older. You'd like it there."

I nodded but added nothing.

Since entering the temple, Huayna Capac and Umu Pilaca stood by the altar, discussing the gold statues they examined together. Finally, after my father nodded, Umu Pilaca turned to address the small audience. "We are ready to begin. Coya Cusirimay, bring your daughter forward."

Still clutching my sister, she slowly took one step forward, stopped, and eventually took a second step. All the while her cold, round eyes were fixed on my father. Huayna Capac, frozen in position beside the priest, held her eyes and willed her forward. Finally, in spite of her resistance, she stood alone before them while Cepi cowered in the doorway. Holding his grip on my mother's eyes, my father moved to her side and clenched her forearm through her shawl. Without saying a word to my mother, he eventually faced Umu Pilaca and the altar.

I'd never attended a ceremony with so few people, and I still didn't understand the purpose. My father said I needed to witness the events, so I sat quietly and watched with Riku and Iska standing beside me.

Umu Pilaca lifted his hands while he prayed in a voice more vibrant than the man.

Most generous Inti, we come with Huayna Capac, your son on earth.
Most glorious Inti, we obediently gather as you command.
Most powerful Inti, we wish to do your bidding.
Most beneficent Inti, come to us so we may show our gratitude.

After lowering his arms and speaking to my father, he said, "We are here today to satisfy the sacred covenant revealed to the great Inca Pachacuti by Inti, the great sun god. As Inti's direct descendant, you are the intermediary between the gods in the Upper World and your subjects throughout the entire empire. You alone can petition Inti on our behalf."

Turning slightly, he spoke to my mother, who continued to gaze at my sister. "Coya Cusirimay, as Inti's direct descendant on earth, yours is a perfect union with the Inca. With Inti's blessing and guidance, you have born a son to follow your husband and now carry the daughter of your union." Extending his arms to both of them, he concluded, "Together, you can ensure Inti's continued grace and bounty for all your subjects."

He turned to face the altar and spoke to the gold statue in the center, a likeness of Inti with the body of a man and a face impressed on a circle surrounded with gold rays. "While Inti's spirit rests in the Upper World, his likeness lives in this world. May he be pleased with our devotion." He slid the icon forward across the stone altar and very slowly caressed every part starting at the head and continuing to the foot before working his way back to its head. When he finished, both the priest's face and the statue carried a soft white glow.

Next he moved to the gold statue on his left, a remarkable likeness of my father. Again he repeated his sacred touch from head to foot and seemed to breathe life into the statue. "Huayna Capac, our beloved leader, in body, you live in this world, but your spirit lives in both. We beg your spirit to come to us that you may witness this ceremony." Finally he moved to the other end of the table where the silver statue of my mother stood and very gently he touched her likeness from foot to head. "Coya Cusirimay, daughter of Inti and sister-wife of Huayna Capac, our most generous mother, from the earth you bring forth life and bless it with your loving care. You alone nurture the seed from which all hope springs. Stay with us that we may honor you."

Perhaps it was just the afternoon sunlight, but through his mystic devotion, all three icons radiated beyond their natural brilliance.

Umu Pilaca very deliberately turned to face my parents, but he stared at the bundle in my mother's arms. When he approached her, she instantly stepped away and huddled over my sister. With an almost inaudible growl she snarled, "You can't have Kaya. She's mine."

"No, she's not. She belongs to Inti," he responded with the authority of the gods.

Undaunted, she glared at him and looked for Cepi's support, but she had already vanished. With outstretched arms my father turned to her. "Give my daughter to me. You can't keep her. It's time to let go."

She backed away again, holding Kaya so tightly she began to cry.

"Coya, you know there is no escape. You must give her to me." He waited for her to respond before continuing, "Give me the child, or face your own death."

She still hesitated, but finally dropped her head and shook with grief. With mother wailing and the baby screaming, she handed my sister to Huayna Capac who briefly held her before passing her to Umu Pilaca. I too began to cry with my mother's pain. Riku placed his hand on my shoulder, but it didn't stop my tears.

With Kaya still protesting, Umu Pilaca lifted her above his head, closed his eyes and prayed again.

> *Most miraculous Inti, you mixed the spirits of sky and earth to create this life.*
> *Most judicious Inti, you demand our obedience and your servants comply.*
> *Most wise Inti, guide Umu Riku as he prepares our most precious sacrifice.*
> *Most generous Inti, accept our offering, Kaya, the one who becomes.*
> *Most powerful Inti, protect your children and grant us your favor.*
> *Most glorious Inti, let us accept the prophecy and live in your grace forever.*
> *Most merciful Inti, hear our prayer.*

When he finished, he gently lowered the still whimpering baby and reverently placed her on the altar between the statues. Without another word, he turned and left. My mother started for the altar, but my father quickly grabbed her arm while Riku and Iska swept Kaya from the altar and disappeared out the door. My mother's voice followed them. "Bring her back. You can't have her." She struggled to free herself, but my father held her with little effort. Finally she collapsed on the floor with my father standing over her. It all happened so fast. I still didn't understand. All I felt was my mother's anguish and my own confusion.

My father helped her to her feet. "Come along, my dear wife, we'll go back to Casana, and you can have a nice hot cup of tea." His soothing voice floated around the temple. "You needn't mourn so. We can always have another daughter."

As she rose, her thin body unfolded and stretched almost to my father's height. Her back and shoulders rigid, chin high and eyes filled with cold hatred, she glared at her startled husband. "No, she can never be replaced. She was our daughter, my only daughter."

I'd never heard this shrill, forced voice. She jabbed her finger into his chest as she spoke, "You have betrayed me for the last time. I am your wife and will act as your queen in public, but you will never again share my bed." Not waiting for his reply, she spun around and marched out the door.

My father held his proud stature until she was out of sight, his eyes following after her as if a part of him had gone with her. Without taking a step, he dropped his shoulders and exhaled slowly until he was empty. After a very long pause he inhaled deeply, again assuming his noble air and title: Inca Huayna Capac, Ruler of the Empire, Son of Inti. Without hesitation he pasted an official smile on his regal face and confidently strode out of the temple.

I remember that day so vividly, it could have been yesterday, but it was years before I understood the importance of my mother's secret or why my baby sister created such turmoil. Forgotten by both parents and suddenly alone, I was stranded on the bench. My ordered, happy life as my parents' greatest pleasure disappeared in one morning. Even though I was still the eldest son of the king and queen of the greatest empire in the world, something intangible had changed forever. Bewildered and afraid for the first time, I picked at my bandaged foot and licked the salty tears from my lips.

Machu Picchu

Kaya

"Kaya, for the last time, come to breakfast." Iska called to me from the cooking area while I still sat on my bed combing my hair.

I'd heard her first and second requests, as I lingered under the blanket, listening to bird calls hanging in the warm spring air. If I rose slowly, Iska usually left my breakfast over the fire and began her morning chores, but today she sounded irritated. Still sleepy, I straightened my dress as I stepped through the doorway into the bright sunlight.

"There you are. Come on, you have to eat, and I need to visit Kinsa. Why are you so slow today?" Her puffy cheeks, broad nose, and smiling eyes always seemed jolly, but she rarely laughed or spoke that way; either she scolded me or more typically, said nothing.

"It's a beautiful morning. What's the hurry?" Unwilling to be rushed, I ambled toward her.

She dished out my hot porridge, filled a wooden cup with tea, and extended each to me. "Here, eat." I took my breakfast, and settled nearby to savor the salty ground maize. "Riku is coming to visit. You must be ready."

"Riku is visiting me? Why? He always comes to see you." I'd seen Riku many times, but only spoken with him once or twice. Typically, he drank *chicha* beer and asked Iska if she needed anything: firewood, cooking pots, more wool, sandals, anything. I noticed her requested supplies always arrived the next day.

She combed her long black hair and deftly braided a single thick cord. "Starting today, Riku will be your teacher."

"Riku will teach me to weave?"

"No. Kinsa is an expert weaver and will train you. And you will continue music with Tawan." She tied off the end of her braid. "It's probably better if Riku explains when he takes you to the sacred plaza."

"When I go where?" I nearly spilled my tea.

"To the sacred plaza. It's just—"

"Why can't he teach me here? Kinsa and Tawan do?" I had no memory of ever leaving the safety of these three buildings and my garden on the terrace below. My stomach twisted into a knot.

"He has other students, and they can't come here. Besides, you'll use the temples for your studies."

"I don't want to learn if I have to leave." I jumped to my feet and ran back into the house.

Iska's voice followed me. "Kaya, you have to go. Quit acting like such a baby."

She couldn't know how scared I was. I knew nothing beyond my garden and couldn't even guess what a sacred plaza might be. Buried in my blankets, I covered my head and whimpered softly. I hid for a long time, hoping that Riku would visit with Iska and forget about me. After he arrived, I heard him talking with her outside the doorway. I squeezed my eyes shut, covered them with my hands, and listened to my heart pound in my head. I just wanted him to go away, but I knew my wish wasn't granted when footsteps crossed the floor mats just beyond my bed.

"Good morning, Kaya. It's a beautiful day, a nice day to watch your flowers grow." His smooth voice drifted to my bed. "I see your orchids are starting to send up flower stems. Pretty soon your garden will be a beautiful paradise with blossoms everywhere. Is your guava tree in bloom? The leaves are so thick I can't see any flowers, but some sweet fragrance is drifting in the window. Will you show me your garden?" He was silent while he listened for my response. He hadn't said anything about leaving the house. Maybe he just wanted to talk to me.

Still wary, I slowly climbed out of my cocoon and darted to the wooden bench beneath a window while Riku stayed at a window a short distance away. Standing on the bench, and, leaning forward, I took a quick whiff before answering. "The guava just started to bloom. I can't smell it right now. The yellow flowers on the buddleia over there are the ones that smell good enough to eat."

Riku followed my pointed finger to the bush near the fence post across the terrace from us.

I loved overlooking my garden from this height. At the end of the terrace to my right, a guava tree spread its branches across the width of my garden, offering protection from rain and sun all year long. To my left stood the stone warehouse filled with wool in various stages of preparation for weaving. Behind the warehouse, a large wooden door sealed the garden from the rest of the terrace. Extending from the warehouse wall into the garden, a thatched roof supported on corner posts created a shelter where I often sat with Kinsa and Tawan for my lessons. A path lined with plants of every description wound between the shelter and the guava tree at the opposite end.

"Oh yes, I see them." He looked around and asked, "What's the reddish clump over there?"

"That's just caladium. It's much prettier when it gets bigger. The leaves look like red and green spider webs."

He pointed to several other plants, and I proudly identified each of them. "You must really like your garden to know how to tend so many different kinds of plants."

Taking care of the flowers seemed very ordinary. It never occurred to me that I was doing anything special. "Iska taught me the names of the plants, but they tell me how to care for them. Usually all they want is a little water and enough room to grow."

"Would you like to see another garden? Perhaps you'll find a new flower that you want to bring back to yours."

"Is the sacred plaza a garden?"

"Not exactly, but you can see many from there. I think you'll like it there, and you'll be back here before Kinsa's visit this afternoon. I would like to show you this place. Will you come with me?"

His gentle unhurried manner wasn't at all scary. I stepped off the bench, and he extended his empty hand to me. "You'll be safe if you hold my hand."

I'd never held anyone's hand, or even touched anyone that I could remember. I cautiously put my hand in his. His warm, soft hand entirely covered mine with a comfort as soothing as my blankets. I instantly trusted him. Together we walked to the ladder to my garden, descended and continued to the huge wooden door that marked the end of my experience. I must have squeezed Riku's hand as he opened the door because he looked down and calmly reminded me. "It's all right. You're still holding my hand, so you're safe."

We wove around two more storehouses on the terrace before reaching an enormous stone staircase. With buildings on both sides of the stairs, I couldn't see much except the long descent to a flat grassy field below us and a shorter climb to a large pile of rocks. “The sacred plaza is this way,” Riku said as he turned to climb the knee-high steps.

The familiar tapping that I heard from my garden was much louder now, and, still holding his hand, my curiosity carried me up the stairs to see what type of bird made that sound. We faced an enormous white rock at the top of the stairs, so we turned and followed yet another terrace. After a few more corners, stairs, and stone walls, the path abruptly opened into a courtyard with the most beautiful buildings imaginable.

“Is this the sacred plaza?”

Riku nodded as we walked across the courtyard to an open building. Since it had no roof, the morning light filled the three-sided building with a tingling glow. My hand fell from his to the cool, shiny walls that radiated like the sun. “Inti, the sun god, is present in everything made of gold, including those walls,” Riku said. “Can you feel him touch your skin? It’s like standing in a warm rain. I feel like I’ve been rinsed clean and yet more is given to me than is washed away.”

All three walls sparkled from the floor to well over my head, as did the high table at the front of the temple. “I like it. It makes me feel sleepy and wide awake at the same time. I want to play my flute and dance.” Humming a bouncy tune, I pretended to do both, while Riku clapped. When the song ended I found myself staring at the table.

“That’s the altar. Would you like to see it?” I nodded and Riku lifted me onto the altar so I could see the image of the sun spreading across its surface, but I was very uneasy sitting there. “We place our offerings here when we ask for Inti’s help, or thank him for his generosity. He cares for us like his children.”

I half listened to him, hoping he would get me off the table. Across the courtyard a more ordinary building with no windows, but two doors and a thatched roof caught my attention. “In that building we store all our special clothes, statues, and containers for the various festivals throughout the year. Sometimes we’ll have our lessons there, but then we’ll use all of the buildings eventually. Do you want to go over there?”

I liked the Temple of Inti, just not the altar, and was pleased to scamper across the courtyard to the next building. I opened the cloth door to let the sunlight in, but after the gold temple, I could barely see anything and waited for my eyes to adjust while Riku caught up to me.

“Go ahead. I’ll hold the door.”

I wandered through the stacks of brightly colored cloth and statues made of metal or painted earthenware. In one corner were several head-dresses covered with red and yellow feathers and still others adorned with long, white plumes.

"During your lessons you will learn about all of the festivals: why we celebrate each one, how we honor the gods with our love and respect, and how all of these precious and sacred ornaments are used." He beckoned me back to the courtyard where he faced the third and final building.

When we first entered the courtyard, I walked right past the temple and the low stone slab that stood beside it. By far the largest of the buildings, it dominated the plaza with its white granite walls, wood doors, and thatched roof. "This is the Temple of Viracocha, the creator of the lesser gods and our entire world."

Inside, the room was much larger than my house and had three windows opposite us that lit the entire area. The building was completely bare except for the straw mats underfoot. Disappointed by the lack of ornamentation, I said, "There's nothing here!"

"Viracocha prefers to be honored with our grateful acknowledgment that his creation beyond these walls is far greater than any portion we could bring into the temple. Come to the window and see for yourself."

I climbed onto a bench, looked out the window, and gasped. "It's wonderful."

Riku stood behind me and held my waist. "If you lean out the window over the thick wall, you can see everything."

I did as he suggested and gawked at the spacious gardens dotted with trees, llamas grazing, and people crossing the open space in every direction.

"It's so big, and there are so many people. Where did they all come from?" From my garden, I'd never seen more than a few farmers and their families.

"Machu Picchu is a lovely city with many people now. They've always been here; you just can't see them from your garden. Do you see all the buildings on the hill overlooking the other side of plaza?"

I nodded.

"Most of the people live there, or on the terraces beyond, but some live on this side of the plaza too."

"Why are there so many people, if they're never in the fields?"

In time, I learned that Riku carefully considered what I thought was a simple question before answering, as he did now. "Do you hear that tapping?"

"Yes, I can hear that bird from my garden."

"That's not a bird; its men shaping stone so they can be fitted together as they do in the walls of this temple and your home. Machu Picchu has several very skilled stone workers, as well as potters to make the dishes like the ones Iska uses, weavers who make cloth to give to the gods, gold workers, animal caretakers, and farmers for many more terraces than you have seen."

I noticed a woman overloaded with pots walking across the plaza. I'd never thought about where my house or dishes came from; they were just always there. Discovering the people, the city, and the mountains beyond was both exciting, and frightening. "The city is so big, but the mountains make it seem small."

"Yes, I suppose they do. Are you ready to see the rest of the city?"

"There's more?"

"Oh, yes. Come with me, but perhaps you should hold my hand."

Now familiar with the warm comfort he extended, I happily put my hand in his as we walked out of the temple directly toward the edge of the courtyard, but I dragged behind as we got close.

"It's all right, I won't let go."

After he tightened his grip, I was able to creep toward the open expanse. "There must be at least a hundred terraces, and they're all bigger than my garden." Most weren't planted yet or even tilled. "How can they finish planting before the wet season begins?"

"You have found another reason why there are so many people. Besides these fields, there is land to be tended near the river at the bottom of the canyon."

I searched the river valley for farm land and spotted something moving. "I see two shapes that look like a man and woman, but they're the size of ants."

"That's only because they're so far away. The man is probably about my size."

The idea that people could be the size of ants so surprised me I thought it must be a miracle.

As if he heard my thoughts, he added, "No, it's not a miracle. Watch the birds soaring above your garden. When they're close they're large, but as they fly higher, they get smaller. The farther away something is, the smaller it appears, even though it doesn't really change size."

It still seemed like a miracle. I said nothing and vowed to watch the birds more closely.

Riku pointed up the stairs leading to the small building above us. "Would you like to go up there?"

Having seen so many fantastic things already, I wondered what else Riku planned to show me. We'd passed the side of the Temple of Inti when

Riku stopped to show me a simple building that shared a common wall with the temple. It had no windows, only a cloth door and a nearly flat thatched roof. Inside the empty building, I saw a rock floor and drab rock walls with several empty niches. Riku told me this was the Temple of Ilyapa, the god of Thunder. After the other wonders of the sacred plaza, I dismissed this temple as uninteresting. Hand-in-hand, we again started up the stairs, passed between two high walls and emerged on a terrace surrounded by a waist-high stone wall.

"Riku, I don't know where to look. Everything is so beautiful."

A warm breeze lifted the life of the city to this highest point. We looked toward the sun across the entire expanse of the main plaza and the houses beyond. In the opposite direction the steep agricultural terraces fell down the mountain toward the river. Between them on the ridge where we stood, I could see the sacred plaza, farmers planting on the terraces near my garden, and beyond them, the city gate perched in a mountain gap. Behind me a mountain rose in a pinnacle that looked close enough to touch. Lush green mountains, like one enormous garden, surrounded the entire city and stretched upward to touch the sky.

"I'm glad you like it. This is a magical, sacred place. Even after all the years I've lived here, I've never tired of it beauty. It's always so peaceful here." We walked around the terrace pointing to each new wonder: massive trees, splashes of color against the green blanket, terraces high above us on the mountains across the river valley and white mountains in the distance. The view was so magnificent, I'd walked around the statue several times before I noticed it.

"What's this? It looks like part of the mountain is covered with gold." An irregularly shaped stone platform dominated the center of the terrace at just the right height for Riku to sit. I'd never seen a bench that shimmered in the sunlight. Much smaller than the base, a strange vertical column protruded from its center.

"It's called Intihuatana, and you're right; it is attached to the mountain. Many years ago, an artist carefully chipped away the mountain to leave this shape. After smoothing the stone, he pounded thin sheets of gold into it so that it looks a large gold finger pointing toward the sky. We'll learn more about it when we start our lessons."

"When will we start? What else will we learn? Iska said that I will learn with other students."

Riku smiled. "You certainly are filled with questions. You will join my other students, Tumbes and Atuk, in three days. They went to the top of Huayna Picchu for me today to get a package I store there. If we look closely, we might be able to see them on the path." Riku pointed to the jutting mountain and searched the surface for their white tunics. Finally, he caught their motion. "There they are, on the left side about halfway down."

I waved to get their attention, but Riku told me that since they were moving, they wouldn't see me. "The trail is too steep. They must watch their feet when they walk."

We followed their slow progress for a while until I asked again, "You said I will learn about the festivals. What more do I need to know?"

"You'll learn about the great deeds of our ancestors and about stories so old, we're not sure who first told them. And you'll learn about the stars, the moon, and the sun." He stopped and studied my face before continuing. "Most important, you will learn the ways of the spirit world." Riku's calm manner made everything easy.

"What are the ways of the spirit world?"

"You'll see soon enough, but now, I think we should take you back to your garden. Kinsa will visit you very soon."

I nodded as I took his hand, and we retraced our path down the stairs, across the sacred plaza and down again. I turned the corner and stepped onto the terrace leading to the main staircase when I saw a llama lying in the grass.

"Whose llama is that?" I asked, really more interested to know why it was in the middle of the path.

"It doesn't matter." Riku dismissed my concern. "Many llamas live in the city. They graze the plaza more evenly when they are allowed to choose where to eat." It watched us as we approached, but made no attempt to move. "You can touch it if you like. The fleece feels different when she's wearing it than when you weave it."

The brown llama with black patches on its face twitched her long ears and slowly chewed the grass hanging from her mouth. Even sitting, her head was higher than mine, but I reached out to scratch her neck. To my surprise, she nuzzled her head into my hand. "She's so friendly! Are all llamas like this?" I scratched her ear as her big brown eyes slowly closed.

"If a llama has been hurt, he may not be so calm, but they're usually gentle creatures."

I reached down to her back and buried my other hand in her fleece. "She's so warm. I can feel her move her neck." Her muscular frame hidden beneath her fleece was a living miracle as wondrous as the gold walls in the temple. I would have sat and snuggled into her, but she stood up and towered over me. I couldn't even see over her back, but she lowered her head to allow me to continue scratching her.

"I think you've made a friend." Riku stepped closer and patted her on the head. "Maybe you'll see her again when we go to the sacred plaza for lessons."

I stood with the llama a while longer, amazed at her size and warmth. Gradually she moved away to graze on the new grass farther down the terrace.

Riku returned me to my home, but I couldn't stop asking questions about the wonders he'd shown me. After he left, I climbed down the ladder, the only access to my garden, and began to clean the lifeless wool as Kinsa had requested. Even years later, I fondly remembered my first visit to the sacred plaza. During that morning, my fear of leaving the safety of my garden dissolved into an insatiable craving for everything beyond it. And yet, in the end, I would long for the seclusion of my garden.

Myths

Kaya

The llama in its mountain pasture was so sad he couldn't eat; he only looked at the sky and wailed. Finally his master came and asked him why he refused the plentiful grass. The llama said that in five days the rains would start and the world would be covered with water. The astonished man believed the words of his llama, so he immediately gathered his family and supplies. The people and their herds reached the top of the mountain just as the rain began. The water filled the valleys, destroying everything in its path. High on the mountain, every kind of animal surrounded them, including a fox and jaguar. The rising sea was so close that it drenched the fox's tail; that's why to this day, his tail is black. Finally the rain stopped, and the water slowly receded. The family and animals returned to the empty valleys and repopulated the world.

Riku told us this ancient story and asked us to think about its meaning before tonight. He said he would come for me at sunset, and we would spend the night beside Intihuatana at the highest point in Machu Picchu. Alone all day in my garden, I sat wrapped in my shawl and rocked from side to side. Staring but seeing nothing, I wondered about the tale. I had never seen rain so hard the valleys filled, but if it happened once it could happen again. We could all die. Maybe Riku would show me where it was safe. How did a llama know it would rain so hard? I thought Riku just made up this story to scare us. No, there must be a lesson I just couldn't understand.

"Kaya, Kaya! Are you all right? What is the matter? Can you hear me? Kaya, look at me?" Iska shook my shoulders.

By concentrating on Iska's worried voice, I returned slowly, shaking my head as if I were emerging from a dream. "Yes, Iska, I am fine. I must have fallen asleep."

"Your eyes were open, and I couldn't wake you. Don't do that. You scare me when you go away like that. It's not normal. Besides, you didn't do the spinning, and you haven't watered your garden."

"I forgot." I replied. "Thank you for bringing my dinner. I want to be ready when Riku comes."

Iska shrugged her shoulders and let out an exasperated sigh. "You are a peculiar child." As she started toward the ladder, she added, "Eat your dinner and bring up your dishes before he comes."

Alone again, I picked at my food. Riku told odd stories, but I didn't care; he always took me away from the confines of my garden, at least for a while. Since that first visit to the sacred plaza more than a year earlier, leaving this small terrace became increasingly important to me, and my lessons with Atuk and Tumbes three times a week were my only escape from this place and its wretched loneliness.

"Come Kaya, it's time to go." His soft, gentle voice floated down the ladder. Anxious to get away, I quickly crossed the terrace and climbed the ladder with my dirty dishes, while Riku patiently waited for me to join him. With no moon and only a faded sunset, my hand slid along the cool wall as we groped down the nearly dark passageway. Since Riku knew every detail, I followed his shadowy movements until we reached the open staircase and climbed to the top.

We met Atuk and Tumbes in the open space beside Intihuatana. Freed of my prison and no longer alone, I drew in a deep breath and shivered in the cool evening breeze rising from the valley. Tumbes spread out blankets on the ground, as I asked, "Can we have a fire? I'm cold."

"No, Kaya, we have plenty of blankets. It must be dark for us to watch the stars."

The chill of the autumn night settled on the mountain as we huddled in a circle doubly wrapped in blankets. As Riku insisted, we spoke very little to one another until the lesson was over. The light from distant fires dotted the city, and above, the stars flickered and grew bright. Riku sat directly across from me with Atuk on his right and Tumbes on his left. He started with a prayer thanking the gods for sharing their wisdom, and then asked me to describe what I had learned about the sun.

"The great god Inti lives in the sun and rules the day," I answered confidently. "We are nearing Inti Raymi when the nights are long and the sun rises and sets in the distant north. Then each day, Inti makes the sun rise a little farther south. In the longer days, the farmers plant their crops as the sun continues to creep southward until the longest day during Capac Raymi. Then during the hot, rainy days of summer, the crops grow strong and the sunrise gradually moves back toward the north. Even after the fields are harvested in autumn, the sunset continues north while Inti takes his rest through the winter. When Inti Raymi arrives, the cycle begins again."

"You have learned your lessons well."

I enjoyed his praise while Riku asked Tumbes to explain the movements of the moon.

"Killa is the goddess who lives in the moon and tells the moon to change its appearance every night. As though Killa were pouring light into her house, the moon fills and grows heavier, so each evening until the middle of the month she rises slightly later. Then one night she appears just as the sun sets and shows her entire face. But Killa is shy, and she increasingly covers her face until she's entirely hidden and can rest. Killa continues her cycle throughout the year and protects the fertility of women and all animals. We honor her rebirth each month with a new name and a festival."

"You speak of her with the respect that is rightfully hers." Riku noted. "Atuk, tell us the relationship between Inti and Killa."

"Some will say that Inti is the greater and Killa follows Inti's orders, but I don't think so. If that were so, Killa would cycle only twelve times during one of Inti's cycles, not twelve times and eleven extra days. The extra days confuse the farmers and make it much harder to plan the festivals. I think that Inti's heat and power rules the day and gives men the strength to grow crops. Killa, with her cool and fickle face, rules the night."

"And so it has always been." Riku replied. "The ways of the sky and the ways of the land are the same. In the sky we see Inti and Killa and on land we have men and women led by the Inca, Huayna Capac, and his Queen, Coya Cusirimay. We can't live without the benefits of Inti or Killa, nor could we live without the order provided by the Inca and the Queen. For everything there is an opposing force, and they must be balanced on earth, and in the sky. Tonight we will learn about the stars and what happens when opposing forces are not balanced."

Riku fell silent, but even on this moonless night, I could feel him watching us the same way a finch watches her fledglings. While not unkind, his gaze demanded that I respond, but I wasn't sure how. Tumbes squirmed and asked, "So when are we going to learn about the stars?"

Not to be rushed, Riku exhaled slowly and began to hum. In time the sound changed to whispered words. "Tonight, as the first step in exploring the spirit world, you will relive a story. Now close your eyes so you can hear me better. Open your ears and your hearts. Feel the mountain beneath you and the cool night air on your face. Notice where I am and where each of you is sitting. Feel the four of us together in a circle and know that you are safe as long as we stay together. Now picture the city below us; find the temples and the main plaza. Imagine the artisan section across the plaza. Remember as much detail as you can. How many trees are in the plaza? Which fields have not yet been harvested? Where are the llamas grazing? Ask the question and let the information come to you."

It all seemed so obvious, and yet, I did feel like I was touching the others and more aware of my surroundings. Riku kept whispering. His careful, halting speech insisted on being heard. "Together we are going to the place and time of the flood. Atuk, you have traveled to Cusco. Ask the spirits to guide you there, and we will follow you. Look around and tell us what you see."

Atuk hesitated, and then in a low voice he said, "I can see Cusco, or at least the valley of Cusco. We are together in the hills. There are no grand buildings like the city I have seen, just thatched huts scattered along the river in the wide valley. Crops, still soft and spring-green, cover the fields. Children laugh while they help their parents tend the land."

"Kaya, you haven't seen the city, can you picture this place?" Riku asked.

In fact, I could, so Riku asked me to follow the river into the mountains. The wide, calm river in the valley moved slowly downstream, but I went upstream. To my surprise, the image unfolded as I described it. "The river is narrower in the mountains and turns white as it falls between the rock walls."

"Good, now go farther upstream."

I climbed up to a still lake nestled in a mountain bowl. Fat llamas grazed contentedly in the new grass, and a family rested near their hut. Riku asked if we were together. Tumbes answered that we were all standing by the hut in the hot sun. Riku asked Tumbes why it was so hot on a spring day in the mountains.

"I'm not sure. Maybe the sun is too close to the mountains."

"Do you feel anything else?"

"Wind! A strong wind carries the sticky heat of the summer jungle. It is so hot I want to jump in the lake."

"Tumbes, concentrate on the family."

"Wait, I can't see them anymore. I can't see my feet. I can barely see my hands. The rain is so heavy I can't see you. Are you still there?"

"We're right beside you. If you can't see, what do you hear, or feel.

"Thunder in the distance. I'm so hot! Even the rain is hot. I can feel the water rushing around my feet and the ground is sliding away."

We all knew the story; the rain would fill the valley. During the lightening flashes, I tried to track the family as they scrambled up the mountain but I couldn't help them. I couldn't stop the rain. I couldn't help the children. All I could do was feel a stabbing pain of terror in my stomach. I wanted to run, but there was nowhere to go.

No longer in a whisper, Riku spoke in his soothing voice. "You have felt the anger and helplessness of a disaster. We cannot help these people and most were unable to help themselves. There is no need to stay longer. Atuk, tell us what you see when the rain stops."

Atuk was silent for a while before answering. "We are still in the same place, but the pasture is covered with rivulets deeply cutting the land into jagged pieces. The llama herd is high above us in the rocky crags. And the family. Where is the family? Oh, there they are on the other side of the valley, just emerging from a rock shelf." He paused again and then shouted. "The lake! It's gone!"

"Atuk, follow the river back to the valley." Riku advised, and we all passed through the mountain gorge to the wide valley below.

"The river covers the entire floor of the valley. I don't see any people in the water or in the mountains surrounding the valley."

Riku sighed deeply. "So now you have all seen the flood. Remember, we are all still safely in the mountains at Machu Picchu. See for yourselves."

Grateful to have escaped, we all opened our eyes to the stars of Machu Picchu. I quietly commented, "It felt so real, like I actually lived through the flood."

I was sure Riku was smiling, although I couldn't distinguish his face. "Yes, the spirits who live in the Upper World are very powerful. They will help us to feel any event as if we were there. Tonight we simply observed the retelling of a story you already knew. In the coming years you will learn to trust the spirits, to learn of unknown stories from the past and future, and to benefit from their wisdom in ways you can't imagine today."

Riku gave us some time to fully return to the present before he continued with the lesson. "With the sun and moon, we have already seen that the events of the sky are reflected in this world. We just saw how the rains destroyed one valley and know from other stories that there was great destruction in all the valleys of the Andes. Now we need to understand the sky story."

We all looked up at the cloudless sky filled with points of light as brilliant as the tiny crystals in the temple walls sparkling at noon. "Who can tell me where the river and the llamas are in the Upper World."

"There's the Mayu, the river of stars that flows between the horizons. In the same way drops of rain lose their identity as they fall to a river, so too, the individual stars blur into the Mayu," Tumbes replied.

I was just learning about stars, so Riku asked him to show me the main features in the bright streak.

"Each night the eastern stars follow behind the sun and moon and travel through the night from east to west. At Inti Raymi, on a winter evening, the Mayu extends from the northeast across the sky to the southwest. Through the year the river gradually falls from the northeast, and by Capac Raymi in the summer the other branch of the river flows from the northwest to the southeast. In summer we can see the source for both river branches. There is a narrow spot, and the river flows down each side of the mountain before the branches join in the south."

Tumbes pointed out the details as he spoke. "Along the river there are many animals. We can see the male llama in the northeast now. The very bright star just on the edge of the river is the llama's head. Its feet are the two dimmer stars just below it. The mother and baby llama are downstream in the southwest. The very black stripe covering the river is the mother stretching her neck over the river to drink. You can see her eyes shining at the end of her neck in the river. Her baby follows her in the dark spot at the river's edge. The fox is the dark patch on the heels of the mother llama, right beside the baby llama. You can see the fox's three legs, his head and his tail extended behind him. The jaguar stands on the other side of the llama baby. We see him in that string of stars."

Riku stopped him again so I could find the star and dark constellations. Because the mountain sky was so filled with stars, it was easier to find the dark figures than to distinguish those made of very bright stars surrounded by dimmer ones. Having finally located all the characters, Riku explained the sky story.

"The male llama says the river will flood, and they all go to the mountains where they find the other animals. We have found all of the animals, the river, and the mountains in the sky exactly as we found them on earth. Can you see how the Mayu flooded?"

None of us could answer the question, not even Atuk who had watched the stars for two years. Riku continued, "The sun follows the same path every year, just as Kaya described. On Inti Raymi, the sun always shines directly into the Torreon and the center shadow of the window always falls on the marker.

At Capac Raymi, the sun always rises on its mark. In Cusco spring and autumn are marked, and the sun always rises in the same place on those days as well. This has been true for as long as our ancestors have marked the sun."

"Now listen carefully," he insisted. "The stars do not rise in the same place each year. Very slowly, the entire night sky is setting into the east. Our ancestors' *quipus* tell us which stars they saw at sunrise. Now those stars have already set by the time we see the sunrise. In the west, our sky is filled with stars, but they too are shifting to the east. Before the Mayu flooded, the sun always rose and set in the Mayu on the longest day and the shortest day of each year. The hot sun dried up some of the river water and kept the river in its banks. In the year of the flood, Inti no longer rose through the Mayu at the winter festival, and the great floods came with the summer rains. So you see, the flood in this world reflected the flood in the Upper World"

"But Riku," Atuk interrupted, "Did the flood in the Upper World cause the flood on earth, or did they just happen at the same time?"

"That, Atuk, is a question we have never answered. Perhaps one day the spirits will tell you. For now, it is sufficient that we watch the sky, day and night, to see if there are changes that foretell our future."

The notion that the stars reflected our stories and may even tell our future was frightening . . . and comforting.

The rest of the night we watched the stars move across the sky while Atuk and Tumbes pointed out other constellations. The Collca was a tight cluster of seven stars we could just see in the northern sky. "This is seed for new stars so we call her the mother of stars. She lives high in the mountains near the source of the Mayu." Tumbes explained to me. "Far into the southern sky, called the Other World, are five bright stars, four in a perfect cross; the fifth is not as bright and falls off the cross pattern. These are the five brothers, four good brothers and the bad one who causes trouble and doesn't respect his parents."

As the starry night faded with the growing light, a very bright, feathery star shone just above the mountain peaks. "What star is that?" I asked.

"Her name is Chaska, a very special star. She's always near the sun, but unlike most of the stars, she is one of only five stars that wander in the sky. Sometimes Chaska follows the sun at sunset and sometimes she rises before dawn," Atuk explained.

Compared to my life of solitude, staying up all night and watching the stars with friends was very exciting. The new stories, new lessons, and mysterious reflections of the spirit world in our world all fascinated and frightened me, but I was getting very sleepy when Iska arrived.

As the sun rose over the mountains, we ate our breakfast porridge while a farmer carried a large bundle of maize across the main plaza. Tumbes jumped up to imitate the man. In his version, the farmer dropped his hoe, and when he stooped to pick it up, three ears of maize dribbled out of his bundle. Tumbes grimaced as he stooped with a straight back to retrieve one ear. To reach the second, he groaned and then teetered under the weight, but rose with the maize in hand. As he reached down for the third ear, his load shifted and rolled off his back. Tumbes landed on his back, splayed across the bundle. Unwilling to let go, he struggled to right himself. Legs flailing and ears of maize sliding out, he finally let go to reassemble his bundle. With help from an imaginary passerby and bent under the weight, he finally waddled away with the hoe in one hand and the bundle steadied with the other. Atuk and I laughed and applauded until Tumbes bolted to a full upright with his arms extended. Even Riku smiled in his quiet way.

The laughter was a fading memory when Riku announced it was time to separate. On the way back to my home, I chattered about the night and asked if all those people were really killed in the flood.

"Kaya, you must completely trust the stories of the sky," he answered sternly. "These are very important to our people, and they should be to you as well. Do you understand?"

I said I did even though I didn't understand at the time. We walked in silence for a while, and then I asked, "Is there a star in the sky that tells my story?"

He stopped, bent down and looked me straight in the eyes. "Yes and when you're older, I will tell you." I was satisfied with his answer, but he stayed crouched like he had something else to tell me. "The Inca wants me to meet with him in the sacred valley, so I will be gone a full cycle of Killa, maybe a bit longer. You will weave with Kinsa and work with Tawan while I'm gone."

I choked back tears. Meeting with Riku, Atuk and Tumbes was my only chance to escape my garden. Iska rarely spoke to me, and Kinsa and Tawan only visited once a week. How could I tolerate being isolated for so long? "You can't leave. I'll be all alone. Can't I study with Atuk and Tumbes?"

"No, Atuk is coming with me, and Tumbes has a special project here. No one else is allowed to take you out of the garden. It's for your own protection."

"Why can't I as least go for walks with Kinsa or Tawan?"

Now, Kaya, I've told you many times. I'm responsible for your safety and your innocence. I can't ask someone else to do my duty."

He stayed with me while I cried so hard I could barely breathe. Finally I blurted, "I can't be alone that long."

He tried to comfort me with a stream of gentle words, but I was tired and afraid of being caged. "I must go. The Inca needs me. Please try to understand. I'm not trying to hurt you."

"Why can't the Inca come here? I could still see you then."

"He is with too many people, and there isn't enough room here. Besides, I serve the Inca and must do as he commands."

"Then take me with you."

"Where I am going is no place to take a precious young girl. Besides, the trip is too long for you."

There was nothing I could do to stop him. I just stood there, rejected by the only person I was allowed to know. He stood again and faced me with his hands on my shoulders.

"Kaya, I have an idea. When I return, you and I will take a trip away from Machu Picchu. We will go to the hot springs in the valley. Would you like that?" Wide-eyed and still choking, I nodded. "You must do very well with your lessons. And this is very important. You must never tell anyone about our trip, not before we go and not after. Never. We would both be punished if anyone knew."

He looked at me carefully as he turned me in a full circle. "You will need to dress as a boy. I can easily find clothes. Can you find a way to hide your hair?"

I nodded and wiped the tears from my cheeks. Dressing as a boy and going to a forbidden place sounded exciting. We returned to my home, where, still dreading the month alone, I reluctantly said goodbye.

Hunting

Ninan

With two hundred men evenly dispersed around an enormous circle, the hunt began with a final drum roll. Still boys, Pacas and I felt honored to be included in this special hunt with our fathers and the empire's military leaders. I could hear my father downhill to my right, but I couldn't see him through the forest undergrowth. One of his favorite captains was on my left. I knew he was an excellent hunter because I hadn't seen or heard him since we were positioned. Before dawn we'd all walked from camp together and were carefully placed around the circle. The drum was the signal for us to start walking toward the center. Moving slowly, I listened to the birds twittering in the canopy as I watched for game. After spotting a deer or other prey, I beat the bushes to force the animal to flee into the ever-shrinking circle. Occasionally one bolted past me, but most ran away from me into the center. Like my father, I carried my short bow and arrows. Pacas and many others carried slings, but our weapons were intended only for self-defense. There would be no killing until we stood shoulder to shoulder.

Having flushed a few deer and a fox very early in the hunt, I had seen nothing for a while. My thoughts drifted back to my father's return a week earlier after a campaign in the south. At full speed, Pacas and I had raced up the mountain road to meet him as he marched into Cusco. Panting and laughing, we stood before my hero as he pretended he didn't know which of us was his son and which his nephew. It was wonderful to have him home again. Sinchi Roca, Pacas' father, ruled Cusco with the authority of the Inca during my father's absence, but it wasn't the same. With Huayna Capac back in Cusco, the city seemed to awake from a sound sleep. The entire city had celebrated his homecoming for two days.

After a while, the circle was small enough that I could see both my father and the captain. Now we could signal each other when an animal headed toward the perimeter. As we continued down the slope, the birds went silent, but the forest floor rustled with the steady commotion of game on the move. Something was always happening. By chance, I noticed motion in the tree behind my father. With the birds already gone, I looked carefully to determine the cause. "Father, look out!" I shouted as I saw a bow stretch and an arrow take flight.

By reflex, my father dropped to the ground just as the arrow passed over his head. Another followed from a tree farther down the slope, barely missing its mark. Still on the ground, my father pointed at the tree and yelled to the captain, "Catch him, but don't kill him!" His command was unnecessary since the captain was already halfway to the source of the first arrow.

In an instant, the captain pulled the assailant from the tree. The stranger caught his balance and turned to run, but the captain slammed him into the tree trunk. His head bounced off the tree, and he slumped to the ground. From the other side of my father, Sinchi Roca heard the commotion and ordered another soldier to join the defense. He chased the other attacker who didn't go far before he suddenly stiffened and fell motionless to the ground.

More curious than frightened, I searched for the arrows in the undergrowth. I bent over the first arrow and had spotted the second a short distance away when my father yelled, "Ninan, don't touch those arrows! They're poisoned. One man is already dead." My father joined me and very cautiously lifted the arrows by the shaft to examine them. They were short with a flint tip, just like the ones I used, but the shaft was painted black. Careful to never touch the flint, he cut off a piece of his mantle and wrapped the arrowheads three times before tying them with a sinewy vine.

The would-be assassin regained his senses to find his hands were already bound. "Take these men and their weapons back to Quispiguanca," my father ordered his soldiers. "We will join you after the hunt." Huayna Capac seemed calm, but his deep voice hissed his command as he handed the poison arrows to his defender.

The captain spoke softly to the other soldier as he finished tying the dead man's hands and feet to a pole. Commanded to do so, the would-be assassin lifted one end of the pole to which the captain tied his hands. With the captain leading the way and the soldier carrying the back end of the pole, the foursome started down the mountain slope toward Quispiguanca, the country palace.

"We'll deal with them when we finish," Huayna Capac announced. "I won't allow them to ruin the hunt by our absence in the perimeter. There are no other attackers. Let's go."

The entire incident happened very quickly, and the rest of the hunters had continued without us. Not nearly as confident that we were the hunters, not the hunted, I jumped at every snapping twig. Now when a fox darted from the brush, I jumped for cover. In contrast, my father stormed through the forest beating the bushes. When a deer tried to pass between us, he yelled, "You will die! You can't escape!" He swung at the deer, missed, but redirected it into the circle. His anger mounted with every step. We caught up to the others and continued to pull even closer together. When we broke out of the mountain forest onto the grasslands we were nearly shoulder to shoulder and could see around the entire circle. Inside, there were deer prancing anxiously and two vicunas nervously standing head to tail. In other areas, the tall grass echoed the movements of the scurrying animals below.

Having completed the human fence, the palace servants entered the circle while we guarded the perimeter. With people so close together we were careful with our weapons. The vicunas were captured first and released, since it was too close to winter to shear them, and their wool was more valuable than their meat. Next, with the help of the deer, the servants located and killed the fox and a puma. Always facing the predator, the deer crowded around their young, defiantly snorted and beat the ground with their front hooves. In the last sort, the does and fawns were released.

Finally the servants swept across the circle killing the remaining animals with clubs, rocks, and spears. My father grabbed the club of a passing servant and joined the sweep. With each wallop he let out a piercing laugh and moved to the next. He hit one deer soundly between the eyes, but it didn't fall as my father expected. He clubbed it again on the side of the head crushing its skull. Still standing, he ran into its side with his shoulder and it fell to the ground. Even though it was clearly dead, he continued to beat the beast, snapping bones and splattering blood. Finally Sinchi Roca broke out of the perimeter, pulled my father off the bloody carcass, and led him back to our camp. The servants collected and dressed the remaining animals before loading the catch on llamas. Already three condors were circling, patiently waiting for the offal.

Pacas and I met our fathers drinking *chicha* in our previous night's camp. Huayna Capac seemed to be almost asleep as he slowly lifted the cup to his lips and muttered, "That's three."

I glanced at Sinchi Roca and asked, "Is he all right?"

"Yes, he just needs to rest after the hunt." His eyes softened as he quietly added, "That was the third assassination attempt, you know." Returning to his normal voice, he finished. "You boys take some lunch and go back to Quispiguanca. We'll return in time for the feast this evening."

Now that we were out of the forest, my skittishness was gone. Pacas and I grabbed the roasted maize and joined the soldiers on the stone road leading to the palace. Not sure who knew about the attack, we didn't speak of it, and the whole event faded like a bad dream. As we walked, we practiced hunting. Taking aim at every acceptable target, no rock escaped Pacas' sling and no patch of grass was safe from my bow. The entire valley between the hunting camp and the palace belonged to my father. Along the road paralleling the river, we passed many irrigated fields and livestock pens. Some of the fields were allocated to Inti and the priests, but most supported Huayna Capac's storehouses and would feed the soldiers, the Inca's extended family, and his servants. There was even a special area set aside for his mother, Mama Oclla, but since her death, her servants and the attendants of her mummy had full authority over this prime cropland.

Most of the harvest was done, so the fields lay still in the afternoon sun. Instead, the activity centered at the homes of Canaris, Quichuas, and Guancabelicas. Their brightly colored headbands and the tunes they sang while they worked easily identified the family origin. Many of these people came from their native lands in the north before my father's reign. When they moved to this valley, an equal number of natives moved to the northern town. This Mitima system, the practice of moving people from their homeland was initiated by my great grandfather, Pachacuti, when he consolidated many cities into the Inca Empire. By moving half the people of a conquered city to another area, the people were less likely to rebel for fear of retribution on their relatives. But more important, even though resettled people carried their religion, customs, and language with them, they were required to learn Quechua, our language. Now Quechua was understood throughout the empire, or so I'd been told.

We could see Quispiguanca majestically situated at the base of the mountains long before we reached it. A massive fitted-stone wall standing taller than four men surrounded the palace grounds. Finally we arrived at the lake and park beneath the southwest wall. Red trim framing the windows of the palace reflected in the pool giving the appearance of underwater doorways. The two real entrances stood opposite one another on the northwest and southeast sides. Identical in design, each had a ramp that led to the guard tower protecting the entrance. The doorway was so tall the soldiers couldn't touch the lintel even with their longest spears, and the tower was twice as high. The palace guards flanked the top of the doorway and could survey the entire valley. Below them, in perfect symmetry, two windowless buildings were used for questioning new visitors.

We followed the captains up the ramp and through the entrance where the guards noted each arrival. The main plaza in front of us was carefully planned with benches under small trees. Thousands could easily rest and enjoy the gardens, so the plaza seemed empty with only two hundred hunters settled there. Pacas and I continued through the plaza to the upper level of the palace grounds. Our homes surrounded a private courtyard with a stream trickling into a small pond. My father's house was in the farthest northwest corner of the palace, and my mother's house, where I stayed, stood beside it. Sinchi Roca's home and another that was used by very special visitors were directly across the courtyard. Riku, the priest from Machu Picchu, and his traveling companion were to stay there when they arrived. A larger building featuring the throne stood by my father's residence. Directly opposite this building was a narrow structure used to store the Inca's insignia, and behind it, the great hall towered over the lower buildings.

Actually there were two great halls, facing each other and opening onto a larger courtyard. Each building could easily hold one hundred people, and another three hundred could relax in the open space between them. Beyond the two great halls lay another courtyard with a pond, stream, and buildings that exactly mirrored the royal homes. These were kept for visiting relatives and important visitors.

Pacas and I deposited our weapons in our houses and headed back to the main plaza on the lower level. We listened to the men talk about the campaign in the south as their women gradually joined them and enjoyed refreshments in the afternoon shade. Later, Pacas and I found the prisoners in one of the guard tower rooms. One sat motionless staring at the wall with the head of the dead man in his lap.

My father arrived after dark on his litter, a chair atop a lightweight platform carried by four sturdy men. As he talked with Sinchi Roca, he seemed to be his typical jovial self again. They immediately headed for our private courtyard to dispose of their hunting gear. In a short while, our fathers returned with their wives, Coya Cusirimay and Pilpintu. In the reddish glow of torchlight, our parents overlooked the soldiers from the stairs leading to the great halls.

My father raised his scepter, and a hush quickly spread across the plaza. "Tonight we celebrate! Our southern campaign was a success and proved the supremacy of the empire. Our hunt today and feast this evening is your reward for your loyal service. Tonight we will forget the hardships and remember only the abundance and grace of Inti. A banquet is set in each hall and the music is about to begin. Enjoy yourselves and give thanks."

The guests cheered their approval, as small groups worked their way up the stairs toward the food. Pacas and I squeezed through the crowd and ran through the royal courtyard to enter the great hall from the far end, right next to the food. The aroma of a steaming pot of vegetable soup accented with the sweet scent of bananas wafted toward us. We helped ourselves to the huge platter of roasted deer and special treats: various bean dishes seasoned with salt and hot peppers, potatoes, llama meat, and fresh maize bread. Finally I found my favorite meal, a dish of boiled peanuts, maize, and guinea pig. Ravenous, Pacas and I had filled our plates and collected a bowl of soup before the first adults reached the banquet table. We devoured the special treats in the plaza, oblivious to the adults around us.

We knew the celebration would last until dawn, and we were free to roam through the crowds, unfettered and unnoticed. With beer flowing as easily as conversations, soon there was no talk of the south or family matters. In the courtyard between the halls the musicians played lively songs on panpipes, flutes, and rattles while in each hall a single drum established the rhythm for dancing. Most were lively group dances; others were all women or all men. Some were provocative dances for couples where each person played a small drum as they wove their way together and then apart. Huayna Capac loved to dance, and he moved through the crowd borrowing a partner whenever needed. He danced with groups of men and in mixed groups, but never with my mother.

My mother stood by the banquet tables with Cepi and Pilpintu while they directed the servants. Occasionally a group of the captains' wives stopped to offer the queen a small gift or to compliment her on the sumptuous banquet. She coolly acknowledged their friendly intentions, but rarely encouraged a lengthy conversation. Before long she had collected a number of fancy jars filled with unknown treasures. Noticing Pacas and me, she signaled us to come to her. As we approached, she said, "Boys, please take these jars back to my house. They're in the way here, and I'm afraid something will be broken."

"Okay. Is there anything you need from the house?" I asked as we carefully picked up as many jars as we could safely carry. She shook her head. Fully loaded and with Pacas leading, we went behind the great hall toward the private courtyard and our house. I'd just heard the soft cries of a young woman when Pacas stopped abruptly in front of me. "What are you doing? I almost ran into you."

"Would you rather interrupt that?" He said as he pointed his chin across the courtyard. I peeked around my mother's house. By torchlight, I first noticed their reflections quivering in the pool. In the doorway beyond it, my father pressed against a beautiful young woman. Leaning against the stone frame she spread her bare legs while her arms rested on his shoulders. My father's tunic was raised to his waist and mingled with her dress. He reached over her head to balance himself against the wall and bent his knees. Then he pulled himself up and into the wall, lifting her to her toes. He pulled away slightly and pushed in again. Back and forth to the beat of the drum in the great hall, my father drove himself into the woman. She squealed softly with each thrust, and he pushed harder and faster until the final release. He exhaled slowly, his back arched, and her legs dangling off the ground. In a short while he gently lowered her to the ground, and they straightened their clothes. It was then that I realized my father was not wearing the usual loincloth beneath his tunic. After a short whispered exchange, they casually strolled away.

Pacas and I giggled at our discovery and patiently waited for them to leave. "Quick. Let's drop this in the house and follow them," I said.

Having found a new game, we ran to our house, hurriedly put the jars in a corner and raced around the end of the great hall to see my father and the young woman enter arm and arm at the opposite end of the building. My mother stood near us talking to Pilpintu and ignored his return. He and his consort retrieved cups of beer and joined the conversation with a group who had been dancing. Huayna Capac chatted briefly and then, leaving the unknown woman with the others, moved down the hall to greet his other guests. He danced with a few of the captains' wives before choosing another cluster. This time he found a young woman who greatly interested him. Her lithe body floated around the dance floor as he held her hand, touched her shoulders and locked his eyes on hers. She encouraged his growing interest and gave him every opportunity to caress her shining hair and brush against her body. They danced nonstop for a while until he whispered something to her. She nodded, and they moved off the dance floor and out the door.

I understood the intimacy, but my father's indiscriminate choice of partners confused me. I knew the law allowed the Inca as many wives and partners as he chose. This was intended to give him the flexibility to marry for diplomatic purposes. It was an act of mutual trust for the daughter of a conquered king to wed the Inca. By accepting the wife, the Inca pledged himself to the service of the conquered. By allowing his daughter to marry, the father expressed his trust in the Inca's word. However, these women he took solely for his pleasure. Even at my age, I knew this was an abuse of his privilege.

"Do you think he'll do the same thing?" Pacas asked.

I hesitated, but Pacas was eager to watch.

"Come on," he said, pulling my arms. We followed the same path back to the royal courtyard.

My father leaned against the same doorway with the young woman facing him. He removed her shawl and nuzzled his face into her neck and hair. She pressed into him and ran her hands along his sides lifting his tunic. She sank to her knees, taking him into her mouth. My father bent over her to fondle her long flowing mane and to tilt her head from one position to another. Finally he settled on a rocking motion rotating his hips back and forth while holding her head in his hands. The beat intensified and then froze. Again he exhaled slowly and relaxed. Finally, he helped her stand and commanded her to swallow the seed of the Inca. She did as she was told while he helped her adjust her shawl. Like the last woman, they strolled back to the great hall to join the others for a cup of beer.

Through the night my father stalked his prey in both great halls while Pacas and I watched. He regularly led a new woman to the same place, indulged himself and returned for more beer and dancing. With eyes as cold as winter stars, my mother watched him from the safety of the women's circle. She kept her back straight and head high as she bore the public insult. At one point after noting my father's return, she clasped her hands on her chest, turned to Cepi and whispered, "Praise be to Inti. At least our secret is safe."

Pacas and I had heard her say that may times over the years, but we didn't know her secret. At the time, I didn't care. I was too hurt by my father's callous philandering and angry that he would treat my mother so poorly. As the sky turned gray in the predawn light my father strolled to his house with Miski, his traveling companion.

Tired, confused and sad that my father was no longer my perfect hero, Pacas and I stumbled off to our beds. Maybe after some sleep, I would understand.

Punishment

Ninan

When I rose at midday, my father and Sinchi Roca were sharing a light meal in the courtyard and discussing the prisoner. They planned to take both men to the military camp by the river at Yucay, since Sinchi Roca had learned they were soldiers, and brothers. Their defense would be heard, and the punishment delivered the same afternoon. Until then, the day was devoted to rest.

It was a short walk to Yucay, and only Huayna Capac and Sinchi Roca rode on litters. The prisoner, still bound, walked between two guards, while his captors carried his dead and now stiff brother, still hanging from the pole. We arrived in the marshaling field as the captains gathered their troops. The rumor of an attempt on the Inca was known to all, and we were greeted with cheers, "Long live the Inca, long live Huayna Capac."

The Inca, the guards and the prisoner stood on a raised platform facing the soldiers while the dead brother lay beside them. My father lifted his scepter for silence and spoke with an authority that seemed to rise from his feet. His deep, booming voice filled the afternoon sky as he addressed the prisoner. "State your name, your brother's name, and birthplace."

In spite of his bound hands and blood-matted hair, the powerful soldier proudly declared, "My name is Samana Wila and my brother's name is Juri Sulka. We were both born in Chuncho on the east side of Lake Titicaca."

"Did you and your brother conspire to kill me?"

"Yes!" he shouted with the defiance of a doomed man.

The soldiers responded with boos and insults, slings ready to fire, but Huayna Capac lifted his scepter, and the crowd subsided. "Why did you break your loyalty oath to the Inca?"

"You disgraced my family!"

Very calmly my father responded, "I'm sure you're able to do that without my help."

The crowd hooted at his joke, but the condemned man responded by spitting at the Inca's foot. Everyone drew a deep breath and stepped back. My father stiffened with the insult but maintained composure. "Please continue your grievance."

There was an audible sigh in the crowd.

"You visited our town last spring and reviewed our service to Inti. We were loyal to Inti and his son, and yet you punished my family. My father was the Curaca, a city leader respected by everyone. You removed him from office and appointed his enemy when the position was rightfully mine."

"Your father was getting old. Your enemy, as you call him, promised greater crop yields and more men for service."

"He promised more than our small village can provide. To win your favor, he has deprived the people, including my family, of sufficient land to support ourselves. He's a lying scoundrel. You will regret your appointment!"

"If that proves to be true, he will be removed from office. You might have replaced him. Surely, you must have realized that. Instead you chose to try to kill me."

The prisoner sputtered and then yell, "You took my youngest daughter and murdered her! My beautiful Chuma was a perfect child. We loved her dearly. You demanded her sacrificed to Inti."

"Then Inti and I have placed great favor on you. Only the very best children can be presented to Inti. Your blasphemous selfishness and disrespect for Inti is a disgrace! Depriving Inti of his rightful reward when your family has been so blessed is disgusting." Without waiting for a reply, the Inca continued, "You shall die for attempting to kill me, Inti's son on earth."

"From the start, I expected to die. I only regret not killing you." His eyes burned with hatred. Suddenly, he lunged at my father with an arrow he had concealed in his tunic. Two guards grabbed him and wrestled the arrow away from him without anyone getting hurt.

The crowd was absolutely silent. My father shook with anger. With the authority of a lightening bolt he bellowed. "Now you will know disgrace. You shall be flayed, and I will have your hide for a drum. Your remains shall be burned to destroy your body and your spirit. You will never enter the Other World! Your family harbored your treasonous acts and will be punished. Your wife and children, as well as your brother's wife and children, shall be stoned and burned. Your sacrificed daughter will be exhumed and destroyed. All remaining relatives will be moved to Canari as permanent Mitimas. For two years, your village will fast and provide twice the goods to Inti as penance for protecting you. For allowing your attack, your captain will be killed and buried."

The crowd gasped and muttered softly. They expected him to die, but the cruelty of the death and the extended reach of the punishment were extreme. Sinchi Roca left us, went to Huayna Capac and tried to bring him out of his rage. Meanwhile, the guards spread the prisoner's arms and legs, tied them to the supporting poles of the platform and tore off his tunic. He stood defiantly facing the soldiers as his captain was brought from the crowd to the prisoner's side.

The captain turned to Huayna Capac and said in a clear voice, "I regret that one of my men put you in danger. I have failed as a captain to be loyal to you and to Inti. Please forgive me before I die."

Having partially regained his self-control, Huayna Capac replied, "You were responsible for your men and their actions cannot be denied. I forgive you for your mistake, but I cannot modify your sentence. Inti sees your contrition and also forgives you."

"I understand. May I have the arrow?" The Inca nodded his approval, and the guard handed him the poisoned arrow. He looked at it for a moment, took a deep breath, and ran it down his arm. By the time it reached his wrist, he dropped to his knees and then fell forward. He convulsed twice and was still.

Huayna Capac picked up the arrow and faced the field of soldiers, "This was a brave man. May his children find favor with Inti." Speaking to the guards, he calmly added, "Now for the prisoner. You may begin."

Before my eyes, the guards used sharp knives to cut the skin across the prisoner's shoulders and down the sides of his back. Drums of every size appeared from nowhere. The frenzied soldiers pounded on them and cheered in ghoulish pleasure. Blood streamed down the prisoner's back and legs as the guards peeled his skin around a short pole. His unforgettable, piercing shrieks rose above the din of the crowd. He tossed his head from side to side, his eyes desperate for an end to the terror.

Expressionless, Huayna Capac stood and watched. My knees collapsed. On the ground, I vomited. Pacas stood beside me, unable to move. By the time the guards were half way down the prisoner's back he stood in a pool of his own blood. Finally he was limp and silent, while the guards finished removing his skin to his waist. When the crowd dispersed to gather wood for the incineration, Pacas and I left for Quispiguanca. Feeling very ill, the acrid smell of burning flesh frequently stopped our trip as waves of stomach spasms overtook us.

Safely back in the palace, Pacas and I sat in silence, flooded with images of the flaying. Everyone expected him to die, but the brutality of the torture and incineration was horrifying. His spirit was lost to this world and the Other World; it would wander forever, never part of either world. The extension of the death penalty to his family condemned them for actions they could not control. In his anger, my father had gone too far. Striking fear into would-be assassins was accomplished, but the extended penalties could justify a revolt.

Lost in thought, I was not aware of the man sitting beside me until he spoke. "Hello, Ninan, Pacas. You boys are very quiet. What've you been doing?"

I jumped at the sound of my name, even though the voice was quiet and non-threatening. I didn't remember his face, but dressed in a plain white tunic with a black cloak, I knew he must be Riku. After a quick appraisal, I asked, "Riku, can I speak to you without my father knowing?"

"Of course. There is no need to repeat your words. Why don't you and Pacas come to my house?"

We walked across the courtyard, and he offered us tea before we began. Pacas and I repeated the events of the past two days starting with the assassination attempt, through the celebration and ending with the punishment we had witnessed just that afternoon. Riku listened and watched but never said a word until we both were silent. Without showing the slightest surprise or excitement he said, "You had two memorable days. What have you learned from these events?"

Learned? I still suffered from the terrible images flashing before me. Learned? "I learned that the Inca has absolute power and can do anything he chooses. No one can contradict him. No one."

"Such is the role of the Inca. Will you rule differently than your father?"

"Yes!" I answered emphatically.

"And how will you rule the empire?" He emphasized each word as he spoke.

It seemed like such a simple question, but I couldn't answer him. I thought of examples of how I wouldn't rule, but what was better? I started speaking several times but never got out more than a few words before my thoughts twisted to an unacceptable end.

"Now you see the importance of these events. This is your time to learn and formulate your own legacy. Never forget what you feel today, or how you reacted to your father's actions but weigh the alternatives. Decide how you would act and what consequences might come from your decisions."

No one had pointed out this stark reality. For the first time I realized how difficult it was to be Inca. Gradually the conversation drifted away from such heavy thoughts. We passed the evening talking about his journey to Quispiguanca and our schooling in Cusco. Exhausted, but much relieved, we left for our beds.

The light of day brought nagging doubts and new promise as we gathered in the throne building. Amazingly, my father seemed completely recovered from the recent events and told Riku the results of the southern campaign without any mention of the previous day. "The entire southern border is secured. The Maule River canyon is a natural boundary leading to the ocean, and forts guard the valley passages between the Andes ridges if anyone were to successfully cross the river. With the refortifications at Pocona and Tucuman, the empire is impervious to our enemies."

"But father," I interrupted, "Doesn't the assassination attempt prove there is trouble in the south?"

Huayna Capac smiled. "Son, those were the actions of an isolated malcontent."

His words offered some comfort, but for the first time, I wondered if they were true. He continued before I could respond.

"On religious matters, the plan is also complete. The temple in Lake Titicaca receives excellent care, and the high priest is devoted to the rituals. The offerings provided by the local people are willingly given, and all are meticulously recorded by the standards set in Cusco. They have even completed the placement of the children in the snows of the southwest mountains."

Riku folded his arms over his chest. "This is excellent news. At least that bridge is complete. Now we'll have more time to finish the other bridge." Nodding his agreement, my father asked how Kaya was doing, and Riku responded that she was still young, but progressing well. He said she had an excellent memory and imagination but added that she was very impressionable and prone to bouts of sadness.

Hearing the visitors in the courtyard, Sinchi Roca interrupted, "I overheard the Curaca bragging about his new house and the abundance of guava he enjoys in Tomebamba."

Huayna Capac furrowed his eyebrows and signaled the servant to allow them to enter.

His cloak flowing behind him, Apu Moche, the Curaca of Tomebamba, confidently strode in carrying the largest basket. His assistants, Conono, with his protruding jaw, and Hatun, a stocky man, followed him carrying additional baskets. After brief introductions, the Inca accepted the generous gifts they brought: long, scarlet feathers, delicate green ones and soft yellow puff balls.

Flattering the Inca was the typical method for opening a dialog, but it didn't seem to distract my father. Interrupting the pleasantries, he asked, "What is the progress at the temple in Tomebamba? Has construction been completed?"

Unperturbed by the abrupt change in the conversation, Curaca Apu Moche responded immediately, "Our great Inca, I am saddened to report that the construction was greatly delayed. In spite of our best efforts, we have not yet completed the terraced platform on which the temple will be built. Last year we experienced disastrous rains that washed out a bridge and a key road. We needed to make these unexpected repairs before we could build the temple." He paused before continuing, "Sadly, I have other bad news. Much of the maize in the Inca's storehouses has rotted. We need your help to rebuild our supplies." Hatun and Conono nodded their agreement.

"Of course we can send supplies, but I'm disappointed to hear of the delays, and I'm troubled that the storehouse did not adequately protect the maize. Tell me, what construction has proceeded."

Pleased that the Inca had taken the bad news so well, Apu Moche replied, "The bridge and road are fully repaired. Now we can haul the timbers needed for my house across the river."

"Your orders were to build the temple first," Huayna Capac interjected. "Your new house is your compensation for completing the temple and yet you have reversed the work priorities. I understand you also directed the workmen to retrieve jungle fruit for your pleasure."

Having witnessed the punishments meted out the previous day, all three visitors begged for forgiveness, "Our apologies. We misunderstood your orders. We'll redirect all our men to the terrace."

Apu Moche was the most contrite, but I suspected he was more embarrassed about accidentally mentioning the house than for disobeying the Inca's orders.

My father lifted his scepter to silence the babbling and said, "You will return to Tomebamba and complete the temple. Construction on your new house will cease. Sinchi Roca, inform our most experienced builder that you will both go to Tomebamba to oversee this project. One month after your arrival, I expect a report sent by you with a full accounting of the situation and a plan for completion. As for the three of you, get that temple built, or our next meeting will be less amicable."

Apu Moche, Conono, and Hatun quickly thanked him for his understanding and departed, pleased to still have their positions, their honor, and their lives. Relieved that the punishments were more appropriate than the previous day, I wondered how far Tomebamba was from Cusco.

Escape

Kaya

I spent every afternoon at the end of my garden watching the city gate at the mountain pass and the road that descended to Machu Picchu. Riku and Atuk would return from Cusco on that road, and I felt sure I would recognize them. Riku had a distinctive gait with steps that didn't start or stop; he just slid forward without swinging his arms or moving the rest of his body. Whether he walked on flat ground or on steps, he seemed to float. Atuk was almost as tall as Riku, but he hadn't quite grown into his legs. His long stride got ahead of his body as he jerked his way forward with a comical rhythm. Such a pair should be easy to distinguish.

I could hardly wait to have them back. The month alone had been terrible. For two weeks I did nothing except sit in the garden and wait for the sunset. Kinsa was angry with me because I wasn't weaving the cloth she needed. She said she stayed up late several nights to do it herself, but I didn't care. Tawan scolded me because I didn't practice the flute and couldn't remember the songs she taught me the previous week. I just couldn't make myself do anything, except count the passing days. After two idle weeks Iska yelled at me and called me a worthless child. She even threatened to give me only porridge to eat, but I still couldn't climb out of my desperate loneliness.

Finally I realized that even more than their return, I was waiting for our secret trip to the valley. I'd forgotten that I needed to find a way to hide my hair. If I didn't have a plan, Riku would cancel the trip, and I might never get off this mountain. Having found a purpose, I struggled to concentrate on my task. I had to get all my hair on top of my head, but it was too long to do that with one, or even two braids. Instead, I curled four braids in circles around my head. Now all I needed was a way to cover it. Choosing an easy brown and white striped design, I wove a band to make the edge of a cap in just one long day. I adjusted it to fit snuggly around my hair, sewed the ends together, and then used scraps of white cloth to fashion a cap.

Having finished the cap with only nine days until Riku's expected return, I worked hard to win favorable reports from Tawan and Kinsa. In a week I learned all of the songs Tawan expected me to know, and I started weaving the pieces Kinsa had requested. I tied the top of the loom to the guava tree, and while kneeling, looped the strap at the other end around my back to provide tension.

With the bobbins of yarn already wound, all I had to do was weave. I lifted the heddle rod, the bar that allowed me to simultaneously lift every other warp thread, and fed the bobbin of yarn through the warp. Next I pressed that yarn in place with the beater. By lifting the shed sword, the opposite warp threads rose, so I could feed the bobbin through in the opposite direction. Again I pressed the yarn in place and endlessly repeated the process. From early morning to dusk, I constantly wove the solid brown fabric intended for a man's tunic, stopping only to retrieve another bobbin from the storehouse at the other end of the garden, or to stretch my aching back and legs. Kinsa was relieved that I was finally doing as she asked, and I'd completed the first piece when I spotted Riku and Atuk late in the afternoon. I didn't expect a visit that evening, but I was disappointed when Iska announced at breakfast that Riku would rest all day. Another day alone. Still, having the extra day gave me time to start the cloth for a second tunic.

When Riku finally arrived, I had already eaten breakfast and was pestering Iska. At the first sound of the gate I ran to greet him, stopping just short. Wearing his white tunic and his black cloak, he still looked tired, although he managed a little smile. The wrinkles in the corners of his eyes accentuated his long nose and narrow chin. We stood facing one another as he stared at me without speaking. He never really looked at any part of me in particular but saw me in the same way I looked at a house without seeing the individual stones or the windows. I was so happy to have him back, I could hardly contain myself, but I knew my manners. He must speak first.

"Hello, Kaya. It's good to see you again. I understand you have learned some new songs." He extended his hand to me which I gladly accepted, relieved that he didn't start with the incomplete weaving.

"Yes, I learned all of Tawan's songs." Wanting to change the subject, I added, "I saw you and Atuk on the road. I shouted your names, but you couldn't hear me. How was your trip? Did you see the Inca? Did you miss me? What did you see in the mountains?" I rattled off questions as we walked to the sacred plaza, barely listening to his abbreviated responses before jumping to the next question. I didn't really care what he said. I just needed to talk with him.

Tumbes and Atuk were already preparing a place for us in the Temple of Viracocha when we reached the sacred plaza. The morning sun flooded the three windows, lighting the entire room. I cheerily greeted them, and they offered friendly replies. Neither one seemed to have changed in the month. I was the only one who was isolated and, except for counting sunsets, had little memory of two weeks. Now I was the only one who craved company. Atuk worked quietly without any expression on his flat face. His small nose, shallow eyes and square jaw gave him the appearance of someone who had run into a stone wall. In contrast, Tumbes showed his perfect teeth through his typical broad smile. Exactly matching his mouth, his laughing eyes bounced precariously on his high check bones.

"It's good to have the group together again," Riku began. "Later, you can share your experiences of the past month, but now you will take another step into the spirit world."

After settling us into the exercise, he asked us to see the image he placed in the palm of his hand. I knew his hand was empty, and yet floating above it, I saw a magnificent stone building nestled between a small lake and a mountain. Riku was very pleased when all three of us were able to describe the Quispiguanca palace, although only Atuk and Riku had visited it. Riku assured us that the gods had blessed us with the ability to know each other's thoughts, and those of the spirit world. I didn't understand the significance, and I was content simply to be out of my garden and with my friends.

At the end of our lesson, Riku walked me back to my house, and I asked, "When will we go to the valley?"

Riku looked at me sternly, "I understand you have not completed all the weaving." I held my breath waiting for him to continue. "Did you find a way to hide your hair?"

"Yes, I can braid my hair and hide it in a cap." I replied with a sigh of relief.

"Then we will go tomorrow. I will talk with Iska. You must be ready before dawn. I'll ask her to wake you early enough to eat before we go."

After waiting so long, I was finally going to the hot springs with Riku. I happily wove all afternoon and braided my hair before I went to sleep. For the first time in a month, I slept soundly, waking only when Iska shook me. In the dark, I jumped out of bed and put my shawl over my head to hide my strange braids. Making sure I had my cap, I raced through breakfast without a word to Iska. Riku said I was not to tell anyone about our trip, and I was afraid I might say something to raise her suspicion. I was ready before Riku arrived.

"What's happening today that's so special?" Iska asked while I waited.

Forced to respond, I chose my words carefully. "I'm not sure, some lesson that will take all day, I guess. Did he tell you when we would be back?"

"Not until after dark. He said he would see that you got to bed, and told me not to wait."

"Well, this will be a long day." I had no idea we would be gone so long. I wondered if it took that long to get to the valley and back, or if he wanted to walk in the dark. Riku greeted me as usual and thanked Iska for her extra effort. She grunted. My shawl still covered my head and hopefully my excitement.

"Kaya, do you have everything you need?" Riku asked, implying a more specific question.

"Yes, it's very cold this morning, so I have extra things."

He nodded his approval, and we left. Our first stop was the storage building on the sacred plaza where Riku recovered a boy's tunic and well-used cloak. Leaving me with a torch, I changed quickly, hid my clothes, and rejoined Riku in the plaza.

He carefully examined me, especially studying the cap. "Yes, you could be a boy. You did well with your cap. Your head looks a bit large, but I don't think anyone will notice." He turned me around to be sure there were no long strands showing and said, "I'll tell people you're from a small town north of Quito. You stopped here on you way to Cusco where you'll study with the priests for a few years. You're traveling with your older brother who is currently visiting relatives in Vilcabamba. You must not speak. You don't know the language spoken in the north, and you speak Quechua too well for a northern boy. Do you understand?" He had a very serious expression on his face.

I opened my mouth to answer him, but his hand rose quickly to quiet me. I settled for a nod.

Still carrying the torch, Riku and I started down the stairs to the main plaza. In typical boy style, the tunic only came to my knees, unlike my dress that nearly reached to my ankles. I was surprised how cool the air was on my legs, and pulled my cloak around my shoulders to keep from shivering. We reached the main plaza, turned to pass the artisan section, and continued toward the terraced fields. Riku walked quickly, while I concentrated on keeping pace. The predawn sky showed no color, but offered enough light for him to leave the torch at the first field. We saw no one as we hurried along a terrace wide enough for several people to walk abreast. From my garden view, I knew the terraces continued up the mountain to nearly the height of the sacred plaza and down the slope as far as I could see. Even though I had watched the farmers in their fields many times, I had no idea the fields were so large, or the walls so high. I wondered if the gods used them like stairs to climb the mountains. On the far end of the terrace, we came to the steps leading to the valley. Each step was knee high, and I struggled to keep up with Riku. No longer cold, I breathed heavily.

He wasn't laboring at all when he noted, "You aren't used to walking the steps around the city. Perhaps we should walk more as we go from your garden to the sacred plaza. This shouldn't be difficult for one your age." He stopped to let me catch my breath and added, "You can speak to me when we are out of earshot. I know some of your tongue and any observers could be told we were speaking in your language. You can always use my name."

Reassured, I said, "I didn't expect so many steps! Now that it's light, I'd like to go slower so I can look around rather than watch my feet."

He seemed rather amused but said nothing as we started again. One step after another the path plunged into the valley. The heavy undergrowth lining the stairs hid the mountainside beyond a short distance, but along the staircase, the plants were familiar, although unremarkable. Most of the orchids and bromeliads needed rain and warmer weather to flower. Still, even the faded green of winter was more inviting than the cold white stone of the city buildings.

We saw two families working on a short terrace. With no one nearby, I asked Riku, "What are they doing in the field? It's too soon to plant."

"A farmer's work is never done," he replied. "They're not working that field, but building a new terrace just above it. Let's find a better place to watch." The trail took us down more steps before we came to a narrow path leading to the terrace where they waved to us as they worked. Standing at the far end of the terrace, three men chipped away on the uphill slope with stone-tipped axes. Closer to us, two women and their maiden daughters were just starting. In a low voice, Riku explained, "The men will use their pick axes to remove the loose rock, and use the natural seams of the mountain to break off pieces. At this end, the men have already dug out the mountain, and the young children have moved the stone out of the way. The women will use the stone to build the next terrace wall. They will work around the natural stone of the mountain to form the base of the new wall and gradually the new vertical wall will stand free. The extra stone will fill the bottom of the cavity created between the new wall and the mountain. Soil from the river bottom will fill the rest."

Headed for the path behind us, two boys about my age herded ten llamas toward us. I just nodded and smiled as Riku asked them, "Where will you get your dirt?"

"At the bend in the river just down stream from Huayna Picchu," one answered without stopping.

"Safe travels to you."

"And to you," he called back as he passed out of sight.

We watched the young children, much younger than I, as they struggled to carry, push or roll the stones to their waiting mothers. Often the stones were so large it took two working together to get them to their mothers. The women carefully placed each stone, taking advantage of their natural shape to pack them together as tightly as possible before filling the cracks with mud.

"By spring, they will have the new terrace completed. You can see by the number of children that the family is growing, so they need the extra field to feed the family. On our way back tonight, we will stop to see how they have done today." Riku paused and added, "We need to go."

Happy to have stopped to rest, I was ready to continue. We returned to the stairs to resume the constant descent. Through the treetops, we glimpsed the river below and the mountain jutting up across the valley. After even more steps, we reached the bridge crossing the river. It looked excessive for the size of the gentle stream below. Seemingly reading my thoughts, Riku asked, "When was the last time it rained?"

"At least two cycles of the moon, maybe three," I said after considerable thought.

"The river is very low during the winter, but rages through this valley in the summer rainy season. I remember when the old bridge washed out. We were unable to cross for months until the river receded and a new bridge was built."

It didn't seem possible the river could ever be that deep.

Seeing my skepticism, Riku asked, "Do you see where the stones of the river edge give way to the brush growing on the bank?"

I nodded.

"Standing here when the water is that high, it sounds like thunder roaring through the canyon."

I decided to listen for the river in both the dry and rainy season.

A few young boys approached the bridge, so we crossed and walked upstream along the riverbank. Carrying enormous loads of firewood on their backs, three women chattered as they overtook us. Even the young girl with them carried a large load. After they passed us, her bundle seemed to have grown legs, since that's all I could see of her. We followed them a short distance to a stream flowing into the river. They continued across the stream, but we turned to follow it uphill past several thatch-roofed houses. They weren't stone houses like those at Machu Picchu but were made of wooden poles. Women filled and carried water jars from the stream, and a baby cried while a young girl ground maize for the evening meal. Something was missing. "Where are the men?" I asked Riku.

"Many men are called for service during the winter. They may be in Cusco building a temple or even farther away repairing roads. Some will be gone a year or longer and will serve as soldiers."

"But the women will have to do all the work. Who will tend the crops? Who will repair the roofs before the rainy season?"

"Some of the men will return in time to do this work, but most of the work will be done by the mothers and children. Besides, doing the work is the best way for children to learn how to satisfy their needs anyway. They'll learn to tend the crops and animals, weave, build, cook and raise children. Everything. The land is plentiful. With hard work, the adults and the generations that follow will do well. If there is trouble, like the flood that washed out the bridge, the village leader, will petition the Inca for help to repair the damage. As the men of this village are helping others, so too others will help them."

"But they work so hard. Don't they ever rest?"

"That's why the festivals are so important. That's when they relax and enjoy themselves, as well as make offerings to thank Inti for granting them good health, good crops, and many children. If their lives are filled with misfortune, they will plead with the gods to forgive their sins. They may even pledge to offer a daughter for a life of service as a Mamacona, like Iska. Her family's crops were destroyed three years in a row. When they consulted their priest, he suggested that they might return to Inti's favor, if Iska were accepted as a Mamacona."

"And was her family blessed?"

"Yes, the next year their village leader reduced their tributes. With one less mouth to feed, and the good fortune of a plentiful harvest, they flourished. In fact her mother had a baby that year, and the following year."

"Wouldn't it be easier to reduce the tributes when their crops were doing poorly?"

"Perhaps, but remember tributes allocated to the religion feed you, and everyone you know, as well as many others. The tribute for the Inca feeds the men working in his service including the soldiers and the builders. Even when crops fail, these people need to eat."

I had never thought about where my food came from. We continued along the stream until the mountain loomed directly over us. The path hooked to the left following the edge of a steep incline. I had already learned more about the people of the valley than I could have imagined, and we still hadn't reached the hot springs. My anticipation mounted with every step.

Healing

Kaya

Before we continued along the path at the base of the mountain, Riku stopped to study me as I tucked a lock of hair under my cap. "Now remember," he said, "you are a boy from the north. Think how Atuk would act and try to do that. Not a word until we are alone again."

I nodded. It wasn't long before we came to a clearing filled with people of all ages. There was a boy about my age with a bone jutting out of his arm, who sat patiently with his mother. An ancient man with a cane hobbled toward the pool at the far end of the clearing. A worried young woman tried to comfort her whimpering baby.

Riku surveyed the ailing before approaching a man treating a girl with a burned foot. The healer wore a black tunic with white and red lightening bolts woven along the bottom edge. On his head he had a black cap decorated with the same pattern, but instead of woven, the streaks were embroidered from his crown down to the edge. Atuk would never have noticed, and I carefully hid my fascination with his clothes. Riku addressed him with great respect, "Good morning, Brother. Your healing powers are much needed here. If I may greet your sister, my friend and I will return to help you."

He continued to wash the girl's foot as he responded, "Your help would be most welcome. My sister is with a young woman at the third pool. She too could use your help."

Just then we heard a high-pitched shriek from the direction he had tipped his head. Riku looked down the path and thanked the man.

We passed the pool, now occupied by two old men, and hurried past a second unoccupied pool. I would have gladly remedied that after our long walk. The sunlight filtered through the canopy to the forest floor, highlighting a white granite boulder on the far side, and a small patch of unfamiliar pink flowers very near us. The shadow of an overhanging vine swooped across the rocks at the pool's edge. Riku didn't even pause, and with the second shriek, I ran to catch up.

Wearing a black dress and a cap of the same design, a woman healer stood beside a pregnant young woman. The patient lay on a blanket, propped up against a rock wall with her legs bent and her feet firmly planted on the ground. Her face, partially covered with tangled hair, was wet with heat.

"Hello, Sister, can we help you?"

"Riku, your arrival is most welcome. I gave her some medicine to weaken the contractions so I can turn the baby around. The boy can hold her hand while we do the work."

"Is she alone?"

"Yes, her husband was called to service just a month ago, and her mother lives too far away to help."

Riku was already on his knees opposite the healer. I knelt beside him, and the woman grabbed my hand. I let her hold it, and tried to brush the hair from her face, but she lifted her head and let out a shrill wail. I thought I had hurt her, and I jumped back.

"She is about to deliver. The pain is caused by the birth process, not our efforts, right?" Riku spoke to me by asking questions of the healer.

The healer nodded, not understanding why he would ask such an obvious question. Speaking and showing me at the same time, Riku taught me how to hold her hand, and still be able to wipe her brow with a damp cloth, or offer her a drink. In no time he was working with the healer to turn the baby. The woman squeezed my hand so tightly my fingers turned blue and then went numb. When the healer's hand disappeared inside her, and Riku started pushing on her stomach from bottom to top, she stiffened in protest but knew this must be done if they were to survive. From the shape of her stomach, something was changing, and they both continued to work even though her screams felt like needles stabbing my ears and my heart. Very suddenly she stiffened again and didn't relax until her face was a deep reddish-purple. Once again, Riku and the healer kneaded her stomach until her belly seemed to collapse into her hips. Much relieved, the healer removed her hand with a gush of water and blood while Riku leaned back, resting on his heels. Exhausted the young woman exhaled a long sigh and allowed me to peel her fingers off my aching hand.

"Our work is done," the healer concluded. "The rest is in her hands, and Pachamama's. You can help her by sacrificing a llama in her name to Pachamama and Inti. Your prayers will comfort her. Riku, do you know where the provisions are?" He nodded.

The pregnant woman turned her head and reached for my knee as I rose to leave. She thanked me in a hoarse whisper. I wanted to offer some comforting words, but I couldn't, so I just smiled and smoothed her hair. She looked so young, and so frightened.

"Come, boy. It's time to go." Riku urged me to leave. We walked down the path in silence, past both pools and beyond to another clearing. Llamas grazed in a stone enclosure, and the embers of their morning camp were still hot enough to rekindle. Riku selected a young llama from the pasture while I worked on the fire. The dry winter wood easily sprang to flame.

"Kaya, sacrificing the llama will be your act. I'll ask the gods to bless your work. Then you'll make the offering and the prayers to Inti and Pachamama."

My heart pounded, and I yearned for the safety of my garden. Finally I stammered, "But I've never killed an animal or offered a sacrifice. What if I make a mistake?"

"This is your opportunity to know life as others do."

There was no possibility of compromise. My stomach churned, and my hands and feet were suddenly cold.

Riku began his prayers. "Inti and Pachamama, you know this to be your daughter, Kaya. Help her to be sincere in her offering, and help the woman of her concern."

After Riku's short prayer he showed me how to hold the llama and to slit its throat so it wouldn't suffer. I did as he instructed, holding her halter in my left hand. The llama's large brown eyes were so vacant and so forgiving, as though she knew her destiny was to die as an offering. She depended on me to be sure the sacrifice was accepted, and her death was not in vain. I looked to Riku for encouragement, but he gave me none. This was to be my task alone. The knife was very sharp and slitting the llama's throat was easier than I expected. She didn't seem to be in pain, but blood covered her chest before she fell to his knees and then lay down. Again I looked to Riku, but he stood stone-faced.

"Pachamama, protector of woman, hear my prayer. This woman faces the terrible pain of childbirth without her family. The baby needs to come out. Riku and the healer helped her, but it wasn't enough. Please help her. Inti, creator of the spirit that lives in all of us, hear me. Please make this woman strong. I give you this llama in her place. Let her live."

Having finished the prayers, Riku helped me lift the llama onto the fire. We watched, knowing it rose to Inti in the flames and smoke. The fire seared through the fur raising a pungent odor, exposing skin and spastic muscles. The cooking meat hissed and spattered as the flames licked the bones clean. I added wood to the fire, watched in fascination and prayed that Inti and Pachamama would be satisfied. Riku ended our offering with a final prayer. "Almighty Inti, may you bless these young women as they live to serve you." He turned to me without commenting on the sacrifice and said it was time to help the Brother.

We found him in the same place, now working on the boy's broken arm. He didn't need our help, but suggested we see to the mother still waiting with the sick baby. Riku examined the baby as he asked the mother about its condition. The baby had refused her milk for a day and was now very hot and weak. Riku consulted with the healer who handed him a packet as he explained how to prepare the medicine. Meanwhile, I was to cool the baby in the pool. His mother undressed him, and I lay on my stomach, holding the boy. The water felt pleasantly warm to my arms, but he screamed as I lowered him into the water. When the infant finally quieted, he started a jerky shake. I called Riku who watched until he was satisfied that the child was not in danger. The shaking continued while the shrieking from the pregnant woman rose and fell in the distance. Finally Riku finished preparing the medicinal tea and showed me how to wet the baby's lips with a piece of cloth soaked in the medicine. He refused it at first, but finally he accepted the warm tea.

Through the afternoon, his mother paced the clearing asking Inti for his forgiveness and promising sacrifices throughout the year, if only he would let her son live. Of course, I couldn't speak to her, so I tended the child, trying to feed him as much medicine as possible. He didn't feel hot anymore and was nearly falling asleep when we dressed him. If he took her milk when he woke, Riku expected he would fully recover. All we could do was wait.

The cries from the distant pool came at shorter intervals. I asked Riku if we could go back and the Brother granted permission. The exhausted pregnant woman lay in the same place, while the healer stood over a small fire stirring a pot. I immediately knelt by the patient who gratefully clasped my hand. Riku assured her that we had made the sacrifice, and everything had gone very well. Now, he said, she needed to concentrate on the child. The healer approached us with a cup and instructed the woman to drink the tea. She drank it without hesitation although her pinched face implied the taste. In a very short time, she threw her body forward, her screams echoing in my head. She struggled to catch her breath between the contractions and finally the healer said she was holding the baby's head.

"Again. Help the baby come out. Push it out. You don't want me to pull." The healer tried to encourage her. At the right time she grabbed both my arms, pulled herself up, and glared at me with the determination of a dying woman. The push was enough to clear the baby's shoulders and the rest just slid out. She collapsed to the ground, relieved she was finally out of pain. I looked at her limp body and swallowed my tears, since no boy would cry.

The healer covered the child's head and cut the cord without emotion. "Your baby is dead. You must rest now."

"Let me see my baby. Don't take him. Let me hold him." Tears ran off her cheeks as she choked on her words. The healer refused her requests and put the baby out of sight. Every part of me wanted to run to the baby and place it in her arms, but I knew I couldn't. There was nothing I could do but hold my breath and try not to cry.

Returning to the woman she said, "He had a withered arm. You don't want to see a baby who suffered so."

She stiffened again and the afterbirth oozed onto the ground. "You must care for yourself. You will have other babies. This one was too much trouble. Be still and rest." She wasn't comforted by the healer's words. When I finally started breathing normally, I held her hand and wiped away her tears. Neither helped, so I hummed one of the songs Tawan taught me. Riku shot a quick look at me, but realized I wouldn't sing the words. Slowly she calmed down and cried herself to sleep, while I continually repeated the same song.

The sun was setting when Riku finally asked, "Sister, may we share your supper before we begin our journey?"

"Of course. You must be hungry. I'll see to the soup." I hadn't eaten anything since breakfast and noticed I was famished. We stayed with the woman until the healer returned with soup for the patient.

The pot of vegetable soup hung over the same fire we used for the sacrifice. It was tasty, but thinned to serve more people. Riku and I spoke together as we ate alone. "What happened to the baby?" I asked.

"When we turned the baby inside the mother, the cord must have wrapped around his arm. By the time the baby was born, the arm was a dark blue. Since a child can't survive with only one arm, the healer didn't allow him a first breath."

"But he could have lived to be a priest or a Quipucamayo. Why did she kill him?"

"His lot was to be a farmer. He would be teased as a child and an outcast as an adult. She will have another child, and this one will be forgotten."

It seemed so cruel, and I doubted that woman would ever forget how she suffered. Then a horrible thought occurred to me. "Did the baby die because of me? Did I not perform the sacrifice correctly? Should I have done something else?"

"You performed the sacrifice exactly as your heart directed you. You asked Inti and Pachamama to accept the llama instead of taking the mother. You never asked for the child to survive. I think Inti had already told you he would not."

I gasped at my omission and wondered if he was right, or if the child died because I had forgotten. I didn't want to talk anymore and finished my soup in silence. Riku startled me when he said, "Brother, you had a busy day. There are many here who benefited from your help." Riku handed the healer a bowl of soup as he sat beside him.

"It is our calling. We go where we are needed. In two days we will travel north in the mountain valleys." He paused to eat and continued between bites. "Thank you for your help. Is there anything we can offer in repayment?"

Riku politely paused. "Yes, do you have any cuchuma cactus? My students are nearly ready for it, and I don't know when we might meet again."

"Yes, of course, we are always pleased to help. Your work is far more important than ours."

From the healing work I had just seen, I couldn't imagine what Riku did that could possibly be more important. When his sister joined us for soup, she told us that the young woman had eaten and was sleeping again. She expected her to recover fully. The fevered baby had also awakened and taken his mother's breast.

It was dark when Riku and I left for Machu Picchu, the package of cactus carefully stored in Riku's pouch. With best wishes for safe travels, we retraced our steps out of the forest, through the village, across the river and up the mountainside to Machu Picchu. Just that morning I had struggled to keep up with Riku as we went down the slope. Going up, the steps were endless. Riku stopped dozens of times so I could catch my breath as I panted and struggled with each step. Part way up, we rested on the terrace to note the farmers' progress. From the size of the dirt pile, Riku decided the boys must have made two trips that day. I struggled to do just one. We continued our climb, stopping about every forty steps until my legs stopped burning and my heart stopped pounding. During those rest periods, a different image of the day flew back to me, and I grew more attached to the people beyond my garden. When we finally reached my home, Riku made sure I was in bed before he left. Sleep came quickly.

Tomebamba

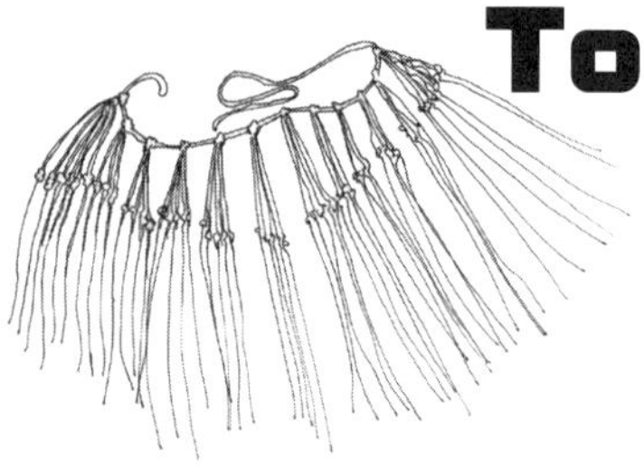

Ninan

Huayna Capac loved Tomebamba, the city of his birth. Set in a lush green valley surrounded by forested volcanic mountains, he claimed that it was even more beautiful than Cusco. He longed to go with Sinchi Roca, but they couldn't both leave Cusco, and since Sinchi Roca was the builder, he was the better choice. Besides, after being away so long, the Inca needed to reestablish himself as the ultimate authority. It was settled; Sinchi Roca planned to leave immediately after Inti Raymi, the winter solstice festival. Listening to their plan and seeking adventure, I asked if Pacas and I could go as well.

"Good idea." My father's eyes brightened. "It's a promising and underutilized region. Who knows, you may choose to establish your *ayllu* there." He turned to Sinchi Roca. "Are you willing to take the boys with you?"

"I'd enjoy their company."

Hiding my excitement, I left to tell Pacas the good news. In that conversation, my father indicated for the first time that I was his choice for his successor. I was his oldest son, and the only one born to his first wife, but that didn't assure my succession. Only a new Inca established an *ayllu*, the family group that included all his direct descendants, and his servants' descendants. A new Inca would provide for these people solely on the wealth that he generated, since his father's wealth remained with his surviving descendants. I hadn't given any thought to where I might establish my *ayllu* when, and if, I became Inca. The Urubamba River valley was getting crowded with the last three Incas all established there. From Huayna Capac's description, Tomebamba might be an excellent alternative.

Pacas and I were ready to leave the same afternoon since all we planned to take was our weapons. Sinchi Roca's preparations were more extensive, and, besides, he needed to stay through the festival. Finally, everything was ready, and we started the three-month trek to Tomebamba with litters for Sinchi Roca, Pacas, Socso, and me. Socso, Sinchi Roca's favorite building foreman, planned to stay in Tomebamba until the project was completed. The servants followed on foot and were responsible for the hundreds of llamas carrying food to Tomebamba. Immediately after meeting with Apu Moche at Quispiguanca, my father arranged for maize and beans to be transferred from Cajamarca to Tomebamba, providing temporary relief in less than two weeks. We carried additional maize, as well as dried potatoes, beans and hot peppers.

Pacas and I thrived on the travel. We walked about half the day until we got tired, and then we rode in our litters. While we walked, we practiced using our weapons or talked with the people we met. For several days, we traveled with two healers who were going to Chacapoyas. As we walked with them, they constantly watched the plants we passed, and frequently stopped to dig up a root or pick seeds for curing one ailment or another. Occasionally a messenger overtook us as he raced toward his destination with information for a city leader. Pacas and I often ran with him for a while to find out where he would be relieved and where the message was headed, but the runners were so fast we were never able to keep pace for very long.

Each day was different as we passed through the valley. Always busy, the village men repaired the thatched roofs, or reset stones in the road while children tended the llamas and women wove cloth. Other days we traveled through desolate rock fields or ascended deserted mountain passes. No matter where we were, a wide, stone-paved road always pointed the way. After weeks of walking, we grew stronger, and our practice targets more distant. We always retrieved our arrows, so we usually took aim close to the road in front of the procession, and we used our slings for targets off the road to the side. All the while, Sinchi Roca and Socso spent their travel time designing the buildings for Tomebamba. During his northern campaign Topa Inca, my grandfather, had brought the region into the empire, but he didn't stay long enough to build much. My father wanted a temple like the Coricancha of Cusco. Of course he also needed a palace, but the temple was to be built first.

Around Tomebamba, the mountains were not as jagged as those around Cusco, and in this milder climate, spring had already arrived. The verdant beauty of the north, especially the valley surrounding the city, was a marvel to Pacas and me. Four rivers wove their way across the plateau from the mountains in the west and south before joining together and cutting a path through the eastern slopes. The town was located beside the largest river at the southern end of the valley. Without any ceremony, we arrived just before sunset at the house where my father was born.

We had finished breakfast when our hosts arrived. Apu Moche, the Curaca, took the lead as he had at Quispiguanca, while the younger Hatun and Conono stood in the background. "Sinchi Roca, good morning. Welcome to Tomebamba, our beautiful city. I hope you find it as lovely as Cusco and worthy of your travel." He smiled and raised his arms as though he was presenting an exquisite view of the city, even though we were still in the house.

"And good morning to you," Sinchi Roca answered without enthusiasm. "Tomebamba is satisfactory. We look forward to overseeing the delivery of the cargo and later inspecting the building construction." He glanced at our small group. "I will introduce you to my traveling companions." Sinchi Roca introduced Pacas, Socso, and me while Conono repeatedly pinched his protruding jaw, and Hatun fidgeted continuously. No one from Cusco had visited in ten years. After their treatment at Quispiguanca, they understood that Sinchi Roca must be satisfied.

Together, we immediately headed for the storehouses where we met the hunchbacked Quipucamayo, the record keeper, overseeing the delivery. There were only three small adobe brick buildings situated parallel to the slope. Each had a thatched roof, no windows, and a wooden door facing west. For each building, the Quipucamayo laid out a *quipu*, the official record. In accordance with Cusco practices, the *quipu* was a long rope with many strings tied to it. The color, type, and number of knots on each string combined to record the information. Each color on the *quipu* represented a different grain while the type and number of knots combined to give the amount. He explained that he stored all the beans and some maize in the first building. The second building was entirely filled with maize while the third had potatoes, squash, hot peppers, salt and small amounts of dried fish and meat.

Pacas quickly reviewed the recording system, and asked how he tracked goods that were delivered or distributed. The changes were recorded at the end of the *quipu* and were kept separate from the original count. He explained that each bin was built to hold enough maize to load ten llamas. So he added or subtracted the number of llamas used to transport the grain and changed the knots accordingly. Conono, Pacas, and I inspected each building with the Quipucamayo and found the supplies stored in bins exactly as he had explained.

Sinchi Roca and Socso spoke with Apu Moche and Hatun about the recent spoilage as they inspected the storehouses. In one building, water had run down the hill, collected behind the building, and soaked through the adobe wall to the grain. In another, the thatched roof had partially blown off during a storm causing the grain to rot. On the third building, the wooden door was inadequate and a driving western rain soaked the beans.

Inside Pacas busily counted the bins of each product. He asked me to remember certain numbers to be sure he didn't make any mistakes. As the llamas arrived, he watched the bins fill and double-checked the accuracy between llama loads and bin counts. The process took all day as each animal was brought to the appropriate building, unloaded into the designated bin and the *quipus* modified to note the change. Pacas precisely followed the entire process.

I was happy to talk with the herders and Conono, the youngest of our hosts. He was a native man with a stocky build and a round face. Even though I was still a boy, as the Inca's son, he tried to gain my favor. "How was your trip? Have you traveled to other parts of the empire?"

I answered politely but was more interested in Tomebamba and Quito. "When will the crops be planted?"

"In the valley the peas are about to flower, and maize will be planted soon. On the hillsides, potatoes are already in the ground, but the quinoa at the highest elevations will not be planted for another month. We can grow almost all year long in many areas." He relaxed a little, relieved to speak of things he knew well.

They were almost a full month ahead of Cusco's planting schedule; growing conditions seemed ideal here. "With such a favorable climate, why are we hauling food from Cusco? Your losses from these storehouses couldn't have caused so much strife."

"Our harvest was much smaller last year than usual. We had constant rain as the maize was coming to maturity. Most of the crop was lost in the field. That compounded the lost bean crop earlier in the spring. The beans had only four leaves when a violent storm washed out the young plants. After the soil finally drained, we could only harvest a single crop in the growing season."

His explanation seemed reasonable. "If you had such a great need, why didn't you ask for help?"

"We did. We asked the Curaca at Quito, but he claimed they had similar troubles and had nothing to spare."

"Why didn't you ask the Inca directly?"

He hesitated, but he reluctantly admitted, "We didn't think he would really help us. We know the claims of reciprocity between the Inca supplies and our tributes, but no other conqueror has treated us fairly. In this area, we simply take what we need from our neighbors."

"But buildings are burned, crops destroyed, and people die."

He shrugged his shoulders. "This is inevitable. When our neighbors suffered, they raided us for food and wood. It all works out."

I didn't understand why someone would choose to fight when there was a peaceful solution. Searching for a less controversial topic, I asked about the weather. The predicable rain every afternoon annoyed me. I didn't like getting wet, especially so close to sunset. Still, even the Inca couldn't change that. As we spoke, the afternoon shower rolled across the valley, so we ducked into the storehouse to find Pacas and the Quipucamayo just finishing the day's records.

Sinchi Roca and Socso had rooted around the buildings all day. The first change was obvious; because the storms came from the west, the current doorways would be bricked in and new doorways made on the eastern side. They also planned a channel to redirect the runoff, and stood in the rain watching the natural flow of the water. By understanding that, they could minimize the work to be done. They marked the ground where a channel would be built and followed it entirely off the plateau, well beyond the end of the existing buildings. Sinchi Roca reasoned that they would need more storehouses in the future, and it was easier to dig the channel now, anticipating the growth.

When the rain stopped, we all slogged down the muddy road back to our residence. Staring at his feet and still stepping in several puddles, Pacas was completely silent as we walked. Reaching my father's house, everyone enjoyed the local beer, and we were invited to a welcoming dinner with Apu Moche later in the evening. Pacas stayed with the group, but spoke to no one. The sun had already set when they finally left. When Sinchi Roca and Socso began to discuss the visit to the construction site scheduled for the following day, Pacas suggested we go outside. After getting a safe distance away from the house, Pacas stopped and carefully checked our surroundings. The street was dark, empty and silent.

"What's wrong?" I asked, getting worried about his behavior.

Almost in a whisper he said, "The *quipu* shows twice as much grain in the storehouses as is actually there, and the Quipucamayo doesn't know it."

"Half the grain is missing? How can that be?"

"The Quipucamayo never reads the total amounts." Pacas sounded scared. "He only watches how many loads of supplies are added and taken away. Twice I made a total count for each grain. I counted the amount of beans in the storehouse and then checked the *quipu* to see if it matched. I did the same for the maize, potatoes and quinoa. Half of the supplies are missing!" He grabbed my shoulders to be sure I was listening.

"All right, I believe you. Are you sure the Quipucamayo doesn't know?"

"I'm sure. He seems like a nice man, and he wants to do a good job, but he's getting old. When I asked him if he ever compared the totals on the *quipu* compared to the totals in the storehouses he said no. It was too much work."

"How can this be? How can the count be so far off? Was the total not adjusted after the spoilage last year?"

"I asked him that," he still whispered. "He said they emptied the storehouses and made the current *quipu* at that time. So the count was correct at the end of last year's harvest."

"Do you think he is so lazy he forgot to record the removal of grain?"

"Possibly, but with the food shortage, I don't think he would be that careless."

"Well, then someone must be stealing from the storehouses. Who could it be?"

"We are strangers here. I don't know." He paused and added, "What should we do?"

I thought about our situation before replying. "I don't think we should tell your father yet. If someone is stealing, he must need it. We can talk with the local farmers to see if they were given enough food from the storehouses. We don't want to get anyone in trouble because he needs to eat." An idea struck me. "Whoever is stealing must be taking it at night. We should watch the storehouses and catch the thieves!"

"We can't do that! We're only boys." I assured him that we would only watch. If we found anything, we would get his father involved.

A plan in place, we hurried back, arriving in time to leave for dinner with Apu Moche and the others. I don't remember much about the dinner, except that at Apu Moche's request, we sat with the men. It should have been an honor, but with the storehouse problems, we were wary of our hosts. As usual, Apu Moche dominated the conversation as he continually spoke of the splendors of Tomebamba in order to promote himself.

The next morning the four from Cusco and the three leaders of Tomebamba set out for the construction site. It was a fine morning, and the short walk through town was refreshing, although the buildings were not as beautiful as Cusco's fitted-stone ones. Most of them were made of cobblestones set in clay mud before being covered with plaster and painted white. The doors and thatched roofs were similar to Cusco.

We reached the open field that was to be the religious center as the workers started their day at the end of the terrace wall. Sinchi Roca and Socso took a brief overview of the entire plateau and then focused on the work area. The water damage was extensive, even to my untrained eye. Water running off the upper slope had crossed the field and formed a shallow lake near the terrace wall. Due to poor construction or the added weight, the earth slumped, and water ran out through the wall. Once the wall was compromised, the mud mortar disappeared, and the rock was dragged downstream. With a channel established, subsequent rains washed a deep gully all the way across the plateau. On returning from Cusco, Apu Moche instructed the foreman to rebuild the terrace wall before our arrival. Now the gaping hole in the terrace wall was rebuilt to waist height, but the spring rains were collecting behind the wall.

Sinchi Roca was very angry, but only Pacas and I knew it. Although he rarely lost his temper, he forgot to breathe when he was upset. He lifted his shoulders and took short shallow breaths in his throat. He raised his right arm and spoke to the workers. "In the name of the Inca, I thank you for your work. You need a day of rest. Go. Enjoy your families. On your way back to your homes, stop by the storehouses and get three days supply of maize and potatoes for your families." As an afterthought he added, "The foreman will stay with us for a while."

The workers were so stunned they didn't leave. Finally Apu Moche assured them that Sinchi Roca represented the Inca and they were free to go. They talked among themselves and finally started toward the storehouses. Sinchi Roca waited until all of the workers were out of earshot and then spoke to the Apu Moche and the foreman.

"There is no reason to waste the men's efforts to build that wall. You must control the water at its source before you attempt to repair it. The rainy season has begun, and water is again collecting behind the wall. By the end of the season it will wash out again."

The foreman nodded, looking in the direction of the wall construction.

Apu Moche responded in his fawning voice, "You are a more knowledgeable builder than I, but we need the wall to begin construction on the terrace. We must complete the wall as quickly as possible, as the Inca requested, and deal with the water later."

Finally understanding Apu Moche's incompetence, Sinchi Roca turned to him and spoke tersely, "I already told you. If you don't control the water first, the wall will again collapse, and your efforts will again be wasted. Apu Moche, you will not be involved with this building project. Socso, you are to act on my orders. Is that understood?"

Apu Moche, the man with the golden tongue, tried to make excuses, but finally turned and left the terrace.

The foreman showed Sinchi Roca and Socso the source of the water and proposed building a series of drainage ditches under the terrace. He wanted to fill the rock-lined troughs with volcanic sand so the water could easily pass under the terrace. At the wall, he proposed setting in large boulders without mud mortar so the water would trickle over stone without damaging the wall. Socso questioned him on the heaviest rainfalls and wondered if even the extra drainage was adequate. The foreman was sure it was sufficient, but Socso suggested they build one additional channel along the uphill slope as the feeding line for his drainage system. It could also spill excess water off the ends of the plateau. The foreman agreed this was a good precaution and could be used as a water source for fountains, streams, or pools around the temples.

Hatun and Conono timidly followed along as we walked the terrace and planned the construction. Sinchi Roca listened carefully to Socso and the foreman. "Excellent! You two will work together well. I'm confident that the work will progress quickly under your guidance."

Socso, comfortable with Sinchi Roca, took the praise in stride. The foreman straightened and displayed a toothless smile.

Sinchi Roca asked the native, "How many men are available for this project?"

"There were four hundred, but only two hundred men are left." The foreman spoke directly to Sinchi Roca for the first time.

"Where are the two hundred additional men?"

"They weren't being adequately fed, so they gradually returned to Quito."

"And why were they not fed?" I could see Sinchi Roca starting to breathe in his throat again.

Pacas and I intently listened to every word. "Apu Moche said the storehouses were empty because of the bad crops last year."

Hatun and Conono looked surprised.

Sinchi Roca tried not to upset the man and continued to question him on another subject. "Do you know of any other construction projects taking place this year?"

"We were building a new house for Apu Moche when the rain washed out the terrace. When he came back from Cusco, he stopped work on that project and started on the wall." Hatun was very intent on the stone he was kicking, while Conono swayed from side to side with his arms folded over his chest as he stared at the clouds.

Sinchi Roca, totally in control, paused and simply asked, "Will you take me to that work site on your way home?"

We all followed the foreman as he walked with Sinchi Roca, and my uncle asked about his farm on the way to the new house. Beautifully situated on the river, the house foundation was in place, and the fitted-stone walls were higher than my head. The skill displayed in shaping and fitting the stone without using mortar was as good as any I'd seen in Cusco. The foreman was excused and headed to the storehouse while we walked back to town. Hatun and Conono needled Sinchi Roca to get his reaction, but he ignored them, and they finally left.

I asked if Pacas and I could join the builders, since a makeshift celebration was certain for the afternoon and evening. Sinchi Roca seemed pleased to be rid of us. We crossed the river bridge and walked along the paths between the fields. Almost directly overhead, the intense sun warmed the dark soil and clogged the afternoon with sticky heat. The field before us promised a plentiful pea harvest, if the farmers were able to clear the intrusive grass. A man and his wife weeded together, while a young girl tended her brother and a baby in the shade of a neighboring tree.

"Good afternoon. You have a fine field there," I cheerily greeted the farmers. The man looked up without stopping his work and managed to say hello. "Will you interplant with squash or maize?"

Seeing that I at least had some understanding of local agriculture, he stopped and leaned on his footplow. "That depends on the rain. If we have a lot of rain, the maize will do better than the squash lying on the ground."

"When will you decide?"

"We'll finish weeding this week, tend our other field on the mountain slope next week, and the following week we will return to plant." His wife stopped working as well.

"What are you growing in your other field?" I asked as we approached them, careful to step on the grassy parts.

"Three types of potatoes. At least two should yield a harvest. Where are you from?" We were dressed as Incas, but he must not have recognized the patterns on our headbands.

"Cusco. We traveled with Pacas' father to inspect the building construction." I nodded at Pacas who stood slightly behind me, as he usually did when I spoke to strangers.

"Now there's a story," he replied, shaking his head.

"His father wasn't very happy about the work either," I added.

The toddler tripped and fell in the coarse sand. His sister lifted the boy to his feet and checked for damage. He was lightly clothed and filthy, but unhurt. His fine hair chaotically covered a head too large for his spindly body. He teetered and dropped to his bottom. His sister, just as thin and dirty, returned to the wool she was carding.

Not sure what to say next, I tried the standard compliment. "You have a beautiful family."

With a sigh of resignation he answered quietly, "They're hungry. We eat only an evening meal now."

Not wanting to offend, I asked, "Have you been ill?" He seemed to appreciate a question about their welfare.

"No, so far we have all been healthy, but the rainy season always brings more sickness. We need to extend our food until the peas can be harvested."

"Have you received maize or any other food from the storehouses?"

He stared at me in disbelief and then broke into a deep belly laugh. His wife dropped her head as her shoulders stuttered, either in laughter or tears. "I have watched my brother's three children die, one by one through the winter. His young daughter went first and then his older son. Finally his wife went dry, and the baby was lost as well. My neighbor lost his dear wife and two grandchildren. The story is the same across the valley."

I looked at Pacas, whose eyes were damp. We knew there was food. Why wasn't it being distributed? Maybe the villagers were stealing from the storehouses, but one look at his children made it clear this farmer was not. "Are any farmers untouched by these difficult times?"

He looked at his wife and then shook his head. "Wait, I understand that two families at the far end of the valley were fortunate to have relatives in Quito. They left about two months ago, and we hear they are doing well there."

"How lucky for them!" I quickly smiled. He started with his plow again and I knew it was time to leave. "We will pray to Inti that his blessings will fill your soup pot with meat and vegetables."

"Only if we weed these peas."

We left on friendly terms, and Pacas and I continued down the path. The houses were generally in good repair, and the crops looked better than most I'd seen in Cusco, but everyone seemed to move slowly with the plodding drudgery. The children were uniformly dirty and scrawny; most sat quietly waiting for the next meal. All afternoon the same scene repeated itself across the fertile valley. The gathering clouds of the late afternoon shower reminded us to head back to the house. There would be no celebration tonight, just a grateful sharing of too little food.

"Pacas, we have to find out where the food is going. These people are starving!" I just couldn't understand why they were dying of neglect.

I knew Pacas had puzzled over this all afternoon, and finally he shared his thoughts. "Someone must be stealing it and taking it out of the valley." He paused and added, "I think we need to tell my father." Sinchi Roca was much more calculating than my father. Huayna Capac would flamboyantly announce the finding and the first person to cross his path would be held responsible. Sinchi Roca could be trusted to find the guilty person before taking action.

"I agree. We'll tell him what we've seen in the fields, and about the trouble in the storehouses." Decisions made and rain falling, we sprinted across the river and up the hill to our house. Sinchi Roca sat alone, watching the rain clouds on the mountain slopes. Since I was the Inca's son, he always respected my requests to speak with him, a courtesy he didn't always extend to his son. Pacas and I implicitly knew this, so I always initiated any important conversation.

"Sinchi Roca, may we speak with you about a serious matter?"

He looked almost amused at my attempt to speak as an adult. "Of course, what have you boys been up to? I thought you were going to celebrate with the farmers this evening."

"There will be no celebration. That's part of what we need to talk about."

I encouraged Pacas to tell his father what he learned at the storehouse and supported him when his father tried to discount his story. We went on to describe the hunger in the fields and how desperately these people needed food. Apparently Apu Moche had not dispersed anything to the needy. I suggested we declare a festival as an excuse to get food to the people, but Sinchi Roca said that if the people were as hungry as we described, they would gorge themselves, and then vomit. We ended the discussion with his promise to walk the fields in the morning and confirm our conclusions. As for the missing goods, we were to meet at noon to devise a plan to uncover the truth. Pacas and I stayed near the house all evening and the following morning.

When we met at noon, Sinchi Roca initiated the discussion, "You boys correctly observed and described the situation. This afternoon I will announce a relief plan to the builders." Very pleased for the farmers, Pacas and I both thanked him before he continued, "As for the storehouse problem you discovered, how do you think we should solve it?"

"The grain must be moved in the dark or the Quipucamayo would know." Pacas answered immediately. "I think Ninan and I should watch the place every night until we see who is taking it, and where it is going. We can hide on the hill above the storehouses and follow whoever is taking the grain."

Sinchi Roca considered the idea. "Ninan, are you willing to help with this plan?" When I nodded, he added a final warning, "You know the penalty for stealing from the storehouses is death. If you see the thieves, you must not confront them. They will kill both of you to save themselves. Is that clear?"

We both nodded, already realizing the danger.

Sinchi Roca collected Apu Moche, Hatun, Conono, and the Quipucamayo on his way to the construction site where the workmen were already digging the trenches. He halted their labor and immediately launched into his plan for distributing food to all registered families in the valley. He told Hatun and Conono to help the Quipucamayo distribute the food in the quantity defined by the family size. The cheer from the builders was loud enough to stop the farmers in their fields across the river. Sinchi Roca then asked for the fastest runner to come forward and instructed him to spread the news. The others were told to finish the day's work, knowing a hearty meal would greet them. When Sinchi Roca was out of earshot, Apu Moche quickly claimed the relief plan as his own; he told the builders his efforts in Cusco had finally brought the relief he sought from the Inca.

With all the activity around the storehouses during the day, Pacas and I met no intruders the first week. By the second week we were getting used to the disrupted sleep and enjoyed our hideout above the storehouses. We watched the moon and stars when it wasn't cloudy, and listened to the panpipe songs drift across the valley. Just before dawn at the beginning of the third week, our waiting finally ended. We hadn't heard anything until suddenly a man said, "Open the door. I'll open the packs." We peered down on the storehouses and saw two shadowy men and their llamas. Well practiced, they loaded the animals and led them off toward town. We waited until it was light and dashed home.

"Father, we saw them! Two men loaded ten llamas and led them away." Pacas exclaimed.

"Did they see you?" he immediately asked, and we said no. He looked relieved and added, "Did you recognize them?"

"No, it was too dark. But we know which direction they came from and which way they went." Pacas replied.

Sinchi Roca thought for a moment and said, "We need to find out where they're going. Locate a new place to hide along their trail so you can follow them after they load the llamas. Find a place this morning, and show me your plans this afternoon."

My stomach tightened with the taste of danger, but this was an endeavor worthy of men, not boys.

When Sinchi Roca left for the construction site, we chose a route we could casually walk without raising suspicion. We reasoned they couldn't be going far since they left the storehouses so close to dawn and would not risk being seen in daylight. We needed a place to hide until they passed us, and then be able to get to the road without making any noise. After checking all our options, we decided on a partially built adobe wall standing beside a house. We could see the storehouses from there and should have plenty of time to completely hide before they passed. It had easy access to the road, and an escape route away from the road if we needed it. Sinchi Roca approved our plans in the afternoon.

By late afternoon we were ready, but very sleepy. Sinchi Roca let us sleep through dinner, and woke us before his bedtime. We headed for our new hiding place, where every sound was a potential threat. A mother walked the street comforting a sick baby. A mouse scurried across a doorway. Someone's llama was loose and aimlessly sauntered past, but there were no thieves. The following night was also uneventful, except it rained, and fog settled in the street.

With a new moon and cloudy skies, the third night was especially black. We could barely see each other even though I could touch Pacas's shoulder. We waited. Just before dawn, we heard noise near the storehouses but could see nothing. We waited. Two men and ten llamas walked right in front of us. My heart pounded, but neither of us moved. The sound of plodding llamas on the street faded before we left the protection of the wall to walk through the black street. We stayed close together since all we could see was the vague shapes of the walls. Moving slowly, we followed the sound as it turned a corner and continued. Hurrying to finish in the light of dawn, they released the llamas in a nearby pen and walked away in different directions.

"Well done boys!" Sinchi Roca offered his congratulations on our successful sleuthing. Pacas and I basked in his praise as he rested his hands on our shoulders. "Let's assume they will wait three days before they strike again. Then we will be ready. Socso and I will join you in your hideout, and the four of us will capture the thieves together. You will be heroes!"

As planned, the four of us waited, and then followed the men to the same place. Pacas and I lit torches while Sinchi Roca and Socso confronted them just as Apu Moche came out of the house to meet his men. With drawn bows, Sinchi Roca shouted, "Who dares to steal from the storehouse."

"Not I. This is a coincidence. I was just going home from my mistress's house. I stopped to see what the commotion was. I don't know these men," Apu Moche maintained his smooth voice even now.

Sinchi Roca asked the other two men, "Do you know this man?"

"His name is Apu Moche. He is the Curaca of Tomebamba, and we are trading quinoa and maize for mullu shells and labor." A sturdy, middle-aged man with a light complexion spoke without reticence.

"Where are you from?"

"We're both from Puna, north of Tumbes."

"Puna is not part of the Inca Empire. Why do you steal from the storehouse?"

"Steal? We are trading with the leading Inca. We are not stealing. Our people need the food. Our crops were very poor last year."

Sinchi Roca lowered his bow. "Enough. You three come with us. Pacas, Ninan, finish unloading the llamas and put them in the corral." With arrows still set in their bows, Sinchi Roca and Socso followed Apu Moche and the two men to our home. Pacas and I took care of the llamas and bolted home in the morning sunlight.

Everyone was eating breakfast when we arrived, except Apu Moche who sat in the corner, sullen and without appetite. A servant had been sent to bring Hatun and Conono. When they arrived, Sinchi Roca briefly described the situation, and told them to gather the entire town in the plaza above the construction site at noon. Meanwhile, Sinchi Roca enjoyed the company of the two thieves. They talked about Puna, an island city where they lived by fishing and growing vegetables. They both had wives and children, but traveled here under the advice of Apu Moche's friend in Puna. He suggested they ask him for help. Even though they were not part of the empire, with a gift and out of friendship, he might comply. Heavily laden with the precious pink spondylus shells, they came to Tomebamba six months earlier where Apu Moche accepted their gift for himself. He agreed to pay them five times the standard rate with food from the storehouses, if they joined the construction crew and worked for it. They moved the supplies at night per his instructions, so the other builders who worked for standard wages wouldn't see. Their work now completed, they were about to return to Puna. Sinchi Roca questioned Apu Moche, who reluctantly confirmed the story.

The plaza was full when Sinchi Roca led the procession, flanked by Pacas and me. Hatun and Conono immediately followed with Apu Moche between them while the two men from Puna were led by soldiers. With the two Puna men beside him on the platform, Sinchi Roca raised a royal scepter for silence and began the proceedings. "These two men are from Puna and have worked with you on various construction projects. They came on their own accord, not as mita laborers, but to exchange their labor for food desperately needed in their homeland. In exchange, Apu Moche promised to pay them in maize and quinoa. These men have completed the work and are free to return with the promised supplies."

There was some grumbling in the crowd, since they too were short of food through the dry season. Others who knew the men as good builders and friends cheered their good fortune.

His eyes filled with disgust and pity, Sinchi Roca studied Apu Moche as Hatun and Conono brought him forward. Speaking to the crowd, he said, "You have known Apu Moche as your Curaca for several years. This is a man with considerable charm and good wit, but unfortunately he also carries a depraved indifference for his subjects and a greed for personal wealth." Speaking directly to Apu Moche he continued, "Contrary to the Inca's instructions, you used mita laborers to build your new house before completing the temples to honor our gods. You have taken advantage of the misfortunes of the Puna men to accumulate a large supply of mullu shells for yourself, and you have authorized stealing from the storehouses to pay them. This alone is crime enough to remove you from your office. However, your brazen disrespect and indifference for the suffering of your own people is contemptible. Do you have anything to say in your defense?"

Apu Moche stepped forward to face the crowd, but the leader with the golden tongue struggled to find his words. "I have lived among you for fifteen years. I have celebrated the birth of your children, and together we have improved our town. You know me as a fair and compassionate man."

The crowd laughed and booed at the same time. Sinchi Roca brought order to the group and Apu Moche tried again. "I am a simple man who has made mistakes. Would any of you have acted differently in my position?"

Again laughter ran through the crowd and Sinchi Roca intervened. Apu Moche knew he only had one more chance to plead his case. "I have learned from my mistakes. Return me to my position and let me prove it."

Most of the insults were drowned in hissing. Apu Moche stood with his chin on his sunken chest.

Sinchi Roca once again quieted the town and spoke dispassionately, "It is impossible for him to justify withholding food from you. There is only one suitable punishment, death by your hands. He will be stoned immediately."

Everyone let out a cheer and quickly dispersed to find suitable weapons. Apu Moche didn't say a word or even lift his head. Hatun and Conono, his only friends, approached him together to wish him a painless death and a safe journey to the Upper World.

Sinchi Roca addressed the condemned man, "Apu Moche, you were trained in Cusco for your position. I am sorry we failed to convince you of the wisdom of reciprocity. You failed to understand that all your subjects deserve your respect and your care. This is our failing as well as yours, but your actions give me no alternative." Sinchi Roca led the silent leader off the platform where his wife and children crowded around him. He calmly accepted their tearful farewells and then walked away from them. Sinchi Roca directed him to sit on the ground, where he covered his face with his hands, and sobbed uncontrollably. The first stone smashed Apu Moche's skull. His body quickly disappeared under a pile of rock. None of the villagers mourned his death.

Immediately following the stoning, a messenger was sent to Quito requesting the Curaca to immediately visit Sinchi Roca in Tomebamba. On his arrival we learned that contrary to Apu Moche's claim, the Quito Curaca was never asked for help. Their storehouses were full, and the Curaca from Quito offered plenty to satisfy their needs. He even offered his son as Curaca in Tomebamba for a few years until Hatun and Conono were schooled enough to take on the role.

We spent another two months in Tomebamba. The story of discovering the miscount and identifying the Puna men rapidly spread across the valley, and we were treated with manly respect by all we met. Along with the grateful farmers, we celebrated a plentiful growing season, and the returning health of the children. During our visit, the terrace for the religious center was completed, and the stones Apu Moche used for his house would soon become part of the temple wall. Very satisfied with the foreman's skill, Sinchi Roca gave him full authority to complete the project. Having established a friendship with Socso, the foreman could always send a messenger if he needed help.

I had made friends with Hatun and Conono and become fond of Tomebamba and its people. The remarkable change in the town in just four months was all credited to us, even though they did all the work. I remembered Riku's advice to learn from the mistakes of others. By providing the help to these people when they needed it, they were able to lift themselves out of their troubles. I had no doubt we would enjoy their loyal support when we returned. The entire town came to wish us farewell when we left for Cusco.

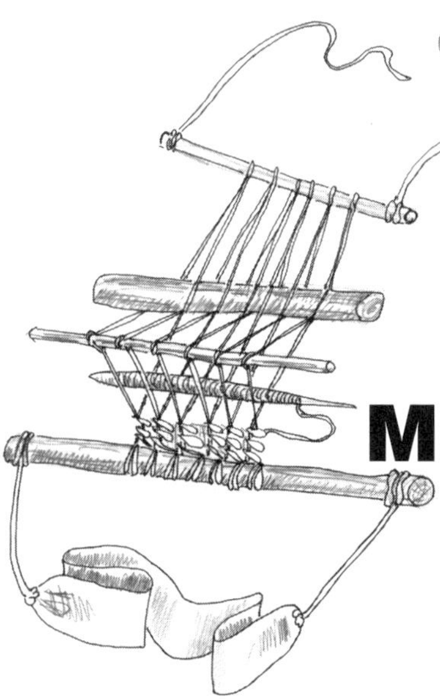

Melancholy

Kaya

Even after an entire year, our secret trip to the hot springs seeped into my thoughts every day. I didn't want to lose even the smallest detail, certainly not the fear in the pregnant woman's eyes, or her gratitude, nor the resignation of the haggard village woman tending her children. The exhausting climb back to my garden perch and the cramps in my legs and bottom were unforgettable. For a day I touched the beautiful fabric of village life. It was disquieting, and yet, my most satisfying memory. Upholding my promise to never speak to anyone about our trip, it seemed like a dream.

Barren by comparison, the year passed quickly. Perhaps because so little happened, the days blended together like the raindrops in the river. No beginning, no end, just a constant flow. The wool became yarn and disappeared into cloth. The crops were planted and harvested while the birds nested and fledged their young in my garden. Weaving with Kinsa and music lessons with Tawan slid by with the same continuity.

During her most recent visit, Tawan taught me a cheery new song. The short melody bounced along on staccato panpipes and then finished with an ascending flurry. Near the end of the lesson, I sang the melody while she harmonized on a deep, mellow set of pipes. The words matched the optimistic melody.

Beautiful channel whose smooth breast
Shall carry the water to our sown field,

Because of you, the plants will flower and
Wonderful fruit shall multiply.

Dance! Sing! Dance for joy!

I liked the song, and it entertained me for a while, but when she left, I found I couldn't play it the same way. Flute in hand, the song trickled out in a slow, plodding dirge. The notes and rhythm were the same, but now it spoke from my heart with a haunting plea. My new words were more soothing than the cloying hope of the original. It wasn't cheerful anymore, but then neither was I. It comforted me and filled my hollow chest.

Lessons with Riku were still the best part of my week, in part because it was the only time I was allowed out of my garden. Atuk and Tumbes were my friends, and they were kind to me, but I could almost see the gateless fence they built around themselves. Grown to his adult height, Atuk was finally comfortable with his new size. His face became his most distinctive trait with his square jaw providing the foundation for his tender eyes and thoughtful demeanor. In contrast, Tumbes exposed something comical in everything he did. One day he used a woman's pin to hold his cloak instead of tying it as was the manly custom. On other day he put his hands in a jar of dye so they were bright red for a week. His eyes always sparkled with the delight of the unpredictable.

In the past Riku's exercises were simple. For instance, he'd tell one of us, the sender, to imagine an animal. The rest of us, the receivers, were to determine which animal. It was easy to receive information when we knew the general topic and who was sending, since every message carried the personality of the sender. When Tumbes was sending, the picture always came with a smile.

One time Tumbes wanted us to see a green parrot with a reddish head and undertail. During the exercise, his imagined parrot landed on my head and then flew over Atuk, splattering his feet. When Atuk sent a picture of a jaguar, a cold shiver rose up my spine ending in my hair. The word jaguar came from nowhere, but I never saw the animal. Tumbes found himself with bow and arrow facing a dense tree. Even though he couldn't see it, he knew there was a jaguar hiding there. Riku said he too felt the fear of a jaguar prowling the forest floor. The images Riku sent were always rich with detail, and we all saw very nearly the same thing. When he showed us a llama, we all agreed the young male was entirely brown, carried two baskets filled with quinoa, and grazed in the main plaza of Machu Picchu while it waited for his master. We also agreed that we strongly felt our gratitude for the perpetual service of llamas.

Now our lessons were more difficult because Riku placed us out of sight and earshot of one another, and we were no longer simply picturing animals. The sender was to take us someplace we had never been. During our last lesson, Riku started by showing us a beautiful lake. We all saw a very long, narrow lake with forested mountains on one side. Savoring the spicy scent of the needled trees, we stood together on the rocky shore to watch the sunrise across the lake. Then we walked through the icy water past darting fish as we descended to the bottom. In absolute darkness we were filled with the spirit of Cochamama, the goddess of all water life. Suddenly we were lifted out of the water to a granite outcropping high above the lake. From here we witnessed the perfect balance in all things. Life ended in death to be transformed into life again, while all emotions blended together as beautifully as the trees in the forest. Joy stood beside sorrow, and fear was offset by courageous hope. When we finished the lesson, we asked him where this place was, but he didn't know. He first saw it as a young boy, and occasionally returned there for inspiration. I felt strangely whole and satisfied when we were at his sanctuary, but I wondered why there were no people. I decided I liked the hot springs with its healing patients better because I felt useful to someone.

On this warm and overcast day, it was my turn to be the sender. Typically, one of us remained in the sacred plaza, while another climbed to Intihuatana, and the third went to the Torreon near my house. Riku usually stayed with the sender, but instead he sat with Atuk. At Intihuatana, I watched the river from my perch beside the statue while the others took their places. When I felt the tingling presence of Tumbes, Riku, and Atuk on my arms, I knew they were with me and I could begin. As Riku had taught us, I closed my eyes and took several deep breaths to firmly establish my place on the mountain. When I was ready, I allowed myself to see us on a raft lazily floating downstream between the canyon walls. Even though they were nearly vertical, the walls were covered with vines, moss and flowers of every color. Just as I spotted a huge spray of pink orchids, the placid river turned white and swept us downstream through its thundering waves.

In an instant I jumped to the top of the canyon wall and watched the river plummet out of the mountains onto a flat plain below. Through the mist I could see it leading away from the precipice and placed myself on the raft floating downstream of the waterfalls. The river grew wider than the entire city of Machu Picchu. Giant trees lined the riverbanks hiding everything on land. In the rain I followed along the bank where the treetops towered above me as they supported vines, shrubs, orchids, ferns and a multitude of other greenery. The individual raindrops gradually stretched into continuous threads of water hanging between the river and cloud. Below me the water was pink, hiding everything under the surface and filling me with a sense of insidious danger. I still continued downstream as the river expanded and swallowed up the land on the far side. Finally the rain was so thick I could no longer see the river or the bank beside me. The overwhelming and uncontrollable power of the place surrounded me with an unknowable fear. I scurried back to my safe haven at Machu Picchu where I opened my eyes and took several deep breaths to slow my racing heart before descending to the sacred plaza and our small group.

After we greeted one another and settled in the Temple of Viracocha, Riku began the review. "Tumbes, where did Kaya start our journey?"

"We were on the river below us."

"Atuk, do you agree?" He nodded in response.

"You were wise to start in a place everyone knows," Riku said with a reassuring smile. "It's easier for the receivers to follow your journey if you start with the familiar. Atuk, what happened next?"

"I'm not sure," he replied. "We were on the river when I heard a loud roar and I fell into darkness. I tried to find you again but was unable."

Never harsh with us, Riku nodded and turned to Tumbes. "And how about you? Did you see more?"

"I don't remember any more about the river. I do remember seeing a flat forested plain that stretched to the horizon."

"That's good. And were you with Kaya and me?" Tumbes shook his head. Riku recounted the journey, exactly describing to the others what I'd seen before returning to Machu Picchu. "Remember, the purpose of the exercise is for the leader to show the group what you see. Journeying can be so interesting, we can forget about the group. Before the leader changes his vantage point, gather the group by calling each person's name and stating your intentions. Kaya, when you changed from the raft to land, Atuk went over the waterfalls."

We all laughed knowing there was no real danger.

"As receivers it is very tempting to explore something that interests you, but it's the sender's journey. You must stay with the leader. Other times we will journey just for the adventure; that will be your time to explore."

With his instructions and practice, our skills always improved.

"Kaya, just before we returned you were frightened because you couldn't see through the rain, the river or the forest. Is that right?"

I nodded and as I remembered every joint stiffened with panic.

"This is your journey, so you can change parts of it. Does it always rain at Machu Picchu?" I shook my head. "Then it probably doesn't always rain there. Did you try to stop the rain, or ask Ilyapa to stop it for you?"

"You mean, simply by asking, I can stop the rain?" The traveling seemed quite ordinary, but the notion of stopping the rain astounded me.

"You can do many things in the spirit world you can't do here. Before you begin a journey, set the rules. You may ask to be shown the journey exactly as it is, or you can ask to change things to another realistic situation, like stopping the rain. Someday, you might ask to change anything in any way. For example, what would happen if Kaya asked to see the river run uphill?"

"Condors on the mountaintops would need to learn to swim!" Tumbes blurted out immediately as he mimicked a bird pulling itself through the water with its wings. Even Riku laughed at the picture of a big lake floating above the mountaintops with the enormous birds flying through it.

Riku allowed Tumbes' fantasy to end naturally and then continued. "You are all too young and inexperienced to journey without setting rules. You must not try this yet, and you must not journey alone. Remember, we travel in a group. Do you understand the danger?"

He spoke so earnestly, I trusted he was protecting us, but I really didn't understand, so I asked, "At the end of my journey I felt more than panic. The place was very powerful and foreboding. Is this the danger you speak of?"

"No, it's not the same, but you've posed a very good question. What you felt is the strength and power of the river basin. How did you get that information?"

I just seemed to know, but slowly I remembered, "I felt the danger in my chest; my heart started pounding, and it felt like a stone was crushing me. And my feet hurt from the cold!"

"That's good. Information will come to you in many ways. Notice all of it, not just the conclusion sent in the message." He paused and started to speak a few times before he was ready to explain. "I can't describe journeying with no rules because it is so different for each person, but the peril is very real. An inexperienced traveler can get lost in a place he can't understand with no hope of returning to this world. It's like being carried to a foreign place and losing all knowledge of who you are. In time, we will go there together, and you will learn by experience. For now, you must trust me and not attempt to do this alone."

Again we all agreed, still curious, but now apprehensive about the wonders of the spirit world.

Having made his point, Riku relaxed and spoke more freely. "Remember, our next lesson will start before sunrise in two days so we can observe the equinox. Ask Inti to shine through these clouds, or we will have little to see." He paused and announced, "We'll also have a visitor from the lowlands that day, so we'll be together all day."

We all asked questions at once, and he raised his hand to quiet us. "Last year while Atuk and I were in Quispiguanca, I asked Tumbes to travel to the town of Vilcabamba. There he asked the Curaca to contact Ixiamas, a shaman of a lowland tribe, and ask him to visit me. He will arrive in two days."

We clamored for more, but Riku wouldn't satisfy our curiosity.

Ever since our trip to the hot springs, Riku had kept his word, and we took an indirect route back to my garden after our lessons. I tried to wheedle out more information about the visitor, but he was not easily influenced by me, or anyone else. In my garden, I returned to my weaving project at the base of the guava tree. Kinsa now insisted I improve my weaving consistency by keeping the yarn and the woven tension the same for an entire piece. She decided I would weave two pieces of light tan cloth with no design, so even small flaws would be visible. Surprisingly, I preferred to weave solid colors; it reflected the monotonous rhythm of my days. Traveling with the spirits to distant places offered some relief, and it seemed real, but I always returned to the same isolating prison. I felt hollow. I thought the sun could shine through me like it shone through the warp on my loom and was always startled to see my solid shadow. Usually alone and always lonely, the days and nights melded into a forgettable blur.

Meeting a visitor, Riku's friend, presented a welcome diversion from the routine. Tumbes had told us amazing things about his trip, but I was never sure whether he was explaining what he saw and heard, or telling a story to amuse us. Could there really be macaws and large parrots that turn into women? I wondered how Riku knew the visitor would arrive in two days, and why he had sent for him. My thoughts wandered back to my journey down the river during the morning exercise, and as I wove, I tried to imagine the river people. Nothing. All I could see was rain and a muddy river, but I heard music in the background. I tried to follow the music into the forest, but soon realized the music was drifting across the terraces in Machu Picchu. It was an eerie song, with a slow lilt, except for a fast, descending passage at the beginning. I couldn't stop humming the song, even long after the player finished. It was familiar somehow. I hummed in time to my weaving, setting the rhythm to match my work and pausing between phrases to be sure the weave was satisfactory. Instead of fading into memory, the song forced itself to the forefront, so I made up words about my guava tree.

Among your leaves my heart nested.

Where do you go when you leave me behind?
Will you ever open your eyes again?

What protective shadow can replace your splendor?
How can I remain so alone?

Finally I stopped weaving and tried to play the song on the flute. It didn't take long to find the melody, but now the sound was even more familiar. Over and over I played the tune until suddenly it was clear. This was the same song Tawan just taught me, except the musician played it slowly, as I did, and he played it backwards. That's why it was so unsettling; it ended where it should begin. I liked playing the backward version first and following it with my version. That way the first verse asked the question, and the next verse answered.

Beautiful tree whose broad branches
Shelter me from dazzling sun and despair,

Awake from winter's slumber to console
This garden's lonely captive.

Bloom again, lovely tree. Live again!

Someone must have heard me playing and responded in a way only I would understand. Who could it be? I searched the fields for someone carrying a flute, but all I saw were farmers planting beans. Disappointed, I resolved to watch the fields carefully the next time I heard music. Was this accidental? Would the musician answer me again? Would he carry me away from my isolation? An afternoon shower was about to drench my garden, so I moved my loom from the guava tree to the shelter. The rain was a nuisance, but it brought the rainbow of orchids and bromeliads that transformed my garden into a paradise for hummingbirds and butterflies.

The drizzling fog interspersed with hard showers continued through the night and next day; only Kinsa's visit broke the gray boredom. A round, middle-aged woman with a stooped neck and lightening-fast hands, Kinsa inspected my work as I wove in the shelter. "Your weaving is much more consistent. Practice. That's all you needed. In another three or four years, you'll be an expert." I sighed wearily at the thought of doing exactly the same thing for several more years but said nothing. She watched me weave for a short while and suggested I roll the cloth around the end rods so I wouldn't have to reach so far when the cloth got longer. "You'll be finished with these tan pieces by my next visit. What color would you like to weave next?"

I could barely maintain enough interest to answer. "Perhaps something very bright; red, green, or maybe yellow would be a welcome change."

"I think there is enough yellow yarn in the storehouse for two pieces of cloth. You can do that next." Without another word, she retrieved the new yarn, restrung the other loom so it would be ready for the yellow cloth, and left.

Alone again, I played my flute and tried to entice an answer from the unknown musician, but the only response was the rain hissing through the new leaves. Even my new song with the inverted beginning and peaceful finish brought no comfort. I slept most of the afternoon and woke only when Iska brought my dinner. Bored and empty, I went to bed early, hoping tomorrow's visitor would enliven me.

Riku arrived well before dawn to find me still sleeping. The fog seemed too thick to see the sunrise, but Riku thought it might clear enough to make the sighting, and he wanted to take advantage of any opportunity. Because the sky was so often cloudy when the seasons changed, it was difficult to measure either the spring or fall equinox. Of course the *quipu* recorded the days between the winter solstice and the equinox, so we knew this was the right day. The previous autumn, we were fortunate to observe it, but Riku wanted us to see that the measurement was the same in the spring.

We passed the early morning reviewing the sun measurements of the solstices and the equinox, but we never saw a shadow. In the past year we were able to measure both solstices. The cold, cloudless sunrise on the winter solstice flooded through the northeast window in the Torreon. Hanging at precisely the center of the window, a thin vine cast a shadow exactly bisecting the marker on the floor. Without any cloud interference for three weeks, we watched the shadow at sunrise and saw it creep closer to the rock marker each day. Finally the shadow bisected the marker perfectly for three consecutive days, and then slowly slid away. On the summer solstice, the clouds allowed us to see the shadow cast for only a single day. A sacred cave in the artisan section of the city had a window aligned to the southwest. Riku told us that for eight mornings surrounding the solstice, the sun passed through the window and illuminated the back wall of the cave. We were fortunate to see it for even a day.

At midmorning Riku suggested we walk toward the bridge. Since the only bridge I knew was the one we crossed near the hot springs, I was surprised when he took us up the mountain past the quarry. I had no idea where this trail led but was satisfied to go somewhere new. We followed the stone trail to the west along a narrow path that fell straight to the river below. Fortunately, we met no one since there was rarely room to pass.

"You can see that the trail ahead is actually the top of a stone wall and is resting on a ledge well below it," Riku stopped to explain. "In the center, there is a span with no wall, and the path falls sharply to the ledge below.

In order for someone to enter Machu Picchu, a wooden bridge must be extended from our side across the gap. We'll put the bridge in place when Ixiamas arrives."

We rested on the trail in full view of the stairs leading down to the gap. Tumbes entertained us with a pantomime of a stranger traveling this path at night. He fell into the gap, but miraculously wasn't hurt. He stood, brushed himself off, and pretended to try to climb the rock wall to get back to the trail. Each time something always prevented him: a snake hiding in the wall, a loose stone or snagging his tunic. With a look of mock surprise, he chastised the impediment, and then fell to the bottom, unhurt, and ready to try again. During his fourth attempt, Ixiamas rounded the curve and started down the steps leading to the gap. Riku stood and walked toward him, greeting him in a language I didn't understand. Ixiamas set down his bundle, and Tumbes threw a rope tied to a log across the gap. With Ixiamas guiding the log, Tumbes pushed it along the trail until it hung half way across the gap. With Atuk firmly planted and holding a rope tied to our end of the log, Tumbes continued to push while Ixiamas pulled the log across the gap. In no time the other two logs were moved into place and Ixiamas carried his bundle and quiver across the bridge.

Unlike any other greeting I'd ever seen, Riku and Ixiamas stood face to face in silence for a very long time. Finally Riku smiled as his shoulders softened and the two embraced. They looked so different and yet there was a strong affection between them. Ixiamas was almost a full head shorter with a slight build that matched his stature. Hanging to the middle of his back, his straight hair was held with a leather band that seemed too heavy for his small, oval face. His jet black eyes, wide nose, and thin lips were pleasantly set on his smooth, light skin. The two friends separated and then embraced again. Finally Riku slapped Ixiamas on the back and turned to face us. "This is Ixiamas. He is a dear friend and a shaman in the lowlands. He saved my life many years ago, and I will always be grateful. Ixiamas, these are my students, Kaya, Atuk, and Tumbes. They are our best hope for the future."

Ixiamas acknowledged each of us with the same warm acceptance so typical of Riku. Oddly dressed, Ixiamas wore a boy's tunic with a man's cloak wrapped around him. A string of white beads with two long pointed teeth hung around his neck.

As Atuk led us back to the city, Riku and Ixiamas spoke slowly in two languages behind us. I heard questions, but couldn't understand the answers, and I was satisfied to know Riku was very pleased to see his friend. Even though he had climbed for several days, we stopped many times so Ixiamas could catch his breath. The daily stairs must have helped me, since I had no difficulty with the incline. The drizzle changed to rain as we reached the sacred plaza and headed for the Temple of Viracocha. Atuk was immediately dispatched for hot soup and coca, while Tumbes went for more blankets. Now that Ixiamas had stopped walking, he wheezed and shivered in his cloak.

"The lowlands are much warmer, and the air is heavier than here. We must keep Ixiamas warm, or he will get sick. It is exhausting for a lowlander to travel up the mountains. The cool damp weather settles in the chest and makes breathing even more difficult in the thin air. Likewise, I find the lowlands very trying. The sweltering heat is inescapable, even when wearing only breeches in the rain," Riku said as he served the hot soup.

Wrapped in blankets and chewing coca dipped in lime, Ixiamas revived and asked Riku about our lessons. They spoke in our language, so we could understand.

"Just a few days ago Kaya took us on a journey into the lowlands. She is becoming a talented traveler. Tumbes is a joyful boy, full of fun and personality; his images are always marked with his character. Atuk is an expert astronomer and a deep thinker. Most of his questions start with why and are becoming difficult to answer. We travel together and learn from one another. And your students, how do they progress?"

Ixiamas dropped into his language, and I understood nothing, except that he was satisfied. Their conversation continued, and I watched them closely. The words they spoke were only partially understood by the other, and yet, they knew exactly what the other meant. There were no uncomfortable silences while one searched for meaning in multiple interpretations; they just knew what the other intended, the same way rain knows to flow downhill.

Tumbes, Atuk, and I sat quietly. Atuk watched our visitor's subtle hand movements and his habit of closing his eyes as though he were falling asleep, and yet hearing the faintest sound outside the temple. The conversation reached a higher level of excitement, and Ixiamas opened his bundle. Inside, he pointed to the packages enfolded in giant leaves and painted with unfamiliar symbols before carefully unwrapping several long sections of a woody vine. Then he opened a leather pouch filled with dried leaves. I didn't recognize either, but Riku lifted each, filled his chest with the vaguely sweet aroma, and gave Ixiamas an appreciative nod. Finally Ixiamas opened a third parcel and carefully displayed a translucent emerald the size of my fist, and an even larger amethyst crystal. These were very generous gifts, and we each examined the stones, admiring their size and quality.

"These gems are beautiful, and anyone would be proud to be given them, but I don't understand the plants. What are they?" Tumbes asked.

"They are even more precious than the stones, and I will guard them carefully," Riku answered with a steady voice. "They will help us to journey in new ways. Ixiamas knew I would need these for your training, and he kindly collected the finest plants at the height of the season. This is a very generous gift, Ixiamas. What can we offer you in return?"

I usually had trouble understanding Ixiamas, even when he spoke in my language, but his first request was easy. "As you know, it rains very hard in the lowlands and is moist even when there is no rain. Salt is treasure that is available only through your generosity."

"You shall have as much salt as you wish, but surely there is something else."

Ixiamas was shy to ask, but Riku waited patiently. "There are villages near us who suffer from a strange illness. I would be most pleased if you could help us."

Riku urged him to continue.

"It seems to strike all people in the village. Healthy children and adults usually recover, but the elders and the babies often die. The trouble begins with a slight fever and sore throat, but in a day or so, most people complain of pain near the ear and jaw, making it hard to swallow. Usually the sickness goes away, but some suffer from very high fevers and severe headaches. If this happens, the person dies."

"Doesn't the fever subside when the person is cooled with water?"

"Sometimes, but not always. Even when the fever does come down, it is likely to rise again. And the headaches are so bad, one woman killed herself to stop the pain."

Riku listened very carefully and thought for some time before responding. "I've never heard of this ailment. Two healers visited about a year ago. I'm sure they would have mentioned it, if they knew of it." He paused and added, "How can I help you?"

"We have tried everything we know without success. My people would welcome any remedies you can offer for high fever or headache. If we can keep the fever low, maybe we can prevent the headaches. If not, at least we can reduce the pain."

"The healers gave me some medicine for fever, and I have seen that it can be effective. I'll happily give you some. They also gave me something for pain. It is very strong and could be deadly, if used incorrectly. I'll show you how to prepare both before you leave."

"Your generosity and concern for my people is a great comfort." Ixiamas sighed with relief.

Riku nodded, invited him to rest awhile and signaled us to leave. He joined us shortly to tell us that Ixiamas was very tired from his travels and needed to rest for two days.

I was disappointed to see so little of this strange man; his visit was the most exciting thing to happen since our secret trip. Still, I knew that Riku would do what was best for his friend. The two days passed slowly, except for Tawan's visit. She bounced across the garden in her usual gait that looked like she was dancing to music only she could hear. I played the song of the secret musician for her, but she didn't recognize it, nor did she like it. She wrinkled up her nose and started the day's lesson, a new melody on the flute. We played until she was sure I knew the song, and she left as blithely as she arrived. The rain droned on for two days while I endlessly wove the yellow cloth and waited.

When we met with Ixiamas again, he told us fantastic stories about the lowland that Riku translated for us. "In the rainy season all the land is covered with water, so the animals live in the trees," he said.

"Even the fish?" Tumbes quipped.

"Well, yes. They swim in the water around the base of the tree trunks. Even the snakes come out of the ground and live in the trees." Ixiamas answered with an unquestionable honesty.

"Where do the people live?" Atuk wondered.

"The houses are built on the highest possible ground, but even then many houses are built on poles above the ground to allow the water to flow under the houses. We move from place to place in boats. Our children learn to paddle at a very young age, much younger than you, Kaya." He told us about jumping spiders with a fatal bite, trees so tall you couldn't see the top, pink dolphins in the river, and fish with teeth so sharp they could bite through bone.

Because Riku had lived in the lowlands, the wonders seemed quite ordinary to him, until Ixiamas began to tell us about some visitors in the north. "Did you see these strange men?" Riku asked.

"No, and I'm not sure whether the story is even true. It's been retold so many times it's hard to know what may have been added."

"Please, tell us everything you've heard."

Ixiamas continued with Riku still helping him explain for our benefit. "If you follow the black rivers upstream, they end in the steamy mountains of the north. Passing over the mountains, the streams flow down to a warm sea. We lowlanders occasionally trade with our neighbors on the sea, as we do with you. They are the ones who tell us stories about these strange men. Some say there are twenty men. Others say one hundred. They live on the sea in big boats, and land occasionally for food and water."

"What do they look like?"

"There are so many accounts, it's hard to know. All of the stories agree they are about as tall as Incas, but their skin is different. Some say they're very pale, and others say they are as red as the morning sun. Some say their hair is black, but others claim it's white and still others insist that it's red. I've been told their faces are covered with hair, but others claim it's just dirt and that they have hairless faces."

"And what did they wear?" Riku looked worried, although I didn't understand why. If the story were true, these strangers were surely so far away, no harm could come from them. For me, the hidden dangers of the lowlands were far more frightening, and alluring, than a few odd men.

Ixiamas raised his hands and said, "Those stories are even more fantastic. Please, I have said enough. Let's speak of things I understand."

Riku nodded and Ixiamas told us about the place where the two great rivers join. The Urubamba River and many others joined to form a very large single channel filled with pink clay, exactly as I saw in my journey. I still didn't understand spirit travel, but I was beginning to trust its veracity. Farther downstream the black river of the north merged into it, making a river so wide, it took all day to paddle across it. He claimed the two rivers flowed side by side in the same channel, one side pink and the other black. When he was a young man, he paddled for two days, and the river was still divided. Riku didn't question him about this story, so maybe it was true. I promised myself that next time I journeyed downstream, I would see if I could find this river.

We met with Ixiamas several times during his two-week stay. He told us about his people, the lowlands, and their religion. He even showed us how to use his blowgun, but mostly he stayed with Riku at the top of Huayna Picchu. I asked Riku what they did up there, but all he told me was that they traveled together searching for answers. As Ixiamas rested and grew stronger, he became anxious to return to the lowlands. Unusual for so early in the year, it had rained almost constantly since his arrival, and he was concerned about crossing the rivers if he waited much longer.

When it was time to go, Riku provided him with two llamas fully loaded with salt. The animals were not well suited for travel in the lowlands, but at least they could carry the load to Vilcabamba. Ixiamas planned to leave the llamas there and haul the precious cargo with his own people. Ixiamas carried the irreplaceable medicines himself. Tumbes wanted to live in the lowlands for a year, and Ixiamas said he would be welcome, but Riku decided he shouldn't be away from Machu Picchu for so long. Riku did allow him to accompany Ixiamas back to Vilcabamba. Satisfied with at least some adventure, Tumbes readily agreed. We walked to the bridge together where Tumbes said goodbye before leading the llamas across. Ixiamas and Riku repeated their silent greeting with the sadness of a final farewell. Both knew they were growing old, and the rigors of the trip would soon be more than either could endure. Besides, the new illness in the lowlands might take Ixiamas sooner.

"Travel under the grace of the gods, my friend. May we have the good fortune to meet again, in this world or the other." With a shrug of his shoulders that fully expressed his sorrow and acceptance of the inevitable, Ixiamas turned and walked away without a word. I think I saw a tear on Riku's cheek as we started back to Machu Picchu. For the first time, I realized he too was lonely. I hungered for a friendship like theirs but knew that was impossible as long as I was confined to my garden. While Tumbes and Atuk were allowed to travel and do as they liked, I was supposed to be content to weave my life out of our spirit journeys, music, and the tales of an occasional visitor. The emptiness of my existence consumed me.

Capac Raymi

Ninan

As the sun rose over the eastern wall of the Coricancha, the nervous whispering dwindled to complete silence, and we who were to become men during Capac Raymi stood perfectly still. In an instant, Punchau, the sacred likeness of Inti, reflected the brilliant sunlight throughout the temple, igniting the gold-lined walls and elaborate, life-sized statues of the gods. In the blinding light, I squinted, then closed my eyes, while the wondrous presence of Inti created in me a reverent union with the immortal. Empowered by this holy place, I was invincible. I could conquer any foe, judge any dispute, resolve any paradox, and sit with the gods. Never had I known such strength, such vitality. Slowly the tingling warmth faded, and I opened my eyes to find five hundred noblemen, a sponsor for each boy, standing along the walls. Umu Pilaca, the High Priest, stood on the left of Punchau, and my father stood on the right.

"Who brings these boys to the Temple of Inti?" my father's voice reverberated through the temple.

"We present these boys to Inti and his son on earth, Inca Huayna Capac," the noblemen responded in unison. "They completed their training and are prepared for Capac Raymi. May they prove worthy to serve the Inca."

"Then it is time. During the next month the boys must demonstrate their strength, courage, and loyalty. Inti, who sees all, will honor the worthy."

My father explained the events of the coming month, and the expectations placed on us. The first event was a procession to the top of Huanacauri Mountain to sanctify our weapons. Next we would go to the top of

Anaguarque Mountain where we must demonstrate our strength and courage. The plaza at Sacsahuaman was the location for the battle reenactment to demonstrate our fighting skills. We were then to take the oath of loyalty at Haucaypata and finally receive the emblems of a nobleman at the temple on Yauira Hill. "We will now join our great forefathers in the temple plaza for the presentation of the offerings," he concluded.

This was our cue to respond in chorus, "Praise be to Inti and to his son Inca Huayna Capac. May we prove worthy."

The Inca led the procession to the plaza just below the temple. In the center, the statues of the gods were all elegantly displayed on special gold and silver tables decorated with feathers and flowers. My father sat on a gold throne with the noblemen on his left. To his right were the mummies of the ancient rulers, Pachacuti and Topa Inca. Each mummy was displayed on a table beside its brother statue, a likeness made during the Inca's lifetime. Mama Oclla, my father's dear dead mother, was even there. Several days earlier, I overheard Huayna Capac's insistence that a single woman should be present to honor Killa, the moon goddess, and no woman could be more appropriate than Mama Oclla. The High Priest was reticent to change tradition and allow a woman, but in deference to his Inca, he made no further objections. As the last to enter the plaza, the rest of the boys and I marched to a single drumbeat and finally stood across the square from the mummified Incas.

Although I was the Inca's son, I was given no special treatment and took my place beside Pacas in the middle of the group. Dressed identically in special clothes and under the watchful eye of the most powerful men in the empire, we all endured the hot sun with adult dignity. My light brown tunic fell to the knee, and had a fine black fringe hanging from the bottom. Made of *cumbi*, a lightweight yet soft and warm cloth, my white cloak hung to my calves, and was tied over my shoulders with a black cord ending with a red tassel. My sandals were made of gold-colored grass and decorated with black yarn. To honor our ancestors who emerged from caves after the great flood, we dressed exactly as they did when they started their new life.

Through the rest of the morning, a procession of one hundred perfect brown llamas was led by young priests to the Umu Pilaca standing next to the statue of Viracocha, our creator. He inspected them in groups of four to be sure they had no blemishes, and then blessed them. Seeking the approval of the gods and allowing everyone to view the animals, the priests and llamas circled the sacred icons four times. Pacas and I noted the regal neck and ears of one, the elaborate garland on another, the finely combed fleece of a third. While they were all perfect, each had a distinguishing characteristic, and each represented the best of the empire. By the end of Capac Raymi, the magnificent beasts would all be sacrificed to Viracocha in grateful thanks for his generosity.

When the review was complete, we showed our devotion to Viracocha by returning a gift he had given us; we sacrificed three llamas. Several young priests built a large fire using specially cleaned and carved wood. In succession, the llamas were meticulously killed and quartered without losing a single drop of blood. Each was totally consumed in the fire without smoke or odor, thanks to a very hot fire. I had never seen such a perfect offering and was grateful for the priests' skill. The High Priest recited this ancient prayer with each llama.

O creator without equal, you are the ends of the world.
You gave life and valor to mankind saying let there be man.
You made us and gave us life. Our children become men.
Hear me, respond to me and consent to my plea.
Give us eternal life through our children and take us in your hand.
O creator without equal, accept this offering.

To end the day, six pure white llamas called aporucos led by prominent noblemen were presented to the Umu Pilaca. In keeping with the legend of our ancestors wandering the country in the wake of the flood, these men and llamas reenacted their search for a new homeland by meandering through Cusco for four days. Meanwhile, we celebrated with our families with feasts and good cheer. If an aporuco llama and his leader came to the door, they were heartily welcomed, fed and asked to join the celebration.

One of those days was exceptionally hot and lazy. Pacas and I were drinking *chicha* in the shaded courtyard of the palace when our mothers joined us. While normally unusual for them drink with us, the daily work routines and formalities were more relaxed during the festivities.

After they were seated, his mother explained, "Pilpintu and I are certain you both will excel during Capac Raymi, and before the trials of the celebration begin, we wanted to give you our gifts."

"Presents. How kind," Pacas answered sincerely in a manner similar to his mother's. "Perhaps you should wait until we have earned our manhood." I liked Pilpintu; her constant smile made her more approachable than my own mother.

"No, son, we'd like you to wear them during the ceremonies," she replied as she and my mother each inserted a hand under her shawl. "As men, you know that you are the protectors of the women and children. One day you will learn that although we seek your protection, we offer much in return. It is only when the character of both men and women are understood and melded together, that the remarkable power and strength of the union, as well as the individuals, is revealed."

As they each handed us a small wrapped package, my mother added, "We ask that you will always wear these pendants as a reminder of your mothers, your wives and daughters, and all the women you encounter."

Pacas and I carefully unwrapped the large silver pendants that hung on an unbroken loop of tightly braided hair. "It's beautiful, and extraordinary," I remarked as I studied the piece and glanced at Pacas' gift.

"Yes, they are identical. You two are such close friends, we decided to make them the same," Pilpintu said warmly.

The round silver pendant featured a sleek puma standing in profile with its head turned to face me. Its two eyes, set with emeralds, accentuated her vigilance. "She looks strong enough to guard her young without the help of a mate."

"True, she rules the night. While her young are safely hidden, she will hunt and secure her territory, but only her mate will protect them against marauding males." My mother's voice carried a hint of some sinister memory that I didn't understand and ignored, not wishing to spoil the spirit of their gifts.

"I will proudly wear this pendant as a constant reminder of my duty and your generosity," I said as I slid the pendant over my head and commented on how perfectly it rested on my chest. Pacas followed my example, and we both thanked our mothers. While we talked about the upcoming events, they finished their drinks and then left as unexpectedly as they arrived. The last time I saw Pacas, many years later, he was still wearing his pendant.

Having feasted for four days, everyone, including the initiates, the sponsors, hundreds of priests, and our immediate families, gathered in the main plaza just outside the palace. Led by the Umu Pilaca and closely followed by the six aporucos, we began the trek to the top of Huanacauri Mountain, high above Cusco. Behind the llamas and on foot, the Inca carried the royal scepter and occasionally helped my mother, who struggled to keep up. Dressed in our royal apparel, the other boys and I eagerly kept the pace behind them. All the other families followed, including Pacas' parents, Sinchi Roca and Pilpintu. Bearers with the provisions and all the animals to be sacrificed brought up the rear. Even though this was a sacred pilgrimage, it was a chance for us to relax a little. "Pacas, who is that kicking stones into the sandals of the boy in front of him?" I asked.

He stretched his neck to see. "His name is Mayta. He's from Cajamarca. I met him yesterday in the plaza."

In front of me boys were intentionally tangling their slings and tickling each other with grass. The lack of respect was beginning to annoy me, but I was their peer and in no position to tell them to stop. My father expected me to set an example, so Pacas and I stayed together and tried to ignore the others.

We spent the night with our families at the foot of the mountain, and began the steep climb to the summit in the morning. Arriving mid afternoon, we gave our slings to the attending priest who greeted the entire procession at the top. At sunrise the next morning the boys all assembled in the temple, while our families gathered wherever they could to see the events. As the sun just crested the distant mountains, the High Priest began.

Inti, my father, let these sons of yours be conquerors of all mankind.
Make them brave and strong.
Make them one with their weapons and the instruments of your will.
Do not allow them to be conquered,
But always be conquerors, since you made them for this purpose.

The young priests led the aporucos around the temple before delivering them to the Umu Pilaca, who carefully cut the leg vein of one llama. Pacas and I led the pairs of boys to the altar where we covered our hands with blood and then coated each other's face. As we did this the priest said, "You will learn the smell and taste of human blood. Be strong and courageous in battle. Trust in one another, and in the will of Inti. Live long in victory."

We returned to the back of the boys' group, where the salty blood quickly dried to a crust. Mayta and his partner were near the end, and as they walked past us to rejoin the group, Mayta laughed as he wiped his hands, still wet with blood, on his friend's cloak. His partner spat insults at him, but the priests were busy tending to the llama and didn't hear him. The sacred blood permanently stained the white cloak, but more important, this gift of life was wasted. I was convinced Mayta did not belong here. If I were Inca, I'd ban him from Capac Raymi and disgrace him and his family.

Wide-eyed, Pacas whispered, "Can't you do something?"

I shook my head and simmered.

When we were all together again, the priest individually returned our slings and reminded us. "Never raise this weapon in anger, but use it only against the enemies of the Inca, son of Inti."

Considering Mayta's misbehavior, it was a timely reminder for me. Mayta continued his childishness while three brown llamas were sacrificed in exactly the same manner and three llamas made of gold were buried to honor Pachamama, mother earth. Finally the priest asked Viracocha to accept the offering and to bless the boys about to become men. I was so distracted by Mayta's continuing antics, that the priests' actions were a blur.

Next, to show their devotion to Inti, a quarter of the boys led individual sacrifices. With the help of his sponsor, each boy said the prayers and cut a vein of his llama's leg. The animal was allowed to wander as it bled and choose its final resting place; the rest of the boys and the families quietly moved out of the way of the wandering llamas. When each llama fell, each boy built a sacrificial fire and presented the llama to Inti and Pachamama. As the animal burned, the boy begged Inti for the strength and courage to be a worthy Inca warrior. Inti must have been pleased to see more than one hundred fires burning on the mountain top. The sacrifices complete, we descended to the camp with the same formal parade, but the boys and sponsors continued into a nearby ravine. "Good luck," Pacas said as we separated.

Like the other boys, I handed my sling to my sponsor, Sinchi Roca, and prayed, "Thank you, wise Inti, for the lesson I am about to receive."

Without ever looking at me, Sinchi Roca also prayed, "Inti, the masterful warrior who leads us, show this worthy boy how to find strength in the pain and endure the agony of battle."

Using our own weapons, the nobles beat us on the legs and arms. The hot, icy stinging brought a flush to my face and then fire to my eyes, but I stood motionless and expressionless. Anger and pain consumed me, but I stared into the distance, seeing nothing for a very long time. My single thought was I hoped Mayta was getting what he deserved.

Still painted with aporuco blood and streaks of our own clotted blood, all the boys suffered silently as the procession walked back to Cusco in the dark. After arriving in the brightly lit temple square and showing our respects to the row of Inca mummies and the gods, all five hundred boys were beaten again in front of our families and the priests. This was not as severe a beating, but our tender bruises and open wounds heightened the stinging misery. A reaction as small as a wince meant a lifetime of disgrace. I thought my head would explode, but I stood my ground, knowing all eyes were on the Inca's son. During the Huari war dance that followed, Pacas and I stayed together. Very repetitive and more like a stylized walk, we danced to distract us from our suffering. I could see the stress in his eyes, as no doubt he could in mine, but neither of us acknowledged our hot, throbbing limbs. After the dance, the *chicha* beer and feast helped to mask the beatings.

Being young and well cared for, the welts, bruises and scabs healed before we gathered six days later in Haucaypata, the main plaza in Cusco. The boys, their families, one hundred Mamaconas and a host of priests nearly filled the square. The maidens were beautiful in their bright red dresses, but we knew better than to approach them. The boys wore the same tunics as before, but a red and white vest covered some of the blood stains, and a new white cloak with blue tie cords hid the rest. Our new sandals were very sturdy, the best I'd ever worn. In the plaza ceremony, we each received the staff given only to Inca noblemen. The long wood shaft was topped with a ceremonial gold hatchet and a red tassel. Staffs in hand, we strutted all the way to the top of Anaguarque Mountain.

The opening ceremonies at the shrine on top were identical to those at Huanacauri, but this time the purpose was different. After the great flood, the spirit of this mountain learned to fly as fast as a falcon, an essential skill in battle. This was our opportunity to show our strength and courage. First, an aporuco was bled, and we carefully painted our partners; I drew wings across the bridge of Pacas' nose that sloped across his cheeks to his ears. Then another six brown llamas were sacrificed to Viracocha and another quarter of the boys led individual sacrifices. Finally, the priest announced, "Inti, we beseech you, bless these boys and make them strong. Spirit of Anaguarque, share your secret speed with them throughout their days as warriors." During another beating to build our resolve, the maidens were dispatched to the base of the mountain well below us. From the bottom they screamed in mock terror and beat drums begging for our help.

With his hands lifted over us, the priest offered his final prayer, "Inti, we beg you, protect our women from your enemies. In your name we will be victorious!"

When he dropped his hands, five hundred boys and an equal number of sponsors bolted down the rocky slope at top speed. Pacas and I ran side by side, using our staffs to steady us and shouting revenge while my heart pounded with the first delicious taste of battle.

Finally freed, Mayta flew down the mountain without care for the rocky slope. When he passed us early in the race, he was laughing and shouting to his friends. He wove between other runners, jumped over boulders and tore around the corners. The best his sponsor could do was keep track of him in the bouncing flurry of white cloaks and gold staffs. "Look out!" he shouted as he tripped and flew forward, knocking over three boys. Somehow he landed on his feet and kept running without looking back. Two of the boys he hit continued to tumble down the slope, getting dangerously close to a precipice before they were able to stop. The third rolled and lay motionless across a large boulder. We slowed to help as we approached, but the noblemen waved us on.

Pacas and I reached the bottom to find Mayta swinging the maidens and cheering his victory as first to finish. "He's not worthy! He can't be a warrior! I'll never fight beside him! I'll kill him myself!" the boys jeered as they arrive.

Mayta instantly changed from jubilant to frightened, having no idea why the group was threatening him. The sight of the nobles carrying two boys down the mountain subdued the crowd, except for one anguished cry. One of the boys was obviously dead as blood ran from his head. Another was badly cut in several places, and his leg hung twisted with the bone jutting out. The third hobbled beside his sponsor.

"It was an accident. I didn't do anything wrong. They fell. It's not my fault." Mayta wailed.

"That may be," one of the nobles answered quietly, "but these boys will never be warriors."

"It's not my fault, it was an accident!" Mayta complained to anyone in earshot.

I was so angry I wanted to kill him, but I held back. Instead, I heard myself yelling, "Beat him! Give him what he deserves!" The walk back to Cusco was joyless, as were the festivities that evening. The Umu Pilaca led Mayta away from the group in the company of his sponsor and those of the three other boys. My father soon followed.

Two days later as we gathered to go to Sacsahuaman, Pacas sputtered as he pointed, "Look there's Mayta. I wonder why they let him stay."

Surprised and disgusted, I added nothing and tried to concentrate on the impending battle. For this event, we wore everyday working clothes and left Cusco without ceremony. The walk was leisurely and most of the boys spoke quietly or not at all. Mayta walked alone.

At the temple on top of Sacsahuaman we started by sacrificing three brown llamas to Viracocha. When that was completed, the priest gathered all the boys together for a final prayer.

Inti, benefactor to us all and the giver of life,
Protect these men in their first battle.
Teach them to fight, not with anger or fear, but
Teach them to fight with valor and courage.
By their conquest, we honor you and your son on earth.

We marched to the plaza below us and took our battle positions. Meanwhile, the spectators stood along the high wall overlooking the plaza. Standing beside my mother, the Inca addressed us, "Today you will be warriors at Ayavire. Inti favored Pachacuti and his soldiers in this hard-fought battle with the Colla when he conquered the lands surrounding Lake Titicaca. You will reenact this triumph with weapons exactly like our great forefathers'. For the honor of Pachacuti and those who fell, we will watch your battle and remember this victory."

We knew weeks earlier that this battle would be reenacted and what each of our roles was to be. Sinchi Roca played Pachacuti, and Pacas' sponsor, an uncle I'd never met from Lake Titicaca, played Colla Capac, the leader of the enemy. The boys representing Incas painted their faces with aporuco blood while the Colla remained clean. Clothes, weapons, and the site were already prepared in the plaza at the base of Sacsahuaman. Major landmarks were designated, and the battle lines were drawn. After a hard fight, the Colla boys, signaled by their leader, were to allow the Incas to win. In other years some boys got so involved that a number were killed. This year we fought bravely but never put each other at risk, except for Mayta. Many boys, including me, took pleasure in fighting him. To his credit, he fought bravely without anger or resentment. None of the Colla warriors helped him, and he always had at least one enemy fighting him. Even so he kept fighting and was one of the last Colla warriors to submit.

We ended the day like the others with sacrifices, more beatings and a feast. The third group of boys led their llamas to certain death and thanked Inti for protecting them through the battle. The beatings were getting more severe, but less traumatic as the pain became the pathway to intense concentration. I replayed every detail of my fight with Mayta. On reflection I realized, I had fought with ice-cold precision, not the hot fury I felt two days earlier. I attacked full force without rancor, and he superbly met each move, defending himself well. When he was on the offensive, he controlled his blows and allowed us to win as dictated. He fought honorably, in spite of the circumstances, and I respected his self-control. The evening events in Cusco included more sacrifices, feasting, singing, and dancing. Tired and relieved the final trial was over, Pacas and I enjoyed the festivities with our families and friends.

The following day the families joined the men and boys in the procession to the next event on Yauira Mountain, making the procession so long, it took half the morning for everyone to arrive. To begin the ceremony, the priests sacrificed six brown llamas to ensure that Inti was present, while the Inca, my father, observed from the highest platform of the shrine. Regally dressed in an elaborately woven tunic, a cloak entirely covered with red feathers that fluttered in the breeze and a helmet with the red fringe covering his forehead, he dominated the group simply by his presence. Even though I knew him as an ordinary man in his daily habits, I was awestruck by his dignified command of the entire audience while he delivered an eloquent speech about the greatness of our ancestors and acknowledging that we, the boys about to be men, represented the future. He concluded by addressing us. "We have prepared you to be honorable men, loyal warriors, and steadfast believers in the glory of Inti. Through your studies, and the trials of the last few weeks you have displayed the strength of youth and the courage of men. It is time to bestow upon you the regalia of Inca noblemen."

After each sponsor called his candidate forward, the initiate was awarded breeches to be worn under his tunic, pendants, and a helmet unique to his city of origin. The Inca himself draped the pendants around each boy. For many, it was the first time they were personally addressed by the son of Inti, and it made a lasting impression. Finally, after everyone was formally welcomed to manhood, we celebrated with our families, carrying a dignity that still felt foreign.

Like the other three events, we finished with a last group of boys leading their individual sacrifices. Pacas, Mayta, and I were among the hundred who each proceeded with the cutting and bleeding of our chosen llama. Bleeding slowly, my llama walked a long time, and I followed him closely as I chanted prayers to Inti and Viracocha.

Most generous Inti, who provides for us all, hear my prayer.
As your warrior servant, I protect those who cannot protect themselves.
Keep me in your care so that I may do your bidding,
And when my work is done, guide me to your side.
Wisest Inti, I return this llama to show my acceptance of your will.

When the llama finally stopped, I stroked his neck as he sank to the ground and slowly closed his brown eyes for the last time. I had never been close to a sacrificed animal, or felt the resignation and complete trust of a gentle beast. It was then that I realized the significance of the act; llamas, and all living creatures, were Viracocha's gift to mankind, and we were obligated to respect and protect them. I ran my hand along his withers and gratefully acknowledged its death on my behalf. Finally looking up, I discovered I was very close to Pacas and Mayta, but since these sacrifices were individual rites, our sponsors decided we should each continue with separate fires. The debarked and exquisitely carved wood leapt to flames, and we each quartered our llamas without interfering with one another. My fire subsided when I placed the llama on it, but the breeze fanned the blaze and consumed my special beast. As he rose with the flames to be rejoined with his maker, I prayed that the gods would accept my offering. Suddenly a piercing shriek jolted me from my reverie.

Terror filled Mayta's eyes while flames rose behind his head. He spun around and raced away from his sacrificial fire, his enflamed cloak dancing behind him like a windswept torch. Mayta was such a fast runner he was hard to catch. Pacas and I bounded after him yelling, "Mayta, stop. Drop your cloak." He tried, but it was too late. The flames jumped to his hair and headband. Fumbling with his cloak slowed him enough for me to tackle him. Pacas threw his cloak over both of us. We rolled on the ground until the flames subsided. The acrid smell of scorched hair and burned flesh lingered long after the fire was out. I had only minor burns, but Mayta was seriously burned on his legs, back and head. I tried to calm Mayta, but he just stared past me, not hearing a word. Others reached us and helped Pacas stamp out the grass fires we had started. His sponsor and several other men tended him as best they could.

"How did this happen?" Mayta's sponsor asked as he carried him to Cusco. "Maybe a spark jumped from the fire or maybe the wind carried a flame."

No one seemed to know. The rest of us completed the ceremony with the ritual beating. I concentrated on feeling the rising welt after each strike, but knew my pain paled compared to Mayta's suffering. His agony must be intensified by the disgrace of never becoming a warrior. I wondered if he would be allowed to live.

The following day the other boys and I were taken to the Calispuquiu baths to wash away the sins of boyhood and to have our ears pierced. Using a fine gold needle, a priest very carefully punctured a hole in each ear lobe and inserted a thread to keep it open until the ear healed. Over time, the lobes would be stretched with ever larger gold ear plugs that would eventually cover the entire ear. Even from a distance, the gold ear plugs immediately identified a man as an Inca, a member of the ruling class. The process was painless, but a misplaced hole could lead to a torn ear and disgrace. Except for the loyalty oath, we were men!

The next day, my father asked me to attend the hearing at the Coricancha with Mayta, his sponsor, and the High Priest. My father began the proceedings, "We all regret the misfortune that has fallen on Mayta and his family. Do you have anything you would like to say?"

His sponsor, who specialized in overseeing bridge building and was well respected by my father, spoke clearly. "Mayta has a quick wit, especially with numbers and building. He was excited to come to Capac Raymi and ran with the speed of the falcon, and, as we discussed earlier, Mayta regrets the accident at Anaguarque. We reviewed that incident and found him reckless, but innocent of wrong doing. Even so, he was badly shaken by the mishap, and vowed to act more responsibly. He fought very well during the battle and can be a great warrior. He is skilled, strong and fearless. He and I have spoken since the fire, and he still wishes to be an Inca warrior."

"What you say may be true, but we cannot have a maimed warrior. By traditional law he should be killed to avoid being a burden to his family," my father reminded him.

"Mayta was unlucky," I said without being asked. "If the family is willing, I would like to suggest an alternative."

My father nodded and his sponsor eyed me skeptically.

"Growing up in Cajamarca away from the sophistication of Cusco, Mayta was perhaps a year too young to go through Capac Raymi. He seems sincere in his desire, but lacking in maturity. I suggest he recuperate for a year and then travel with a healer for another year. If his recovery is sufficient and he chooses, he could be allowed to go through the rites. Of course the Inca and priests would review his recovery before granting his right to participate. If not, his experiences may make him an excellent healer."

"Good idea!" His uncle jumped at the suggestion, and even Mayta brightened a little.

Ultimately it was my father's decision. He weighed his options and concluded, "Ninan was involved with Mayta throughout the past month. I trust his judgment. If the family is willing to accept responsibility for Mayta's recovery, the boy can live. As for participation in Capac Raymi, we will review that in two years."

"Huayna Capac, you are a generous man. I am certain his family will accept your terms, and I know you will not be disappointed with Mayta as a soldier or a healer." He turned to me with a grateful smile and said thank you.

The judgment complete, Huayna Capac and I walked without speaking to the main square where the sound of celebration replaced the serious timbre of the Coricancha. The square was packed with my peers swaggering through the crowds in the full dress of soldiers. Everyone who lived within a week's traveling distance of Cusco came for the final four-day celebration. My mother stood with Cepi and Pilpintu, apart from the other wives with their horde of children scurrying underfoot like guinea pigs. The noblemen wore their finest *cumbi* clothing, accented with gold and silver ornaments, while everyone else was clean and proudly adorned with the head gear of his homeland. Everyone was already drinking *chicha* and eating the best of the kingdom while music and singing arose sporadically.

Conch shells quieted the crowd and drew attention to the Inca standing on the podium in the center of the square.

"Welcome to the final celebration of Capac Raymi."

The cheer reverberated off the stone building before dying out.

"You represent everyone in the empire, and here on the podium, the mummies of our Incas welcome all our returning ancestors. Tonight, in the presence of the living and the spirits of the dead, the new men will pledge their loyalty and lifelong obedience to Inti. Everyone else will renew his pledge and beg Inti for his continuing favor."

A raucous cheer traveled in waves across the plaza and back, accentuated by the thundering conch shells.

That was the signal for us to surround the podium. Umu Pilaca replaced the Inca on the podium, and one hundred Mamaconas arrived with cakes on gold platters. These were distributed to everyone and held in both hands overhead. The cheering turned to singing as the women worked their way through the plaza. When everyone was served, the priest accepted his cake and raised his hands as well. The crowd calmed down and he said, "These are very special cakes made with flour ground from maize and llama blood. They are gifts from Inti to all his children. When you eat this food, it will always be present in your bodies and will stand witness to your every action. If you ever speak evil of Inti or the Inca, it will be known, and you will be punished. By eating this food you pledge your loyalty and obedience to Inti and his son on earth."

With that he ate his cake and everyone in the crowd, including the Inca, followed his example. A song of praise started up spontaneously in several places around the plaza, but soon we were singing and swaying in unison.

Eventually, the Inca moved back to the podium and called for attention. "The honorable group of young men who have just completed the rigors of Capac Raymi stands before you. These men will lead you in your civic work and will bring us victory in battle. This is your chance to meet them all before they return to their home provinces."

One by one a sponsor led his initiate to the podium and announced his name and native city. The final act was announcing his new adult name. The crowd cheered enthusiastically with each new name. When it was his turn, Pacas stood beside his sponsor as he introduced him. "Pacas, son of Sinchi Roca and Pilpintu, is a worthy young man whose excellent memory and logical reasoning are witnessed in his ability to recite the entire history of Pachacuti and delve into the details of its *quipus*. An expert with the sling and a skilled archer, Pacas, who is named for the town where he was born, will be a trustworthy warrior and loyal servant to the Inca. From this time forward, let him be known as Pacas Amachani, Pacas the defender."

I was so proud of my friend, I cheered louder than anyone else in the crowd.

I was the last to be named, and I stood between Sinchi Roca and Huayna Capac. There was total silence as my uncle spoke about me. Getting to the end, he spoke slowly, "My nephew Ninan is an honorable man, who has accomplished much for one so young. He is an excellent marksman and is knowledgeable in all the great battles of our ancestors. A man of reason, he asks difficult questions and seeks truth in the answers. Together as boys, he and my son used their skills to root out the injustices in Tomebamba. During this ceremony, he showed his willingness to consider unconventional solutions that demonstrate his compassion and wisdom. Together these traits will combine to create a fine leader." He paused before concluding to allow the echo to die out. "From this time on let Ninan be known as Ninan Cuyohi, the man who moves fire."

I liked my new name.

Before cheering took hold, Huayna Capac raised his arms and the crowd hummed with an anxious whisper. In his deep, resonating voice, he spoke very slowly so that everyone could hear. "Ninan Cuyohi is a worthy name. His uncle and I are very pleased with the man he has become. When the time is right, his name will change one more time." He paused, "His name will be Inca Ninan Cuyohi, my successor to the empire."

The cheers burst into a deafening roar. I reveled in the privilege and promise of one day leading the greatest empire in the world. Oblivious to the unspeakable turmoil in store, it was the best night of my life.

Pule

Kaya

My garden was very quiet for two weeks. The cold fog hung on the mountain as thick as the fleece covering a llama. Rain wasn't falling, but the dampness clung to my clothes, my skin, and my thoughts. Every breath encouraged the fog to invade me and merge with the cloud seeping through my skin. I couldn't hide from the encroaching gloom nor find solace in my normal distractions. No one worked in the fields, at least not anyone I could see or hear. I tried to find a tune to comfort me, but every song was too lively, too cheerful. I just couldn't make the music express my misery. I'd played for the mysterious musician every day for two years, and still there was no answer. Tawan's chest cold canceled her visits, and Kinsa was in Pisac trading our cloth for new dyes. The Inca called Riku to Cusco two weeks earlier, so there was no schooling in the sacred plaza, and no opportunity to escape the hollow loneliness and unbroken monotony of my garden. I didn't even want to practice sending images to Atuk or Tumbes.

Having recently advanced to making *cumbi* cloth, I practiced handling the finer, softer vicuna wool at Kinsa's insistence. For two months I was to do nothing but card, spin and weave the new wool. No patterns. No colors. Plain white cloth. Her instructions during her last visit rang in my head, "*Cumbi* cloth is the best fabric in the empire. Only the elite wear it. You should feel honored to weave with the long fibers of vicuna wool, and you must learn to do this perfectly. You'll easily learn to card and spin, but it will take practice to weave with the finer yarn and make the fabric suitable for a nobleman." With that, she filled my shelter with wool that waited to be cleaned, waited to be carded, waited to be spun, and waited to be woven. For weeks I moved among the tasks only to allay my boredom. Working with the finer wool was hard, and I didn't really care whether the cloth was good enough for use.

Nothing suggested this day would be different from the others. I expected to languish alone and forgotten in my garden. In spite of the cool mist, I arranged my large baskets under the guava tree to get as far away from the mound of wool in the shelter as possible. With the raw wool on my right, cleaned wool on my left and waste in front of me, I picked the burrs and grass from the wool on my lap. Take a clump of raw wool, pick out the debris, put the puff in the other basket and start again. Repeat. Repeat. Repeat. Humming to the rhythm of my fingers offered no relief. Sitting by myself with nothing to do but a simple task, the tedium stupefied me even more than the fog, and I worked by touch with my eyes closed.

After a while, I faintly heard a bird in the valley, the first on this solitary and oppressive day. When it stopped, I listened carefully for the chirping without opening my eyes. Another bird began a conversation as I took another piece of wool. A third bird twittered a different song. I waited for an answer in kind. Listening as intently as the bird, I nodded when its mate finally responded. Soon there were too many conversations to distinguish one from the next, and the tweeting, chirping, trilling, and singing all blended into a confusing chorus. They sounded so content, and I imagined them flitting cheerfully in the treetops, until the chatter grew louder and more excited. As quickly as it grew, it also faded to its original volume. The placid singing continued while I cleaned two more pieces of wool, and then their activity increased and subsided again. This time it sounded like they were flying towards me and then back to the valley. As they repeatedly approached and retreated, the volume and variety of their voices increased. I took another piece of wool while I placed the cleaned wool in the basket and wondered why the birds were acting so strangely.

Finally, they were close enough that I could see hundreds of birds as they flew up and down the mountainside. With each trip, they lifted the fog higher and dissipated the dreariness with their song. The flock continued to press up until the fog clung only to the tallest peaks, just below the billowy white clouds. As if on command, all singing stopped, and the birds retreated to the valley once again. I felt a smile creep across my face, and I removed wool from the basket without thinking. Suddenly the sun streamed through a small opening in the clouds, and the crystals in the rock terraces sparkled like jewels. The dew on every flower, every leaf, every blade of grass, and even my basket glistened in the morning sunlight. Trapped in each droplet, miniature rainbows replaced the drab gray of the morning. I took a deep breath and slowly exhaled my own gloom.

The chorus in the valley sang with joy as they all took flight and streamed up the mountain once again. Near the end of the rising flow, I heard a loud, authoritative caw and spotted a powerful bird shooting up the mountain like an arrow. All the birds circled above the mountain cradle in the sunlight, diving, dancing and singing just for fun. Gradually the finches, cocks-of-the-rock, parrots, and cotingas settled in small groups around the terraces, trees, and buildings. One of the last to descend, the large macaw landed ceremoniously on the wooden post marking the corner of my garden.

When Ixiamas visited us, Riku described macaws, but I'd never seen one. From head to tail, this bird was almost as tall as me, and its wingspan was nearly as large as my extended arms. Every aspect of this macaw was stunning, from its long, graceful tail to its enormous gray feet, but most extraordinary was the color of its feathers. On top, they shimmered in the sunlight more intensely blue than the zenith in the late afternoon. Underneath, the feathers were the same color, only darker, like the sky just before dawn. I hummed a song, and my hands continued to tease the wool, but the bird held my full attention. Its dark brown eyes were surrounded by the same yellow as the stripe at the base of its beak. Very gently, it used its enormous black beak to preen the feathers first on the wings, then the back, breast, and tail. Meanwhile, it inspected my work as closely as I watched it clean and comb its feathers. My tune found words that I repeated in a singsong way, "Pretty bird come to me. Can I fly? We shall see." I picked slowly, careful to make no quick movements while more types of birds than I'd ever seen sang around me.

"Kaya, would you like to fly with me?" asked the bird. I kept singing, not believing what I'd heard. Birds can sing, twitter, warble, hoot, screech, whistle and caw, but they can't talk. Perhaps I was dreaming. I listened to the other birds around me greet one another, squabble, and signal danger, but none spoke to me with words. I must have imagined I heard a bird talk. I watched my work while I sang. Perhaps there wasn't really an enormous macaw sitting on my fence post. How could there be? They only lived in the lowlands; at least that's what Ixiamas told us. "Kaya, would you like to fly with me?" I slowly lifted my head and looked around. Other than the shining sun, everything looked exactly the same as it had for the last two weeks, except for the enormous blue macaw still sitting on my fence post!

I kept working and humming softly. Now what was that story Tumbes told us? The one he said he heard when he went to Vilcabamba. A man living at the edge of the mountains lost his wife in the great flood. During the day, the man went into the fields to care for his animals, but when he returned, his dinner was waiting for him. After several days, he decided to hide near his house to discover who was cooking for him. He saw a macaw fly into his house. He waited for a while, but the bird didn't leave, so he went to the house, saw his dinner and captured the bird. The bird turned into a beautiful woman, and he married her. "Kaya, would you like to fly with me?"

I must be dreaming. How should I answer a bird that can't possibly be here? What do you say to a bird that can't possibly speak? What bird knew my name and perched in my garden? I quietly whispered to myself, "I don't know how to fly."

"What's that? I can't hear you."

I continued to stare at my work. Dream or not, anything was better than the loneliness of my garden. "I said I don't know how to fly."

"How very odd," the bird said as it plucked a particularly well-shaped feather from its wing and dropped it on the ground. "Do you know how to dream?"

I nodded as it removed another plume.

"Then you know how to fly. Stand up, stretch your arms and close your eyes."

Still incredulous that I could understand a bird, I did as it asked.

"Now turn around slowly," it prompted me. "Slower. Do you feel the sun on your face?"

"Yes, it feels wonderful after the damp fog." The warmth bathed my face and lit my closed eyes.

"Do you feel the breeze?"

I studied the air and noticed a slight, damp breeze rising from the valley. "Yes, but it's not very strong."

"It doesn't matter. Now turn around slowly one more time, and when you feel the breeze directly on you face, take two steps into the wind."

As I turned I felt a weight lift off my shoulders. I hesitated, then took two steps and floated off the ground. "I'm flying!" I was so excited. I opened my eyes and promptly fell to the ground.

"Well, barely. Standing in the air is no different than standing on the ground. You just allow it. Now try again, but this time, when you feel yourself lift off the ground, open your eyes slowly and look at your feet."

Still bursting with the possibility of flight, I forced myself to concentrate as I closed my eyes and turned in a circle. When I felt the breeze on my face, I stepped forward confidently as the ground disappeared beneath me. My smile stretched across my face, but I held my position as I slowly dropped my head and opened my eyes. Everything I felt was true. I was hanging just above the top of my baskets. I quickly looked at the bird and said, "I did it!" And then fell to the ground again.

"Kaya, the moment you question your ability, the dream ends. Now try again and ask the spirits to help you."

I did as the macaw instructed, and soon I was able to stay in the air and even drop my arms. Through that glorious morning this remarkable bird showed me how to move up, down and forward. Giggling constantly, I even did somersaults in the air. "This is the most wonderful thing I've ever done! I still can't believe I can fly."

"Then how did you get to the top of that fence post?" it asked as I landed.

There was no drudgery pressing on me. The heavy and yet hollow feeling that had haunted me for years had disappeared. I was lighter than a butterfly. "I think I simply wished myself here."

"Good. That's what natural flight and being whole feels like. You simply express your desire, and it happens."

I looked around my garden from my new perch. Somehow everything was different, and I said, "For the first time ever, I feel content, and free! Every part of me is singing—even my toes." I flew to the post on the other side of the bird and asked, "What's your name?"

"My name is Pule. I live far away." She spread her wings and extended her black tongue as though she were hot.

"Are you thirsty? I have some water. I'm not sure I know what you like to eat."

"I'll have some water, but I'm not hungry." I immediately hopped down from the post and got a bowl of water from the shelter. She fluttered down to the ground, drank deeply and then returned to her perch. "Well, I must be going."

"Oh, please. Don't go yet. Can't you stay long enough to take me to Salcantay Mountain?"

Her head turned abruptly to face me as her oval eyes opened to big brown circles. "One day I'll show you the way, but not today." She sighed, "We can go to the city gate if you'd like," she said fluttering her wings.

We left immediately and flew across the agricultural terraces directly to the city gate. We perched on the roof at the entrance where I could see my garden and the sacred plaza beyond it. Through the mountain pass behind us, the road still shone in the lingering dew. We could see much farther from here than from Intihuatana, and still the mountains extended to the horizon in every direction. "Where's Cusco?" I asked, somehow expecting Pule to know.

She hopped around to face southeast and said, "It's that way, but it's well beyond our view."

"You mean there's more than we can see, even from here? Where does the world end?"

She laughed, if that's possible for a macaw. "Where the spirit world begins." She hopped up and down on one foot as if the roof was hot. "Come on, it's time to go back."

The view was wonderful, but flying was even better, so I happily followed her. When we got back to my garden, I was afraid that she might leave right away, so I asked, "Can I touch you before you leave?"

"Of course! In fact, there is a spot at the base of my neck that I can't reach." She dropped her head to me, and I scratched the skin beneath the short, fluffy feathers all around her neck and head. "Ah, that feels good," she sighed contentedly. "You can feel my tail too, if you like." I petted and scratched her long tail, as well as her wings and body. Each feather lay perfectly against its neighbor to form a covering softer than flower petals, and yet resilient to my touch. She even sat on my shoulder with her tail draped down to my waist. For her size, she was surprising light, but somewhere there was also a graceful, invisible power.

In a very short time we had become friends, and I'd never been happier. We talked about the farmers and their families on the terraces. I even told her about the mysterious musician. She laughed when I tried to imitate Kinsa's remarkably fast hand movements as she wove. When I described the tedium and loneliness of my days, I cried until I ran out of tears. To comfort me, she settled on my forearm and rested her head on my chest. Mostly, she listened and just let me talk. "I miss Riku and Atuk and Tumbes. I miss walking with him and meeting in the sacred plaza. I even miss my lessons with them."

She lifted her head and looked straight at me. "That's good. Maybe when he comes back, you'll try harder to learn more quickly. Riku's instruction is the most important part of your life."

I blinked slowly and held her stare. "Why? His lessons are fun, but I never considered them important."

"He's the wisest man in the empire, and you are very lucky to be his student," she insisted as she hopped off my arm to perch on my overturned basket. "He's the best one to show you the ties between this world and the spirit world."

"How do you know that, and why do I need to learn such things?" She didn't reply but ruffled her feathers and watched me with her big brown eyes.

"Obviously Riku hasn't told you much. Now I know why you called my here."

"I called you here? How did I do that?"

She studied me for a while and seemed to look through me the same way Riku did. "Well, you're certainly filled with questions and emptiness," she said slowly. "Are you sure you want to know why you've called me? You might not like the answers."

The lump in my throat made it hard to swallow. I closed my eyes and shook my head hoping she would be gone when I opened them, so I'd know this was a dream. It didn't work. She was still standing on my basket waiting for my reply. Maybe I should ask her how to tell if I was dreaming or not. No, everything she said was a riddle. Still, if I didn't ask her to explain herself, how would I ever find out what she was talking about? Who could tell me what a talking bird meant? "What hasn't Riku told me?" I wondered, or did I say it?

She scratched her breast with her claw, hopped from one foot to the other and fluttered her wings a few times. "Are you sure?"

I hesitated. What could be worse than the lonely isolation I'd endured my entire life? I nodded timidly. Cawing softly, the macaw sounded like a baby whimpering. She tipped her head to one side and finally said, "There's no way to tell you except to just say it. Your first mother, the woman who gave birth, is Coya Cusirimay and your father is Huayna Capac, the Inca of the empire. You are their daughter."

My chest blew apart as I gasped in confusion. My head throbbed with a million questions. I burst into tears and clutched my chest to keep my heart from disintegrating. "What did I do to make my parents abandon me? Why aren't I in Cusco with my parents? Why am I treated like a prisoner? Why can't I have any friends?" Blurry eyed, I stared at the talking macaw before me. "You're lying! It can't be true. My own parents wouldn't punish me like this."

I threw the wool, the baskets, whatever came into my grasp. "You're just a bird. How could you know such a thing?"

Pule flew up and circled just out of reach. I tried to catch her, but tripped on the debris and landed in the mud. Angry and wailing with a pain I'd never known, I stayed there until I could hardly breathe. Fine, I'll just stop breathing. Everyone had abandoned me anyway. Who would care? Why did Pule lie to me? I thought we were friends.

She landed on the ground. "You must believe me. This is true and exactly explains why you live as you do. It is also why Riku's teachings are so important," Pule almost whispered. She tried to calm me with soft comforting words, but how much could a bird do? I felt like I was sinking into the mud that oozed through my hair and fingers. Why, was the only word I could find.

"If you are to understand, I must tell you the rest."

Not sure I could tolerate more, I covered my ears. It wasn't enough.

"When your parents willingly gave you to Riku, you were just a baby, absolutely innocent, pure, and perfect. You live in isolation for your own safety, as Riku has told you. Until you become a woman, you must remain as beautifully untarnished and true of heart as you were when you were born. This is only possible by living apart from all others."

I uncovered my ears and watched her. She turned her head away to avoid looking at me and continued, "The Inca will carry out the sacred tradition to honor the gods. The tradition demands that the Inca's daughter is sacrificed to Inti when she becomes a woman. This extraordinary gift is given with humility and piety, demonstrating that all noblemen are devoted to Inti. If the Inca's pure and precious gift pleases him, then Inti will grant prosperity and honor to everyone in the empire for the Inca's entire reign. Crops will flourish, labors will be fruitful, and the soldiers will be successful in battle. With the installation of the next Inca, the cycle begins again. So, you see, you must learn the ways of the spirits. Like me, you'll need to talk with those of this world." When she finished, she finally faced me, and I knew from the sadness in her eyes that she was telling the truth.

I wanted to disappear into the mud. I covered my head with my arm and sank into myself. "I'm not the Inca's daughter. This can't be true. I can't be the Inca's daughter. There must be some mistake. I don't want to be given to Inti. You must be wrong. Go away and leave me alone. Just go away."

Prophecy

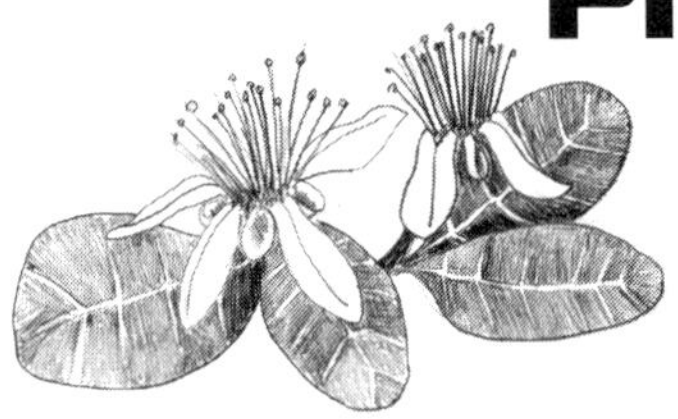

Kaya

I must have lain in the chilling mud most of the day. I remember the horrified look on Iska's face as she dragged me to dry ground and wrapped me in a blanket as the sun dropped behind the mountains. Shivering and caked with mud, every joint ached. My legs were so stiff, I couldn't straighten them. I don't know how Iska got me up the ladder and into bed. Whenever I woke, Iska tried to feed me hot soup or tea. Neither held any interest, and I fell back to sleep after a sip or two. Sometimes I woke from dreamless sleep to see her adding another blanket to my bed. My teeth chattering and riddled with throbbing pain, I fell asleep again before she could pick up the ever-present bowl. Other times I woke as she dabbed a damp cloth on my fiery face and arms. I begged her to stop punishing me, and she would agree only if I would take some tea. At least the tea didn't hurt. I was getting so weak, I needed Iska's help to roll over during my few lucid moments.

Riku must have heard my plea. I learned much later that he interrupted Huayna Capac in the middle of a prayer and announced that he must leave immediately. Rather than walk back to Machu Picchu as he usually did, he asked Huayna Capac for a litter and the fastest carriers he had. He left immediately and traveled the entire distance in less than four days, a trip that would normally take twice as long. I woke to his gentle voice and his hand lifting my head. "Kaya, you must drink this medicine. It will reduce the fever and the pain."

The calm confident voice rambled like a lullaby, insisting that I stay awake long enough to finish the tea. The bitter taste burned my mouth; I only drank it so I could sleep. After that it was Riku I heard whenever I woke. I found comfort in hearing a steady stream of words telling me that Iska was eating or Kinsa had visited while I slept. Anything.

When I finally started to feel better, Pule's visit returned as a foggy dream. And yet, there was something compelling about her message that I needed Riku to explain. I waited until I was well enough to concentrate on his response. "Riku, am I the Inca's daughter?"

He shot a piercing glare at Iska across the room. She faced him staring through her pudgy cheeks. Her normally slit eyes were now wide open, and her jaw hung to her chest.

"You need to get well. Please don't worry about such things now. Drink some tea." His steady voice was reassuring, and troubling.

I weakly pushed it away and asked again, "Is it true that I'm the Inca's daughter and will be murdered?"

Riku would never lie to me, but I'd learned he also rarely revealed everything he knew. "Tawan will visit this afternoon and play your favorite music. That will help you feel better."

I saw pity in his eyes and felt his regret as he patted my hand. I didn't need to hear him say it.

"Why should I get well when you're going to kill me anyway?"

With a furrowed forehead and half-closed eyes, Riku looked worried for the first time ever. Looking older than I remembered, his hands tightened around the cup, and his face sagged with the weight of my question. With some success he steadied his voice. "Kaya, you've heard something about your destiny, and your questions deserves answers. If you knew the whole story, you wouldn't be so upset. It's a long and beautiful tale, but you can't fully appreciate it while you're so weak. When you're well, I promise I'll tell you everything and answer any questions you have. Please get well so I can share the truth with you."

He was right about one thing; I was still too weak to concentrate on his words for very long. He had said enough to confirm that at least part of Pule's story was true. I rolled away from him and instantly fell asleep in blankets damp with fever.

It was another week before I was well enough to get out of bed to eat. With her round, strong body, Iska helped me stand on legs I didn't recognize as my own. Unsure of my balance and alarmingly weak, I hobbled across the room and sat, exhausted from the effort. My sallow hand held the spoon, and I finished the soup unaided before falling asleep where I sat. Again Iska helped me back to bed where I slept continually, barely recognizing the passage of days or nights. Still, I knew I was getting better. When

I woke it was Iska, not Riku who tended me, and I could turn myself in bed. I recovered slowly, but in Riku's promise, I found the will to get well.

The day she found me in the garden, Iska had combed the mud from my hair and cleaned me as best she could, but after lying in the same clothes and blankets for so long, I was disgustingly dirty and smelly. One day she smiled kindly and announced, "I'll warm some water and give you a good scrub. You'll feel better when you're clean." That same morning Kinsa stopped to give me some new clothes and blankets. I gladly parted with the old ones and thanked her for the replacements. Being clean and sitting in the sun was the final cure. I was exhausted from the effort of bathing, but I knew that was temporary.

Riku looked genuinely relieved to see me outside combing my hair when he arrived. "Kaya, what a pleasure it is to see you looking so well!" I stared back at him without saying a word, and he quickly added, "No, I haven't forgotten my promise. In five days, you and I will go to a private place, and I'll tell you the secrets of your ancestors."

Relieved that I would finally learn the truth, I recuperated in my garden. No one had even been in my garden since I became ill, much less tended it, and the weeds had exploded in the humid weather. They were so tall, they were even overtaking the orchids hanging on the fence posts. Still, the occasional bursts of color proved that at least some of my flame red and brilliant yellow bromeliads survived the choking mass. Each day I weeded and loosened the soil in a small area to reclaim the begonias, asters, or fuchsia. It would take at least two weeks to work my way to the guava tree at the far end. Kinsa and Tawan both visited me, but neither tried to teach me anything, or required me to do any work. Mostly, I just sat and let sleep overtake me as I discarded the lingering weakness.

As he promised, Riku came to my garden on the sixth day, and for the first time in over three months, I left my home. He offered his arm, which I gladly accepted for balance, and we walked to the main staircase leading to the sacred plaza. Instead of climbing, Riku descended to the terrace of the Torreon where he turned away from the temple to follow a wide terrace with fitted-stone buildings as grand as the temples around the sacred plaza. "Riku, what is this place?"

Without looking at me, he replied, "This is the house of the Inca when he visits Machu Picchu. He hasn't been here since you were a baby, but it's always kept ready for his arrival."

We passed through a serpentine entrance to an open courtyard enclosed by high walls and flanked by buildings at each end. "If you wish, we can explore the buildings later, but it's a lovely day. Let's sit in the courtyard."

We had walked less than the distance to the sacred plaza, but still weak, I readily sat on a sun-warmed bench. The garden was beautiful with dark green ferns complementing the purple bougainvillea that lined the stone walls. Neatly planted in front of them, pink and white cosmos added the fragile cheer of their short-lived bloom, while orchids hung along the top of the wall with sprays of white flowers alternating with the vibrant pink ones in perfect symmetry.

His sandals lightly tapping on the stone floor, Riku paced back and forth with his hands behind his back and his head lowered. Finally he settled beside me in an awkward silence. "Where did you hear that you are the Inca's daughter?"

My visit with Pule seemed so fantastic to me, I didn't want to reveal the story to Riku. I picked my cuticles.

"Did Atuk or Tumbes tell you?"

I turned my head and stared at him. So, they already knew! No wonder they were so distant. "So it's true. I am the Inca's daughter."

Riku sighed in resignation, knowing he wouldn't get an answer. "Kaya, you are the only daughter of Inca Huayna Capac and his sister-wife, Coya Cusirimay. Huayna Capac has other daughters by other wives and women, but you are his only daughter by the queen."

"Do I have any brothers?"

"Yes, they have one son who is five years older than you. Again, the Inca has many other sons by other wives and women."

"What's my brother's name?"

Riku was not going to be rushed or badgered. He fell silent without answering, and I knew this was a signal to be quiet. "Kaya, I have promised to answer your questions, but I'd like to tell you about your ancestors first." Riku closed his eyes and looked directly at the sun as though he were asking Inti for something. I waited patiently without interrupting him.

"You know my name as Riku, but do you know my full name?"

I shook my head, not understanding what his name could possibly have to do with my ancestry.

"My full name is Umu Riku, which means the priest who searches. Actually, I am the leader of a special group of priests called Prophets spread across the empire. One of our duties is to train the next generation of Prophets as I am doing with Atuk and Tumbes. Our most important role is to find answers to the puzzles in the empire. The gods speak through us to tell the Inca about the future and things beyond our understanding. We know how to ask the questions and to interpret their answers. It was a Prophet who taught the Incas how to build and irrigate terraces to maximize the crop yields and protect them from frost. It is also a Prophet who consults the gods about ambiguous predicaments facing the Inca." He stopped to study me. "Are you sure you're strong enough to hear the entire story today? Perhaps we should go more slowly."

"Whether I am totally recovered or not, I must know the truth." I looked away from him and closed my eyes for a moment to gather my resolve.

Lifting his hands with his palms facing the sun, he seemed to be pleading with Inti. He lowered them, shook his head and muttered something under his breath before continuing. "There are two other types of priests, the Healers and the Temple Priests. You met two Healers at the hot springs, but you have never met any Temple Priests. The Healers also have divining abilities, but their skill centers on medicines and treating sickness. Pachamama, the Goddess of the Earth, showed a very ancient Healer how to use coca to combat the fatigue caused by the cold, high mountains. She also showed Healers how to reduce fever, calm an upset stomach, heal a wound, and hundreds of other cures. The Temple Priests are responsible for recording the events of the sky. This allows them to tell the farmers when to plant and a wide variety of other agricultural events. They also determine the tributes to be paid by the people and the offerings returned to the gods. The elaborate religious ceremonies during the festivals are all painstakingly planned and performed with exquisite precision. Their effort on behalf of all of us demonstrates our devotion to the gods and asks for their continued blessing." He paused to ask me, "Do you understand the differences between the types of Priests?"

"Yes, I think I understand. Still, I don't understand how this relates to my ancestors." I fidgeted with my hair.

"In many ways, everything about you rests with the Prophets. Please be patient so I can tell you the entire tale. You now know that the Inca is your father, so your grandfather was Topa Inca. His father was Pachacuti Inca who was in turn the son of Viracocha Inca. Do you remember the difference between Viracocha Inca and Viracocha?"

"Viracocha, our creator, is the greatest of all the gods. He walked in this world after he created it, but returned to the Upper World long before Viracocha Inca was named to honor him," I replied, satisfied that we were finally getting to my ancestors.

"That's very good, Kaya." He paused. "Kaya. That's a beautiful name. When you become a woman, you will be known by your full name. It has already been chosen. Would you like to know it now?"

"Oh, yes, please."

"Your full name will be Kaya Chaka, the one who becomes a bridge."

"I like the sound of the name, but I don't understand. What does it mean?" Usually names emphasized the person's work, the place of her birth, or something unique about her appearance or her childhood. I'd only seen two bridges in my life, and I found nothing to connect me to the name.

"It's all part of the story I'm about to tell you." He took a deep breath and exhaled slowly before starting again. "We'll start our story with Viracocha Inca and his Prophet. In the time of Viracocha Inca, the empire was limited to the valley surrounding Cusco, an area you could across in a single day. The Inca way of life was a peaceful blend of the agrarian tradition of the Tiahuanaco people near Lake Titicaca and the more aggressive influences of the Chanca people to their west. For most of his reign, the other people who lived in the valley were isolated from the warring factions surrounding them. Devoted to their religious traditions, Viracocha Inca and his people prospered. Late in his reign, his Prophet gave him an extraordinary message that has been known only to a select group surrounding the Inca in each generation."

Riku hesitated as though he didn't want to continue. He held my hands and his gentle eyes scanned my face. Knowing he would keep his promise, I waited.

"Kaya, I would have chosen to wait a year or two to tell you this secret. By then you would be old enough to understand how important it is that very few people know of it. That's also why I want to know how you learned your identity." He stopped and stared at me, but I offered no information. He shrugged his shoulders and said, "I'm certain you'll tell me when you're ready. I trusted you not to disclose our trip to the hot springs, and you have honored that promise. Now I must insist that you keep another secret. You can talk with me about this, but absolutely no one else. Can you keep this to yourself?" He emphasized each word and looked deep into me.

It was impossible to lie, and I desperately wanted to know. I held his gaze without blinking. "I'm not sure I will recover if I don't know the secret, so I will keep it to myself."

He continued to hold my eyes until the words were etched in memory. Finally he blinked and turned to the courtyard. Again I waited, knowing I passed his test and was worthy of his trust. "The Prophet told the Inca that during the fifth generation, Viracocha, the creator and most powerful god, would return to this earth as a man. By his judgment, the entire empire and its religion would be destroyed."

I gasped in disbelief. No wonder I was sworn to secrecy. People couldn't be told that everything they cherish would vanish. "How can this be? The empire is so strong."

"It is now, but remember, it was only the size of Cusco when the Inca was told this. On hearing this as an old man, Viracocha Inca was ruined. He lost all desire to live or rule just at the time when the Chanca threatened to attack Cusco. His son, Pachacuti, was a fearless young man who defended Cusco and eventually defeated the enemy. As the new Inca, he fully believed the prophecy and sought ways to alter Viracocha's judgment. In a vision of his own, he discovered that Inti could act as an intermediary between the Inca and Viracocha, so he proclaimed Inti to be their primary god and dedicated his reign to pleasing Inti in order to gain favor with Viracocha."

Riku sighed deeply, but continued without prodding. "Pachacuti was a great man who established the foundations of the Inca Empire as we know it. He expanded the empire into the Urubamba River Valley, including Machu Picchu, but his greatest achievement was the solidification of the pact between the Inca sovereignty, the religious organization, and the peasants. Each group provided an important service to the empire and in return, each was assured an equitable benefit. The peasants provided food, wool, and labor to the Inca sovereignty and the religion. In return they received food and clothing in years of famine, civic improvements, and protection. The soldiers defended the peasants from marauding neighbors and designed the agricultural terraces, irrigation systems, roads, and temples. The religious group tracked the sky and worshiped the gods. They established the calendar for the peasants and honored the gods with festivals and sacrifices. Having found favor with Inti and Viracocha by caring for everyone, the empire prospered. Pachacuti's plan was to expand the empire and prove to Viracocha that the Incas brought peace and prosperity throughout the world, and were worthy custodians of his creation."

Riku stood to stretch his legs. When he finally sat again, he leaned on a staff he found behind the bench. I understood this system already and I wanted him to get to the part that affected me. Still, I respected Riku and calmly listened as he told the story in his own way.

"Topa Inca accepted the challenge of unifying the entire world and expanded the empire, first to the south and later to the north. Often he was able to explain the system of reciprocity to the neighbors, and they peacefully joined the empire. When he met resistance, and assimilation could not be negotiated, his strong and well-trained soldiers attacked and took the city by force. After defeat, the captured cities were left undisturbed, or the leaders were killed and the citizens dispersed to other parts of the empire, depending on their willingness to pledge their loyalty to the Inca and the ways of Inti. Moving at an exhausting pace through his entire reign, Topa Inca consolidated cities from the southern border of the empire to those as far north as Quito, each a three-month march from Cusco."

I had no idea the empire was so large and now understood why Pule laughed at me when I expected to see Cusco from the city gate. Riku's story was remarkable, and I tried to remember every detail, in spite of my illness.

"Now under Huayna Capac, famine has been eliminated throughout the empire. The roads are complete, although in need of constant repair, and almost all of the temples are built. The religion continues to worship the gods and makes great offerings to thank all the gods for their many blessings. Except for isolated areas where the leaders are corrupt and must be brought to justice, the empire beats with a unified pulse. To finalize the preparations for Viracocha's return, Huayna Capac must still expand the empire in the north. When Viracocha left this world, we believe he traveled to the ocean down a river that started in the mountains just north of Quito. This area is not yet part of the empire, and Viracocha's judgment of the Incas could be severe if he is greeted inhospitably by our enemies."

I tried to hear beyond his words and asked him, "If the empire is doing so well, and Huayna Capac captures the river, why does the Inca still fear Viracocha's return? He'll see how well the Incas have ruled and honored his teachings. He'll be pleased with the Incas and the prophecy will be proven wrong."

Still bent over the staff, Riku's drooping head and bony hands made him look frail. His dark, sad eyes studied the mountains across the valley.

"Do you remember the tale of the great flood?"

I nodded.

"Do you remember that the earth is a reflection of the sky and that by watching the sky we can learn what will happen on earth?"

Suddenly I understood. "Something is wrong in the sky. Riku, tell me what you see." I held my breath as I waited for his answer.

"In your lessons we talked about Viracocha leaving this world by traveling out to sea during the winter solstice and crossing into the Mayu, the river of stars that leads to the Upper World. In ancient times during the summer solstice festival, the sun always set in the Mayu in the southwestern sky. During the winter solstice festival, it always set in the Mayu in the northwest. Because the stars are falling to the east, the sun no longer sets in the river of stars during the solstices. When Viracocha tries to return, he will be unable to pass into this world because the sun and the Mayu are not aligned. The bridge no longer exists."

"Then how will he return?" I asked without hiding my apprehension.

"That is precisely the question Pachacuti asked when he heard the prophecy. We are facing total destruction if we cannot build another bridge for Viracocha to use. Besides, the gods are not the only ones to use the bridges. In the southwest, the spirits of all people except the Incas pass at birth from the Other World into this one. And during Capac Raymi, the bodies and spirits of their dead cross the bridge and travel back to the Other World. Only the Incas and the gods use the bridge in the northwest. When there was a bridge, the gods and the Incas crossed freely during Inti Raymi. Today, although the gods can pass spirits into this world, body and spirit cannot travel together to, or from, the Upper World."

A cold chill passed through me. I hoped it was just the end of my illness. My feet felt tied to the ground, but every instinct told me to run. Suddenly I dreaded the rest of the story and felt sure Pule was right, they were going to kill me.

Riku's apologetic voice labored with the weight of each word. "Pachacuti asked his prophets to find an answer. After fasting, prayers, and journeys, they returned to him with a solution based on a vision. All people in the empire, except the Incas, would build a bridge in the southwest, while the Incas would build a bridge in the northwest. In the vision the prophets saw streams of beautiful children. These elaborately dressed innocents were pure and perfect in every way. They were free of blemishes, healthy, happy and the pride of every parent. The children represented the hope for the future and the greatest blessing the gods ever gave to the people. The vision was very clear; returning the children was the purest and greatest sacrifice they could offer."

With my eyes tightly shut, each word came to me like thunder echoing through the mountains. He lovingly put his arm around me before he continued. "In the southwest the native people were already returning their children to the gods before they became part of the empire. In times of strife the gods were begged for forgiveness and during prosperity they were thanked for their benevolence. With the expansion of the empire, Pachacuti and Topa Inca embellished the sacrifice without altering the ancient ways and explained the changes as the Inca's way of showing his respect for their beliefs. With a very solemn ceremony, their most virtuous and innocent children were placed in the snow-capped mountains in the southwest. The priests were instructed to feed the children and kill them without pain. Then they were buried in the perpetual snowfields with food and coca leaves to sustain their spirits and bodies until their crossing. Silver statues and special cloth were placed beside them as gifts for them to take to Inti. The final prayer captured the beauty of the gift."

Inti, we beseech you, listen to our prayer.
With these children you gave us hope and we are grateful.

Unsoiled by this world we return them filled with our love.
We surrender them to you and eternally promise to worship you.
Use these children as a bridge to bring us closer to you.
Inti, we beseech you, listen to our prayer.

I couldn't move, and inside I felt nothing. There were no images of children, or ceremony, or snow-capped mountains. There was nothing, cold, black, nothing.

"There aren't as many Inca noblemen, so fewer children need to be presented. In fact, the obligation rests solely with the ruling Inca. Starting with Pachacuti, each Inca has extensively trained his eldest daughter in the ways of the spirit world so she can act as an intermediary between this world and the gods. Following her passage to womanhood, she is returned to Inti during the Inti Raymi celebration. This grandest of all sacrifices thanks Inti for a generation of prosperity and pleads for continued grace. Collca, who was named after the mother of stars was the first to be returned. Machu Picchu was a new city then, and her ceremony was the very first offering ever made here. Topa Inca also gave his lovely daughter, Chaska, who was named after the star that always stays close to Inti as he sits in the sun. As Huayna Capac and Coya Cusirimay's sole daughter, you too will take your place in the snows of Salcantay Mountain. With this great honor you will be part of the bridge that all noblemen, including your parents will use to pass to the Upper World. If we are successful, Viracocha, returning as a man, will also find this bridge suitable and will reverse his ruinous judgment. Kaya Chaka, you will have the honor to complete the bridge and to welcome Viracocha back to this world. You are our best hope for the survival of the Inca Empire."

"I am just a child." How could he ask so much from such an insignificant girl? I'm just a child. How could I refuse? But I am just a child. That's the last thing I remembered with any clarity. "I am just a child."

Brothers

Ninan

The multi-colored strands of the rope spiraled together just as life, death, earth, and sky were intertwined. During the dance, the women carried the rope on one side and the men on the other as we wound through the streets of Cusco and finally into Haucaypata Plaza. Seated beside our mummified ancestors, my parents, the Inca and his queen, listened to each dancer chanting his prayers as we passed.

Powerful Inti, grant the Inca a long and reverent life.
Most generous Inti, forgive our sins.
Wise and protective Inti, spare us from illness and the wrath of Viracocha.
Benevolent Inti, let us live to honor you until we return to our creator.

Carrying the end of the rope that was elaborately decorated as a snake's head, Umu Pilaca led the grand procession while we continued to dance and chant into an ever-tighter spiral. Finally reaching the center, the priest stopped and silently lifted the serpent rope above his head as a signal for everyone to do the same. As the serpent climbed into the sky, Umu Pilaca sent our prayer with it.

Viracocha, our magnificent creator, hear our prayer.
Only you balance the forces of life, death, earth, and sky.
We place this rope to show our desire for you to lead us out of chaos.
Grant us your favor so we, your children, may serve you.
Viracocha, our merciful creator, hear our prayer.

Everyone lowered the rope to the ground and stepped away from the perfect coil. The dancers formed a circle around it to admire their ordered work as Umu Pilaca said, "Together as one, we danced to demonstrate our devotion to Inti and to beg him to petition Viracocha on our behalf. Surely they will forgive our sins and grant us good health."

We all cheered, satisfied that we had performed the dance perfectly. Splintering into smaller groups, everyone drank and sang through the night, but even the most inebriated were careful not to disturb the rope.

Easy for several hundred to carry, it was a heavy load for ten of us to take the rope from the central plaza back to the Coricancha Temple the following morning. Pacas led the group with several loops slung over his shoulder. Lugging an equal load, I followed behind him with a short stretch of rope sagging between us, while the other eight men followed on the tethered line.

As we entered the temple two groups of Mamaconas, the chosen women, worked in the courtyard. My mother oversaw four young beauties as they roasted peanuts over the sacred fire, while across the courtyard Miski, my father's favorite mistress, chatted with the others as they mashed *mulli* berries. I caught a glimpse of the young women as we passed and almost tripped over Pacas, who completely stopped in the doorway. Startled back into motion, he continued down the stairs to the storage room and carefully placed the rope on its stone bench. Pacas fussed with the coils, making sure none were misplaced or entangled. The others were satisfied and gradually drifted off.

"Ninan, help me straighten out this coil. It's still not resting properly."

This fastidious behavior was not typical, but I humored him, making the meaningless adjustments he requested. He puttered with the rope and then with the ceremonial blanket that covered it. He even smoothed out its wrinkles and made sure the blanket was square to the bench.

As the last of the carriers left, I asked, "Are you satisfied yet? The rope is expertly stored."

He glanced at the doorway and with a furtive gleam in his eye, he answered under his breath, "Finally they're all gone. Now we can go watch the women."

His sly plan revealed, I chuckled to myself, but spoke sternly, "Well, I'm sorry to see you're not sincere in your concern for the sacred rope. Of course, we shouldn't spy on the chosen women, and I should report you to Umu Pilaca for even suggesting it."

Pacas stepped away, hurt by my threat, and I continued before he could answer. "I could tell the priest about your disrespect for the rope and your impure thoughts of the Mamaconas. That would likely ban you from the temple for at least a month and destroy any opportunity you might have to meet the girl you incessantly worship. Maybe he'd even let me watch when he poked your eyes out." I relished the moment.

Motionless and mouth agape, he stared at me. With a wide grin, I flippantly continued, "Or I could show you a secret place to hide where the priests can't see us, and you can show me which of the chosen women has given you this reckless fever."

He stood with his feet spread and his hands ready to throttle me. I laughed and grabbed his arms. "Pacas, you're my best friend. I'd never intentionally endanger you. I was only teasing. All you've talked about lately is this girl, and I don't even know which one you favor."

Pacas sighed in relief. "That was a nasty trick. I'd never do that to you. Promise me you'll never do it again." His grave voice refused to dismiss my prank.

Suddenly I realized how unintentionally cruel I had been. One day I would be Inca, and, officially, he would be my servant. It would be within my rights to destroy him. He deserved my respect and my absolute promise not to betray him. I needed his friendship as much as he needed to trust me. Ashamed of myself, I started slowly, "Pacas, I truly regret tricking you. From this day forward, I promise never to deceive you in any way, or betray your trust."

Men for only thirteen months, we stood at arms length willing to acknowledge the end of our childhood friendship and eager to establish an even stronger relationship as adults. Except by birth, he was in every way my equal: strong, very quick with numbers and genuinely interested in serving the empire. I couldn't ask for a better friend and ally.

Looking directly into my eyes, he finally answered, "I accept your apology, Ninan. We grew up as friends and nearly brothers. With the blessings of the gods, one day you'll be the Inca. I know you as an honorable man who searches for the truth and passes judgment with compassion. Your strength and courage will serve you well, but as Inca, yours will be a lonely life. Remember to take comfort in the company of your friends."

Touched by his compliment, I said nothing. We stood together in the depths of the Coricancha at the center of the world. No matter what was to come, Pacas and I would be loyal friends working for the good of the people and by the will of the gods. I'd known him my whole life, but only now did I realize how important he was to me.

The intensity faded as a smile spread across his face and his dark eyes lightened with a sparkle. "Let's find the women."

Unseen, we raced up the stairs before slowing to a quick noiseless step. Pacas followed me down the corridor behind the courtyard. Hidden between the wall of the temple and the wall of the priests' sleeping quarters, a staircase led to the top of the temple wall. Several years earlier I watched a builder fix the roof and grew curious to know how he was able to appear and disappear from the top of the wall. I found the stairs, and the builder showed me the enclosure at the corner of the courtyard. Because there were actually four walls meeting in the corner and the abutting roofs created a valley, the builders had ingeniously designed a bowl for rainwater to collect and run through a crevice in the rock rather than flood the courtyard. Combining two functions, they made it extra large so it could also be used as an access point to the roof. We climbed the stairs and discovered the bowl was just large enough for both of us to sit. By stretching around the roof beams, we could see and hear the Mamaconas in the open courtyard below, but were well hidden from their view.

Fortunately, the women were still engaged in their morning work. My mother and the peanut roasting continued to our left while the brewing was in the opposite corner to our right. All clothed in the same simple white dresses, Pacas scanned the girls' faces to spot his favorite one. "There she is," he whispered, "She's the one at the mortar pressing the berries."

She was a beauty. Her thin lips and small nose gracefully balanced her rounded cheeks and gentle eyes. Small in stature, she kneeled gracefully over the mortar and slowly rocked the pestle from side to side as she added berries with her other hand. Following the contours of the stone, the juice drained away from her and funneled into a waiting bowl. She worked steadily as the other girls carried and sorted the berries, emptied the bowl and prepared the juice for fermentation. Mostly they were listening to Miski as she talked about men. "Men are as intoxicating as the beer you're making. Some of you will be Mamaconas your entire lives, but some of you will be given to noblemen as gifts for their deeds."

The tallest of the girls carried berries and dreamily added, "I hope I will wed a brave soldier, a strong and handsome young man. I could please such a man."

Miski raised her eyebrows and asked, "And how would you please such a man?"

"The gods will show me what I need to know." The girl's wavering voice belied her confident words.

"Why depend on the gods for something I already know? To interest a man you continually show him how desirable he is, but you never look at him directly. Here I'll show you." Miski pretended the tall girl was an attractive man as she displayed her considerable charm. Keeping her head slightly down and her eyes diverted from the "man," she sauntered past him, allowing her shoulder to slightly brush his arm as she stooped to pick up a stone. She straightened and made sure his hand touched her hair before she slid past. "You see how easy that was? I never looked at him, and yet he knows I find him desirable."

Showing no signs of womanhood, the youngest girl poured the juice into the fermenting jar. "But we are the chosen women. We can't touch a man. We would be beaten and disgraced for what you did," she squealed.

"Oh, I was showing you how to entice a man you already know, but you can still show your interest from a distance. Let's say you wanted the attentions of a man standing where the queen is. Continue your normal conversation, but speak a bit louder and slower than usual. When the man turns his head to see you, drop your chin and look at something half way between you and him. If you're standing, you can freeze in a flattering pose. Here, I'll show you."

She started again, her voice a little louder as she nearly sang the words. "We need to bring in more mulli berries from the temple doorway." She turned toward the queen and then struck a provocative pose as she looked toward the entrance. Her head was still lowered, but she swung her arm toward the door and gracefully stepped to the side, showing the queen a profile of her face and body. She stood that way for only an instant before continuing the natural flow of the gesture. As soon as she raised her voice, the queen looked up from her work and then shook her head in disgust. Miski giggled with the girls at the queen's response. "You see, you can draw attention anytime you like. You were chosen because of your natural beauty. You just need to learn how to use it."

I watched this demonstration, fascinated with her subtle and yet very effective ploys. Pacas ignored the banter entirely and saw only his favorite as she crushed berries. "What's her name?" I asked.

"I don't know. We've never spoken. This is the first time I've really even seen her without being watched by her guardians. She moves so gracefully and is so intent on her work. I wish I could touch her face."

"That would be the last time you'd see her. The priest would certainly take your eyes, if not your life." Resigned to that situation, he nodded and settled his gaze on his girl again.

Miski continued her demonstrations on sitting and turning her head to get attention. They imitated her as she stood up, turned to pick up a bowl and carried it to a convenient bench. All her motions flowed with a natural rhythm, but something always held my attention. She slightly exaggerated her hand movements, brushed her hair from her eyes, or bent her leg to straighten her dress. I realized she was very enticing, even though she was an older woman. Unpracticed, the girls' clumsy attempts were almost comical. On the other side of the courtyard, the girls watched the display and commented quietly.

"Get back to work! What's the matter with you?" my mother commanded as the smell of burned peanuts rose to our hideout. Her scowl and reprimand set a stark contrast to the frivolous woman opposite her. "Feed the burned nuts to the birds." She turned to face the girls grinding the roasted nuts into a fine powder. "These two containers are full. Take them to the Temple of Inti. The priests will mix them with the ashes and spices there."

Two girls obediently carried the jars across the courtyard and disappeared into the temple. They returned immediately to tend the fire and transfer the newly roasted nuts into the mortar. My mother stood rigidly between her girls and Miski's antics.

Pacas was aware of everything in the courtyard, but he couldn't take his eyes off his favorite. We both saw her stop working just as Umu Pilaca walked in the main doorway. Miski's womanly demonstrations abruptly stopped as the priest continued toward my mother. It was fortunate that Pacas's girl was behind him when she looked directly toward our perch. I pulled Pacas away from the edge, and we fled down the stairs. It was far too dangerous to stay, even in such a good hideout. We ran to the corner and then slowed to a brisk walk as we left the Coricancha behind.

"She is a very pretty girl, Pacas, but we are too young to marry, and so is she."

"I know, but I worry that she might be promised to another before I have a chance to ask for her."

"Are you sure she is the one? You've never even talked with her and you don't know her family."

"I don't care who she is. I know she's the right woman. Did you see how she looked at us? We were being very quiet, so she had no reason to search our corner. She just knew someone was there. I've never spoken to her, she has no idea who I am, and still we know each other. How could this be if we were not intended for one another?" He was absolutely certain of his decision and my questions did not dissuade him.

"Well, you'll at least need to know her name. If we knew that, we could talk to my father and see if he will grant your favor."

We walked downstream away from the temple as we concocted ways to learn her name. Without noticing, we crossed the river and found ourselves strolling beside the rock-walled pastures of the Mamaconas. A llama stood on a small rise, accentuating his size, his long straight neck and attentive posture. His entirely brown coat hung on him like a royal cloak. Well fed and under-worked, there was no doubt he was the dominant male as he watched the entire flock and dismissed us as a threat. His attention was drawn to the opposite side of the field, over the rise and beyond our view.

"Pacas, what do you think he's watching?"

"I don't know. Let's circle around so we can see."

We followed the wall as it paralleled the river and then turned away. It was a sunny morning, but because of the festivities the previous evening, no one tended the animals or worked the fields. Just as we rounded the corner we saw my half brother Atahualpa, son of Miski, and his friend Rumi leading a very young llama through the pasture gate. Amazed that they were able to lure the animal away from its mother, we watched as the two boys headed away from the pasture. The pure white llama between them obediently traipsed along as it looked back to the safety of its mother. Together the miniature threesome was proportioned exactly as grown men would be with an adult llama but, barely school age, the boys and llama pranced with a playfulness I had nearly forgotten. Pacas and I smiled with delight, and, lacking any immediate task, we decided to follow them to a grassy spot in the shade of the basswood trees. We circled around using the walls and shrubs as cover until we were close enough to hear.

Rumi tethered the llama to a small branch while Atahualpa puffed up his chest, pointed his chin to the sky and strutted away from him. "I am the Inca, and you are my servant. I can make you do anything I wish." Atahualpa picked up a stick to use as a scepter and marched back to Rumi, who was already on his knees. He rested the scepter and his foot on Rumi's back.

Rumi dropped his head to his knees and in a muffled voice replied, "I will always be your trusted warrior. With your blessing I will kill your enemies, and their lands will be mine."

Pacas nudged me as we exchanged amused glances. Pretending to be Inca was every boy's recreation, and their pretentious play was filled with childish sincerity. As Atahualpa removed his foot, he commanded, "Stand my loyal servant. Today we celebrate! We captured the leader of our strongest enemy and killed all his soldiers. Praise be to Inti and me, his son."

Standing proudly, Rumi added, "Praise Inca Atahualpa! Ruler of the earth and sky."

"We will celebrate by killing the leader of our enemy." Atahualpa shouted while parading around the grassy knoll with Rumi in lockstep behind him. He lifted his stick and Rumi obediently cheered. When he stopped to greet the imaginary dignitaries, Rumi waited at a respectful distance. Atahualpa approached the llama and Rumi moved to face him with the llama between them. "I am the Inca. Only I am worthy of killing our enemy's leader."

Pacas and I, still hidden, watched this fantasy with the humor of adults. I never saw the knife. With one fatal swipe, Atahualpa slit the llama's throat, and it dropped with blood spurting everywhere. As though practiced at the art, Rumi fell with the llama and held the dying animal with its ribcage exposed.

"I will have his heart as my trophy," Atahualpa proclaimed. He too dropped to his knees and with Rumi's help, expertly extracted the heart and held the still throbbing, bloody mass above his head. They had successfully killed and mutilated the llama faster than any priest had ever completed a sacrifice. Pacas and I stared at each other, knowing it was too late to save the llama.

"Inca Atahualpa will destroy all who oppose him. In the name of Inti, I will reign supreme!"

The childhood game was no longer amusing, and Pacas and I stood stunned by their vicious and well-practiced attack. When Atahualpa lowered the heart and began to lick the blood, we both bolted into action.

Rushing out of our hiding spot, I yelled, "Stop that! You will be punished!"

To my complete surprise, Atahualpa and Rumi started laughing. It sounded more like a mocking, hysterical squeal than children laughing, but it didn't stop our charge. Rumi grabbed the knife and tried to stab Pacas with an underhand forward thrust. Stronger and eight years older, we had no trouble disarming him without injury.

Pacas held him and I turned to Atahualpa. Still standing with the pulsating heart, Atahualpa swallowed his laughter to taunt me. "Punished? By you? You're too soft to punish me. You have no taste for blood. I'm not afraid of you. I will be Inca, and this will be your heart in my hands."

The brazen audacity! With one perfectly aimed kick in his stomach, I sent him flying. "If you weren't my father's son, I'd kill you right here for insulting me. We'll take you back to Huayna Capac and your mother. They'll punish you."

Through the kick, short flight and hard landing, Atahualpa still held the now quiet heart. His hands, arms, and face covered with blood. I grabbed his free wrist and yanked him to his feet. Struggling to breathe, he was silent, but his eyes blazed with hatred, not tears. I held the front legs of the llama with my free hand. Pacas kept one hand on Rumi and held the llama's hind legs in the other.

No one spoke as we began the long walk back to Casana in the center of Cusco. Bent from my kick, Atahualpa hobbled and carried the heart the whole way home. Rumi kept eyeing the knife, now carefully hung out of reach at Pacas' waist. Pinched to slits, his eyes and mouth carried a ruthless grimace that was especially unnerving in so young a child. Over the dead llama, Pacas and I exchanged glances that reflected the cruel brutality of these children. As we got closer to the palace, people watched us pass, but no one interfered with two warring sons of the Inca.

Miski was just leaving Casana as we reached the doorway. At the sight of her precious son still bent and covered with blood she dropped her basket of wool and ran to him in panic. "What have they done to you?"

Still tightly holding his wrist, I answered for him. "He's not hurt. We caught them killing this stolen llama."

Bending before her son, searching for the source of the blood, she snapped back, "You're mistaken. Rumi must be responsible. Atahualpa would never do such a thing."

"I assure you, Pacas and I saw the entire incident. Your son is a practiced murderer. Where is my father?" Atahualpa was right; there would be no punishment if his mother resolved the situation. I wasn't prepared to ignore the incident, especially after parading through Cusco.

Satisfied that Atahualpa wasn't seriously hurt, Miski rose slowly, brushing my arm with her bare shoulder. "Ninan, my dear, there is no need to trouble your father with the trifles of child's play. Surely we can overlook this just once." Honey sweet words flowed from her lips. "He was imitating the sacrifices he saw at the festival. He's too young to understand that what he did was wrong. I'll talk to him." She paused and struck a provocative pose as she brushed her hair from her face, exactly as she had shown the girls earlier in the day. Using the wares she knew best, Miski added, "Ninan, you're a man now. You can decide this. You and I can discuss this privately and come to an arrangement."

I was flattered by her attention and understood exactly what she was offering me. Had we not witnessed her antics earlier, I might have been duped by her seduction.

"This is not child's play. These two have done this many times and they must be disciplined."

Miski and Atahualpa were both startled. Miski considered me an innocent, and her charms always worked with the men, as her son had no doubt witnessed many times. Still holding the culprits and the victim, Pacas and I passed through the hallway into the courtyard. Huayna Capac, Sinchi Roca, and two noblemen I didn't recognize continued their serious discussion as they entered the main courtyard from my father's favorite meeting room directly opposite us. Miski, still trying to avert the confrontation, murmured sweet promises behind me as we approached. Seeing us with a llama and bleeding children, my father halted in mid-sentence.

"Father, we need to talk with you about Atahualpa and his friend. Pacas and I saw them steal this llama from the Mamaconas' pasture and cut out its heart." We dropped the llama and released the boys. Both scurried toward Miski as she gracefully flowed past me to ingratiate herself at Huayna Capac's side.

After dismissing the unfamiliar men, Huayna Capac acknowledged the llama, the dried blood flaking off Atahualpa's limbs, and the sticky heart he moved from one hand to the other. He turned to the carcass, Pacas and me and said, "Tell me what happened."

In full detail, Pacas and I described Atahualpa's apparent innocence when he took the llama and pretended to be Inca. We finished the story with the expert killing and dissection of the llama. Huayna Capac examined the animal, both impressed and dismayed at their skill. "Why did you kill the llama?"

"So I could eat the heart and grow up to be the Inca." Atahualpa answered with childish puffery.

Huayna Capac smiled, amused by his presumption. "And why do you think you will be the Inca?"

"I'm your son, and my mother told me I would be Inca."

Huayna Capac glanced at Miski, who carefully avoided his scrutiny, while a muffled laugh escaped my mother as she stepped to my side.

"Why does eating the heart make you the Inca?"

"The Inca must be strong to kill his enemies and the heart will make me strong. When I am Inca I will eat the hearts of my enemies." My stomach turned in revulsion.

His face as inscrutable as stone, my father continued, "And how did you learn to kill the llama and remove its heart?"

"We have seen many llamas sacrificed. A priest told me how to take out the heart."

"How many times have you done this?"

"I ate a heart each day of a full moon for a year. Is that long enough to make me Inca?" His hopeful eyes searched Huayna Capac's face for affirmation.

Huayna Capac ignored the question. "What did you do with the rest of the dead llamas?"

"We hung each one in the tree. It was always gone the next morning."

My father stared at the heart in Atahualpa's hand and Rumi hidden behind Miski. "Do you understand that what you're doing is wrong?"

Atahualpa gasped as he looked at his father and then the ground as he answered. "You are the Inca and can never be wrong. I will be the Inca, how can I be wrong?"

Huayna Capac glared at Miski but spoke in a gently firm voice to Atahualpa. "You're just a child and still too young to even be considered to be the next Inca. You were wrong to steal the llamas from the Mamaconas, and you were wrong to kill innocent animals without the blessing of Inti and a priest. Your plan to eat the heart of your enemies when you are Inca is ridiculous. No civilized man, and especially not the Inca, would ever eat human flesh. Never, not even an enemy's. It's revolting and a sin against Inti." Huayna Capac was very fond of Miski, and he'd never scolded Atahualpa. Usually he ignored children, preferring to leave them with the women.

Miski moved closer, trying to divert my father's attention while Atahualpa stood alone to face his first reprimand. "You'll see. I'll be the greatest Inca of all!" he defiantly proclaimed

"Enough of your insolence! Today you'll be punished. The future is in Inti's hands." Atahualpa had surpassed my father's limited patience for children. "Atahualpa, you will have no contact with your friend. Rumi, you will move to Quito. If your family wishes to move with you, arrangements will be made. If not, you will be raised by the priests."

My father turned to Sinchi Roca who had quietly observed the entire proceedings. He nodded his response, knowing he was responsible for finalizing the details. Huayna Capac turned back to Atahualpa. "You, my son, need a lesson in humility. For the next year you will pray to Inti for forgiveness, and at each full moon you will sacrifice enough hay and grain to feed all the llamas you killed. Through the next growing season you will work in the fields of the Mamaconas to compensate for the llamas and the grains."

Atahualpa did not understand how difficult the next year would be, but Miski did. "My dearest, must you punish our son so harshly? Isn't there another way to discipline him?" she pleaded with him, still clinging to the power of her sensuous influence.

"Yes, there is another way. In addition to repaying his debt, Atahualpa will travel on foot, as a servant, during our journey to the Temple of Viracocha at Cacha. We leave when Camay Raymi is over. And rather than accompany us, Miski, you will stay in Cusco."

Miski stepped away, visibly shocked that Atahualpa's childish behavior had caused her to fall so far from his favor.

"Don't leave her with me," my mother complained. "She is a poor excuse for a mother and a disgrace to the Mamaconas. Today she showed the girls how to entice men. Only Tinkha, who was crushing berries, ignored her antics. Send her to Quito with Rumi."

Tinkha! So that was her name! Pacas must be pleased to know the name of his favorite girl. I didn't dare to even glance at him.

"You are the queen and my first wife. You are the head of this household and the ultimate authority of the Mamaconas. What did you do when she disrupted the work? Discipline her! She will not go to Quito. She has other uses here when we return."

Even I understood that my mother was just given permission to subdue the Inca's favorite mistress as she wished. She sneered in delight. Eyeing my mother with dread, Miski was visibly relieved that she hadn't lost her place in my father's bed. "Sinchi Roca, Ninan, Pacas, and Atahualpa will accompany me to Cacha in four days. We will be gone for about three weeks. Now clean up this mess and finish the preparations for Camay Raymi." Huayna Capac waved his hand over the dead llama and bloody children, and then signaled Sinchi Roca to follow him as he stormed across the courtyard and out the palace door.

Teary eyed, Miski gathered up the boys and headed toward the bath, while Coya Cusirimay called two servants to collect the dead llama for the evening meal. Pacas, grinned broadly but said nothing as we headed away from the discord. There was much to discuss, including the unexpected trip to Cacha and saving Tinkha for Pacas. Too bad Atahualpa would travel with us, but at least the presumptuous bastard got what he deserved.

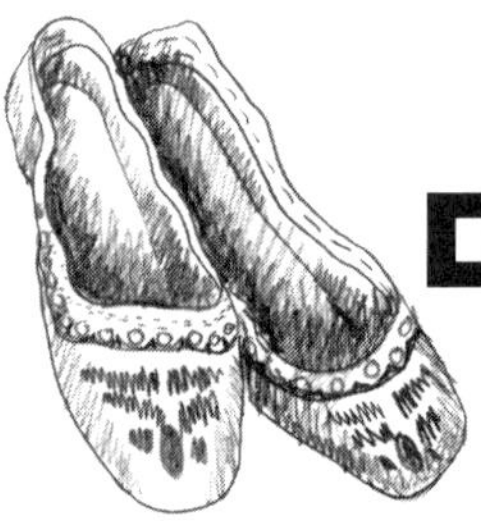

Diplomacy

Ninan

With its fitted-stone buildings, golden temples, and Inca nobility, I considered Cusco my home throughout my life. Still, traveling away from its luxuries into a world peppered with adventure, always rekindled my desire to discover the empire for myself. Our trip to the Temple of Viracocha in Cacha was no exception. Compared to Tomebamba, this was a short trip, an easy six-day walk. The journey began by following the Huatanay River downstream to its junction with the sacred river. From there the river flowed downstream as the Urubamba River, while upstream it was called the Vilcanota River. Our journey paralleled the tree-lined Vilcanota River as it spilled out of the southeast mountains. Riding side by side in intricately carved and painted litters, Sinchi Roca and Huayna Capac led our procession to Cacha. Shaded from the sun, each litter rested on four bearers all dressed identically in white tunics trimmed with red. On top, their continual conversation touched on preparations for the upcoming Inti Raymi festival in Cacha and the nobles they encountered at the recent Camay Raymi festival.

Litters for Pacas and me were immediately behind them, although we walked most of the time. Mama Runtu, another of father's favored wives, followed on her litter. She was invited along to care for Atahualpa as well as her own son, Tito, since Miski stayed in Cusco. Tito, another of my many half brothers, was a year younger than Atahualpa but almost as tall and stronger. With Atahualpa confined to foot travel, Mama Runtu walked as much as she was able, but unaccustomed to travel, she tired easily. Pacas and I often watched the boys so she could ride in comfort.

Late on the second day, Pacas and I were following Atahualpa and Tito, when suddenly Atahualpa turned and started hitting me with a stick. Eight years his senior and twice his size, I had no trouble defending myself and getting him to keep up with the group. "You're as fast as a puma, and as vicious. Is there something you'd like to tell me?" I asked.

"I should be riding on a litter, but because of you, I have to walk like a servant." He spat his words at me as I walked backwards in front of him. I still had trouble taking the young boy seriously.

"There is no shame in walking. It will make you strong much faster than eating a llama's heart."

Atahualpa rolled his eyes.

"I like to walk," Tito said in a voice louder than his size. "There are always interesting spiders along the road, and with the trees, I've found lots of other bugs, and a few toads. Besides, people won't talk to you if you're riding in a litter." He veered to the edge of the road where he bent down to move a loose rock but found no prize. His high cheek bones and long, strong nose were hidden under a tangled mass of stringy, black hair. He bent again to pick up a stone.

Atahualpa watched him with disgust. "You're such a child. Don't you know anything? Riding in a litter means you're important. Everyone knows you're a nobleman."

"I know, but I still like the walk. It's more fun."

Neither Pacas nor I knew either boy very well. We were men after all, and they were only children. Still, I liked Tito's lack of pretense, and he found interesting creatures that I'd never seen before.

Pacas started to unwind his ever-present sling from his head. "Tito, how are you with a sling?"

"Only fair. Will you teach me?"

Pacas nodded as Tito extracted his sling from the pouch he carried.

With his chin high and his eyes directed toward the distant mountain, Atahualpa tried to ignore us.

"Atahualpa, do you prefer the sling or the bow?" I asked.

He seemed to consider that a worthy question, since he actually looked at me when he answered. "I like the bow." At least there was one thing we had in common.

"I don't see your bow. Where is it?"

He winced. Even a boy his age knew he should always carry a weapon. "Mama Runtu said she would put it on the litter."

Leaving Pacas and Tito, the two of us quickened our pace to catch her litter before going to the front of the procession. From there we shot down the road and retrieved our arrows as we reached them. Not very strong, Atahualpa had trouble pulling his child's bow. He was tenacious though and kept practicing. I showed him how to nearly lock his forward arm and pull back with his other arm rather than push with one arm and pull with the other. We practiced for a few hours every day, and by the fifth day he was starting to improve. Unfortunately, his hatred for me didn't mellow. "Why are you mad at me?"

"You disgraced me in front of my father. Now he'll never choose me as Inca." He was on the verge of tears but refused to succumb.

"Atahualpa, you are too young to worry about that. Besides, I only made your actions known. You were the one stealing and killing llamas. It's appropriate that your secret was discovered during Camay Raymi. I hope you asked Inti for forgiveness."

He shrugged his shoulders and mumbled. "I don't need Inti's forgiveness."

"We all need his forgiveness," I reminded him, but he shook his head.

"Since Inti tells the Inca what to do, Huayna Capac can do no wrong. I'm Huayna Capac's son, so I'm always right too. Inti will always tell me what to do. I don't need to ask for his forgiveness."

I marveled at his absolute conviction. In my experience, the directions coming from Inti were usually unclear, and the Inca struggled to understand his meaning, even with the help of the priests. Convinced that I was his enemy, there was no point in contradicting him. "Atahualpa, I think you should let your teachers help you understand Inti's lessons."

I wanted to dismiss his arrogance to youth, but I couldn't. I'd never had such certainty, and I wondered why not. Other than in the lessons about our forefathers, I had no experience with divine guidance, nor was I ever certain I was right about any spiritual matter. At Camay Raymi, the cleansing festival, I always asked Inti for forgiveness, even though I never felt that Inti heard my request or forgave me.

Atahualpa practiced his archery, and my thoughts drifted back to the Camay Raymi celebration we left in Cusco. Because of the heavy rains this year, the final event was spectacular, and I was glad my father decided to leave after the flooding. Each year, a temporary dam was built in the hills northwest of Cusco. Downstream from this primary dam, but still above Cusco, several smaller dams created holding ponds. While the soldiers and mita workers constructed the dams, the Mamaconas and the priests prepared the offering. Throughout the year, a small amount of the ash from every sacrifice in Cusco was saved for Camay Raymi. The peanuts that Pacas and I watched the Mamaconas roast were ground and used as a binder for the ash.

Ground hot peppers, coca, and salt were added as an offering to Viracocha and crushed flower petals were added to help track the flow of the offering.

Except for the boys who just reached manhood, everyone from Cusco gathered at the highest dam just as the sun dropped behind the mountains. Fortunately, I was standing beside my parents when Tinkha passed us carrying a jar of ashes, so I casually asked my mother her name. She eyed me suspiciously, but told me her full name was Tinkha of Cana. When I told Pacas his girlfriend's name the next day, he danced around like the sparks in a fire.

To begin the ceremony, Umu Pilaca thanked Viracocha for his blessings in the past year and asked him for the good health of his worthy children. Next he asked for forgiveness on behalf of those who had been sick, since illness was punishment for those who were blind to their transgressions. On his nod, the Mamaconas threw the offering into the river as the priests broke the dam by pulling out a key timber, releasing a torrent toward the city below. As the deluge rushed past beside us, the High Priest offered a final prayer.

Sacred river, carry these ashes to the ocean.
Let the winds lift them to Viracocha in the Mayu.
Generous Viracocha, forgive your children and accept our tribute.
Let us live in health and your children will always worship you.
Hear our prayer, Viracocha, our merciful creator.

Meanwhile, the small dams broke with the advancing waters, adding the ponds to the flow. In Cusco, the water flooded through the streets and houses, washing away the sins and illness of the previous year. At the bottom of the city, more flowers and coca leaves were added to the river by the boys who became men the previous month. Racing by torch and moonlight while sweeping any floating petals back into the flow of the river, the new men followed the flood until the water was entirely within the river banks. It was late afternoon the next day before the last of the runners returned to Cusco. They swept the banks twice as far as Pacas and I had done the previous year.

As we traveled to Cache, I realized that Camay Raymi was one of my favorite ceremonies. Atahualpa's indifference baffled me. Even more than becoming a man, this annual act gave me a fresh start, a chance to leave my mistakes behind. Atahualpa completely rejected the practice, and the need for it. I decided he was just too young to appreciate its significance and hoped he would understand when he was older.

Without further outbursts from Atahualpa, our trek ended with a royal welcome at Cacha. People lined the road to spread branches of coca all the way up the slope to the town. Dressed in their finest clothes, the priests and Mamaconas lined one side of the street while the soldiers and administrators lined the opposite side. Interspersed throughout, but always behind the nobleman, the clean and well-fed farmers and families spontaneously added their exuberant cheers to the chorus as we approached. "Long live the Inca. Health and prosperity to the Inca."

Even with all the attention, I couldn't resist staring at the majestic temple towering over us. "I knew the Temple of Viracocha was large, but I never imagined this," Pacas shouted over the noise of the crowd.

From a distance I estimated the temple was more than a hundred paces long and almost thirty wide. The remarkable roof peaked along an impossibly high ridge at least as tall as seven men. Where it joined the long walls, it was still as high as a man could reach with a spear. To this height, the fitted-stone walls used the dark stone so common in the area, but at the end, stark white adobe ascended to the peak. Two large wooden doors framed in red, echoed the red trim on the windows lining the entire length of the building. I wanted to explore its interior, but instead we followed the welcoming parade away from the temple to the palace tucked into the hillside.

Similar to Quispiguanca but much smaller, the palace had a pleasant courtyard and easily accommodated our group.

"New friends and old, we are delighted to visit your beautiful town. Thank you for your generous welcome." My father's booming voice echoed off the walls. "Your noble leaders planned a feast for this evening, and you're all invited!"

The crowd cheered their good fortune until he quieted them by raising his ever-present scepter. "I look forward to renewing old friendships and beginning new ones, but first we must rest after our journey. At sunset we will join you in the temple plaza."

After a final cheer, the crowd dispersed, and we settled into the palace. Atahualpa found a shady spot and slept soundly. He looked so innocent and harmless, I almost felt sorry for him. Not nearly as weary, my father called for *chicha,* and we all rested quietly in the courtyard, enjoying the warm sun and the gurgling water of the nearby fountain. Tito was tired too, but he sat with us rather than trail behind his mother, who left to meet the servants.

"Why is the Temple of Viracocha here? I thought it was on an island in Lake Titicaca." Tito didn't address the question to anyone in particular, but my father answered.

"Your schooling has only just begun and already you know there is a temple on the island. Viracocha rose out of the lake and created all that we know, and to honor him, the ancients built a beautiful shrine on the island. After admiring his creation, Viracocha left Lake Titicaca and wandered through the mountains dressed as an old man. When he reached Cacha, the people didn't recognize him, but instead feared the stranger and plotted to kill him because he had light skin and a hairy face. Our creator knew of the plan and made the mountain spew fiery stone. Terrified, the people begged him to stop before they were all destroyed. Viracocha, often a merciful god, spared the town and all the people. They built a shrine here to show their thanks."

My father paused to finish his beer. "When I first became Inca, I traveled throughout the empire, meeting the local leaders, inspecting properties that belong to the religion, and verifying the tributes paid by the people. In Cacha, I heard this miraculous story and saw the small shrine they had revered since Viracocha's time on earth. Their enduring devotion deserved to be recognized, so I decreed that this beautiful temple should be built. Sometimes we hold the Inti Raymi ceremonies here, and you may come here again when you are older." His story sounded complete, but he continued as he helped himself to more beer.

"Building the temple not only honored Viracocha, it gave me a way to reward their allegiance to all the Incas since the time of Pachacuti. Visitors traveling here for the festivals bring generous gifts of gold statues, cloth, and exotic foods for their hosts. In addition, maintaining the storehouses and the Temple provides work to the citizens beyond traditional farming. I benefit because this is an excellent location for storing maize, and the storehouses are protected by some of our strongest allies."

Tito listened to his explanation while he pushed a beetle with his feet. He would have been satisfied to know we needed a temple to celebrate Inti Raymi, but I liked the story. I decided this was a good time to ask. "Father, why are we visiting Cacha? What needed your attention so urgently that you decided to make a special trip rather than wait until Inti Raymi in five months?"

He sighed deeply. "Did you recognize the Curaca Checa when we entered Cacha?"

I nodded; he was the man who was with my father when Pacas and I brought Atahualpa and Rumi to the palace.

"He visited Cusco to invite Sinchi Roca and me to Cacha. As fine as this valley appears, our close friends are struggling and have asked for my help."

When he reached for yet another beer without further comment, I nudged Pacas, and we left with Tito, leaving my father and Sinchi Roca to themselves.

As arranged during the evening feast, Pacas and I joined our fathers at noon the following day in the palace courtyard. In a short while Curaca

Checa, the leader of the Hanan group, and Curaca Pusani, the leader of the Hurin group, arrived together. Having been introduced at the feast, this morning we greeted one another as friends. Checa and Pusani were so similar in appearance, they could have been brothers. Both in the prime of life, they were the same medium height and stocky build with black hair worn in the standard Inca style, short and bound with a headband. Their tunics were the same white with a black and yellow woven pattern, and even their gold earplugs were nearly identical. The only visible distinguishing mark was the scar on Pusani's left shoulder.

Huayna Capac initiated the plan for the visit. "My understanding is that in spite of a good growing season and industrious people, Cacha isn't able to sustain itself and pay the tributes to the religion and to the state as you have in the past. You asked for the tributes to be reduced, but you're unable to adequately explain your situation. You're trusted friends, and we're here to help find a solution. Today the four of us will walk with Pusani. He can show us the workings of the Hurin section. Tomorrow we will review the Hanan section with Checa." The plan was satisfactory to everyone, and after agreeing to meet us for the evening meal, Checa left to attend to his usual business.

"As you know the people of this area are excellent farmers, and the women specialize in intricately woven patterns. We'll start by reviewing the goods in storage, and then we'll inspect the fields," Pusani began, choosing his words carefully so he wouldn't have to speak any more than necessary. His voice seemed to come from his nose, not his mouth. Even though it wasn't particularly high-pitched, a nasal whistle accompanied every word.

When we passed the Temple of Viracocha on our way to the rows of storehouses, I asked if we could look in the Temple.

After an almost imperceptible nod from my father, Pusani responded, "Of course, I'd be honored to show you."

With that he swung open one of the huge doors and we stepped onto the black sand floor inside. Immediately in front of us was the first of eleven huge columns. Each one supported the roof as it ascended to its peak atop a long wall that ran down the center of the building. Like the walls, the columns were fitted-stone construction to a height well above my head and painted blood red.

"This room is huge. At least a thousand people could easily stand in just this half! And these columns are beautiful!" I said.

"Yes, I believe we have enjoyed the company of as many as five thousand visitors for the Inti Raymi ceremonies, although I couldn't say if they were all in the temple at the same time," Pusani replied with his chin held high. "It's a high honor to participate in the event. I never tire of it."

"The paintings on the columns show exquisite detail, and they're all different," Pacas noted. "Each seems to show the life of a different plant or animal."

"That's right. Snakes, toads, chinchillas, pumas, falcons, condors, and, of course, llamas are all represented, among others. You'll also recognize the maize, potato, squash, pepper, coca, the baccharis shrubs and several other plants we depend on for crops, fuel, lumber, or medicines. As you know, Viracocha created all these creatures, and we have chosen to honor him with their likeness on the columns."

"I can't imagine anything more magnificent," Pacas said as he encircled the column with the llamas.

Pusani nodded and added, "Do you see those windows in the white center wall above us?"

We nodded.

"During the celebration, torches are suspended from them and the top half of the building glows a soft yellow, like the sun. There are banners hanging from the wood beams and lots of other decorations. And the sound! When the drums play, the music is so loud, you can't hear yourself sing. You really must return for Inti Raymi, the building seems so lifeless now."

"Perhaps we will," I replied. We wandered through both halves of the building passing through enormous doors in the center wall and tried to imagine the temple filled with men singing, dancing and celebrating the gifts of life so generously given to us all.

"Come along. It's time we addressed the issues at hand," Huayna Capac called to us from the entrance as he and Sinchi Roca stepped into the sunlight.

Behind the temple, one hundred and fifty identical buildings stood in fifteen perfectly straight rows. Each round, fitted-stone building was nine paces across and taller than two men. "We can open any or all of these storehouses," Pusani began as the Quipucamayo joined us. "One hundred and twenty of them are entirely filled with maize, but at the end of last year's harvest they were all filled. Throughout the year we distributed maize as requested for various festivals and sacrifices, as well as to feed the mita workers building roads in the area. Fifty of these buildings belong to the religion and eighty belong to the state. Twenty are used for storage for the farmers." We wandered through the maze, randomly opening the storehouse doors.

"This is a remarkable storage area. Where does the maize come from?" I asked.

"We store all the maize grown along the rivers from Lake Titicaca in the south to the Urubamba River in the north. In the past twenty years, we've built more storehouses and increased the amount of maize kept here almost every year. We only suffered from drought twice in that period."

Next we toured the work area for the Mamaconas and watched as they carded wool and wove fabric suitable for tunics. Curaca Pusani took us to the two buildings at the far end and showed us the storage area for the finished cloth. Stacks of tunics, capes, blankets, dresses, shawls and clothes for children were piled on reed mats from the floor to the roof. There were alpaca and *cumbi* pieces in every color and in hundreds of woven designs. The smaller building was entirely filled with *cumbi* cloth for the ceremonial costumes the priests and Mamaconas wore, as well as magnificent stacks of fabric intended for sacrifice.

Puzzled, I struggled to understand their problem but refrained from asking, hoping the answer would become obvious. We left the storage area and walked to the terraces where Pusani resumed his review. "These crops are irrigated by the small stream that flows into the river behind the temple. The others to our left are also irrigated, but the water flows naturally from a spring near the highest terrace."

The maize was just starting to tassel and rustled softly in the late afternoon breeze. There were farmers in a nearby field, and I walked over to greet them. "Good afternoon, that's a fine crop. Do you expect a good harvest?" I'd never met a farmer who wasn't happy talk about the land he tended so lovingly.

A tall middle-aged man with a sun-worn face stood to answer me. "The ears should be bigger by now. We planted later than usual because of the heavy spring rains. If the recent dry weather continues, we'll have an average crop, but with more rain, the ears could still reach full maturity before the cold weather begins." He started working some food scraps and manure into the soil again. Already preparing the field for colder weather, the decaying material extended the growing season by keeping the soil warm.

I wished him well and returned to the group. The crops looked good this year, and Pusani said that the harvest increased each of the past ten years. Why couldn't they pay their tribute?

We continued to walk the fields while Sinchi Roca examined the terraces. "How many men were called to mita service away from the valley?" he asked Pusani.

"Ten of every hundred men were called. Most were assigned to the roadwork through the mountains to the west," Pusani replied with the thorough knowledge of an experienced administrator.

"And even with the men away, you met your required tributes?"

"It was difficult, but yes. Twenty of every hundred baskets of grain were stored for the religion and another twenty for the state. For the weaving, the women decided how to distribute the work, since some women preferred to weave patterned fabric suitable for the state and others were more skilled at *cumbi* weaving needed for the religion." The tributes seemed reasonable to me.

We continued along the terrace to the stream before heading to the hilltop while Sinchi Roca asked, "How many of the fields are irrigated?"

"The system brings water to more than half of the fields. Managing too much water, like this spring, is unusual. The only solution is to wait for it to drain off or soak through the terraces." His answers were short but always complete.

With so many irrigated fields, it was clear why the valley had only two poor years. As we climbed the terrace stairs, I marveled at the splendid view of the fertile valley below.

Noting my pleasure, Pusani added, "Yes, it is a beautiful valley. People have lived here since the time of Viracocha. We take care of the land, and the gods reward us with plentiful crops and many healthy children. Look up there. You can see the new terraces that are being cultivated this season for the first time. Beyond them is the area where more terraces will be built this winter."

Still looking for answers, but uncertain where to find them, I replied, "Those fields look too high for maize. What do you grow there?"

"We have a variety of maize with small ears that will thrive there."

"And do you build new terraces every year?" I was getting used to his voice.

"If we have a good harvest, we will build more terraces," he answered simply.

"I would have thought you would expand when crops were poor to ensure more growing space during the next year."

"That seems reasonable, but we have found that the men are stronger and healthier after a good harvest, and so are able to work harder through the winter. Besides, when the harvest is very good, more babies are born and survive the cold season. We must plan to feed them, so we build additional terraces. Remember, we must add nearly twice as much space as we need to feed the people in order to pay the tributes," he said without expression.

Sinchi Roca had walked away, but Pacas and Huayna Capac were listening to our conversation. Seemingly knowing my thoughts Pacas asked, "Below us over there I see some land that isn't terraced. Why don't you expand there instead of up the mountainside?"

"That looks like dark rich soil from here, and we can walk down there if you wish. Actually, that's coarse volcanic stone with no soil.

Viracocha put it there as a reminder that we must follow his ways. We cannot disturb that area without inviting his wrath again."

Pacas and I searched the rest of the valley for other areas to cultivate. Other than the high terraces Pusani said they intended to use, there was no more land.

Sinchi Roca rejoined us, and we started back to the palace as the valley fell into mountain shadow. Pacas and I intentionally lagged behind. "I never expected there could be more people than the land could support." I said. "How can they be faulted? They live exactly as they should. They work hard, and they're devoted to the Inca and the gods. What more can Huayna Capac ask of his subjects?"

We walked in silence, each searching for a solution. "Maybe Curaca Checa will tell us something different tomorrow."

As planned, Checa and Pusani joined us for the evening meal where the conversation carefully avoided the problems of the day, and we enjoyed the company of loyal friends. My father suggested we play a betting game. Each player took turns throwing a handful of dried beans painted with either one or two dots on each side. The others bet on the sum of the dots, with the closest guess winning. Atahualpa and Tito joined us after the meal and were allowed to throw the beans and shout the official dot count. They both enjoyed being with the men, especially as the center of attention. Pacas and I soon lost interest and left for bed while the others drank, and Huayna Capac allowed his hosts to win by intentionally guessing too high or low.

As the midmorning sun rose over the southeastern mountains, we met Checa in the palace courtyard. A skilled diplomat, Checa applied his charm to the Inca, but he also knew when to address the day's task. "Inca Huayna Capac, I am fully prepared to show you anything you wish to see. I understand you reviewed the current tribute levels and the stored goods for the state, so unless you have additional questions, we can move on to the other aspects of my leadership. I can provide the records showing the building projects we have completed, or I can show you the cooperative trade agreements we have with the towns between here and Lake Titicaca. If you like, we can also review the judgments of the past three years.

"Let's begin with the judgments for the past year. Since nothing needed attention from Cusco, you must have handled everything." My father matched Curaca Checa's overly friendly tone as we settled in a shaded area of the courtyard.

"The people in the valley are remarkably well behaved. We had the standard number of marriages and deaths to administer and the tributes were all assessed and collected." He relayed the details before continuing. "There were a few spats between neighbors, but nothing out of the ordinary. Would you like to review them?"

Huayna Capac nodded and Checa detailed several incidences, saving the most interesting until the end. "A stranger was caught stealing from a storehouse. Because of our history with Viracocha, we are very tolerant of strangers. He was a mita worker who had permission to go home because his beloved wife had died. We fed him and gave him a place to rest while we verified his story. After three days, we let him go with provisions so he wouldn't be detained again." With a broad smile, Checa paused to give the Inca a chance to compliment him.

"Well done. He must have been grateful for your generosity. Was there nothing more serious? Were there no fights or murders?"

Checa thoughtfully stroked his chin as he checked his memory. Finally he replied, "There was a death, but we declared it an accident. A young father was felling a tree by the river. The trunk split, twisted and dropped in an unexpected direction crushing his young daughter who was gathering reeds nearby. He'd planned to use the tree for the roof beam of his new house, but it was worthless after it split. Just as well. Can you imagine living under a beam that had killed your child?" He tried to shake off the image.

"And how did you judge the father's actions?"

"Everyone knew he was very fond of his daughter, and there was no question it was an accident. He and his wife prepared a huge offering to Inti, begging for his forgiveness. Work is always the best healer, so he asked for twice his usual service. He's currently with the road builders. His family and fields are well cared for by his brother's family, and his neighbors finished the roof on his house." Checa finished his story with a sigh.

My father allowed a respectful pause before responding, "That's a tragic story. Be sure he receives triple wages for his service and tell him that I've asked Inti to forgive him for his carelessness." Huayna Capac stood and stared down at Curaca Checa. "Considering how peaceful everything is in the valley, there doesn't seem to be any reason to reduce the tribute."

Startled by my father's abrupt change, he sputtered, but recovered quickly. "Inca Huayna Capac, we are peaceful, loyal subjects. If we continue as we have, we'll soon be short of food. We must be allowed to keep what we need. The storehouses for the state and the religion are full. Surely there is no reason to stockpile more."

Questioning the Inca's judgment was never wise, but my father continued in an even voice. "Your concern is the people of this valley. You don't understand the affairs of the empire."

Contrite and realizing his mistake, Checa immediately lowered his head and asked, "Inca Huayna Capac, you are the wise one. This is the reason we asked you to visit Cacha. How can we meet the tributes and feed the people?"

"Show me the *quipu* that records the number of Hurin and Hanan noblemen, and the peasants living in the valley for the past ten years."

Curaca Checa scrambled to his feet, explaining he didn't remember all the details. He needed to summon the Quipucamayo to be sure of the specifics.

My father dismissed him, and we all stood to stretch while I considered my father's diplomacy. I watched him the previous day with Pusani when he simply listened to everyone else as we asked questions and the information was provided. This morning I watched my father with Checa as the conversation shifted from irrelevant to essential. The Inca never relinquished his dominance, in spite of Checa's best attempts to build a closer relationship. My father's skills merited my respect, but I still wondered how he intended to solve the problem. "What do you expect to find?" I asked, hoping for some insight.

"For the valley to flourish, we must maintain the balance between the Hurin noblemen, Hanan noblemen, and the peasants. We need to know if all groups are growing at the same rate and when the increase began." He declined to say more, so I talked with Pacas until Checa returned.

Somewhat flustered, he arrived with the Quipucamayo and immediately began the review. In addition to the total number of Hanan, Hurin, and peasants in the valley, the Quipucamayo also recorded the information for the residents by sex in each of the nine age groups: baby in arms, able to stand, less than six, six to eight years old, eight to sixteen years, maize pickers ages sixteen to twenty five, able bodied workers roughly twenty five to fifty, light workers for another ten years, and the elders. Because the crops were especially bountiful for five years in a row, there were a very large number of children under six years.

Huayna Capac smiled broadly but made no comment when he learned there was another large group between sixteen and twenty. The Quipucamayo added to my father's pleasure when he speculated the increase really extended between fifteen and twenty-one. The older age groups showed only minimal increases over the ten years. Much to Checa's surprise, the ratio of the peasants, Hanan and Hurin was very consistent. The total number of peasants increased more quickly than the others, and he thought this was a problem until Pacas took him aside and explained the concept of ratios. Satisfied that he had all the information he needed, Huayna Capac dismissed the Quipucamayo and invited Pusani and Checa to join us in the morning when he would tell them how to resolve the situation.

Checa looked confused and delighted at the same time. "Inca Huayna Capac, we will happily return. We're eager to hear your solution and learn how we can best serve you, the gods and the people of our valley."

"You are worthy and loyal subjects, and Inti has blessed your efforts with years of prosperity."

Pleased to have received such high praise from the Inca himself, they left just as the clouds delivered a drenching rain. Fortunately it only lasted a short while, stopping well before Checa and Pusani returned for dinner.

By the light of grass torches, the group laughed and enjoyed the meal. Pusani was content being quiet, but spoke when addressed. Checa prattled on about their valley but always ended by demonstrating his subservience to Huayna Capac. Now that the work was done, even Sinchi Roca smiled and spoke occasionally. Happily sated, everyone rested with the comfort of an excellent beer and good company. Under a starry sky, the Curacas left in good cheer.

The following morning we gathered once again. After friendly greetings everyone was seated except Huayna Capac who addressed the Curacas in his deliberate, commanding voice. "It is time to reveal the plan for the Cacha valley."

It was a curiosity for me, but implementing it was entirely their responsibility.

"The tributes to the state and the religion will remain the same for the next five years; twenty of every hundred baskets of maize will go to the state and twenty to the religion. Over the next five years you will require more storehouses, and Sinchi Roca will provide a plan for the number that you'll need to build each year. The young men will provide the labor for building the storehouses, and will be compensated from its stores. In addition, these men will go to Cusco for two months each year for military training." He paused, but no one dared to speak. "There will be no additional housing built for the Mamaconas or the priests, since the total number will be reduced to the number of five years ago. As need arises elsewhere, Cacha will be notified of the opportunities for priests and Mamaconas to move to other parts of the empire. When the former number is attained, a person will be added only on the death or departure of a member."

Pusani and Checa quietly listened to his plan without any indication of discomfort.

"The farmers will only build the additional terraces you have planned for this year and next. For the following three years they will serve double mita service through the dry season. By doing so, they will be fed and paid from the state storehouses. Your increasing population will easily manage the crops in their extended absence."

Again my father paused and peered down on the Curacas. They could have asked for clarification, but Checa had already felt the sting of questioning his decisions.

"Finally, your prosperity is a gift from Inti and his maker Viracocha. Your abundance clearly shows that the gods are pleased with your dedication. Inti has told me that you must now demonstrate your gratitude for his blessings. During each of the next five Capac Raymi celebrations, the residents of Cacha will show their thanks by sacrificing one hundred children to Inti."

Checa gasped, but he said nothing.

"The children will be chosen by both of you, and will fairly represent the Hurin, the Hanan, and the peasants. In five years we will review the situation. We'll likely have additional lands to develop, and the loyal people of Cacha will be the first to be given the opportunity to move to new lands. My son and Pacas will remain in Cacha to work through the details. Are there any questions?"

Pusani was predictably silent, and Checa was speechless. The group dispersed without objections, or even comments. Their quiet, peaceful valley was suddenly to see continual and unsettling change. Even I was stunned. It was clear the valley could no longer support an increasing number of people, but I expected that the tributes to be reduced. I had not expected my father's solutions. Reducing the demands for food by killing children and disguising the act as sacrifices of thanksgiving? That seemed like a cruel "reward" for honorable allies. Building more storage for even larger stockpiles when there was already several years' supply? Preparing young men to be soldiers? He never said it, but I suspected my father was preparing for war.

Pacas and I remained with Checa and Pusani to work through the details of the plan. First we located where the ten new storehouses would be built, and estimated how long it would take the designated men to build them. We did the same for the terraces and calculated how many men would remain to work the fields with the women when the mita service was doubled. Together we all confirmed that if there was no drought, my father's plan would cause no hardship. If the harvests were poor, food might be scarce, but then they would receive food from the storehouses.

The most controversial aspect of the Inca's proclamation was the annual sacrifice. We didn't choose the specific children. All we decided was how many would be Hanan, Hurin, and peasants. Even so, it was difficult to agree on the division. They already mourned their loss, even though some would live another five years.

Going back to Cusco, Pacas and I traveled as the senior adults for the first time. We had complete freedom and no responsibilities, and yet, Pacas and I spoke continually about the details of our visit to Cacha. My father had asked very few questions and received no more information than we did, but with it, he announced a radical new plan that would eliminate the problems in the valley. Although I thought his plan was harsh, every aspect of it helped to maintain the balance between the available resources and the number of people, as well as the balance between the needs of the community and the needs of the religion and state. In spite of the substantial changes, nothing undermined the fundamental structure. Still, Riku's questions from years earlier haunted me. "What have you learned from these events? Will you rule differently than your father?" I knew I would, but how? What was better?

Acceptance

Kaya

With Riku's explanation, my child's world vanished as quickly as raindrops landing on a hot stone. The sounds of my beating heart and shallow breath suddenly disappeared into the void of a starless night. No images of Riku or my garden penetrated my timeless despair. None of Tawan's songs rose from my memory. Nothing touched my lifeless existence: no fear, no anger, no self-pity, and no hope. Nothing. Locked in my own nightmare, the ember of my fate slowly burned through my chest before it flared into icy streaks that encircled my throbbing head and flashed like lightning behind my eyelids. Even the physical pain was better than the undying emptiness. The burden of my sacrifice would kill me before the act. In this absolute isolation, I was blind to my own hand reaching out.

"Pule! Where have you been? I need your help." I found myself standing in my garden, my hands feeding wool to the half-filled spindle that spun near my feet.

She sat on her favorite fence post calmly cracking the shell of an enormous nut. It popped open in her powerful beak, and she ate it before responding. "Hello, Kaya," she said casually as she looked around. "You have such a beautiful garden and the mountains are magical. I almost forgot how much I like it here. What a lucky girl you are!" She eyed the second nut in her gray claw and decided to eat it as well. "Could I have some water? These are always better with a drink." Pule was the only one who could help me, so I quickly brought some from the shelter. When I came back, she was still turning the fist-sized nut in her mouth. A few rolls later, her beak crushed the shell sending fragments in every direction. She carefully eliminated the remaining bits of shell and swallowed the nut. After fluttering to the ground to drink, she returned to the fence post to preen her wings.

Without thinking, my hands continued to spin the wool to yarn, while she dropped bits of leaves, a few bugs and a beautiful long feather to the ground. Pule had finally come, but now that she was here, she wasn't interested in helping me. Why did she come, to eat nuts and torment me? I couldn't wait any longer. "Pule, I need to tell you about Riku."

She kept picking at her feathers. Without interrupting her cleaning, she finally answered, "Well? What about him?"

I wasn't even sure she was listening, but the horrific truth poured out of me. I told her about the prophecy of Viracocha's return and his judgment on the Incas. I stopped to give her a chance to comment, but all she did was switch to the other wing without uttering a word. She showed no surprise when I explained that I was the Inca's daughter, or that I was to be murdered to become part of the spirit bridge. Finally, bursting into tears, I told her how empty I was.

She carefully completed her primping and repeatedly tipped her head sideways to stretch her neck. "So, why are you telling me this? I already told you half of it and would have finished the story if you'd let me."

I thought Pule was my friend, but she wasn't very sympathetic. She didn't even seem to care that I was going to die. How could this magnificent and yet mysterious bird have known what Riku would tell me? Then I remembered Riku's description of priests. "Are you a diviner too?"

"No, I'm just a bird, and you're a spoiled child. Do you have any idea what a bother you've been? For the past six months Riku has walked you to the sacred plaza everyday where he fed you a bowl of soup. He was the only one who could get you to eat at all. With Atuk and Tumbes, he placed you in the sun, and prayed to Inti to help you find your way back. Have you thanked him for helping you get well?"

She fluttered to the next fence post. Her words felt like thorns jabbing me. I looked around and discovered it was early spring; the last thing I remembered was listening to Riku in the Inca's courtyard in late summer.

"You've wasted six months. You're way behind in your training. Now Riku will need to accelerate his lessons. He's not a young man, you know. Getting you ready in time will not be easy. And what about Iska and the others?" Her words drifted away.

This wasn't why I wanted Pule to visit. This wasn't right at all. Why was she scolding me? I was the one to be sacrificed! "Pule, did you hear me? They're going to kill me! I want you to protect me. Tell Riku how evil this is. Make him change his mind."

She discarded another feather with an exasperated sigh. With her head cocked to the side, she said, "Riku described the prophecy very well, and still you don't understand. You're younger than your years." She tilted her head the other way and shifted her weight to one foot. "I guess I'll have to show you how greatly honored you are. Maybe then you'll accept the inevitable."

"Why won't you listen to me?" I threw down the spindle and defiantly crossed my arms. "You're the one who doesn't understand. I don't want to die. I don't want this great honor."

Her raucous caw sounded more like laughing than a normal bird call. It took awhile for her to settle back into words. "Will you come with me? I want to show you some special places. Perhaps you'll understand if you see for yourself."

Flying with Pule was wonderful, but I wasn't sure I trusted her this time. Still, if I stayed, I was going to die. What could be worse? "Yes, I'll go."

She bobbed her head forward. "Do you remember how to fly?"

Wondering how I could possibly forget something so liberating, I nodded and asked, "Where are we going?"

"Follow me."

She spread her great wings, flapped twice and was airborne. I spread my arms, turned into the breeze as she had taught me and lifted into the sky. We spiraled up into the clouds hanging over the mountain peaks. "Stay close to me. It's hard to see in the clouds."

I did as she asked, following slightly behind and below her. She flew to the left and then slid back to the right as we continued to climb into the darkening cloud. Finally she leveled out and flew straight along a ladder of light. Outlined by two white streaks and crossed with short rungs of yellow, red, green, and blue, the path stretched before us. Pule followed the ladder as it twisted and curved, exactly like a road. "Kaya, stay on the path. I'll follow behind you." She circled up and fell in behind me. I was content to lead, but looked back occasionally to be sure she was still there.

Even as we passed out of the clouds into the bright noonday sun, the light path steadfastly led the way. Finally beyond my grief and everything familiar to me, I relished the wind blowing in my face and across my bare arms. Unlike walking the stairs at Machu Picchu, flying was effortless, and I could happily drift forever. I stayed with the trail as it dropped back to the ground and ended beside a small stream meandering through a narrow valley. Beside the water, pink daisies and grass gradually faded into yellow sand painted exactly the same color as the canyon walls towering above us. Just downstream the water fell over a cliff and crossed a desolate plain. In the distance and far below us, a huge blue lake disappeared into the haze.

"Where is this place?" I asked as Pule perched on a rock beside me.

"This is the great western ocean in a time before Viracocha Inca. Do you see the city on the plain below us?"

I nodded and studied the unusual buildings, especially the enormous rectangular platform with the sunken courtyard in the center. "You can imagine it took thousands of people to construct such magnificent buildings. They had a flourishing community here with new temples always being planned and hundreds of fields of cotton and beans growing in terraces along the river. Unfortunately they displeased the gods. This life-giving river is now only a thin trickle. We can go down to the fields without being seen, but you must stay beside me."

I nodded and Pule flew off. We landed halfway to the ocean on a terrace wall overlooking a farmer tending a pathetic crop of beans. The yellow soil imparted its color to the wilting stems and sparse leaves of the sickly plants. The farmer shuffled unsteadily through the rows, trying to extend a thin stream across the entire field. As the water seeped into the soil, he carefully lifted the dampened earth and placed it at the base of a plant. With painstaking care, he worked his way down the entire row, while the scorched air stole the precious liquid almost as quickly as he could move the soil. "Why doesn't he open the weir and bring more water onto the terrace?" I asked.

"There is no more water. You saw how small the stream was in the mountains. He diverted this water from much farther upstream and directed it across the sandy soil to his terrace. He has worked very hard to get this much water. You can see the other terraces around us are even drier." Pule watched him work.

No one worked the surrounding terraces, where dusty stubble stood defiantly in the relentless sun. At least his plants had leaves. Still his efforts were wasted, and I said so. "He can't possibly grow the beans. There isn't enough water. Why does he even try?"

Pule looked around without answering. "That looks like his house over there. Let's go find his family."

We flew the short distance and landed on his shack. The stench of rotting flesh seized my throat as I coughed and relieved my stomach. There were no trees or animals, but two emaciated children slept in the shade of the house. The older boy was about my age and his distended belly stretched over his thong. Skin hung from his arms and legs, barely covering his protruding bones. Flies infested his hair and walked through his nose as he slept. The other boy, a few years younger, looked much the same, except he lay in a writhing bed of ants. "Oh Pule, he's dead and they haven't even buried him."

"No one has the strength. Their mother died a week ago. She still lies inside."

"Why don't the leaders help them? There must be food and water somewhere." I knew I couldn't help them, but there must be someone who could.

"Let's go down to the city and see the leaders." We flew again and landed at the edge of the sunken platform. Saturated with death, the acrid sky hung over the platform like an invisible shroud. The entire courtyard reeked with half-burned trees and charred body parts. With piercing indifference the condors and buzzards squabbled over the choicest pieces. My watery eyes stung, and my stomach heaved with no relief as we overlooked the open graveyard. To imagine this place as a thriving city, while a condor rose from the pyre with a child's leg in its claws accentuated the hideous contradiction. I gawked in silence, unable to move or look away.

Pule perched on my shoulder, "Several months ago the leaders divided the town into two groups. Half the men, women, and children left with half the remaining food and water to try to get help from a nearby city. They walked for days across the desert headed for the next river valley to the north. Many died on the trip, but those that survived found the city in worse condition than the one they left."

I sobbed as Pule spoke.

"Those that stayed fared no better. With no help returning, they gradually succumbed to starvation and sickness. They tried to cremate their dead to reduce the spread of disease, but over the years they had cut most of the trees lining the river. At the end, there was no water, no food, no wood and no one to perform the rites of passage." With no hint of compassion she lifted her beak to point to the city. "This was once a thriving community. Unwittingly, the people destroyed the land, and their gods punished them by taking the water." Pule surveyed the village. "What a waste. The insects will clean the place. Let's go." She dropped off my shoulder and was airborne before she reached my feet.

Still feeling sick, I was ready to leave and try to forget I'd ever seen this place. I lifted off the ground and followed Pule away from the sorrow. No matter where she led me, it couldn't be as awful as this. I wanted to feel the jubilant freedom of flying, but the devastating memories haunted me. Pule flew along the lighted path, and I floundered behind her feeling guilty for the joy of flying and having abandoned a disaster, even though I was powerless to help.

I followed Pule as we fled the lifeless desert, and sighed in relief as the coastline below turned greener with every wing beat. Grasslands gave way to bushes that led to continual forest broken only by the broad rivers flowing to the sea. As a squawking flock of green parrots burst from the trees, we finally landed on a sprawling frond of a palm tree overlooking a bend in a river. Opposite and below us, the river curled around a small village spread along an uplifted bank. Light-colored children with straight black hair squealed with delight as they dashed between the wooden poles supporting the houses. They laughed as the smallest was finally allowed to catch her older brother. Nearby, several women chatted as they prepared the evening meal. Two young maidens cut fruit while others loaded crabs into a steaming pot hung above the fire. Their round faces and small noses perfectly suited their healthy petite bodies. Sitting in the shade, two wrinkled women wove reed mats, and an old man contentedly whittled a monkey from a nut. In a clearing behind them, a small group of men planted a root crop I didn't recognize. "Pule, who are these people? They're not Inca."

"No, they've never even heard of an Inca. They enjoy an isolated life among the mangroves. Their village is high enough to withstand the flooding rains in the wet season, but still close to the seas where the fish and crab are plentiful. The jungle provides almost everything they need, but they supplement their stores by growing manioc. They are especially fortunate to have a spring. Do you see it? There are two girls filling jugs at the end of the field."

Ten dugout canoes, two in the lead and the rest scattered behind them, lazily worked their way upstream along the riverbank. A lilting tune drifted up to us as three men in each canoe paddled to its rhythm. After the two lead canoes disappeared into the mangrove, only their muffled voices marked their approach. In no time they tramped into the village loaded with fish and bundles of reeds. I was about to ask where we were when Pule started without prompting. "This is the mouth of the northwest river where Viracocha traveled out to sea when he left this world. When he returns, he will cross from the Upper World to the sea and arrive on this river. Even though these people have never heard of the Incas or Viracocha, they will soon be your enemies."

"But why? They seem like good, happy people."

"The same could be said of any enemy. Always the majority of the people are worthy and decent." Pule looked upstream and added, "You've only seen one aspect of these people." Some canoes drifted downstream staying very close to the opposite shore. Weaving through the shadows, it took a while to realize there were actually six canoes, each carrying four men. Getting closer to the village, the two men in the center crouched down and covered themselves with reed mats. Without a sound the paddlers wove into the mangrove and disappeared.

The village women set to work cleaning the newly arrived fish while the men examined the bundles of green thatching reeds. One pointed to the brown thatched roof of the closest reed house while the other pointed to the equally needy roof of the house beside it. The men argued with increasing acrimony until the village elder rose to join them. He was a bent man who walked only with the support of a child's shoulder. The two men immediately stopped bickering and bowed their heads, acknowledging the elder's approach. He turned to the first man and listened quietly to his story before hearing the opposition's argument. He nodded at them both and pointed at the closest house indicating it would be repaired first and the other would follow. Both accepted his decision and helped him back to his shady seat before they headed toward the half-loaded canoes.

Silently and without warning, the men from upstream burst out of the jungle into the village clearing. Each carried a burning torch in one hand and spears in the other. They raced to their targets and hurled torches onto the dry, thatched roofs. All twenty houses were immediately covered with flames. The villagers scrambled to reach their weapons. A woman grabbed the conch shell and sounded the alarm. Three loud blasts wailed through the trees before a club cracked her skull and the shell in a single blow. Still, it was enough. Downstream, the canoes double-timed their strokes and threw their cargo into the river to lighten the load.

In the village, the invaders clubbed the elder and squabbling builders first. Digging tools in hand, the men from the field dashed to the rescue only to meet their enemies' spears. Shrieks of agony and terrified children mixed with the cloud of choking smoke. Instinctively, older children grabbed the hands of younger siblings and ran into the mangrove. Armed with burning sticks and stone knives, the village women courageously joined the defense, stabbing a few attackers in the back as they faced the men in the fields. Others turned to the women only to be skewered with a burning stick in the stomach.

Not part of the initial assault, four old men had hidden in the jungle. Now they methodically moved through the village killing the feeble whittler and his protective wife. The children too scared or small to run were quickly silenced with a spear through the heart. Anyone who could ever be a threat was killed.

Finally the canoes landed and the men charged with savage revenge. Fearless, they cut off the invaders from the remaining women and children. The last two canoes paddled past the village and blocked any attempted retreat. With no hope of escape, the attackers coalesced to a single purpose; kill as many men as possible. Working in threesomes and dodging the falling embers, the primary attacker charged the selected opponent. The second delivered the killing blow and the third protected his partners. In response, the villagers used their familiarity with the battleground. Trees were large and in places easily climbed. From this height, village men threw spears targeting the enemy and jumped down into critical battles. It was enough of an advantage to quickly defeat the remaining invaders. With the last of the attackers finally dead, the villagers clung to the living and wailed their losses. Together they picked their way through the smoldering ruins and the children gradually returned.

Angry, I begged for an explanation, "Pule, why did those men attack?"

"They wanted the land because of its ideal location. The leaders of these two groups are brothers. Their father said they should both live here in peace, but after his death, one son decided to leave, taking his family and any who chose to follow. They live upstream in a less convenient site. Their leader wanted this village, which he considered to be rightfully his." Pule shifted to another branch and plucked a palm nut with her claw. She split the hard shell, swallowed the nut and reached for another in a single movement.

I tried to understand the useless destruction as the villagers tied all their enemies' bodies across a canoe and set the corpses adrift among the waiting crocodiles. "But why should the Inca care which brother lives here?" The branch I was on was hard, and I turned so I didn't have to look at the burning village, but the inconsolable grieving still rose with the billowing smoke.

"He doesn't care, but Viracocha must have a safe passage when he returns. You've seen how they treat their neighbors. They're even less tolerant of unarmed strangers. Viracocha will return as a man who could be killed. The Inca must bring this area into the empire or be judged an unworthy ruler. It will be a hard fought battle. These people have no desire to be part of a foreign empire, and the Incas aren't adept at fighting in a mangrove swamp. There are hundreds of ways to kill a man in the jungle."

Dread of the confrontation raised bumps on my arms, and a shiver passed down my spine, in spite of the sweltering heat. "But Pule, why have you shown this to me? I can't fight these battles. You tell me I'll be dead anyway."

"We have one more stop in the Urubamba Valley. Are you ready to go?" She continued to consume the nuts.

Directly below us, the men collected all of their own dead and lined them up along the riverbank. Knowing that they were equally responsible for their plight and would soon be the enemy of my people, I was no longer sympathetic to their loss. The battle that transformed those beautiful creatures into bloody, torn masses seemed completely avoidable and absolutely pointless. "There is nothing else I want to see here."

Pule dropped the empty shell and flew off. I followed her at just the right distance to watch her powerful, graceful flight. Mesmerized by the rhythm and whispered song of her wingbeats, the gruesome images of famine and war flashed before me. I was barely aware of our flight as we swept back over the mountains and down to the Urubamba River Valley. The plentiful maize stood in the fields ready for harvest. In other fields, the yellow squash swelled to maturity, and flaming red peppers hung on verdant plants. Pule finally landed on the roof of a farmer's home as he and his wife returned from the fields carrying massive loads of potatoes. Their five children, ranging from a son almost reaching adult height to a stumbling toddler, followed behind them carrying something; even the youngest dragged a cloth sack. Pule gave a sigh of relief, as did I, and asked, "What do you see?"

"I see two parents and their five children returning from the fields."

"What can you tell about them?"

"They worked hard today, and the loads they carry are heavy. I feel sorry for them."

"Why?"

"At Machu Picchu I've seen how the farmers work. Day after day, year after year, they toil endlessly to grow their crops." I shook my head in sympathy.

"Are these people healthy?"

I studied each of them more carefully. The father dropped his load beside the adobe wall of their house. In his prime, his muscular arms and legs extended beyond his tunic as he stood to stretch. His pregnant wife rummaged the fire pit for a hot ember and easily coaxed the wood to flame. Already unloaded, the oldest boy and girl headed out with jars for water while the younger ones played in the sandy soil. "Yes, they're healthy, so they must have plenty of food. Their clothes and shoes are dirty, but they are in good repair."

"So why do you pity them? They are satisfied with their lives. The couple has a large happy family that will never want for food, clothing, or a place to live. They tend their land and crops with a love that fulfills their lives and satisfies their needs. Pachamama and Inti nurture them with the same compassion they find for each other and the land. Where do you find them lacking?"

"They work so hard just to stay alive."

Pule squawked and shook her wings. "To be able to work is a gift. Ask the starving man if he would be willing to accept the strength to work his fields and provide for a healthy family. Ask the women who died in battle whether they would prefer to prepare the meals for their children. What could be better than work that provides for your family, gives purpose to your life and pleases the gods?"

I couldn't find anything to dispute, but there just had to be more to living than endless work. On their returned, the two oldest children practiced a dance step as the full jars splashed water on them. Their mother nodded her appreciation as she dreamily stirred the dinner pot. "Perhaps they are satisfied with their life, but I can't live that way."

"I know. No one asked you to live like this. Everyone's work is different. Here you see a farmer. Kinsa is a weaver, and Tawan mixes dyes when she isn't with you. Riku is a priest, and I am a teacher."

"But what am I?"

Pule just stared at me. She wasn't scolding me, but she hopped from one foot to the other. "Kaya, it's time to go, but on our way back to Machu Picchu we'll go past Cusco. Perhaps you'll find your work there."

Without another word she took off heading upstream through the fertile valley past magnificent palaces and then across a narrow mountain range. In the distance Cusco shimmered in the afternoon heat and reflected sunlight. We swooped down over the main plaza, and Pule showed me where my mother and father lived. It was very nice palace, but a fantastically beautiful building stood short distance away.

"Can we please rest there for a while?" I pointed to the building, and we soon alighted on the roof overlooking a central courtyard surrounded by rooms lined with gold. Men hurried across the courtyard wearing the beautiful *cumbi* tunics that Kinsa made. Everywhere I turned I saw another marvel; flowers as brilliant as a rainbow, water fountains made of gold, and superbly cut stone doorways leading to rooms lined with silver statues as tall as me. With so much glittering splendor, I almost overlooked the most astonishing item. Hanging on the wall was a likeness of the sun. The center was a disk of gold engraved with a benevolent face and outlined with emeralds. Emanating out from the center were rays of gold, each inset with gems in colors I'd never seen. "What is this place?"

"This is the Coricancha, the most important temple in the empire. The likeness of Inti you were admiring marks the center, the navel, of the entire world. The Temple of Ilyapa is over there, and the Temple of Killa lies across the courtyard. The other gods have their temples as well." Everywhere I looked I found something more beautiful than anything I could imagine. Wide-eyed, I stared at my surroundings as Pule continued, "Now do you see how important a single person's work can be? If there were no farmers who could provide food for many, no one would be able to cut or move the stone to build this temple. No one could mine the gold or create these beautiful works of art. There could be no priests or Mamaconas, and the gods could not be honored or thanked for their many blessings. No one person could possibly learn to do all these things. Millions of people working together created this. You must learn that everyone's work is equally important, and difficult. The leaders, including the Inca, oversee all of this and have obligations no less trying than the farmer plowing his field or building a new terrace."

I sat next to her and tried to accept my work. "Riku told me the Inca must honor his obligations to the people. He must beg Inti for continuing grace by sacrificing his daughter. Me." My heart sank with the inevitable.

"Yes. Your promised death and completion of the bridge for Viracocha is the only hope of reversing the prophecy. Without it, famine, disease, and war will completely destroy the empire. There will be no hope for these people. Pleas for forgiveness will go unheard."

The significance of my sacrifice was finally becoming clear, and a faint drop of pride splashed into the pool of dread. "Your work is much more than dying. Riku will teach you to talk with the spirits of the gods. You are a gifted student, but you lack the will to learn. You must learn the way of the spirits before you return to the Upper World, so you can still speak with Riku, Atuk, and many others after you die. With the grace of Inti, you will be able to guide them and give them knowledge beyond this world. You will have the privilege and responsibility to stand between Inti and the Inca. You will help the Inca understand Inti's will."

Riku told me this in the Inca's courtyard, but the revelation of my certain death was all I heard. Finally I realized the importance of my death and just how many people depended on me. Like the waves of a pebble dropped in a pool, the pride mixed with a sense of responsibility and honor filled my heart with purpose, even though I still feared dying. I closed my eyes to savor Pule's teachings. When I opened them and turned to thank her, I saw my garden sparkling in the morning dew instead of Pule. Disappointed she had left without good-byes, I turned toward a familiar rattling to see Riku climbing down the ladder.

"Hello, Riku. I'm sorry I've troubled you so. You've given me such loving care. I don't know how to thank you."

Riku stopped and stared at me. Beneath his eyes, his cheeks sagged more than I remembered, but a smile gradually replaced his furrowed brow. "Welcome back." He took my hand as though the past six months never happened.

I felt his love surround me, and I asked, "When do we start lessons again?"

He straightened his back as though he just set down a heavy bundle, took a deep breath and replied, "Soon, very soon."

Reunion

Ninan

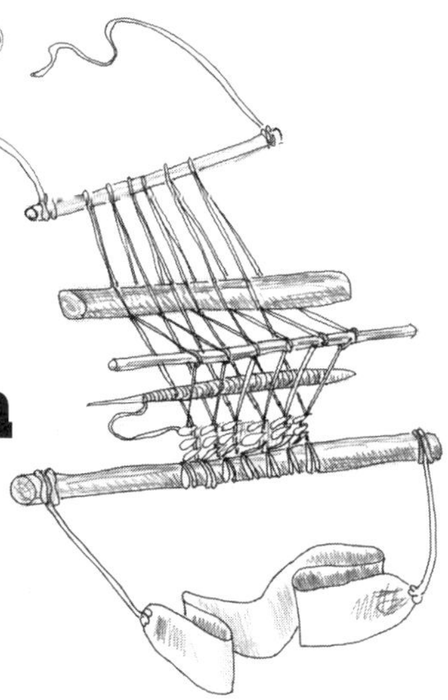

Standing at the mountain pass of Machu Picchu's city gate, the sparkling granite buildings in the distance rested like jewels on the lush forest. The elegant brilliance of the city that lay before us lacked the pretense of Cusco, but its natural grace radiated an eternal calm. "It's beautiful, much nicer than my father described," Pacas gushed. "The city looks like an embroidered blanket on a giant llama standing in a river. Can you see it? Behind us the mountain Machu Picchu rises like the llama's rump and the pinnacle, Huayna Picchu, on the other side of the city stretches upward like his neck. In the lower, narrower strip between them, the city lies across his back like a precious cargo. We can only see the river canyon from here, but we know the river parallels the city on our right, curls around Huayna Picchu and then continues through the mountains on our left. Isn't that like the llama and river in the sky?"

"I think so, but you'll have to ask Riku," I answered, more interested in my father. Having dismounted from his litter, Huayna Capac instructed the guards at the gate to take care of the servants and llamas. Looking tired, excited and worried all at the same time, my mother waited without dismounting.

"Do you remember your sister?" Pacas asked.

"Only vaguely. How well do you remember any baby? I remember my father and mother fighting. She was very angry about losing my sister. They haven't spoken of her since, at least not that I've heard." The afternoon sun warmed my back, a welcome change from the exceptionally cold winter in Cusco.

With instructions complete and my father remounted, we wound down the mountainside toward the city. At the edge of the first terraces, the Inca disembarked and greeted the cheering crowd. Progress slowed as the people clamored to see the Inca and his queen. Huayna Capac always thrived on the attention, but my mother remained in her litter, above the dust and smells of the masses. Generating little interest, Pacas and I followed on foot. We exchanged smiles with the curious bystanders until we reached the main plaza where Riku met us. When Riku announced the evening feast from the steps leading to the Inca's residence, the crowd cheered and finally dispersed.

After the crowd noise diminished, Riku formally greeted us while Atuk and another priest stood silently behind him. "Huayna Capac and Coya Cusirimay, welcome to Machu Picchu. It is a pleasure to at last return the gracious hospitality you have always extended to me during my visits to Quispiguanca and Cusco."

Huayna Capac placed his hand on Riku's shoulder and patted him like an old friend. My mother answered as she stepped from her litter, "While it is a blessing to leave the mountain winter, I would never forego the opportunity to see my daughter."

Riku acknowledged her formally, with respect but no warmth. Coya Cusirimay, whose name meant the queen who speaks of happiness, never seemed to find any. Her distant, defensive ways didn't allow many, if any, to approach her.

"Accompany me to my house. I would like to rest," my mother ordered Riku who dutifully led my mother to her house just behind the Inca's residence. Huayna Capac continued toward his home with a string of servants trailing him.

The formal introductions complete, I turned my attention to my peers. "Atuk, it's good to see you again. Machu Picchu suits you." It had been five years since he accompanied Riku to Quispiguanca, but I easily recognized him.

"And you certainly have grown," his now manly voice responded. "This is Tumbes, my friend and Riku's other assistant."

Boasting an easy smile, Tumbes eagerly interjected, "Ninan, nice to meet you. And you must be Pacas, the numbers wizard."

Pacas responded immediately, "I'm pleased to meet the comic. I hope to enjoy your humor, even if it comes at my own expense."

Tumbes was surprised his reputation had reached us and equally delighted to have a new, appreciative audience. The bantering continued as Atuk and Tumbes led us to their house next to the Torreon Temple where we enjoyed *chicha* and snacks as we rested. The afternoon passed quickly while we exchanged tales of travel and compared a young man's life in Cusco and Machu Picchu. Eventually the conversation returned to the purpose of our visit.

"After more than a year, Kaya is finally healthy again," Atuk offered. "Her fever was so high, Riku thought she might die. When she finally started to recover, she fell under a spell. She looked all right, but you'd get a better response from a stone wall."

With that, Tumbes jumped to his feet and spoke to the wall. "I hear you've fallen on hard times. What's that? Your girlfriend is very cold and won't talk to you? She thinks you should split apart? Maybe you should move away. We saw some lovely young walls just standing around near Quispiguanca. There's no reason to fall apart over this one. There are plenty more stones in these mountains." He leaned on the wall with one hand and used the other to accent his words while we laughed.

As we left to go to the feast, I asked Atuk, "Is Kaya a good student?"

He turned to me and answered with an unassuming honesty second only to what I always received from Pacas, "She is an excellent student. I have studied five years longer than she has and have difficulty keeping up. Riku is right. We need her to stay with us as long as possible. There is no way to underestimate the potential benefits. She's old enough to be a woman, but because of the illness she looks younger. No one would question a decision to postpone, and I see no reason to perform the sacrifice any earlier than is absolutely necessary." My thoughts were a mixed pleasure of developing another trusted friend and hearing of her talent. Meeting my sister in the morning promised to be interesting.

By midmorning the following day we were assembled in the garden beside my father's house. It was rather plain, but the bougainvillea added a delightful charm. The Inca sat on a bench near the center, while my mother paced from one end to the other, anxiously glancing toward the entryway. I leaned against the staircase leading into the house, with Pacas hidden above me. Officially, he wasn't supposed to be there, but my father recanted, providing he stayed out of sight. The sounds of a busy city drifted over the walls. In the distance someone pounded a rock, shaping it for a mortarless stone wall while children laughed and women chattered as they descended the stairs toward the plaza.

My mother halted as footsteps approached through the entryway. Atuk appeared first and saw the three of us spread across the garden. Tumbes followed, looking somber and ill at ease. Finally Riku and Kaya stepped into the opening together. Her head lowered in respect, they both floated toward my father as mother and I joined Huayna Capac standing opposite the new arrivals. Kaya was very thin, presumably from her illness, but her waist-long black hair sparkled in the sunlight. Her frailty overlaying her prestigious heritage created a curious manner.

"I am very pleased to present your daughter to you," Riku began. "She is recovering from her illness and has begun her studies again. She is an accomplished weaver and can sing more than one hundred songs, or accompany another musician on the flute. Most important, she is a gifted traveler and reports vivid detail of her visions." He paused, expecting my father to speak, but the Inca only stared at her, so Riku continued. "Kaya, this is your father, Huayna Capac and your birth mother Coya Cusirimay. Your only full brother, Ninan Cuyohi, the man who moves fire, stands with your parents." A parrot squawked as it flew over head, interrupting the awkward silence.

Kaya stood with her hands at her side. Her large blue dress hung on her, obscuring her shape from neck to ankles. Everyone, including Riku watched Kaya, waiting for a response. Finally she lifted her head. Staring at Huayna Capac, she seemed to memorize every part of him as she studied him from his feet to his head, returning her eyes to hold his stare. My father allowed a gasp to escape as a look of surprise and possibly fear crept over his face. She turned her attention to our mother and repeated the foot to head perusal before locking on her eyes.

Tears streamed down my mother's face as she spun without uttering a word and fled to the Inca's house.

Next Kaya turned her gaze to me. Her eyes felt like the softest *cumbi* slowly floating across every part of my body until she reached my face. I held her gaze and watched her shoulders drop as the tension melted away. Her narrow nose and thin lips were lovingly set in the smooth skin of her oval face, but the depth of her eyes accentuated by long, dark lashes and high cheekbones was impossible to ignore. She filled me with a warmth I'd never known.

"Huayna Capac, did you have any questions for Kaya?" Riku's voice pulled me, and even more slowly, my father back to the business at hand.

He stammered and then asked, "Kaya, are you well?" He had already heard a health report, but at least it initiated a conversation.

"Even though it has been several months, I'm still weak and tire easily on the stairs of Machu Picchu, but the illness is gone. Riku saved my life, and I'm certain I would be dead without his excellent care." She spoke with a melodious sincerity and a genuine respect for her teacher.

"Tell me about your studies with Riku." He choked trying to maintain his official Inca voice. He didn't want to look at her and frequently lifted his eyes to look at the wall behind her.

"Riku is an excellent teacher. Atuk, Tumbes, and I are learning the ways of the spirits," she replied with a voice that didn't know how to lie. She turned her head to glance at Riku who nodded his encouragement. "We're learning to travel together to places beyond Machu Picchu. We go to the times of Pachacuti, and Riku promised we'll travel forward next," she calmly answered, as though everyone knew how to do these things.

"Have you spoken with any spirits in the Upper World?" He asked, hardly aware that she had answered his last question.

"Not yet, but Riku tells us that it is possible. Since it was easy to learn to fly and find the various roads, I'm sure we will soon. It will take practice, but Riku will show us how to reach various spirits. So far, we still need his help."

Riku stared at her, his eyebrows furrowed. Kaya caught his expression and knew she had said too much.

Trapped by the lust I'd seen so many times, my father stuttered as he tried to speak. Riku saw it too and turned to me. "Ninan, do you have any questions for Kaya?"

Forced to speak, I blankly asked, "Can you tell me about Riku's other students? Are you able to work with them as you do with Riku?"

"It's easier to contact Riku. He's able to find me no matter how I ask for him." She spoke easily with the same fluency as music. "With Atuk and Tumbes, we still need to know in advance that the other will send information. In time, both sending and receiving will get easier."

Huayna Capac finally rejoined the conversation. "Do you understand your future?"

"I will be sacrificed at the first winter solstice celebration after I become a woman. With more training, I will be the conduit between the worlds. My task will be easier than those I leave behind for others." She looked at me as she spoke.

A chill with the bite of winter ran across the back of my neck, but I shook it off. Before we left Cusco, my father told Sinchi Roca he wanted the sacrifice to take place at the next winter solstice, whether she had become a woman or not. Now I asked my father, "What's your hurry? Who knows what could be gained with an extra year."

Riku gave me an appreciative glance.

Huayna Capac considered the options before speaking. "We'll wait a year. Next winter, we will review your progress again. Riku, Kaya, make the most of the extra time. You are excused."

Riku nudged Kaya, who seemed surprised by the rapid decision. The four turned to leave, and I watched her disappear through the entryway. My father paced with his head down and hand supporting his elbow as he drummed his chin with his fingers. Pacas joined me, and we discreetly followed the foursome out of the courtyard. Back on the staircase, we turned away from them and descended to the main plaza. Avoiding the small cluster of women exchanging the daily news, we continued to the now vacant llama pastures immediately below Intihuatana.

"Pacas, you must help me. I need to talk with Kaya alone."

He spun toward me. "Are you crazy? She is one of the Mamacona. You can't talk with her. It's impossible. Being caught alone with her is certain death."

He was right, but that didn't alter my resolution to see her. We walked around the pasture to the steep cliff behind the sacred plaza towering above us. "I helped you when you wanted to see Tinkha, and I convinced father to save her for you. In a year or two she'll be your wife. Help me. All I want to do is talk with my sister."

He stared out over the river valley. I knew he'd agree, but he must decide without coercion. We continued along the harvested terraces following the arch of the cliff. After a long silence and completely exasperated, Pacas replied, "I don't see how it's possible. Do you even know where she lives or spends her days?"

"Except when Riku escorts her to the sacred plaza for lessons, by day she is alone on a terrace above the priests' houses where we visited with Atuk and Tumbes."

He squinted at me, waiting for an explanation.

"Atuk told me yesterday during the banquet."

"Show me where she is."

I knew he'd decided to help me, but I concealed my delight. We walked along the terraces beyond the temples and then climbed the narrow stairs to top of the ridge and followed the path to the main staircase separating the agricultural terraces from the urban sector. The pleasant melody of falling water, laughing children and gossiping women echoed off the stone walls lining the stairs. Halfway down, we left the stairs again, heading away from the city across the terraces to find the best view of Kaya's garden. Turning to face the urban sector, I guided his search. "Do you see the Torreon?"

Its perfectly round walls were easily identified, and Pacas nodded immediately.

"You can see Atuk's house on the terrace just above it and the others beside it. Now follow that terrace until it abuts the staircase we just descended."

He had no trouble following my directions and replied, "The terrace ends with a stone wall dropping vertically to the stairs."

"That's right. Now follow that wall up the stairs past the next terrace with the field of coca. Just above it, do you see the lush garden with the guava tree at the end? Kaya spends her days there and lives in the house on the terrace above that one."

"How can we possibly get there without being seen?" Pacas stared incredulously at the garden. "At night we could climb a rope from the coca field, but during the day when she's in the garden, surely someone would see us. The only other way is to enter from the Mamaconas houses above it. That's suicide."

He was right of course. Her perch was unapproachable during the day. We stood studying the problem, unable to find a viable solution until Pacas asked, "Why not just ask Riku if you can see her? He's responsible for her care. You're her brother, and you only just met her. Maybe he would let you visit. I could keep him occupied while you talked with her."

I liked his plan but wasn't at all sure Riku would allow it if he knew my real intent. I wondered if I should even tell Pacas but decided it was only fair that he should know. "Pacas, I must tell you. I don't feel the same affection for Kaya as I do for my other sisters."

"That's only natural," he replied. "You've only just met Kaya. You watched your other sisters grow up."

He didn't understand. Staring straight at the garden terrace, I tried again. "I think I love her as you love Tinkha. I want her as my queen. She is my only full sister, so rightfully, she belongs at my side."

"Have you lost your senses? You can't have her. You know her role. This is impossible. I don't think you should visit her. There are many pretty women, even among your half sisters. Choose another. Any other would be honored to be the queen."

"Pacas, that's why I must see her, I need to be sure she is the right woman. She didn't look into your eyes, you can't understand. Besides, she would fare better with me as her husband than my father."

In spite of his tanned complexion, Pacas' face instantly flushed to a brilliant pink. "What! Not again. Would he risk bringing the wrath of the gods to the entire empire for a whole generation? Your father wouldn't jeopardize everything just to have another wife, would he?"

I'd never seen him so angry, but I shrugged my shoulders and stared at my feet. "I don't know. He seemed very attracted to her."

"She's too skinny. Maybe when she's healthy she'd be attractive, but now she looks half dead."

"To you perhaps, but I know that yearning look he gets before he chooses a woman. Kaya deserves better, and I think she'll be a wonderful queen. With her by my side, I'll be the best Inca since Pachacuti."

As we walked back to the main plaza, Pacas denounced my father's behavior, which he considered an obscene abuse of privilege, between his rants about my imbecilic notion of loving a doomed woman. He tried every way he could to convince me that it would be better if I didn't speak with Kaya. His logic was impeccable. Why grow attached to a woman you may never be able to wed? Why risk catching the illness that still lingered with her? Why risk Riku's suspicion, or worse, his wrath? Why risk disgrace and losing the right to become the next Inca? The more he talked, the more I knew what I had to do. We found Riku just as he was leaving the Temple of Inti.

"Riku, with your permission, I would like to spend the afternoon with Kaya. She is my sister after all. I'd like to get to know her before she dies." I concealed my real intent and felt bad about deceiving him.

His hands clasped behind his back, he watched me closely as he considered my request. I stood casually and hid my thoughts from him. I didn't dare to even think about Kaya while I talked with him. He was far too good at hearing, or seeing, or feeling, or whatever it was he did to get his information. He answered slowly, emphasizing each word. "She is still recovering from her illness and is very fragile. She can't tolerate being upset." He shifted his weight to his left foot.

"Perhaps I can cheer her with some stories of our travels. She must get lonely being in her garden all day long." I smiled brightly, hoping it didn't appear false.

"All right, you may see her, but you cannot be alone with her, and I have to visit your father."

"Pacas could stay with us," I volunteered quickly as I waved my hand to my best friend who stood a short distance away. I held my breath as Riku studied both of us.

He thought a moment, eyed each of us and finally said, "I'll take you there. Iska would never allow your entrance without my approval." He stooped to pick up a small bundle, and we headed toward the stairs. As we turned off the stairs on her terrace, he cautioned me again. "Now be gentle with her and don't scare her. She needs stability and friendship, nothing more. Do you understand me?"

I nodded and the three of us passed into the Mamacona housing. Kneeling with her loom wrapped around her ample waist, Iska struggled to stand to greet her unexpected visitors.

"Ninan, this is Iska. She cares for Kaya. Iska, do you recognize Ninan, Huayna Capac's son and his friend Pacas?" Riku introduced us in his calm, quiet voice.

"Yes, I saw you both at the banquet last night," she said as she approached us wiping her hands on her dress. "Ninan, you look just like your handsome father." She acknowledged Pacas with a nod and a smile, although it was hard to tell through her pudgy cheeks. "It's a privilege to meet both of you. What brings you here?"

"Ninan asked to visit with his sister, and I have given my approval as long as Pacas is always with them," Riku said gently, but firmly.

Iska coughed slightly as her slit eyes opened to the size of platters. She stared at us and then Riku before she timidly asked, "Are you sure? No one except the Mamaconas and you has ever visited her garden. No one."

Riku gently reassured her. "It's all right. Both are honorable men. I've known them since they were babies." As she relaxed somewhat, Riku continued, "I must meet with the Inca so I can't stay. Will you show them the way?"

Still unconvinced, but unwilling to confront Riku, she slowly responded, "Please follow me."

With that, Riku said goodbye and left the same way we came. We followed Iska to the edge of the terrace where she showed us the ladder that hung down the terrace wall. "You'll find Kaya in the garden. Do you need me to show you?"

"No, I'm sure you climb this ladder often enough. We'll visit with Kaya and climb out when we're ready to go."

I politely thanked her, and she ambled back to her weaving, but looked back occasionally to watch us and shake her head. We easily descended to her garden that rested on a long, rather narrow terrace overlooking the agricultural section beyond it. Even during these winter months, birds and butterflies flitted among the profusion of greenery, while Kaya knelt at the far end. Half-filled with a red serpent design in a white background, her loom was tied to a tree at one end and wrapped around her waist at the other end. Her hands continued to weave as she followed the condor soaring high above us. I didn't want to startle her, so we stood by the ladder, and I spoke in a voice loud enough for her to hear. "Pacas, this is a beautiful garden."

It needed tending even to my untrained eye, but he understood my intent and replied, "Yes, it is, and the view of the valley is very pleasing."

She gracefully extracted herself from the loom and glided toward us. "You're too generous. I alone tend this garden, and, with my illness, I was unable to care for it as I like, but it will improve as I get stronger. Still, you are most welcome." She was so calm and so beautiful. "Can I offer you some *chicha*? I asked Iska to bring some down this morning."

"You knew we would visit?" I asked.

"Ninan, you told me this morning when we were with our father. Pacas, it's nice to finally meet you too. I asked Riku your name as we walked back here."

Atuk was right; she was learning Riku's talent for knowing other people's thoughts. We settled in the shade of her shelter overlooking the full length of the garden.

"This is a beautiful place. It's much bigger and friendlier than it appears from the terraces." I struggled to initiate a conversation, although I would have been content to simply watch her flawless face and elegant hands.

"It is nice. Still, having spent so much time here, I long to escape." She served the drinks with the refinement of a practiced servant and the air of a princess. Never knowing hard work, her thin fingers finished each task without effort or hurry. "Please tell me about your lives in Cusco. Tell me about our parents."

Pacas squirmed beside me, uncomfortable with his role as chaperone. I ignored him entirely and tried to memorize Kaya's eyelashes caressing her clear, dark eyes as she slowly blinked.

"I know our father much better than our mother," I heard myself say. "As queen, she directs all the tasks of the Mamaconas, but she finds no pleasure in it. In fact, I don't think she finds joy anywhere. She is cold and unfriendly to everyone, including her husband and me. Until this morning, I didn't think she cared for anyone, but she certainly was taken with you. She must miss you terribly."

Kaya listened intently as she knelt with us, but made no gesture. "We are her only children, is that right?"

I nodded.

"It must be very difficult for her to always be alone. You follow your father's path, and I am here. She is not a strong woman. Until today I never understood why I wasn't allowed to stay with my birth mother. It was difficult for her just to see me. She hasn't the strength to raise me and then let me go. Iska, Kinsa, and Tawan, my other mothers, are very caring, but I'm not attached to them as I would be to my birth mother." She paused to drink and then added, "Mother also carries the weight of a secret. Do you know what it is?"

"How do you know that?" I asked, now even more impressed by her skills.

"The same way I knew you would visit me. She told me."

The ways of spirits were beyond my understanding, and until recently, my beliefs. "No, I don't know the secret, but I know there is one. I've heard her mention it to Cepi a few times." I turned to Pacas. "Our mothers are good friends. Do you know the secret?"

He shook his head and I shrugged my shoulders.

My sister intently stared at her cup and concluded, "As Riku always says, we can hide what we don't want others to see. We'll know the secret when we need to know." She carried a radiate smile when she lifted her head. "And Huayna Capac, what is it like to live with the Inca?"

I wondered how much I should tell her. Riku insisted I not upset her, but still I couldn't lie to such a trusting innocent. "Huayna Capac is a jovial man who takes the responsibilities of Inca very seriously. He's an excellent diplomat and fair in his judgments. Visitors from all over the empire steadily flow through Cusco where they seek his advice or require his authority to settle a dispute. Sinchi Roca, Pacas' father is a great friend of Huayna Capac. He takes control of Cusco when our father travels. We traveled with him to Tomebamba once." Absorbed by her beauty, I stopped to watch her adjust her dress as she shifted her legs to the other side. Atuk was right. Her illness had arrested the development of womanly curves. Still, she possessed a noble charm that compensated for her childlike figure.

"And when will you become Inca?" Her direct question carried none of the envy or intrigue so commonplace in Cusco.

"Probably not for a very long time," I responded with the same honesty. "Huayna Capac is still a robust, vital man in prime health."

Pacas snickered beside me, and Kaya turned her head to stare at him and looked back to me. She waited, and I felt obligated to explain. "Our father enjoys the company of women. He continues to take more wives and has sired more children than I know. Many women ask for his aid, claiming their children are his. Some are his, but others are just looking for his generous gifts."

Kaya looked frail, but she absorbed information like a thirsty llama taking water. "When you're Inca, will you take many wives too?"

"It's the Inca's prerogative to take as many wives as he wishes, and there are diplomatic reasons for doing so. Still, I'd never ignore my queen the way he does." I had said more than I intended, so I changed the subject. "How do you like your lessons with Riku?"

She looked out across the garden to the mountains beyond. "They are my escape. He shows us distant lands. Sometimes he doesn't even know where the places are, but we always learn from our traveling."

"What is it like to go with him?" I knew she never actually went anywhere and struggled to understand.

She glanced at Pacas and me before studying her intertwined fingers in her lap. "I've never tried to explain it to anyone." She played with her fingers some more and at last began, "Do you ever dream?"

I nodded.

"Do you remember where you were during your dream and who you were with?"

I nodded again.

"Do you ever find yourself in places, or with people you don't know?"

I looked at Pacas and tried to remember. "I don't think so. Usually my dreams replay the people of the day, although events may differ from the daytime outcome."

"I have that type of dream too. Usually I'm working with Kinsa on a new weaving technique by day and at night I dream the piece is already finished." She brushed a lock of hair from her face. "Unfortunately I wake to find it never is. Traveling with Riku is similar but still different. When I dream at night, I'm directing the dream and the outcome. When I travel with Riku, I see what someone else or something else chooses to show me. I'm fully aware that I'm at Machu Picchu, but I can see, hear, smell and touch another place and time. All four of us go to the same place, but what we experience is somewhat different."

"How is that possible?"

She shrugged her shoulders. "I don't know. Riku is very skilled, but it's not entirely his doing. Maybe the gods make it possible. I've traveled without him." Fear flashed in her eyes. "Promise you won't tell him. I'm not supposed to do that. That's why he looked at me strangely this morning. I accidentally mentioned something from my own traveling."

"Will you tell me if your traveling caused your illness?"

Surprised, her hands covered her mouth. She dropped them slowly and continued softly, "Actually, it cured my illness, but Riku can't know that." I had no skill in Riku's ways and understood even less. Still, it was important to her, and I promised not to upset her, so Pacas and I agreed to keep her secret. Her small round mouth relaxed to a smile. "Tell me about your trip to Tomebamba."

Pacas joined in, and we retold our adventures of trapping the thieves and restoring the town to the standard ways. She even laughed a few times at Pacas' fanciful descriptions of our hiding places. We talked about Quispiguanca and Cusco and the fun times we had playing together as children, carefully avoiding any unpleasant memories. The afternoon passed quickly, and she began to look very tired. With a prearranged nod, Pacas excused himself to enjoy the view from the other end of the garden.

Kaya and I stood facing each other by the ladder. A few years younger, she hadn't reached to her adult height and was a head shorter than me. I gently brushed a strand of luxurious hair away from her face. Her hands at her sides, she gazed up at me with those magnificent eyes. "Kaya, may we visit you again?"

"Please do." Her tired eyes sparkled. "You have given me great pleasure, and I'd like to know you better."

To thank her, I placed my hands on her shoulders and lightly kissed her forehead. Although an appropriate farewell, I wanted more. I gently kissed her lips while her sweet scent filled my head. She awakened in me an unfamiliar desire that flared into an intense heat pulsing through my body. I stepped back and my hands dropped to my sides. I was helpless to do anything but stare at my sister's simple beauty.

Kaya noticed Pacas' approach and stepped aside to include him. "Thank you for allowing us to visit you. I have enjoyed your garden," Pacas politely concluded before starting up the ladder.

I mumbled an appreciative goodbye without touching her again. Climbing reluctantly, I turned back to say, "I will carry your fire until we meet again."

Women

Ninan

We left Machu Picchu before Kaya and I met again. Riku insisted that she maintain her training even while we were there and additional visits were too strenuous for her. As much as I wanted to see her, I respected his judgment. Even so, I planned a secret midnight visit, but Pacas convinced me to abandon the attempt for Kaya's sake. He insisted that if I loved her, I would never endanger her. If we were discovered, she would never recover her honor, and she might be killed in disgrace. As the Inca's son, I thought I could dissipate any trouble, but he persuaded me not to take the risk. I decided I could wait, if it increased the possibility of taking her as my wife when she came of age.

Back in Cusco, I thought of her daily, in spite of my new responsibilities. Huayna Capac appointed me as judge for Cusco's civil issues. I heard and settled the grievances of our Inca neighbors squabbling over water usage, a husband's indiscretions, drunken fights, unruly children, and a myriad of other minor concerns. Sinchi Roca sat with me for two weeks overseeing my procedures, advising me before I pronounced a judgment, and reminding me of obscure laws and penalties that applied to the immediate circumstance. After two months experience, he visited me only occasionally, or when I requested his presence.

All hearings were held on a raised platform in Haucaypata. The plaintiffs stood before me as each person presented his or her complaint. I presided from a high-backed chair covered with hammered gold designs and red feathers arching over my head to shade me. The crowd surrounding the platform changed constantly as people wandered past, greeted friends, cheered a plaintive and then continued their daily routine. My next case was about to begin when Huayna Capac, Sinchi Roca, and Pacas walked past with a visitor from the coast. They were negotiating a trade agreement, and Pacas was acting as Quipucamayo. An expert supervised his work, but this was his first opportunity to record proceedings. How much cotton equaled how many loads of maize? When was the llama convoy loaded with the squash and guava to arrive in Cusco and then return with *chuno*? If a crop failed, what would be traded instead? Pacas glanced at me briefly as they slowed to file through the doorway into the city palace. I wished I were joining them, but instead, two rancorous middle-aged women ascended the platform, glared at each other and then faced me. I began the proceedings as usual, pointing to the elder standing on the left. "State your name."

"My name is Tancar Apachini, the first wife and widow of the great Mananam." She stood proudly in her finest dress covered with a blue and white shawl fastened over her chest with a large silver pin. She crossed her arms in front of her and lifted her chin.

"And you, state your name." I pointed to Tancar Apachini's opponent standing defiantly beside her.

"My name is Sonco Sullul, the more beautiful and favorite wife of the handsome Mananam and mother of his four children." Short and rotund, she firmly planted her hands on her flaccid hips.

Tancar Apachini shook with anger but suppressed a verbal response.

"Tancar Apachini, state your complaint," I said, ignoring their mutual animosity.

"As principal wife and the mother of Mananam's eldest son and daughter, it is my right to establish the distribution of my husband's wealth. Sonco Sullul was a worthless wife. She begrudged her position and refused to follow my household orders. She was a poor cook, a sloppy weaver and an indifferent mother. I was forced to discipline her children constantly. Because of her indolent behavior, I have decided she will receive none of my loving husband's property, and I demand that she leave my house immediately." She stomped her foot and pretended to push Sonco Sullul off the stage while the crowd cheered her indignation.

Having daily witnessed similar acrimony, I simply continued, "What is the extent of Mananam's property?"

In a proud, clear voice Tancar announced to the entire plaza, "Mananam's property includes a house and household goods in Cusco, a dozen fine gold statues, and a large emerald that he earned by his service to the Inca. On the edge of Cusco he owns two irrigated terraces and a herd of one hundred llamas grazing in the high sierra."

Several in the audience recited the holdings with her word for word.

This was a household that needed nothing, except family harmony. I addressed Sonco Sullul, "State your case."

"Tancar Apachini is a cruel taskmaster who beat me without cause. She hates me because Mananam preferred me."

Her whiny voice grated like a squealing guinea pig, but I tried to listen impartially.

"I did all the cooking, the marketing, and weaving for the entire family while I raised my four children. Tancar was never satisfied with my work, and when I suggested she hire a servant to help, she refused saying a second wife should be capable of managing it all. Meanwhile, she did nothing except work with the Mamaconas. For my loyal years of service to Mananam and the four children I bore him, I am entitled to at least half of his holdings. Besides, Tancar misstated his wealth. I know there are *three* fields under cultivation and *two* herds of one hundred llamas each." Her fat cheeks and protruding stomach bounced to accent her words.

As the accusations continued, I realized neither of the women mourned her husband and neither had a charitable thought for the other. I wondered if they had ever felt the love I so recently discovered with Kaya. Were all marriages doomed to such discord? Certainly my parents marriage was strained as were all those I met on this platform. The squabbling attracted a crowd, equally split between the two wives. I raised the judgment scepter, and the noise gradually subsided. "Tancar Apachini, can you explain the discrepancy in the accounting of your late husband's holdings?"

Regaining her composure, she loudly announced, "The extra field and additional herd of llamas are mine. They passed to me from my dear mother who now sits with Killa in the Upper World."

Sonco Sullul sputtered but said nothing.

Addressing the audience, I inquired, "Are there any others who might have a claim on the properties of Mananam?"

A whispered hush shuffled through the audience and then ceased.

I was about to continue when a small voice answered, "I loved Mananam, and now I carry his child."

Finally united, the wives shouted insults calling this woman a liar and a whore while I beckoned her forward. She waddled through the crowd and struggled to climb the platform stairs. A pretty young woman, who would hold her newborn within the week, she meekly stood behind the two wives. "I am Mirani, lover and neighbor to Mananam. He grew so tired of his bickering wives that he chose to stay with me." She hung her head to avoid the hateful glares of her neighbors.

In my new position, I had heard vulgar insults and witnessed spitting, hair pulling and occasional fistfights during the proceedings. Partially hardened to it, I still winced to think these were Cusco's elite and questioned the timid woman, "What evidence can you give that the child you carry is Mananam's?"

The crowd hung on every word as their fickle support found an unlikely heroine. "My new husband was in Cajamarca for six months overseeing the construction of a bridge. Living alone in the house next to Mananam, he often chose to spend his evenings with me in my husband's absence. Mananam didn't hide his preference. Both wives and several of the children saw his visits." She tipped her head toward the two feuding women. "I was with child when my husband returned three months ago. He is an honorable man and will accept this child as his own." When she finished, she shied away from the other two. The crowd had expanded with each new discovery, but now stood waiting for a conclusion.

I turned my attention back to the wives and queried, "Will one of you corroborate her story, or must I delay my decision until I hear from your children?"

"Mananam did visit Mirani regularly, but there may have been other men visiting in her husband's absence," Tancar Apachini replied.

"To remind you, perjury during this hearing will result in the loss of all your property. Did you see other men entering her house?"

Tancar looked at Sonco Sullul for support, but got none. With the sigh of defeat she simply answered, "No."

One final question bothered me, and in sympathy for the tormented Mananam, I asked Tancar Apachini, "How did your husband die? He was in the prime of his life."

"He was walking along the road heading for our country fields. He tripped over a loose stone, fell and hit his head. He died before we reached him." Tancar Apachini covered her face with her shawl as she spoke to affect at least some semblance of public grief.

"Can anyone in the audience confirm this account?" I searched the crowd for a respondent and saw two hands rise.

"Yes, we are his brothers, and we were with him when the accident occurred. I ran back to get his wives while my brother stayed with him."

I thanked them and was satisfied that neither wife was responsible for his death. "Mirani, you are indeed fortunate that your husband will keep you. For the compassion you have shown a troubled man and to support his child, the emerald and four gold statues will become the property of your husband." Next I addressed the wives with as much disgust as I could muster. "As for you two, you must learn to live civilly when you remarry. I do not want to see you before me again," I said sternly, hoping to make a lasting impression. "Tancar Apachini, as principle wife, you will retain the house in Cusco, four gold statues of your choosing, one field and fifty llamas. Sonco Sullul, you and your children will vacate the house by the full moon. You may choose four gold statues after Tancar Apachini has made her selection. One field and fifty llamas will help support you and your children until you remarry." I stared at the women and concluded, "You are dismissed."

The three women left without acknowledging one another, while the crowd reviewed the judgment and ambled back to their lives. Meanwhile my assistant approached me with two men. This case was simple; one man's llamas had trampled and devoured a field of new beans. I ruled he would provide new seed and help the farmer replant the field. The planting season was only two weeks past, so there was still time for the replanted crop to mature properly.

Having completed the cases for the day, I crossed the plaza and allowed my thoughts to wander back to Kaya. I wanted her as my wife but worried that her lot might be as bad as Tancar Apachini, or even worse, my mother. I had just resolved to be a better husband, although I didn't know how, when Pacas met me at the palace doorway.

"Ninan, you're finished. So am I. Let's go." He bounded past me, expecting me to follow. "Come on. Today's the day!" Preoccupied with the morning's rulings, I'd forgotten my promise.

"Pacas, she'll wait for you. If you let me get a drink first, I'll be much better company." Resigned, he followed me into the palace, chattering like a schoolboy. At least he was reviewing the negotiations instead of babbling about Tinkha. "The maize we grow in the mountains is much heavier than the coastal cotton. So, to increase the weight from the coast, we needed to substitute peanuts for some of the cotton." I knew the value of the exchanged goods was partially determined by the number of llamas needed to transport it. "They also wanted quinoa, and by weight, quinoa is most closely matched to the cotton, but quinoa is much more valuable. To increase their value, we negotiated to get some of that red dye they extract from beetles. So, by balancing the weight and value of the goods, we were able to agree on an arrangement where we ship maize and quinoa from the mountains to the coast and in return, they ship cotton, peanuts, and dye to us." Still exuberant, he continued, "We even traded gold for fresh fish! Can you imagine? We will have fresh fish three days after the full moon for the next six months! The runners will deliver them and return with small weights of gold." I finished my *chicha* as he jabbered, but seeing that I was still brooding, Pacas asked, "What's wrong?"

He worried every time I mentioned Kaya, so I told him about my morning. "Three women were fighting over property. The two wives were too busy hating each other to notice their husband had found another woman. Neither wife mourned her husband. The third woman was alone and only interested in his wealth. Poor man. I hope we do better."

Pacas jumped to his feet and cheered, "Let's find out."

I laughed at his enthusiasm, content to leave the brooding for another day. "Where are you to meet her?"

"In the main courtyard of the Coricancha. Are you ready to go?"

We left immediately for his first visit with his promised bride. He practically ran from the palace to the temple.

When we arrived, Tinkha sat surrounded by her friends. They all talked and worked together, but quickly dispersed while we removed our sandals at the courtyard entrance. She remained, carding wool with an absentmindedness developed from years of practice. Pacas immediately joined her, choosing his location carefully so he could watch her with his back to the prying eyes scattered around the courtyard. I was to supervise their visit, an unnecessary role considering our location. Pacas awkwardly stared at Tinkha but said nothing. Completely inexperienced with men, she drew back with a sudden need to direct her full attention to carding. After two false starts, Pacas successfully initiated a conversation. "Coya Cusirimay is very pleased with your work. She mentioned your fine weaving and careful preparation of the ceremonial beers." He waited for a response, but in spite of the dark brown complexion typical of her heritage, she blushed at his high praise. "I understand you're from Cana. Did you ever visit Lake Titicaca?" he tried again.

A slow smile spread across her face, and her pleasantly low-pitched voice glided through the words. "I was young when I was brought to Cusco, but I remember visiting my uncle who lived on the shore. We fished from their wonderful reed boats and waded in the icy water. I never imagined there was so much water in the world!"

Barely aware of the courtyard surrounding him, Pacas listened intently and added, "My mother is from the southwestern end of the lake, but I've seen it. I've lived my entire life in Cusco, although Ninan, and I traveled with our fathers as far south as Cacha. Do you remember the Temple of Viracocha there? You would have passed it coming to Cusco."

She shook her head slowly, and her eyes moistened. "They took me from my family when I was only six, and I walked to Cusco with strangers. Most of the girls were my age or younger. We were so frightened. I've tried to forget that trip, but during the night I still wake with a start, terrified that I'll be killed."

Pacas glanced at me but just as quickly returned to Tinkha. In a whisper he asked, "Do they treat you well here?"

She nodded. "I miss my family, but we are well cared for."

They sat together for a long time, sometimes silent, sometimes exchanging small bits of their lives. In typical fashion, Tinkha's black hair covered most of the back of her unadorned dress. The other girls were getting bored with their entertainment and returned to their work. My mother, Coya Cusirimay, walked by us, saw that I was staying close and continued without interrupting. I was thinking they made a handsome couple when Pacas quietly asked her, "Do you know that I have asked to marry you?" He sat very still, watching her, anxious for her answer.

She stared at her work. Her hands hesitated and continued. "Yes, Miski told me. Being so close to Huayna Capac, she seems to know everything." She placed the cleaned wool in its basket and took another puff to clean.

"You are very well respected as a Mamacona. Would you prefer to remain here or become my wife?" Pacas managed to ask the question without faltering or moving anything but his lips. The tension was enough to keep his back absolutely straight as he waited.

"I learned to be satisfied with my life as a Mamacona, never expecting anything more. Being a wife and mother seemed impossible." She stopped her work and chose her words carefully, her kind voice barely above a whisper. "Now you, a strong, handsome, young man with unlimited prospects, want to take me as your wife. I couldn't be happier, and I joyfully accept your proposal." She lifted her head to see Pacas grinning. His shoulders dropped slightly, and they talked with a new ease.

Close enough to hear their conversation if I tried, I leaned against the temple wall and relaxed. Listening to them, I didn't notice Miski's approach from behind me. "They're a well matched couple." Her honey-sweet voice hung over me. "They'll be happy as man and wife. Too bad they have to wait so long."

She came closer, but I held my position. I could feel her warm breath on my neck. I responded coldly, but my face flushed as I answered, "What do you know about their wedding date?"

"Nothing, except that I overheard your mother tell Umu Pilaca she wouldn't release Tinkha until after some big festival at Machu Picchu in a year or two. She needs her help with the preparations." Hidden by her body she slid her hand across my lower back and down my buttock. I wanted to step away, but her advances weakened my knees and strengthened my groin. Her cloying voice settled in my head. "And what about you? Who will you choose to marry? Many would gladly be your wife, but they don't know you're completely inexperienced with woman." As she spoke her hand drifted even lower and her chest pressed against my back.

A man for nearly three years, her insult was even more biting for its truth. I stepped away as I faced her and hissed, "My private affairs are none of your business! I will choose a queen when I'm ready, and you'll be the last to know."

In a brazen move she stepped forward and whispered, "When you are man enough, I'll teach you the ways of pleasure." She passed close enough to discover I qualified for her lessons, grinned provocatively and was gone. I glanced around the courtyard, relieved that no one had noticed her advances. My attention returned to Pacas and Tinkha, who were rapidly building a friendship. It was too bad they'd have to wait so long to marry. Perhaps if my father cancelled the celebration at Machu Picchu, they could marry sooner.

While still mulling over Miski's proposition, Coya Cusirimay approached in her usual stiff and distant manner. "Ninan, I need Tinkha's help with the preparations for Homa Raymi. She has wasted enough time with Pacas, and as chaperone you must end this visit."

"Dearest mother, you were generous to allow them this meeting. I will send Tinkha to you shortly." I smiled and tried to thaw her icy request. Satisfied that her demands were met, she abruptly turned without even glancing at the happy couple. Walking away from me, her jerky steps looked unnatural, and I wondered if her joints were stiffening.

Presuming the reason for the queen's visit, Pacas and Tinkha rose to say goodbye. In a single conversation Pacas had awakened a timid girl to find a cheerful young woman. He secretly held her hand and whispered so only she could hear. She responded in kind and after a brief pause, she picked up her baskets and disappeared across the courtyard without looking back. His pining eyes followed her retreat, oblivious to the snickers around him. He just stood there with a ridiculous grin on his face, until I led him out of the temple before he embarrassed himself any further. "She wants to marry me!" Pacas bounced down the street before me, as giddy as a young boy after his first beer.

"Well of course she does. You're a fine man with a bright future. Any young woman would be proud to be your wife." I tried not to spoil his pleasure, but realistically, other than marrying the next Inca, he was the best prospect in the empire. After all, he was the son of Sinchi Roca, the man who represented the Inca in his absence.

"Oh, it's not that. We like each other, and we'll be very happy together." He must have seen me wince. "What happened?"

"Miski said that my mother won't release her until after the big celebration at Machu Picchu more than a year from now. She claims she needs Tinkha for the preparations."

He slowed to a plodding walk, thought a moment and resolved, "I'll wait." We walked a little further in silence as he considered what I said and added, "Oh, I'm sorry." Now we both considered my predicament. Preparations were already beginning for the death of the only woman I loved.

Even worse, I hadn't proven myself capable of pleasing any woman and was therefore unprepared to be a husband. An afternoon shower approached from the east emptying the streets of the normal foot traffic. We were alone when I confided in my best friend, "Miski offered to give me lessons in pleasuring women."

Pacas coughed quietly, took a deep breath, and burst into laughter. The clouds opened and drenched us instantly while I stared at Pacas, completely befuddled by his spastic response.

"What's so funny?" Soaked, I wasn't particularly amused.

He inhaled, started to speak, but chortling still overtook him. He held his stomach and rolled against the wall under the eave. Annoyed, I followed him to get an explanation. Still grinning, he sputtered, "You and the conniving viper! You could be Atahualpa's new daddy. You could punish him the next time he eats raw hearts. Better yet, you could sire another potential heir and further legitimize her claim. That would give her an even better reason to dispose of you."

I hadn't considered her motives, but now that Pacas pointed them out, her proposal was obscene. I joined him in a hardy laugh that outlasted the shower.

"Too bad," he added. "From what we've seen, the lessons should have been most enjoyable!"

I had to agree with him, she was an alluring woman. Still, I couldn't help but wonder aloud, "How stupid does she think we are?"

"Just ignorant enough to be seduced. There must be safer ways to learn," he concluded.

I stepped back into the street, and we continued our stroll. This was a serious topic, and we both needed to consider our options. Traditionally, one of his father's secondary wives taught the son, so I had many options, but Pacas' rightful teacher was not appealing. "I think you should ask your father for advice," I suggested.

"You're right. He'll know who is most suitable." We watched the rain hanging from the distant clouds like the hair of a young maiden. "What about you? Will you ask Huayna Capac?"

"He is so indiscriminate. He might suggest I try them all."

Pacas nodded and thought a moment before suggesting, "How about asking my father?"

"Perhaps, but I think I'll ask Mama Runtu, Tito's mother."

"Good idea. She is a lovely woman with no political aspirations." With the decisions made, Pacas reverted to his favorite topic, Tinkha. I teased him mercilessly while he valiantly defended her. Mostly, I was jealous that there were no obstacles, except time, between him and his future wife. From what I could see, Tinkha and Pacas would have a marriage worthy of emulation, and I hoped I would have the one woman who could offer me the same.

The weeks passed quickly as we both fell back into the daily routine. Pacas studied with the Amautas and continued his training as a Quipucamayo, while I continued to preside over the civil matters. After judgments one day, I met Mama Runtu walking alone in the main plaza and asked if she would teach me the ways of pleasuring. She said she was honored that I had chosen her, and we agreed to meet. The prospect of my first intimacy interfered with my work and interrupted my sleep. Watching my father over the years wasn't adequate preparation. Nervous and intrigued, I waited impatiently for our first meeting.

Mama Runtu met me at the door of her house in an older section of Cusco. Her family lived comfortably, but not extravagantly. "Ninan, welcome to our home. You honor me with your visit." She led the way into the one-room house with a kitchen on the right and sleeping mats on the left. I noticed she took special care to use beautiful new blankets on a mat large enough for two. "You can be sure we are alone and will not be disturbed. My neighbor is a good friend and will watch the children," she continued.

I stumbled along, uneasy with our new relationship. "I am grateful for your discretion, and your willingness. I have watched men and woman many times, but I have no experience." I took the *chicha* beer she offered and sat on the floor as she requested. Mama Runtu was a young woman, perhaps only ten years my senior. Like my father, I too was attracted to her easy smile and quiet manner, although she was not particularly pretty. There was nothing memorable about her face. All the parts were there, but it almost seemed like the gods used the leftovers. Her eyes held no shine, her two front teeth badly overlapped one another and her large nose somehow didn't match the rest. Still, she carried herself with an unassuming dignity that drew me to her.

"Watching and doing are very different." She lowered herself to my side and asked, "May I kneel beside you?" She wore only an oversized yellow dress and had draped her hair over her shoulder.

I quickly emptied my cup of beer, and she leaned slightly toward me to take my cup and refill it with more *chicha*. I knew this woman as my father's partner and the mother of a promising young boy, and yet before me now she was as seductive as Miski. While I continued to drink, she caressed my shoulders and back, which helped me relax and yet heightened my awareness of her every move. She said very little, but gently and gradually showed me how to touch her. She took my hands in hers and drew them to her lips for a kiss so light I saw it more than felt it. Her face against the palm of my hand, she filled my other hand with her hair. Still guiding my hands, she lifted her hair to my face and told me to breathe deeply. Her long soft mane slid across my cheek, enveloping me with her earthy scent. Unfamiliar yearnings stirred and goaded me on, so I closed my eyes to kiss her hands, but she offered her lips. I reveled in the exploration as she guided my lips down her neck and my hands to her hips. In a single motion, my hands slid up her sides lifting her dress over her shoulders, while my eyes feasted on her soft curves and glistening skin that begged me to touch every part of her.

She comfortably posed and allowed me to gaze at her lovely, remarkably youthful shape before extending her hands to me. As I approached, she placed my arms on her shoulders and I kicked off my sandals. With a practiced ease, my tunic and thong disappeared under her gentle touch. I stood naked and eager as she guided us toward the blankets. Her supple breasts brushed against my chest, shooting a warm tingling throughout my entire body. Even during our first full embrace she positioned my hands and body for our pleasure as we fell to the blankets still wrapped together. She knew the intensity of my arousal and allowed me to penetrate her quickly. The fire of passion coursed through me with an uncontrollable urgency and release was immediate. With my eyes closed, I lay on her, my heart still pounding, and asked for more. She laughed, waited a short while and began again more slowly.

Over the months I eagerly anticipated my visits to Mama Runtu, and we became friends as well as lovers. I never noticed her crossed teeth or misplaced nose again. Somehow they disappeared into the woman in the same way a withered stalk of maize is overlooked in an otherwise bountiful field. Still, something was missing. Even saturated with pleasure and in the company of a loyal woman, loneliness flooded over me with each arousal. As kind and respectful as Mama Runtu was, she couldn't satisfy my emptiness. Kaya was the one I wanted to please.

Ayahuasca

Kaya

The petals of my favorite fuchsia nodded their approval as a brown and white wren landed at the base of a flower. His soft, high-pitched voice sounded more like a timid mouse than a gregarious, tail-flitting bird. Another wren answered his call and fluttered into the bush, ignoring my presence entirely. They danced among the branches, snatching small insects and repeating their minuscule song. My garden never looked better, and I was as content as the wrens. Blessed by misty rains interspersed with warm sunny days, every plant flourished with abundant vitality. At the end of my terrace, the guava tree drooped under the weight of the maturing fruit, while beside it the red amaryllis spikes filled the air with their sweet scent. In the months since Huayna Capac's visit, the tilling, planting and weeding consumed my solitary afternoons. Working with my hands to nurture the neglected residents healed my broken spirit and allowed the trauma of learning my destiny to blossom into a humbling pride.

My studies also benefited from my renewed vigor. In nearly daily lessons, I struggled to memorize the legends I had forgotten, and to relearn the skills of traveling. Atuk, Tumbes, and Riku helped me practice. Kinsa and Tawan visited regularly too. Kinsa taught me the techniques for weaving all the remaining traditional patterns and, of course, helped me to meet the continual need for additional cloth. We made cloth for sacrifices, for the priests' clothing, and for blankets. Tawan's lessons were harder because it took months before I could breathe deeply enough to sing or play the flute without getting dizzy.

I enjoyed the lessons, but I liked working in my garden the best. After being neglected for so long, there was always something to tend, and it gave me the freedom to reminisce about my family. Ninan was such a handsome man with a muscular body, shiny black hair, piercing eyes, and straight nose. Huayna Capac was shorter and less commanding than I imagined. No wonder Riku spent so much time with him; the Inca didn't seem strong or wise enough to lead on his own. And why did he have so many women? Pacas thought something was wrong, even if Ninan wanted me to believe it was all right. I remembered my mother too. I thought being the queen would be an easy, comfortable life, but she looked tormented and lonely. Pule was right. Everyone has his own work, and the troubles to go with it.

Mostly, I thought about Ninan. I liked listening to his travels with Pacas, but he surprised me when he left my garden. Do siblings normally kiss when they say goodbye? It's a nice custom, but Pacas looked distressed. I'd never kissed Atuk or Tumbes that way, and they were becoming friends. Were brothers and sisters naturally closer? Was it normal for me to want to touch him? I'd never had those desires with anyone else. Did I hear what he said as he left? What does it mean that he will carry my fire? Would my brother light the fire when I was to be sacrificed? Even if I was to be killed by fire and he started it, surely that wasn't what he'd say when he met me for the first time. When Riku told me the prophecy, the truth felt like a hot ember buried deep inside me. Did Ninan mean to take that burning away? How could he have known about that, and if he did, how could he carry my ember? It was the burden of my fate. Day after day I tried to decipher his meaning, but I was never satisfied with my musings. For all I didn't understand about Ninan, Pacas' expression when Ninan kissed me did tell me one thing; this was a secret not to be shared with Riku or anyone else. Enough. I had to stop daydreaming, complete my work and prepare for the trek the following morning.

Riku, Tumbes, Atuk and I were going to Riku's sanctuary near the top of Huayna Picchu. The needle-like peak jutted out of the earth at the north end of the city, forcing the river far below to bow around it and nearly surround the city. Riku asked that I wear my warmest clothes, carry a blanket and a large jar of water. The others would carry food, firewood, and other supplies. We were to have a special ceremony, and Riku insisted we eliminate salt and hot peppers from our food for the past week. Iska, of course, had complied, and I was weary of the bland diet that left me with no desire to eat the breakfast that she had risen early to prepare. "Good morning. Are you ready to go?" Riku greeted me cheerily, even though the fog and misting clouds masked the first signs of morning light.

Iska helped me tie the blanket holding the water jar around my shoulders. "I'm ready. Is there anything else we need?" I tried to sound enthusiastic in spite of the heavy jar on my back.

"No, everything else is prepared. Iska, we'll see you in three days." We said our good-byes and descended the stairs toward the main plaza where he stopped at the Torreon to collect Atuk and Tumbes before continuing. There was no one in the plaza this early, and the only sound we heard was the dampened reflection of our footsteps off the terrace walls. Tumbes and Atuk were as sleepy as I was, so we walked in silence as we passed through the plaza and shortly reached the path to Huayna Picchu. When we started to climb the stairs leading to the top, Riku warned, "Be careful here. The mist makes the stairs very slippery, and there's nothing to grasp for balance."

Tumbes had a difficult task, since he carried a large bundle of firewood that scraped along the mountain as he tried to stay away from the sheer drop at the edge of each step. For balance, I slid my hand along the moist, moss-covered granite wall but found no handholds. I continually stared at my feet, securing each foothold to steady the shifting weight of the water jar on my back. This was the first time I had climbed Huayna Picchu, and even though we were accustomed to the stairs in the city, we all breathed heavily to keep Riku's pace on the knee-high, seemingly endless steps. We stopped to rest as a breeze cleared the fog surrounding us, but the river valley and even the city below us were still obscured in the billowing clouds. At last the sun edged over the mountains, contrasting the shadowed, nearly black slopes with those in direct sunlight. Kissed with sun, the slopes flaunted their verdant foliage of spring green orchids, blue-green ficus and the purplish-green bromeliads. Even the sheerest slopes were covered with vines and lichen. Moving again, we slowly and carefully ascended the peak under Riku's patient and watchful eye. Painstakingly built into the mountain, the path wound around the peak and still continued to climb. My legs burned with the exertion as it became increasingly difficult to catch my breath.

When we finally completed the last set of thigh-high steps, a house clinging to the mountain appeared before us. It seemed as precariously situated as the condor's nest, but the small, sturdy structure was built to endure forever. Behind the building there was a flat area where we could put down our gear and walk around without fear of falling. Atuk was the first to unload and walked straight to the edge. "This is magnificent! You can see the escarpments across the valley and beyond to the mountains in the distance. And now that the valley is clear, you can see all the way to the river."

I joined him to see the river, but quickly stepped away. "Not a good place to fall." I crept forward to the edge again. "The river looks so small. Look, there's a man. I can barely see him."

Tumbes joined us at the edge of the mountain. "Does anyone care to follow me?" he said as he spread his arms, pretending to fly with a circling hawk.

Riku, busy with the bundles, called us back, "I could use your help preparing a fire and a bit of food." He didn't need, or even want our help. He just wanted us away from the edge, so we busied ourselves with the tasks he requested.

Atuk found a pot in the building and filled it with water to put on the fire. "You must be very fond of this place. When did you first come here?" he asked.

"When I was about your age, my predecessor, Cascani, brought me here with Chaska and Ixiamas, my friend from the Amazon. We performed the same ceremony we will do tonight." Riku unwrapped some ground maize and other vegetables from his bundle and added it to the water. Unfortunately he neglected to add any salt or pepper, but anything would taste good after our climb.

I hadn't realized Ixiamas or Riku knew Chaska, my predecessor to the spirit bridge. In fact, I knew almost nothing about Riku's past. Afraid he would ignore my question, I reluctantly asked, "How did you come to be a student with Ixiamas and Chaska?"

The question seemed to send him into his memories. Just as curious, Tumbes and Atuk were silent as they listened and pretended to busy themselves with the fire.

Riku studied us carefully, trying to decide how tired we were. Satisfied that we were alert, he shrugged his shoulders and stirred the pot. "When I was a boy, I traveled with my parents from Cusco to the jungle downstream. My mother needed to visit my ailing grandmother who lived in the village that Ixiamas now leads. We planned to leave the lowlands before the rainy season, but my grandmother grew progressively worse and then suddenly died. With the rivers raging, we had to wait until the end of the wet season to travel back to my father's people in Cusco." He stared at nothing as he dredged up the memories, but his voice softened with an ancient pain. "On our return we needed to go over a suspended bridge well downstream from here. So many people wanted to cross the bridge that we were forced to wait all day. Finally my father led the way with my mother close behind. I followed at a distance to avoid the swaying they caused. We were all on the bridge when one of the main support lines snapped. Both my parents lost their balance and fell to the river below. I would have followed except my foot got caught in the reed mat of the bridge floor. Hanging upside down, I heard my mother screaming until they hit the river and disappeared. Finally I realized my own predicament and grabbed a dangling rope while those on the riverbank yelled instructions. I dragged myself across the half-demolished bridge and back to safety." He paused to taste the porridge as we each expressed our condolences.

His harrowing experience stunned me, and I felt sorry for him, but being an orphan didn't explain how he came to know Chaska, my father's eldest sister. Curious, I pressed to hear more. "It must have been terrifying to see your parents' death. Did you travel back to Cusco by yourself?"

Gazing at the mountains leading to the jungle, his voice was unchanged, but his drooping, searching eyes were haunted with raw memories that still carried the sting of red ants. "No, I was on the jungle side of the river, so I returned to my mother's family. I was happy there. Ixiamas and I became even better friends. Unfortunately the lowland climate didn't agree with me, and I suffered continually from congestion in my chest. After the bridge was replaced, I again said goodbye to the village people, and my uncle took me back to Cusco. With no relatives living near Cusco, my only opportunity was to become a priest. Besides, my experience in the jungle was valued by the High Priest. Even so, nobody really noticed me until I was struck by lightning a few years later."

None of us expected such remarkable stories from Riku, the tranquil man we knew as our aging teacher. Given such excellent new material, Tumbes would typically provide a comic reenactment, but instead, with watery eyes he asked, "Did it hurt? How did you survive?"

"Inti must have protected me. I was standing in the courtyard of the Coricancha Temple during a light afternoon shower. Thunder rumbled in the distance, but there was nothing nearby. I did notice that my hair felt like it was lifting off my head, and my feet itched." Riku served each of us a cup of maize as he spoke. "They told me I lay motionless for three days before I woke in my bed with Topa Inca and the High Priest at my side. I was amazed when they told me I survived a lightning strike. It took a month or so to fully recover, and they both visited me regularly. At first I was stiff and walked with great difficulty, but soon the dreams were the only symptom of my encounter." He paused to eat his cooling soup.

"Two near-fatal accidents while you were still a boy. Remarkable. We always knew you were touched by the gods," Tumbes commented. We ate and spoke among ourselves, while Riku nibbled slowly.

When he finally set his empty cup aside, I asked, "How were your dreams different after . . ." I stopped unsure what to call it, "the accident?"

"I never remembered my dreams before the lightning strike. Afterwards, I frequently dreamt of exotic places like the lake we visited. There were many others: vast stretches of grassland that thundered with the trampling of massive woolly beasts, snowfields extending to the horizon, red deserts devoid of any life, foggy, cold mountains blanketed with gigantic trees whose spicy scent cleared my nose and lungs, and islands with waving trees and rainbow fish swarming in emerald water. I remember all of these, and many more in the minutest detail. In fact, I still dream of these places." He hung his head. "There is one odd thing about the dreams. I've never seen any people."

"But your gift of traveling is remarkable!" Atuk said. "The High Priest must have been pleased."

Riku rubbed his hands together and chuckled, "Yes, Topa Inca and the High Priest often listened to me describe every dream, fascinated with the color of the sky, the acrid taste of the desert air, or the depth of the icy snow. The priest was so trusting, I could have totally fabricated a place with fire-breathing monsters and orange rivers, but I never did." He grinned at the thought of it. "It was Topa Inca's suggestion that I join Chaska at Machu Picchu for training with Cascani, the master diviner."

We rinsed the dishes and tossed the scraps over the mountain edge. Riku filled the pot with water and set it back in the fire. We all quietly performed our tasks as he continued, "So, the High Priest brought me to Machu Picchu to meet Cascani and Chaska. She was just beginning her training and about five years younger than I was. Kaya, you look so much like her. Even some of your mannerisms are the same: the way you tilt your head to the side while you listen, and the way you rock back to your feet after kneeling. Huayna Capac was also struck by the similarity when you met him."

I wondered why he fumbled through the review. I thought I'd done something wrong. He was remembering Chaska. "What was she like? Was she a good student?" I asked.

"She was a beautiful, happy child." Riku seemed pleased to talk about her. "She could sit for days in your garden, singing constantly as she did her weaving assignments, but she was not a traveler. She simply had no interest. Still, as she got older everyone was amazed at her healing gifts. One day Cascani happened to mention a baby in the city who had a most distressing rash. Chaska asked him to describe it thoroughly, and she immediately told him which leaves to pick to make a salve. Skeptical, he did as she requested and the baby was cured!"

"How did she know?" Tumbes asked.

"She said the trees talked to her and told her what to do." He shrugged his shoulders. "I had no expertise with medicines, so I suggested Ixiamas join our training, since that's one of his specialties. He actually spent a year at Machu Picchu, but like me, he was unable to adjust to the new climate and returned to the lowlands." As he spoke, Riku meticulously unrolled one of his packages and removed a length of vine. After rewrapping the others, he started to pound it with a rounded stone on a smooth, slightly concave stone slab.

"Were you ever able to contact the Upper World when you were with Chaska, Ixiamas, and Cascani?" Atuk asked.

He stopped smashing the vine and stared at his work. "No, I'm sorry to say we did not. Chaska and Ixiamas identified several new cures, while Cascani and I explored new places. We all helped Topa Inca with numerous delicate political situations and a few military problems, but we never received any information about the prophecy of Viracocha's return."

"Well, we can do it, maybe even today. We must be half way to the Upper World already," Tumbes optimistically replied.

I wasn't as confident but neglected to say so. "What are you making?" I asked instead.

His gentle eyes lifted to meet mine, and almost apologetically he said, "It's time to accelerate your training." A quick glance to Tumbes and Atuk confirmed that they also noted the darkened tenor. "Tonight we'll travel in a new way. This is the vine Ixiamas brought from the jungle, and by adding the other plants in my pouch, I will make *ayahuasca*." He carefully collected fragments that bounced out of the stone mortar, resumed the pounding, and continued, "You have prepared for this journey with many years of study and each of you brings unique abilities. For the past week you eliminated salt and hot pepper from your food. The climb up Huayna Picchu proves that you are strong and can tolerate physical discomfort. Tonight we will ask the Upper World to show us Viracocha's return."

I wondered how Tumbes had guessed our purpose and gave him a questioning look, but he looked as surprised as Atuk.

The yellowish mash on the mortar oozed with a thin white liquid. Riku worked his way up the remaining section of the vine, reducing the entire piece to a damp fibrous mass. He explained that Ixiamas picked the vine early in the morning following a day of rain when the juice was most potent. Atuk helped him transfer every last drop to the pot of hot water. With equal care he added a handful of dark brown dried leaves and five very ordinary looking oval leaves. "Together these three plants represent our three worlds," he explained. "The dried plant grows close to the earth and knows the secrets of the Other World. The oval leaves are found only in the forest canopy, which touches the sky and the Upper World. The vine connects the worlds with its roots in the ground and its highest tendrils reaching for the sky. It alone contains the milky sap, the river of life in this world. Together they become more powerful than anything you can imagine." He stirred the pot to wet all three components. Satisfied, he carefully placed the wooden spoon at his side.

"Are we ready to begin the ceremony?" Tumbes asked.

"No, the mixture will boil until after dark. Then we will begin. You may explore the area, if you like, but we'll be awake most of the night so I suggest you get some rest."

In the distant west, the same snowy mountains that I saw from the sacred plaza dominated the horizon, but now I was high above the city. For the first time, I could see Salcantay Mountain jutting into the southern sky, its massive, snowcapped peak glowing in the afternoon sun. Repulsed and yet drawn to it, I wondered where Chaska and Collca were buried. Knowing that one day soon I would join them, a peaceful, grateful pride settled in my heart. I too would eternally rest on the magnificent bridge between this world and the Upper World. The mountain was so alluring, I closed my eyes and tried to fly there, but Tumbes interrupted my reverie and invited me to explore Huayna Picchu with him.

The area around the house was really very small with nowhere to go except up to the top along an even steeper path, or down to the city. Inside there were a few jars, cooking pots, and several threadbare blankets. In the corner, carefully placed on a stone slab off the damp ground were three curious items: a small drum decorated with snakes, a gourd rattle painted as the head of a puma, and a gold cup with geometric silver designs on it. We'd never seen instruments or a cup decorated like that, but when we returned to the fire circle to ask Riku about them, he and Atuk were napping. I stirred the clay-colored brew, fascinated by the yellow foam gathering on the surface, and Tumbes spread out his blanket to rest. It was nearly dark before I heard Riku adding more water to the pot and stoking the fire. I woke easily, anticipating the ceremony. "How is the *ayahuasca*?" I asked, smelling the slightly tangy brew mixed with the usual aroma of smoke.

Riku tasted it by the light of a flaming stick. "I have added water for the last time. When this boils down, we will be ready. Please bring four of the empty water jars from the building." I gladly obliged and spaced them evenly around the fire as he directed. With nothing more to do, I stared at the fire and waited. Orange and yellow flames shot up as he added wood and then melted into white-hot embers before he added more. As the night chill descended on the mountain peaks, Atuk and Tumbes awoke and quickly joined us by the fire. We waited in silence until the stars glistened through the thin clouds, and Riku finally announced, "The *ayahuasca* is nearly ready. Please empty your water and tend to any other personal needs. It will be a long night."

When we returned, Riku had spread out a ground cloth for each of us around the fire. Our own blankets were neatly folded and placed beside an empty jar on the cloth. The snake drum sat on a rock to his left, and the cup and puma rattle lay on his blanket to the right. He seated me to his right, Tumbes to his left and Atuk opposite him. When Riku was satisfied with the arrangements, he said, "We are about to begin a most important journey. *Ayahuasca* is a gift from the gods, and if they allow it, we will see the return of Viracocha. You must remember three things through the entire journey. First, we are traveling with the grace and guidance of Inti. Second, we must stay together and always be aware of each other. Third, never stop listening for the rattle and the drum. You will need them to find your way home." He shook the rattle and beat the drum to be sure we all understood. "Oh, one more thing. *Ayahuasca* may upset your stomach or cause other bodily inconveniences. Use the jar to relieve yourself, but do not leave this circle. You could easily step off this mountain in the dark." He paused, looked at each of us, and asked if there were any questions.

No one responded. We were all excited and apprehensive about this new type of adventure. Riku had never made such meticulous preparations, nor been so specific about his instructions. After a nod to each of us he began.

Almighty Inti, hear us your servants.
Grace us with your guidance as we seek the wisdom of the Upper World.
Show us what you will about Viracocha's return.
Help us search for lessons that will benefit all of mankind.
Almighty Inti, grant us your favor and a safe return.

Riku handed the special cup filled with *ayahuasca* to Atuk and said, "Sip this slowly. You will gradually feel its affects. Now remember to listen for the drum and rattle." When Atuk finished, Riku filled the cup for Tumbes and then me before taking one himself.

I looked across the dying embers to Tumbes while Riku maintained a regular rhythm, alternating a drumbeat with a single shake of the rattle. The drink smelled like cold ashes and, considering its deep brown color, had remarkably little taste. Nothing seemed to happen. Maybe the vine had lost its potency over the years. Around me Atuk swayed from side to side, and Tumbes stared into the fire. Warmed by the fire, I removed my shawl and let it fall to the blanket. Riku's drumming faded into the distance, but the rattling moved closer. I could hear each seed as it hit the side of the rattle with maddening regularity. The powerless seeds jumped to the top of the gourd and then tumbled to their resting-place on the bottom, only to be forced to take the dizzying trip again.

Tumbes pointed at the fire and laughed hysterically. He held his stomach, screeched his delight and tried to catch his breath. I searched the fire to find his amusement and immediately saw an enchanting dance. With the drum, the blue flames shot up and then dropped, while the red flames jumped and fell with the rattle. The colors were more transparently vivid than any flower or any gem I'd ever imagined. The delightful bobbing and weaving of the flames ended with a dizzying display, and I reached for my jar to empty my stomach. Even with my eyes closed, I could still see my trusted companions retching beside me while the paired flames gracefully danced and the tormented seeds screamed in anguish.

I lay down on my blanket trying to relieve my stomach spasms when great streaks of lightning blazed before me. Bolts of purple, red, and green flashed and vanished. With each drumbeat a new pattern raced from side to side, then directly toward me. At first jagged bolts alternated with gently curved waves in colors I couldn't name. Then swirling pools created iridescent radial spines. They sparkled more intensely than direct sunlight reflected from a gold plate. Not only could I see my friends and the fire with my eyes closed, I could feel the lights. They tickled my bones, burned my fingers, caressed my breath, cramped my stomach, froze my blood and pinched my eyebrows. As I watched the display of lights, each pattern touched and awakened parts of me that were unknown. Suddenly aware I was made of many small pieces, I felt strangely whole and complete. I wondered if Atuk and Tumbes saw the same lights, but before I could even formulate the question, Atuk replied that the lights were beautiful.

Riku continued the rhythm of the drum and rattle. Hundreds of rays pulsed to the beat forming a circle as each vibrantly colored streak overlapped and yet remained distinct from its neighbor. Through the lights, an eerie dirge drifted into view. The lights continued to flash on and off, and with each renewal, the streams accelerated and collapsed into an ever tighter circle. Finally it coalesced into an intense bluish white ball that appeared and vaporized with the rhythm. Then the sphere spun slowly, flared and expanded to a huge ball before immediately collapsing into a faster rotation. With each rattling cycle, the ball grew bigger until I was totally inside it. I grew and shrank with the pulsating sphere, feeling the immensity of a mountain, the insignificance of a single grain of sand, and the identical essence of both. Reluctantly, I stepped out of the ball. With a horrific explosion, the dazzling sun burst apart into four spinning circles that fell to the ground like shooting stars and spun across the valley in pairs.

As the four of us stood together on a neighboring mountain, I watched the mysterious procession as an anxiety crept into my chest. Had the sun fallen to earth? Where was the sky? I looked up to find the sun setting over the dusty mountains across the valley. The spinning circles on the ground filled my view, but now they carried a glistening, blood-red platform heaped with a tangled jumble of gold and silver statues. Each precious and unique piece was perfectly shaped because the statue held the life of the object inside it. There were stalks of maize, complete with roots, green leaves, mature ears and fine hair, all meticulously encapsulated in gold and decorated with silver. The fragrance of the plentiful harvest filled my lungs even though the golden potatoes, peanuts, guavas, beans, quinoa, peppers, and coca were all similarly entangled on the platform. And yet, fear and anger pounded in my head when I realized the life-giving spirits of the entire empire were unceremoniously dumped on that platform.

In front of the platform a bearded man led four enormous llamas. Compared to the magnificent platform and spinning circles underneath it, they were drab and colorless, as though they were traveling after sunset when color disappears. My angst turned to a sobbing grief when the procession continued north getting smaller and smaller until it disappeared behind a mountain. Exhausted and very thirsty, I listened to the beat of the rattle and drum until I slid into a dreamless sleep.

It was midmorning before I woke in the warm mist. Atuk, Tumbes, and Riku were already drinking a hot tea, but no one spoke. Riku looked exhausted, and Atuk's face was as gray as the ashes surrounding the fire. Sullen and distant, Tumbes stared at the ground. I forced myself to sit up only to discover every muscle ached.

"Have some tea. It will help you feel better." Riku extended a cup to me. "We will rest today and return to the city in the morning. This afternoon, after we have all slept and eaten, we will talk about last night. There is a pot of vegetable soup, with salt and hot pepper when you feel hungry." With that Riku leaned back on his blanket and was asleep instantly. None of us spoke or even moved. I finished the tea and slept until early afternoon, and the others came to life in their own time. It was late afternoon before Riku called us together to review the previous night.

"Kaya, tell us as much as you can remember." Riku spoke slowly, as though his tongue was too big for his mouth. He was always interested in the finest details of our travels, so I precisely recounted everything I could remember, being careful not to embellish the original vision and perhaps alter its meaning. The sun exploding and falling to earth interested him the most even though I assured him the sun was still in the sky. Satisfied he turned to Atuk and asked him the same.

Atuk's description began much like mine, but his account of the moving platform was different as he explained. "I stood with all of you on the mountain, but I was also with the farmers in the valley watching the procession. Fear filled the hearts of all the people, even as they cheered the procession. When it was out of sight, the women cried and the men beat the ground in anger." Filled with their angst, Atuk punched the air and shouted obscenities. After a while he was able to add, "The red platform with the gold statues floated through the air. I didn't see the sun explode into four circles or anything else below the platform." Excited, he told us that he turned into a falcon and followed the procession. His description of flying was different than my trips with Pule, but the exhilarating sense of freedom was the same. Riku asked where the procession went, but all he could remember was north into the green mountains. Then he questioned him about the platform and anything in front of the platform. He said he hadn't examined it because the farmers' reaction was so intense.

Finally Riku turned to Tumbes who had intently listened to our visions. It took no prodding for a broad smile to spread across his face and the story to fall out. "The flames, I want to start with the flames."

Riku nodded.

"At first the flames danced as Kaya described, but later they turned to children, laughing and singing as they covered each other with paint. They tickled and teased one another as they tumbled and played. They were so happy, so content, so innocent. I joined them and danced again as a child. I could have stayed with them forever, but you were all leaving, so I hurried to catch up." He sighed with a lingering sense of loss, and Riku gave him a while to recover before urging him to continue. "I saw the red platform, but I don't know what it carried because the strange llamas preceding were so remarkable. The skinny-legged beasts were huge, at least twice the size of a llama. They looked like they'd fall over with such a large body supported on such thin legs ending with only a single hoof. They had the same long neck as a llama, but were short haired, except along the neck and tail. I asked them what they were, but they couldn't understand me."

"Did you see the sun split and fall to the ground?" Riku asked.

Tumbes shook his head. "No, the sun stayed in the sky, but I did see the spinning circles below the platform." He closed his eyes trying to remember. "I did forget one detail. As I left the children dancing in the fire, all of the children painted red lay down and went to sleep while the blue ones kept dancing."

Riku didn't seem to have any more questions of Tumbes, but looked puzzled. I asked him what he saw. He closed his eyes and rocked as he tried to decide something. "My gift has always related to seeing a place. Even though I saw no people I knew we were in the valley approaching Cajamarca and that Viracocha once again walked as a man. In my vision, the intensely red platform carried only one thing, the Punchau, the icon of Inti that hangs in the Coricancha in Cusco. It is a beautiful likeness made of solid gold and accented with emeralds on the sun's rays. The eyes on the face are made of aquamarine and almost look real as they follow you across the courtyard. In my vision, the colorless, lifeless Punchau lay on the bloody platform entirely devoid of its grandeur."

Still feeling weak and addled from the *ayahuasca*, I tried to focus my thoughts on the similarities and differences in our accounts. The others also pondered in silence as we tried to find the truths that had been revealed to us. Riku was much more experienced at interpreting visions, and I wanted to hear his explanation. "Riku, what does it mean? The stories differ in several places. Is all the information true, or should some be disregarded because of our inexperience?"

He took his time to speak. "That's an excellent question. The voice of the gods is always true, but our perceptions are limited. Look at the view across this valley. The mountain is so steep we can't see the river below and now the clouds cover the peaks. Our view is accurate, just incomplete. We know the river and peaks are there, we just can't see them. In our visions we may or may not know what is hidden." Riku squirmed to find a more comfortable position. No doubt we all suffered from the same stiffness. "I'm certain the *ayahuasca* confirmed that Viracocha will return to earth. Kaya and I both perceived the man. The statues tell us something very valuable will be moved north, causing anger and grief to the people. I know Huayna Capac has considered duplicating Cusco at Tomebamba, so we may simply have seen some of Cusco's treasures being moved. Maybe the people were upset to see so much going to Tomebamba, or they might have been angry for some other reason. The presence of Cajamarca is a mystery. It's on the way to Tomebamba, but if the procession were going to Tomebamba why did Cajamarca appear in my vision at all?" He trailed off and we sat in a stupor again. He startled me from half-sleep when he continued. "We all saw the bright red platform moving in the procession. This must be very important, but I don't understand its significance. Nor do I understand the exploding sun. Still, we should all be grateful to know that the sun will survive Viracocha's return. Everyone saw the sun in the sky, even as the platform moved north." He looked around the circle at his exhausted and fragmented students. "*Ayahuasca* is a trying teacher. We'll rest until morning, but don't forget even the smallest detail of your travels. And now, I will close our ceremony with a prayer." We resettled ourselves and drew a few deep breathes to help us concentrate as he prayed.

Most gracious Inti, thank you for guiding us and sharing your wisdom.
Once again you were generous beyond all measure.
Help us to understand your truths so we can eternally honor you.
Most merciful Inti, thank you for this journey and for our safe return.

Riku added a few sticks to the fire, as Atuk lay down beside it. I wrapped my blanket around me to fend off the damp air and watched the fire. Still uneasy, I tried to stay awake and concentrate on Riku's explanation. Somehow his interpretation didn't seem quite right. From the farmers' fear and my own, I felt something sinister, or false, in Viracocha's return. I was sure there was a much more important message than anything we discussed. Maybe I would be of more use in the Upper World. Maybe because I knew my fellow travelers so well, I would be able to send them the information they needed in ways they could understand.

Inti

Ninan

Riku looked up at my father still seated on his litter, smiled and said, "Welcome back to Machu Picchu." He showed no annoyance or surprise at our premature arrival, a full month in advance of Kaya's scheduled review. Huayna Capac, Pacas, and I had planned to stay at Quispiguanca until then, but we departed without any explanation, while Sinchi Roca stayed behind to host our guests from Quito. After the bearers lowered the Inca's litter to the ground, my father turned on the chair before attempting to stand. Nearly falling as he stepped off the platform, he hobbled toward Riku on the outer edges of his feet.

As usual he rested one hand on Riku's shoulder to greet his old friend. "It's good to be back. Your warmer climate grows more appealing with each passing year." Delighted, he gazed across the city. "Simply glorious. Machu Picchu overlooks the edge of the world. It's as pristine and mystifying as always." Acknowledging Riku he added, "And how are you, my friend?"

"Very well. This place has a way of nurturing those who choose to live here."

Since our arrival was not expected, there were no crowds, only an occasional passerby following his daily routine. Without ceremony, my father and Riku turned to ascend the stairs leading to the Inca's dwelling. I dismissed the bearers, and, hoping to find some *chicha*, Pacas and I followed our elders. Trying to hide his dependency, the Inca leaned on Riku as they walked. Riku allowed the ruse until my father was comfortably seated in his private courtyard and the servants dispatched for refreshments. "I see you're having trouble with your feet again." Riku dropped to his knees to remove my father's sandal. "How long have you had these sores?" he asked as he carefully examined the brown patches covering the reddish skin on the sole of my father's left foot.

"I had a similar sore about two months ago, but it went away. This just appeared last week. I thought it would heal by itself, but it just keeps getting worse. I expect bathing in the hot springs will heal it. Do you have a better cure?" he asked, fully expecting an immediate response.

Riku found that his right foot was also inflamed and without answering Huayna Capac's question he asked, "How do you feel? Have the discussions been going well?"

The Inca tolerated insubordination only from Sinchi Roca and Riku. He relented and answered, "The delegation from Quito was boring and gave me a headache. Rather than go on a hunt, they wanted to finish the agreements. I get tired just thinking about them. Well, now they can wait for my return." He lifted his hand to wipe the sweat from his forehead and caught sight of his palm. "What is this rash? Now there's a spot on my palm."

Riku examined the single sore on his left hand and finally answered, "The healers have told me about it. There is a possible cure, but it doesn't always work. I'm glad that you decided to come to Machu Picchu early. We need to treat this quickly." Two servants returned to the courtyard with *chicha* and popped maize, a special treat for the Inca. We all rested comfortably in the shade and enjoyed the fluffy white delicacy. When the servants left, Riku resumed the conversation. "Have you seen sores like this on any of your women?"

Huayna Capac had already dozed off, but roused himself enough to consider the question. "No, I don't remember seeing any recently, but about six months ago Miski had a few sores on one foot. Do you think it's related?"

"Probably. She must also be treated, or your rash and sores will return."

My father jumped to his feet and exclaimed, "She made me sick? I should have her killed!" Rediscovering his discomfort, he sat immediately.

"Calm down, it's possible you gave them to Miski."

"She had sores before I did. She must have passed them to me." My father huffed.

"It's not that simple. Besides, what is most important is that you're both cured, and all the women you have recently enjoyed are also examined. For now, you must rest while I prepare your treatment. I'll see all of you in the morning." He was gone before I even had an opportunity to ask him about Kaya. I resigned myself to sulking all evening in the courtyard, while Pacas searched for better company with Atuk and Tumbes.

Early the following morning, Riku returned as the servants delivered our breakfast. Much revived by the rest, my father remained seated as he greeted him. "Good morning, Riku. Just being here has improved my health, and I think I'm already healing."

"I'm glad you are feeling better, but we must care for those sores," Riku insisted. "We can deal with the other matters later."

"All right. Inti would surely cure me, but I see no harm in offering a helping hand." Huayna Capac shrugged his shoulders, resigned to endure Riku's cure, whatever it might be.

"Good. We'll leave for the hot springs when you've finished eating. I've already alerted your bearers. Anyone care to come along? We'll return in two days."

I was about to ask if I could visit with Kaya when Pacas eagerly responded, "Ninan and I would like to go. I understand the warm waters are very enjoyable." His pleading eyes begged me to agree. If I visited Kaya, he would have to stay to supervise. I'd waited a year already; I could wait a few more days.

We descended all morning to the river, crossed a bridge, and continued up a streambed on the other side. The trail was only slightly steeper than the road from Quispiguanca, and the bearers had little difficulty carrying the litter. A vigorous man, my father would usually walk such a short distance, but the sores on his feet made that impossible. After passing a small village, we followed the path into the forest. Riku must have sent word ahead, since no one else was at the springs. Pacas wandered up the path beyond the main pool. "Ninan, come look. There are two more pools back here!" Muffled by the dense forest, his voice was barely discernable.

I looked at Riku, and he pointed with his chin. "You may use the third pool." With Riku's help, my father stepped off the litter, and I followed Pacas deeper into the forest.

Since I wouldn't see Kaya for a few days, I might as well enjoy this lovely place. I paused at the second pool where a vine hung in a shaft of sunlight until Pacas backtracked to find me. We walked the short distance to the third pool that was just large enough for four people. Surrounded by well-worn stones, the pool abutted a moss-covered granite wall. Along the edge of the rest of the clearing, ferns and low bushes provided a tranquil privacy. I had already removed the sling from my head and my cloak. The rest fell off as quickly, and we slipped into the clear, warm water.

"When you are Inca, I think you should build your palace around a hot spring." Pacas grinned as he leaned back until his head dropped to the stone behind him.

"If I did, I'd never get you out of it. I suppose you want me to hold all negotiations in it too. Wouldn't it be hard to keep the *quipu* dry?"

"I'll manage," he said without opening his eyes.

I spread my arms on the rocks behind me and relaxed. Overhung by motionless trees, the place had a small fire circle at one end, a bench opposite me near the path, and our clothes strewn between them. Totally limp and empty headed, I joined Pacas in a short nap. What was enjoyably warm when we entered seemed hot when I awoke. I nudged Pacas who was also ready to get out. We dried quickly in the cool air as we dressed and then headed toward the main pool. My father wasn't enjoying the pools as we had. "Ow, that hurts. Must you do that?" Huayna Capac sat sideways to the pool, one foot dangling in the water and his other leg extended along the rocks on a blanket.

"Yes, we need to remove all the scabs to be sure. Now hold still so I can finish." Riku saw us returning. "Did you enjoy the waters?"

We both enthusiastically answered and asked if we could help. "In fact, you can. By my cloak over there you'll find a large jar wound with cloth. I'll need the jar, a large shallow bowl, and a cup from the fire circle."

We collected his supplies and joined them by the pool.

"Pour about a quarter of the maize into the shallow bowl."

After carefully removing the cloth and cap, Pacas estimated the amount as he poured the finely ground maize interspersed with a gray powder.

"Add some of the warm pool water to the bowl and stir it up."

The instant the water touched the powder, the sickening stench of rotting grain overlaid a familiar sweet and sour scent I couldn't place.

"That smells bad enough to be a cure," my father remarked.

"Yes, I think it will be strong enough," Riku responded unemotionally. Having finished with father's second foot, Riku allowed him to soak them in the pool. He stirred the mash, took a deep whiff and added some more water. He studied my father's haggard face and said, "The medicine is prepared, so whenever you're ready, we'll bandage your feet and hand."

Huayna Capac sat for a moment enjoying the water and then nodded. Riku pressed the mash into each of the open sores and then across each foot. Using the cloth from the jar, Pacas and I bound his feet and tied the ends together as Riku instructed. My father looked relieved, if not comfortable, when we finished.

"The bandages will remain overnight," Riku told us. "Tomorrow we'll repeat the process in the morning and again in the evening. By the following morning, your feet should be healing, and we can return to the city." Riku looked satisfied, but tired. He gave us some instructions for the meal before slowly heading toward the upper pools. My father lay on a blanket and slept instantly.

The following day, Riku cared for my father continuously. I still wanted to ask him about Kaya, but he was always preoccupied with the Inca. Pacas and I lounged in the pools, explored the forest beyond them and circled back to the river. The day was enjoyable, but my thoughts continually returned to Kaya and the original purpose of our visit. The year had passed quickly, and her fate would be decided very soon. As expected, Huayna Capac's feet were substantially better on the second morning, and we left for the city after Riku bandaged them yet again. My father chose to ride to the top, but I challenged Pacas to a race. Knowing that each rising step took me closer to Kaya, I ran until my legs and chest burned. Having reached the main plaza in record time, Pacas stood with his feet spread and his hands on his knees. "That's the fastest," he inhaled, "you've ever run. What's your hurry? Did Riku give you permission to visit Kaya?"

My arms folded over my head, I too struggled to reply, "Not yet, but I'll ask him as soon as they arrive. I want to spend the entire afternoon with her."

He still gasped as he spoke, "Let's go to your father's house to wait. We can get something to drink, and we won't miss their arrival."

Saving myself the effort of speaking, I nodded, and we slowly crossed the plaza and climbed the stairs to the Inca's house. We were fully recovered when my father's deep voice announced their return. Riku helped him to a bench, and the servants immediately served his favorite bittersweet beer.

Looking exhausted, Riku wandered to a distant bench on the opposite side of the courtyard. I strolled over to sit beside him. "Thank you for curing my father. He looks tired, but much better than when we arrived."

"Yes, he does. I think the medicine will completely cure him, but his love of women will no doubt cause the illness again. Did you see how I treated him? You may need to instruct someone in the future."

I hadn't considered the possibility of a reoccurrence. It was inconceivable that my father, the Inca, son of a god, could be seriously ill. "Yes, I saw the treatment, but what was mixed with the maize?"

He chortled wearily. "It's exactly what you thought. Did you get a deep enough whiff that you would recognize it again?"

I nodded.

"As you know, maize can rot if it isn't stored properly. Sometimes, when it's warm and moist, a grey hairy moss will grow on it. The maize I used was rotting in this way. I had the maize and moss ground together into a fine powder. You must remember the smell. If it's not the same smell, the medicine won't work."

Astounded that rotting maize could be so useful, I promised to remember. Together we watched the servants caring for my father. "You look very tired. Will you rest today?"

"As soon as I finish my beer, I'll advise him to sleep, and I'll go rest as well. Tomorrow will be an important day." He lifted his beer slowly, as if it were a great effort.

I hoped he would continue, but when he didn't I asked, "What will happen tomorrow?"

He slumped forward resting his elbows on his knees. "The Inca wants to review our progress. On the way back, he decided to meet with Kaya, Atuk, Tumbes, and me in the morning. She is learning so quickly, we could all benefit by keeping her longer."

I thought I'd have more time! I had to meet with Kaya before the review. My head pounded harder than when I was running. I tried to casually ask, "May I visit with Kaya this afternoon? I'd like to see her before tomorrow's review. Maybe I can help you influence my father."

Riku considered my request for what seemed like a long time and thoughtfully responded, "Yes, perhaps you can help, but remember, tomorrow is an important day. You can't upset her." He finished his beer and added, "I'll take you and Pacas there." A wave of relief rolled over me, but I held it inside. When Riku was ready, the three of us ascended the stairs to Kaya's terrace.

Kaya faced the barren winter fields and watered a bush near the end of the garden. I scrambled down the ladder as she turned to wave to Riku standing above us. She was so beautiful, I could do nothing but stare. Healthy again, her gracefully rounded face complemented her broadening hips and swelling chest. She put down her watering jar and glided towards us with her arms extended.

Pacas descended, and reminded me to move away from the ladder so he could step to the ground. In a hushed voice, he said, "She's absolutely stunning, and no longer a child."

"Ninan, Pacas, how nice to see you again." Surprising both of us, she quickly embraced Pacas and then me, adding a kiss to my cheek. "Come, sit in the shade and tell me about yourselves." The lovely, long eyelashes and penetrating eyes were all that remained of the skinny young girl I fell in love with. Not only had she grow considerably taller and initiated her womanly curves, her entire being blossomed into a cheerful young woman. The transformation was even more evident in her carefree movement as we walked together to her shelter. Under her charming direction, I sat directly opposite her, and Pacas sat nearby. She immediately reached for the cups and jar of beer as she spoke. "I saw you arrive a few days ago and heard from Iska that you were going to the hot springs for our father's health. How is he? Is he recovering, or are you about to become the Inca?" She beamed with playful enthusiasm.

"Riku is an excellent healer. The Inca is regaining his health and will no doubt live a long life," I answered, ignoring her presumption.

"And mother? Is she happier?" She sincerely wanted to know about the woman she had seen for only an instant.

"I'm afraid we left her with visitors to entertain at Quispiguanca. She is no doubt annoyed with father for leaving, but she didn't realize how sick he was. She has plenty of help and will manage." Our eyes locked. "And how are you? You look healthy—and beautiful."

A radiant smile spread across her face that seemed to reverberate through her. "I've never been better. I'm healthy, and I love it here." She talked about her work and even showed us one of her recent, very impressive *cumbi* weavings. When she asked about Pacas and me, I told her about presiding over civil disputes. She laughed at the trivial arguments I shared with her and their ignoble reactions to my judgments. She thought they sounded more like children than the elite of Cusco. She was equally interested to hear Pacas' explanation of the intricacies of recording the proceedings of various trade negotiations. At first he was uncomfortable speaking with her, but noting her sincere interest in a skill where he excelled, Pacas soon relaxed and spoke freely.

As the afternoon passed, my fascination grew with each turn of her head and waving hand. Well schooled in womanly activities, she was also wise beyond her experience. Her head tilted to one side, she absorbed every word, every gesture and every thought, and somehow she even understood the political intrigue that defined Cusco. Drawn to her like a bee to the hive, I doubled my resolve to have her as my wife, although I still hadn't asked her. Pacas stood to wander through the garden, and I suggested we walk as well. We chatted as I guided her partially down the terrace and then back until we stood just under the roof of her garden shelter. At a natural break in our conversation I turned her toward me and gently began, "Kaya, I need to ask you something." My quiet voice and serious expression immediately subdued her demeanor.

She glanced at Pacas at the opposite end of the garden, and then reached for my hands, "What is it, my dear brother?"

I couldn't look into her eyes, but instead stared at our interwoven hands. "Our father is a healthy man, but one day he will die, and I expect to become the Inca." She already knew this and waited for me to continue. "Since the moment I first saw you, I've loved you. We have spent very little time together, and yet, you know me better than anyone, except perhaps Pacas."

"Yes, I feel the same bond. It's as if we have known each other our whole lives. We understand one another. I even hear your voice when we are apart." She fell silent, continuing to hold my hands.

I didn't think this would be so hard. Why did I hesitate? She waited. "As Inca I will need a queen. I want to marry a noble woman who will bear many children and will lead the work of the Mamaconas. More importantly, I want a partner, someone I love and trust. I need someone who will help me as the Inca, someone wise, someone with visions, someone like you." I finally lifted my head to see her placid eyes perfectly suited to her radiantly soft face. "Kaya, will you marry me and become my queen?"

Her hands went limp and slid back to her sides, while her eyes opened so wide, I could have seen her soul. Perfectly still and suddenly pale she stared at me in total disbelief. "I am honored you consider me worthy to be your queen, but you know I'm to be killed." Then she added, "How could you be so cruel to even suggest such a thing? How can you think this is even possible?"

I'd considered many options, and gave her my best answer, "I will ask Huayna Capac to spare you. Surely he can find another to take your place." I didn't mention, but I had heard a rumor that might help her.

With a furrowed brow, she leaned toward me. "Have you told Riku your plan?"

I shook my head. "I understand someone must be sacrificed, but why must it be you?"

Kaya turned away, walked a few steps and turned back. "The training, the expectations of the people. Can we really ignore them?"

"Why not? I will be Inca. I can change the rules. I can command Riku to find another."

"Ninan, being your wife and a mother is a dream I never even allowed myself to consider. I would be honored to marry you, but it seems impossible."

"I will find a way." I took her hand and drew her close. In a tight embrace, her head nestled into my neck, and her small breasts pressed against my chest while her soft, mellow scent filled my hollow body. When she pulled away slightly, I leaned into her for a passionate and illicit kiss. Deep and warm, she gave herself to me completely. Finally I'd found what was lacking with Mama Runtu, an unbreakable intertwining of two lives.

"Iska is coming. I can hear her above us." I hadn't really noticed Pacas' footsteps quickly approaching.

Reluctantly, but without hesitation we separated. The longing in her eyes drew me closer, but Pacas held my shoulder. Iska's shape hovered over the ladder in the lengthening shadows.

At a brotherly distance I softly said, "Kaya, be patient. I have much to do. Tomorrow, you must do exactly as Riku expects. I will address you formally like a distant acquaintance. But remember, I want you as my wife."

She nodded as Iska stepped off the bottom rung of the ladder. "Hello, Iska, how are you this evening?" Kaya spoke in a completely normal voice.

After saying our formal good-byes, Pacas and I climbed up the ladder, and I was confident that she would play her role perfectly.

The following morning, the sun hung in a flawlessly blue sky when I joined Pacas and my father in the courtyard for a late breakfast. The shrubs and ferns surrounding us looked brighter than I remembered; in fact everything sparkled with new vibrancy. After meeting with Kaya, the dread of her review was entirely gone.

My father looked up from his plate and casually commented, "You look well rested today. The hot springs brought you back to good health as well." He returned to his plate.

"Yes, I believe you're right. The springs and warmer weather here are most enjoyable." I couldn't disclose the real cause for my improved disposition.

"Come, eat. Riku and his students will join us shortly."

Preoccupied with his food, Pacas didn't look very happy. We had avoided talking about our visit with Kaya the previous evening, since he didn't approve of my advances. Still, I knew he wouldn't betray me. I ate quickly, and the servant cleared the dishes as Riku arrived. He glided across the courtyard, apparently entirely recovered from the rigors of treating my father. If he were anxious about the review, he hid it completely. In fact, he looked relaxed as he greeted us, "Atuk and Tumbes are bringing Kaya. They'll be here very soon." Speaking directly to my father he queried, "Is there anything else we require?"

"No, I'm ready." He stood and walked with only a slight limp to his favorite bench along the north wall which still lingered in the morning shade. I followed and stood beside him. Pacas observed from the doorway into the house.

Riku drifted over and stood in the sun facing us. "You appear to be healing well," he said with a smile. "I'll change your bandages later. Perhaps in another few days, your treatment will be completed."

My father hated to be inconvenienced in any way and being dependent on Riku displeased him. He grunted an ungrateful response. Behind Riku, Atuk entered the courtyard followed by Kaya and Tumbes. Kaya joined Riku, and Atuk stood on her other side. Tumbes took his place next to Atuk. Even lovelier than the previous day, Kaya captivated me. Her white dress featured a unique green and black design along the bottom. Even though she ignored me, my eyes wanted to follow her every movement. I forced myself to see the entire group.

Huayna Capac initiated the conversation without the stumbling of the previous review. "Good morning to all of you." They responded similarly, and he continued, "Atuk, Tumbes, you've grown strong in the past year. Inti must be pleased with you. Kaya, Riku didn't exaggerate when he said you regained your vitality and added womanly features." Bowing her head, she blushed without answering.

"You must visit Kaya's garden. She transformed a weed patch into a piece of the Upper World." Riku said to break the Inca's intense stare.

My father closed his eyes and shook his head before replying. "Well, yes, perhaps I will." Regaining his composure, he continued. "Kaya, we are here to review your progress. What did you learn in the past year?"

"I learned all of the standard woven patterns including those representing each of the crops, each of the moons of the year and, of course, all the symbols of the gods and the great Incas. I even created a few designs, as you can see in the bird pattern in my dress." Unhurried, her motions were entirely natural as she held out her dress for examination. "Unfortunately I forgot several songs, but I relearned them, and many others. Riku, Tumbes and Atuk helped me relearn the Inca histories and several of our traveling practices." My love's voice was a higher pitch than I remembered, but no one seemed to notice the slight tension.

"And what do you think was your greatest accomplishment in the past year?" My father tested her maturity. I'd seen him ask the same question to leaders from all over the empire.

She blinked slowly and motioned to her companions. "Under Riku's leadership, we traveled many times. We continue to expand our ability to send and receive information accurately." She looked at Riku for approval. "During our greatest vision we saw a moment during Viracocha's return."

Huayna Capac glared at Riku, who continued to watch Kaya. Apparently Riku hadn't reviewed this important new information with him. My father was forced to turn his attention back to Kaya as she relayed their remarkable vision. All my life I heard stories of healers who envisioned cures, and diviners who dreamed of the future. I never believed any of them; there was always another explanation. These were four people I respected, and none was capable of deception. Now I was certain I wanted Kaya as my queen. Her gift would benefit the entire empire. She completed her story, and silence settled over the group.

Riku waited for my father to comment, but when he didn't, he summarized, "Inti generously allowed each of us to view the same event, giving us more detail to interpret than a single person could receive. We spent many sessions reviewing the vision and concluded several important messages. First, we are all certain the ancient prophecy is correct, and Viracocha will again walk on earth as a man. We also think it is very important that the people along the road were afraid and outraged, but we don't understand why. It is essential to note that although she was the only one to sense it, Kaya feels certain there is something false about this event. Finally, we know that a large amount of gold, and perhaps even the Punchau will travel north after his arrival."

My father, the son of Inti, and Riku considered various possible reasons for the people's response. Maybe they were angry to see so much of their hard work moving north. Maybe they were afraid Viracocha would punish them for their wrong doings. Maybe they didn't recognize Viracocha and thought the gold was stolen. Maybe they were afraid of the strange beast she mentioned. There were so many possible reasons. The students respectfully stood through the entire discussion until I noticed Tumbes whisper something to Atuk.

Riku continued, "There are other troubling aspects to this vision as well. Perhaps you understand them." The Inca puffed out his chest a little farther and simply told him to proceed. "We don't understand why Viracocha was traveling alone. Why is there no escort, or the Inca himself? Surely, the Inca, son of Inti, would meet our returning creator. Secondly, the platform was a vivid, unforgettable red. That must be significant since all four of us clearly saw it. What is so important about that platform? The last question is the identity of the strange beast in front of the platform. Why would Viracocha arrive with a monster when llamas are so plentiful?"

The conversation continued between Riku and Huayna Capac. I only partially listened to the increasingly preposterous interpretations until my father mentioned the Quito visitors. Pacas and I had only just arrived at Quispiguanca when my father decided to leave for Machu Picchu, so we didn't participate in any of the discussions with them.

"Perhaps the northern visitors are right," my father offered in a halting, quiet voice. He hated for someone else to have better insight than he did. "They were complaining about the Inca leaders in the north and implied that I don't know what they are doing. They claim the Curacas overwork the people and then refuse to pay them according to the agreements, so the people see no benefit to paying tributes."

Riku listened intently, trying to reconcile the vision and the information from the visitors. Atuk whispered back to Tumbes, and they both stared at something in the sky behind me. I glanced back, but was too close to the wall to see anything. My father continued, "They think the Cayambis and Carangues will overthrow their leaders, and that such an act would threaten the stability of the entire north."

Riku rested his forehead on his thumb and forefinger. With a furrowed brow, he stared at the ground and asked the Inca, "And what do they propose you do about it?"

"They want us to form an even tighter alliance in order to stop a rebellion before it starts. For gold, they will provide soldiers, if I provide the leadership. In addition, they want me to build a city like Cusco in either Cajamarca or Tomebamba."

How I wished I had met with them. Ever since our trip to Tomebamba, I tried to stay current with the events of the north. This poor leadership contradicted everything I'd heard about Hatun and Conono, my friends who now governed Tomebamba.

"And what have you decided to do?" Riku asked. Tumbes and Atuk were getting restless. Tumbes kept shifting his weight from one foot to the other, while Atuk crossed his arms on his chest and then dropped them to his side. Distracted by their restlessness, Kaya glanced at Atuk and then followed his eyes to the sky. She looked puzzled.

"The bridge to the Upper World will be successful or Viracocha couldn't have returned," my father replied. "To be traveling north, he must have crossed the bridge, traveled south to Cusco to collect the gold and then returned to Cajamarca in the north. We can conclude from his safe passage that I will be successful in securing peace in the north."

"So your visitors' requests concur with the vision," Riku said, accepting his logic.

The restlessness was changing to worry, and I fought to concentrate on my father's conclusions. "I will agree to their plan. My preference is to enhance Tomebamba, my birthplace. We already have a presence there, but if you're sure Viracocha was heading to Cajamarca, I'll consider building there instead." Riku nodded as my father continued, "If we are to do battle with the Cayambis and Carangues, it is risky to use only northern soldiers and Inca leaders. We will use their men, but most must come from the south. Otherwise the Quito leaders could claim the victory as their own, depose Inca rule, and establish sovereignty themselves."

"Your plan seems flawless. I'm pleased our group helped you formulate your response. Now, we have Kaya's situation."

Fully alert, I tried to ignore the increasingly distracting whispers and constant motion among the students. "We have made exceptional progress in the past year. Kaya is very gifted and keeping her with us will benefit your planning and increase the possibility of communicating with her, and Chaska, in the Upper World. Besides, she has not begun her monthly cycles."

Riku stated the case very well, and, wanting to help without revealing my motive, I suggested, "Father, it will take you over a year to prepare for your march north. Where's the harm in waiting another year?"

Huayna Capac seemed inclined to agree with us as he considered his answer. He closed his eyes to think.

Kaya started to cry. First tears started to trickle down her face and then her body shook with sobbing as she stood with the others. Tumbes and Atuk could barely contain themselves even though they tried to regain their composure before the Inca noticed. Riku moved closer to Huayna Capac and in his whispered tones the only words I heard were Chaska and Kaya. My father was nodding his head. Muffled cries carried over the wall of the courtyard from all directions. "Praise Inti. Forgive us. Don't forsake us."

Atuk fell to his knees and Tumbes pointed to the sun and screamed in anguish, "Inti, don't leave us!"

I stepped out of the shadow of the wall and turned around. Nearly half the sun had vanished leaving a crescent shape like a half moon. "Father! Look! The sun is disappearing!" I shouted.

In spite of the bandages, the Inca sprang to his feet and ran to the center of the courtyard. Riku trembled, and his knees collapsed as tears built in his eyes. The howling and pounding on the drums beyond the walls grew to a feverish pitch until I could no longer hear myself. A gray cast filled the courtyard like a threatening storm, except there were absolutely no clouds in the sky.

My father bellowed over the roar. "We will go to Intihuatana and plead for Inti's return." He turned on his bandaged feet and without breaking into a run, ascended the stairs to the sacred plaza, continued past the Temple of Ilyapa and up to the highest terrace. Riku kept my father's pace, as did we all. Normally the gold-plated monolith dazzled in the sunlight and even the moonlight, but its wonder faded in the increasing darkness. We encircled Intihuatana and faced the sun, now almost three quarters gone. Riku led the chant, and we shouted in unison.

Inti, don't abandon your children.
Inti, forgive us.
Inti, we beg you, return to us.

In the main plaza below and across the terraces, people shouted, beat their drums, sounded the conch shell trumpets and invented ways to make as much noise as possible. We must get Inti's attention and show him our devotion. We must convince him to return. An eerie chill settled on the mountain as all color turned to gray. The western sky grew ominously dark, enticing a few stars to shine through the glowing twilight.

With only a small, brilliant point of light remaining, Huayna Capac fell to his knees beside me. No longer chanting, my father prayed to Inti in his deep, booming voice. "Inti, my merciful father, I beg your forgiveness. Do not punish all your servants for my transgressions. As you have commanded, I will give you my daughter. She will be yours at the next winter solstice. Inti, my merciful father, return your favor to us and we will honor you forever."

Instead of the unison prayer, I railed at Inti's cruelty, blamed him for the ills of the world and dared him to take her from me. I couldn't hear myself over the increasing din, but through my watering eyes, I saw my dearest sister halfway around the circle still chanting with Riku and the others. She couldn't have heard our father on his knees beside me. With his prayer, the sun stopped as Inti considered his promise. Still on his knees, and his eyes closed, he repeated incessantly. "Inti, my merciful father, she will be yours. She will be yours."

I screamed obscenities, stamped the ground and hurled rocks at the sun. Slowly, very slowly, as though Inti still hadn't decided what to do, the sun peaked out and grew to a thin sliver. The pall of death gradually lifted, and the anguished shouting changed to grateful cheers. Riku's new chant gradually spread around the circle.

Inti, our almighty father, we thank you.
Inti, our merciful father, we love you.
Inti, our benevolent father, we will honor you always.

The cheers, chanting and drums continued with the same intensity until the entire sun shone brightly, and Intihuatana once again reflected its brilliance.

Gradually, the shouting subsided, but the disappearance of the sun was a sign of Inti's displeasure and an omen of disaster. Riku and Huayna Capac were already discussing the sacrifices to be made to thank Inti for returning and to mitigate his anger. Not only would there be sacrifices here, but in Quito and Cusco. Runners would deliver the instructions, and the coordinated ceremonies would continue for a week. Kaya stared across the valley, now bathed in sunlight.

Suddenly Pacas was by my side and whispered, "Come with me. You don't want her to see you like this." He led me past the sacred plaza, down the stairs and back to Atuk's house.

"He promised to kill her at the next Inti Raymi. In ten months she'll be gone," I wailed. "I can't live without her. I must save her." I couldn't believe what just happened.

Passage

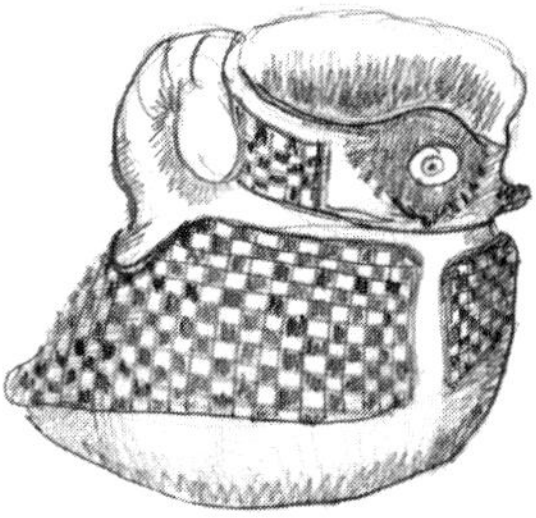

Kaya

Because we hadn't foreseen the disappearance of the sun, I was scared and confused. If we were diviners, surely we should have known of an impending disaster, even if we hadn't specifically asked about it. I wondered if Huayna Capac had recovered from his illness, or did he only appear to be healthy? Riku once mentioned that such an event foretold the death of an Inca, or his heir. Ninan. Maybe that's why he hadn't visited me immediately, or even the next day. No, he was all right; although I couldn't distinguish his words, I occasionally heard his voice rise from Atuk's house on a terrace below me. When the sun reappeared, Riku immediately went to Huayna Capac's side. Seeing me alone, Atuk brought me back to my garden, but I'd heard from no one in the day and a half since he left me. No one remembered that I even existed.

Unable to concentrate, I chose a task that required little attention, cleaning and carding wool, and listened to the eerie sounds around me. The birds hid in my guava tree without song, although I could hear an occasional flutter as they moved among the branches. On the stairs below me, the frightened women spoke in hushed, anxious voices while unattended babies whined beside them. Beyond them, the farmers should have been preparing the fields for planting, but instead they stood in small groups, leaning on their plows. Occasionally one shook his head, stamped his foot, or extended an arm toward the sun. Everyone was badly shaken by the sun's disappearance. Even though it returned to the sky, the event surely warned of a catastrophe.

All day I sat under the guava tree in a muggy heat that was too warm for early spring. At first the wool I carded was fairly clean, but in the afternoon it was filled with stickers and bits of dung. Instead of a rote task, cleaning wool became a filthy chore that annoyed me with constant pricks and the nasty taste of the dust emanating from the wool. Adding to my discomfort, the acrid smoke of the sacrifices had saturated the air since dawn and would no doubt continue until sunset for many days. The odor of burning flesh and wool cloth disagreeably mingled with the stench of rotting maize they must have discovered as they prepared for the sacrifices. Maybe it was the heat, or the stink, or the mandatory elimination of salt and pepper for all witnesses. Whatever the reason, my stomach hurt with a constant, dull ache, and my head throbbed in protest. I planned to stay in my garden until the moon rose over the mountains, anticipating that the cooler, cleaner air would heal me, but aggravated with my work and Ninan's absence, I decided to go to bed early. I climbed the ladder, passed Iska who completely ignored me, and went directly to my bed. I pulled the blankets over my head to put an end to the day. Still uncomfortable, I lay on my side, drew my knees to my chest, and wrapped my arms around them. The nauseating smell still clung to the house as I fell asleep.

"Pule! I'm so glad to see you. What a pleasant surprise," I welcomed her as she landed on the garden fence post.

"I thought you might like some company during these difficult times," she responded as she flapped her wings, causing a loose feather to drop to the ground.

"Very true. I've been forgotten in the excitement of the sun's disappearance. Did you see it?"

"No, where I was, the sun shone brightly all day, but I heard about it."

"Does this mean Huayna Capac will die?" I asked.

"Well, of course he will die, at some point. How else will he return to the Upper World?" She plucked another feather as she looked around my moonlit garden. "I see you've been tending your garden. It looks much better than the last time I visited. And what else keeps you busy?"

"I finally met my father and mother," I hesitated, "And my brother, Ninan. He said he would visit me, but I haven't seen him since the event."

"He's probably busy helping your father. Maybe we should go for a trip since no one has demands on you at the moment."

"Where should we go? Anywhere away from here would satisfy me."

"You once said you wanted to visit the mountains. Let's go to the highest peak and then down to the ocean. Have you ever been to the ocean?"

"I saw it from the mountains when you last visited. I'd like to get closer."

"What are we waiting for?" she asked as she stretched her wings, pulled twice and was airborne.

Just as easily I spread my arms and followed her. "Why can't I fly unless I'm with you?" I asked as we passed over the city gate. "I've tried many times, but I've never even felt light on my feet."

"Flying is a gift that can only be granted by the gods. Perhaps you forget to ask for permission, or perhaps you wanted to fly to escape rather than to discover."

"My intentions affect my ability to fly?"

"They influence everything you do, not just flying," she answered solemnly as we continued to rise toward the gibbous moon. With a nostalgic sigh she added, "Flying in the moonlight is best. Everything sleeps so peacefully."

"I like it too. You can't see the colors of the flowers at night, but the soft shadows are comforting. Killa gives us just enough light to fill the darkness." I looked down on the treeless mountaintops drifting away from us as we crossed one range and approached a grassy plain. "Where are we going? We passed the mountains already."

"There are even larger ones in front of us. Besides, this is the way to the ocean." She continued while I variously marveled at her wings shining in the moonlight, the passing villages, and the dark forests below us. We climbed again in the shadow of the western range until we finally sailed over the top to be suddenly flooded with light almost as bright as day.

"This is wonderful! Can we stop here for a while?" I asked.

"Not just yet. We'll go down the other side and find a place to stop." I followed her until she landed on a flat rock beside a sparkling field that I assumed was covered with snow. I could see the snow on the mountains from Machu Picchu, but I'd never been close to it. "You can walk on it, if you like," she encouraged me.

I immediately stepped down off the boulder to find myself in knee-deep snow. "It's soft . . . and cold!" I said laughing as I lifted my sandaled foot and bare leg out of the snow to take another step. "And it's slippery," I added as I ungracefully landed on my bottom and slid down the slope.

"That's why I wanted to find a solid rock. Sometimes the snow is packed hard, but at other times it's as light as your puffs of wool, and deeper than a tall building. At night it's difficult to judge."

Still sitting in the snow, I threw my hands into the air and watched the delicate snowflakes gently floating back to me. I even threw some at Pule, who was much less enthusiastic. In a short while, I shook with the cold, so I stood carefully and clambered up the slope to Pule's rock. Covered with snow, I stamped my feet and brushed it off my dress and skin. The snow on my arms turned to drops of water. "It's just cold water!" Maybe someone had told me that, but either I didn't remember, or didn't understand.

"Yes, remarkable isn't it? Ilyapa is very clever to freeze the water into snow so it will stay on the mountains in the winter. Then through the spring and summer, when Inti is strongest, it slowly melts so it can find its way to the valleys below. With the water and the blessings of the mother earth, the farmers are able to grow their crops and prepare for the cold, dry winter. Meanwhile, the river flows to the mother of the ocean who welcomes the gifts from the land and promises to share her infinite waters. Without the generosity of all the gods, living in these mountains would be very difficult for the trees, your garden, the crops, and the people."

Little bumps covered my arms, either from the cold, or this beautiful plan. "I assumed the trees and wild plants would always thrive. It never occurred to me that they suffered from drought like the crops."

"It's impossible for any living thing to live apart from the others. Viracocha planned it that way." She looked at my wet clothes and concluded, "We need to find a warmer place for you. Let's go down to the ocean."

Sad to leave the snow behind, but anxious to be warm again, I followed Pule through the mountain pass and down the western slope. I dried quickly as we watched our shadows dive into chasms, disappear, and then suddenly hop to the opposite edge and continue to follow us. To enhance the shadow dance, Pule flew in loops, dove and powered straight up. One time she flew fast enough to pace a vicuna running across the slope. It looked like her shadow was actually riding it. I followed her antics, laughing and playing like the child I was never allowed to be. As we descended even lower, we played shadow tag, and I giggled as our shadows touched although we were distant from one another. I chased Pule, who easily evaded me, until she allowed me to catch her. After letting me rest, she immediately tagged me, and again I began my frolicking pursuit. Passing over grazing alpacas, freshly plowed fields, rivers, and wide stretches of barren rock, we descended gradually to a sandy beach surrounded by rocky cliffs beside the ocean. Pule gracefully landed on a bone-white log that jutted out of the sand, and I sat beside her. "Look, now the moonlight is playing tag with the water. Each wave rises to touch the moonlight and then falls into darkness to hide."

"Even the gods like to play," she replied. "Let's stay here and watch them for a while."

The rolling, gurgling waves stumbled onto the beach to release a sheet of water that climbed out of the ocean and wet my feet before slithering back to its depths. New waves formed with a steady rhythm, but knowing the sea was their home, they gradually receded as they rocked the sea to sleep. On the sandy shore, stranded plants and conical shells glistened in the moonlight until they dried in the warm, sweet-scented breeze. Falling toward the horizon, the brilliant moon lit a path directly to my feet. Even though the heaviness in my belly still bothered me, I yearned for more. "Pule, can we follow the path across the ocean to the horizon?"

She shook her head as though I had woken her before answering, "We have followed the snowflakes from the mountaintops to their home in the ocean, and still you ask to explore farther."

"Killa lights an enticing path. How can I refuse?"

"With no idea where it goes, you wish to follow it." She paused. "We can go, but you will lead. It's time you understood the implications of traveling alone."

That sounded like a warning, but I immediately left our roost and headed out to sea. Pule flew behind me at a distance. How difficult could it be? The path was so bright, I could easily follow it out and back to our shore. The sea stretched before me, and I gladly watched the sparkling waters of the endless rolling waves filled with millions of small fish and an occasional family of enormous ones. High above us, seabirds soared effortlessly among the wispy clouds. Enjoying my adventure and content to lead across the watery expanse, I pressed on to find the horizon. Fish jumped so high, they seemed to fly beside me and birds dived into the ocean and disappeared. There was always something new and in my excitement I almost failed to notice the clouds gradually covering the moon and obscuring our path. I turned to Pule and said, "I think we should return before the path disappears." She didn't answer, but followed me as I circled around and headed back to shore.

I hadn't realized how far I'd flown and now hurried to reach land before the path entirely vanished. When the moon shone, I made special note of its direction because at times the clouds entirely hid the light, and I flew unguided. The hazards of traveling alone were obvious, and I'd learned Pule's lesson. I was about to ask her for help when I was finally saw the dark outline of the coast. Now even without the lighted path, I made my way to shore, but to my dismay, I wasn't at the place I'd left behind. I had no idea which way to turn. I landed in a huge tree and stared down at a small fire on the beach. By the light of the fire, I saw motion emerging from the shadowed forest. A single man, silver from head to foot, walked along the shore carrying a large piece of cloth attached to a long pole. He strutted back and forth with his arm extended toward the ocean. Finally he stuck the pole in the sand, dropped to his knees, bowed his head to his folded hands and muttered something I couldn't understand.

Pule landed beside me and without rancor said, "You were wise to turn back when you did. At least you were able to find the land. If you'd gone much farther, you could have wandered over the ocean forever. We need to return to our beach. Leave this place with me."

With no idea where our beach was, I happily followed her as she headed south along the coastline. When we arrived, the moon had set and the waves seemed very distant in the darkness. Always facing the warm breeze rising off the ocean, Pule preened her feathers and said, "We'll rest awhile before returning to Machu Picchu."

I sat quietly trying to memorize the fresh salty smell of the ocean intertwined with a fading flowery aroma and drying seaweed. I wanted to remember every detail for my lonely days in the garden: the shapes of the fish, the sounds of the waves, the sand being pulled through my toes, the mysterious northern beach and its resident.

At last Pule asked, "Do you see Mayu lighting our path?"

"Yes! The river of stars lifts out of the ocean and ends behind us in the mountains. From Machu Picchu I've only seen a small stripe between the mountain peaks. I never imaged the path was so long."

"The pathway of the spirits is lit by your ancestors' souls in the Upper World. If a spirit follows the path, it will go all the way to Inti, but today we'll follow as far as Machu Picchu. Are you ready to go?"

I enjoyed the warm, damp air of the sea, but I knew we needed to leave. She explained that the trip back was a different kind of traveling.

"Take a deep breath," she started, "Look around you, and close your eyes. Now remember your bed at Machu Picchu and place it on top of this beach. Open your eyes slowly."

"We're back!" I exclaimed, again amazed by her magic. Pule was perched on a bench right next to my bed. We talked about our trip to the ocean, and I asked her what she knew about the strange man. She said she wasn't permitted to tell me because she didn't guide me there. She warned me that finding things you couldn't explain was another hazard of traveling alone. After a while, I could no longer distinguish my blankets from the seashore, so I gratefully thanked Pule for visiting me and fell into a deep sleep.

I woke slowly to see a sunbeam pouring through the doorway, and I snuggled in deeper to enjoy the memories of our voyage along the life-giving rivers of two worlds. In the comforting warmth, I noticed dampness between my legs. Did I wet my bed in the depth of my dream? In disgust, I sat up and threw back the covers. A red stain covered my clothes and bed.

Refusal

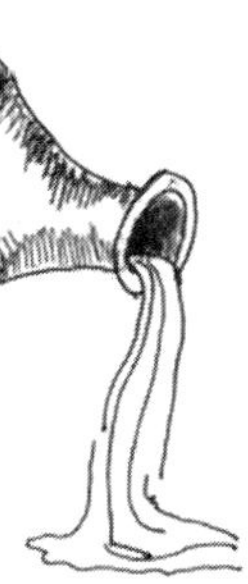

Ninan

I wanted to visit Kaya, but how could I? The Inca vowed to return her to Inti at the next Inti Raymi celebration. Although I was still determined to have her as my wife, I couldn't face her knowing how he promised to appease Inti. I waited a full day, hoping that after initiating the rituals, the Inca would be willing to listen to me. However, not knowing when he would choose to leave Machu Picchu, I had little choice other than to approach him on the second day. The stone walls of his throne room were entirely covered with vibrant weavings, giving warmth to an otherwise cold room. He sat alone on a bench beside his throne eating his breakfast as we exchanged greetings. After taking a deep breath and before I lost the courage, I stated confidently, "Father, we need to talk about my future wife. Pacas already made his selection, and it's time I made my wishes known. You have publicly announced your intention to appoint me as Inca when your long and distinguished reign comes to an end. As you have rightfully chosen your full sister as your wife, I too choose to marry my full sister, Kaya."

He didn't seem surprised, nor did he stop chewing when he replied, "You can't. She will be sacrificed at Inti Raymi. Inti is impatient. His disappearance must have told you that. I think we better declare her a woman this year and get on with it. Riku wants more time, but I don't think the gods will allow it. Choose another."

"Did you hear me?" I repeated without raising my voice, "I want to marry Kaya. You can't murder her now or anytime. I need her when I become the Inca. She's more valuable alive than dead."

He swallowed slowly as he regarded me. "She's more valuable to whom? To you? That's what this is about? Who cares what you need? You'll be responsible for the empire. Your needs are insignificant. How can you expect to gain the trust of your subjects when you're prepared to ignore Inti and the traditions of your people? How can you expect to be Inca when you ignore the voice of Riku?" He waved his spoon at me and continued, "You're too selfish to be Inca. I must be mad to think you'll ever be fit to rule."

I ignored his threat, "It's easy for you to dismiss her. When was the last time you actually loved a woman? I don't mean took her for political reasons, or to fill your needs. Even Miski is merely a toy for you to flaunt in public. When did you last say a loving word to my mother?"

"She rejected me, you insolent brat." His eyes bulging, he added, "What business is it of yours how many women I enjoy?"

"How can you lecture me on love for the empire when you're a self-centered rake? At least I surround one woman with love. She needs me and I need her," Resolute, I stood with my arms across my chest.

Suddenly on his feet, he shouted, "If you've soiled that girl, I'll have you burned in disgrace."

"I don't need to copulate to have feelings for a woman," I blurted out, immediately regretting it.

Shaking from head to foot, he hesitated with indecision, then spun away from me. He collected himself and continued softly, "You're not the first to love deeply. Kaya is the image of Chaska, my only love, and my father's gift to Inti. She was radiantly beautiful with the same sad eyes, greedy for life. I loved my sister with a pristine passion. She consumed my breath, my every thought. I wanted to die with her that day, and part of me did." He turned to me, his shoulders rounded and his eyes softened. "Do you think I felt differently than you, that I *chose* to marry your mother? Do you think I want to get diseases from every harlot who needs to legitimize a son or relish political alliances based on someone's pitiful daughter? With my eyes closed, every woman I've loved has the face of Chaska. I wish they had her soul, her gentle nature, her wisdom. Inti had better be pleased. My father gave him the very best, and I will give him Chaska's double. Do you think it's easier to sacrifice a daughter than a first love or that I feel nothing for that abandoned shell of a daughter? Can you imagine the pain in suffering this loss not once, but twice?" He paused, looked directly into my eyes and said, "What you want is completely irrelevant. We must do what the gods demand. Now leave and find another woman to be your wife."

In one final plea, I repeated what I had overheard in Cusco's plaza, "I'm told that Kaya has an elder twin. Take her. She's the one who should be sacrificed. Help me save Kaya for the sake of the empire."

"So you've heard that old lie. There is no twin. Now leave."

"Father, please, stop this madness. How can Inti expect us to give our best children to him? Why can't we serve him better by having our finest children set the example for the rest of the empire? You are the Inca. Change the rules. Pachacuti did it. Why can't you?"

"First you insult my affection for women, and now you challenge my leadership decisions and imply my infidelity to the gods. How dare you question my authority? How dare you think I would arbitrarily change the ancient ways simply to satisfy your selfish desires? How dare you imply that I don't have the courage to make the changes in the best interest of the empire, or recognize the difference between your lust and the empire's needs? Get out of here before I have you killed for treason."

I left without another word, knowing I had wasted my opportunity to save Kaya. How could I be so stupid? What would I tell her now? I was going to lose her! No, there must be a twin. In a daze, I wandered into the main plaza before I remembered Tumbes mentioning that Riku often visited the top of Huayna Picchu. There at least I'd be undisturbed and away from questioning eyes. I headed straight for the path, followed it into the forest, and climbed to the building near the top in a misty rain.

"What have I done?" I screamed into the valley. Hurling stones into the void above the river wasn't enough. I ripped up all the blankets, smashed the water jugs on the floor, kicked in the fire pit, and tore down the door. I boiled with anger for my father, these ridiculous traditions, and my own incompetence. How could I have failed so miserably? How could I ever face Kaya? I found a supply of *chicha* and finished it.

The sun was setting when Riku turned the corner to see me sitting in front of his disheveled refuge. He calmly sat down beside me and began, "You talked with your father about Kaya, and he upheld the tradition. Now you want me to intercede and save her." I nodded, hoping he would comply. He put his hand on my shoulder, sighed, and added wistfully, "I know how you feel to have someone you love slip away from you."

"You? I refuse to believe you've joined with Kaya, and wonder if there's ever been a woman in your life."

"Until you arrived, I never even thought of Kaya as a desirable woman, but as a young priest I was hopelessly in love with Chaska. She was a remarkable healer, and so kind. It was obvious your father loved her too, so even if she were spared, we would never wed. For the last twenty years I've tried unsuccessfully to contact her." He paused. "Do you think it's easy to see Kaya every day? She walks like Chaska and holds her head to the side like her. She even speaks like Chaska. I see Chaska and know that Kaya will meet the same fate. Ninan, everyone in the empire knows she is promised to Inti. They depend on your father to offer his daughter to Inti on their behalf as Pachacuti decreed years ago. They won't hold to their obligations to the Inca, or to Inti, if he doesn't honor his obligations. You're asking your father to destroy the foundation of the empire you will one day inherit."

"Without Kaya, I'm not sure I can be the Inca." Saturated with beer, I rested my head on my hands and tried to find a way to persuade him. "I need her visions of the future, and her loving support. I can't do this alone."

"You don't have to do it alone. Dead or alive, Kaya will always be with you. That's the basis of our work, and she is very talented."

I looked straight into his eyes and replied, "You just said you have never reached Chaska. Why do you expect to reach Kaya? Even if you do, I'm untrained. I won't be able to find her."

"She will come to you. All you need to do is be open to the possibility. Besides, Chaska had a talent for healing, but Kaya's gift is prophetic. Oracles are always easier to reach."

Shaking my head, I again dropped it to my hands. "It's not the same."

"No, it's not, but it's as much as you can hope for."

"What if she refuses to be killed?"

"She would be drugged and killed anyway. There is no honorable way your father can thwart his obligation."

"I've heard Kaya has a twin. Take her."

"There is no twin. You know better than to believe street tales."

"But if there is a twin, who would be taken?"

Riku fingered his chin. "Well, there is no precedent for twins, but only the eldest daughter is taken when there are several daughters, so I think only the elder twin would be sacrificed."

I desperately wanted to believe Kaya had a twin, but if neither my father nor Riku knew of her, she probably was only a myth. Unable to think, I said, "You won't help me save Kaya, even though you lost Chaska and will lose your link to her through Kaya."

"You're not hearing me. I expect to maintain contact with Kaya, and with her help find Chaska. I'm confident we can reach Kaya in the Upper World, or she can reach us." He sighed deeply and added, "I owe it to Inti, to your father, to the people and to Kaya to be sure the sacrifice is carried out on the next winter solstice at Inti Raymi."

"But she's not a woman yet. My father can't take her so soon."

"Her bleeding started in the night. She is fasting and in seclusion."

"Oh, Kaya, why now?" Intoxicated, exhausted, and consumed with rage, I sobbed uncontrollably.

Battles

Ninan

"It's always a pleasure to have friends visit, especially our allies from Quito." Huayna Capac initiated the farewell with Apu Tacana, the Curaca. Once again healthy, the Inca had regained his congenial temperament. "Unfortunately your return was delayed, but it was imperative that I witness the fading sun at Machu Picchu." My father excelled at using the circumstances to enhance his aura of power.

"We understand completely. These are dangerous times and none of us can afford to fall from the grace of the gods. Sinchi Roca's suggestion that we use the runners to contact our people was very helpful," Apu Tacana replied. A tall man for a Quitoan, he was dressed in his bright red and blue traveling clothes. Standing between Masi, his assistant, and his litter, he added, "We are grateful for your extended hospitality, and your pledge of support."

"Your knowledge of the northern volatility is essential. Together we can preempt a rebellion. If we can't win their compliance peacefully, then we'll win in battle," the Inca responded, finally accepting the validity of their information.

"Then we'll welcome you to Quito within two years. If there are significant developments, we will send coded messages as we have arranged." Turning to leave, he paused, stared directly at my father and added, "We understand your extensive preparations, but we urge you to come as quickly as possible. I can't overemphasize my concern. Our enemies are growing stronger every day."

"And because we may not recognize all of our enemies, there is no need to preannounce our arrival." Huayna Capac responded with equal fervor. "The less information known about our strategies, the more quickly we will succeed. You know our plans and can assume we are proceeding as expected."

Framed with an embroidered cap, the visitor's round face softened slightly as he nodded, "Then may you continue to walk in the blessings of Inti."

"And may your travels and homeland remain under his protection," the Inca concluded with equal sincerity. The visitors bowed slightly and started the trek home.

For the past week, Huayna Capac and Sinchi Roca were constantly with the Quito visitors, and although Pacas and I were also present, we weren't encouraged to participate. As a result, neither of us understood the final agreement. In the years since we were initiated as men there were no battles, so we had no knowledge of war beyond what we learned from the histories. Now that they had finally left, we were anxious to query our fathers. We ambled back to the royal courtyard where they talked about the visitors. "Apu Tacana certainly enjoyed the *chicha*," my father quipped. "There are few men who can drink as much as I can."

"You couldn't have kept his pace when the sun disappeared. That night he could hardly walk. Still, discovering his preference for *mulli chicha* made it easier to keep him occupied during your absence," Sinchi Roca reminisced.

"I'm sure it did. And Masi, did he stutter while I was gone?"

"He tripped over his words even when he was alone with Apu Tacana. Too bad he's so hard to understand. He's a clear thinker, and Apu Tacana depends on him. I would have liked to talk with him more."

Comfortably seated by the pond in the royal courtyard, the lighthearted conversation continued. Knowing better than to interrupt, I waited until they began to review the agreement. For fifty llamas loaded with gold and two hundred loaded with salt, Apu Tacana agreed to align his troops with the Inca in the inevitable battle with the defiant tribes. He also agreed to support my father in subduing the people living along the river north of Quito that led all the way to the northern coast, although he didn't know that territory very well. To support the effort, my father would establish a substantial city in the north. He wanted to expand Quito, since it was the perfect city, but Apu Tacana was adamant that there was only space for a small palace and that he should instead choose either Tomebamba or Cajamarca as his primary site. Huayna Capac chose Tomebamba because it was his birthplace, and it was closer to Quito.

"One hundred thousand men will be difficult to train and assemble without the Cayambis knowing." Sinchi Roca said bluntly.

"True, but even if they do find out, will they believe it? No one has ever gathered so many men. If they do believe it, imagine the fear such a large army will cause. Still, I think we should try to keep our plans a secret as long as possible, even from the Inca leaders of the Cayambis and Carangues. If they do intend to revolt, the less time they have to prepare, the better."

While Sinchi Roca considered my father's strategy, I took the opportunity to ask one of my questions. "Father, why do you need such a large army? Surely the Cayambis and Carangues aren't that numerous, or that formidable."

"Ninan, you forget, we are expecting to fight in two areas. The Cayambis and Carangues live in the mountains and down to the coast around Tumbes. We will also attack along the river north of Quito. We know little of that area and must be well prepared."

"You alone want to initiate the war north of Quito. Why do you insist on bringing this area into the empire?" With so little known of the jungle, I struggled to understand its significance. I anticipated a simple answer explaining some bit of information I had forgotten.

My father's hesitance baffled me. He studied Sinchi Roca, who looked sad and undecided, but finally he shrugged his shoulders and nodded. My father sighed, and in a soft voice he finally continued, "Ninan, Pacas, come closer. It is time you learn the secret of the Incas."

My father's unusual voice and ominous eyes sent a cold chill down my back, although the sun shone brightly. Excited and yet dreading to hear such an important secret, Pacas and I moved in so close we were nearly touching.

Huayna Capac glanced around to be sure no one was in the courtyard even though the trickling stream nearly obscured his whisper. "You heard Riku describe the vision at Machu Picchu."

We nodded, and he reluctantly continued, "Riku described a time during Viracocha's return to earth and confirmed that the prophecy is true." Everyone knew that our creator was to return, and Riku's vision was interesting, even fascinating, but not a new revelation.

Pacas and I exchanged glances while sweat inexplicably rose on my forehead.

"Do you remember the story of Pachacuti defeating the Chanca because his father, the Inca Viracocha, refused to fight?"

Why was my father still speaking in a whisper? Everyone knew the histories of the great Incas, and, failing to see the connection, I replied, "We learned he refused to fight because he was Hurin class and the soldiers would not follow him. Pachacuti was only able to take control because he convinced the warriors that Inti commanded him to lead."

"That's the official story, the one recorded in our histories, but there is another reason he refused to fight. In a dream, our creator revealed that he would return as a man during the reign of the fifth and final Inca." He stopped and held my eyes. "Ninan, you will be the last Inca. The world will end during your reign. Riku's vision confirmed that, and Inti himself warned us by temporarily disappearing."

It couldn't be. There must be another interpretation. The empire was in its prime. Yes, there were trouble spots, but the future was so promising. I stared at my father, then Sinchi Roca. Both carried the same sympathetic, resigned expression. Pacas stared at me, his jaw slack, and his eyes bulging out. I was suddenly on my feet, challenging my father. "You're wrong. The prophecy is wrong. If the world were going to end, why would you bother to go to war in the north? Why would Pachacuti and Topa Inca expand the empire at all? Why not live quietly and wait for the end?"

My father, the fourth Inca, grabbed my wrist and pulled me back down. His voice still muted he replied, "That is precisely why Pachacuti replaced his father as Inca. Viracocha Inca chose to do nothing for five generations. Pachacuti, like you, couldn't accept the prophecy. What if it's false? What if we can alter the prophecy by our actions? Since Pachacuti, all the Incas have dedicated their lives to reversing Viracocha's judgment. If we can welcome his return and show him how well we have ruled, perhaps I—" He corrected himself. "I mean, *you* can convince him not to end the world."

How could I possibly convince a god of anything? Even as Inca, I was still Viracocha's child, not his equal. Why would he listen to me? My father started talking again, and I forced myself to listen. "We must fight in the northwest to be sure that Viracocha, the man, can return unharmed. You see, Quito is the perfect city because at high noon on the spring and fall equinoxes, there is absolutely no shadow. For a short time each year Inti shines on every living thing with no trace of darkness. Viracocha passed through the perfect city as he left and will surely return by the same route. That's why we must bring the north river into the empire. How could we, ah, you, change his edict if you can't assure safe passage to your most honored guest?"

Pacas sobbed beside me, repeatedly mumbling Tinkha's name. His father tried to comfort him as they stood and walked away together. Questions and revelations raced through my head. Why wasn't I told? So that's why Huayna Capac was planning for war when we visited Cacha. Why should I believe this nonsense? No wonder he wanted us to travel to Tomebamba at such a young age. How could I possibly lead the people to the end of the world? How long do I have? No wonder Kaya was so surprised with my proposal. Kaya. I must have Kaya. I said, "Kaya and Riku know all of this, don't they?"

"Riku knows everything, and he has probably told Kaya, Atuk, and Tumbes by now. It was his prerogative to determine when to tell them." He paused before returning to the history. "Since the time of Pachacuti, the reigning Inca, his primary confidant and a divining priest knew the entire truth. When Pachacuti promised the people to sacrifice his eldest daughter to Inti, the public reason was to demonstrate his devotion and to ensure that Inti would direct the other gods to help the people. Inti accepted Pachacuti's offering and ended a terrible famine. And so the public tradition was established that the Inca would give his eldest daughter to Inti as suppliance for the entire generation."

"And was there a secret reason for the sacrifice? Do I remember Riku talking with you about this just after your return from the south?" Puzzling memories from my childhood flooded back to me.

"I did tell him the bridge in the southwest was complete, leaving only the northwest bridge unfinished. I'm surprised you remember. You were quite young."

"What does Kaya have to do with the bridges?" I asked urgently.

"You have studied the stars only for agrarian and navigational purposes. The diviners study the sky to understand the relationships between this world and the worlds beyond," he answered reluctantly. "In the time of our ancient forefathers the sun rose and set in the Mayu, the river of stars, during the winter and summer solstice celebrations. The Incas and the gods used the bridge in the Northwest during the winter solstice to go to the Upper World. Everyone else in the empire used the bridge in the Southwest during the summer solstice to go to the Other World. During Pachacuti's time, the sun no longer set in the Mayu during summer solstice and Pachacuti's diviner told him that the spirits could no longer pass. We sacrificed and placed many of the people's children on the highest mountain peaks in the southwest, as close to the Other World as possible. Now the spirits of the dead can enter the Other World through their sacrificed children and the grace of the gods. Known only to a few, Viracocha was the last to pass to the Upper World before the original northwest bridge was also lost. All of our mummified Incas are patiently waiting for the bridge to be replaced. Until then their devoted families will feed and care for their bodies and lingering spirits."

He took a deep breath and avoided looking at me. His eyes heavy with regret, he tilted his head back and spoke to the sky. "To solve this horrific problem, Pachacuti built Machu Picchu to serve as the sacred foundation for the bridge to the northwest. The Urubamba River flows toward the Upper World in the northwest from the Incas' country estates to Machu Picchu. This secluded location is perfectly situated near a mountain that is eternally white with snow. As with the bridge to the southwest, the northwest bridge is being built with our most precious gifts, the eldest daughter of each Inca. Pachacuti's daughter, Collca, was the first. My precious sister, Chaska, followed, and Kaya will be the last. When completed to Inti's satisfaction, all our forefathers will pass to the Upper World and Viracocha will return."

No wonder Kaya was so surprised by my marriage proposal, but how could I face such a disaster by myself? Now I must have her beside me. Speaking more to himself than to me he prayed, "My dearest Chaska, I still love you. Soon we will walk together." He looked directly at me. "Chaska is the only woman I've loved, and I worshipped her purity until the day she left this world. No other woman was her equal, certainly not your mother or any of my other women. I try, but I find no comfort in any of them. As you have chosen Mama Runtu, my mother, Mama Ocllo, was my teacher. She was the only woman who ever satisfied me."

I winced when he mentioned Mama Runtu. I didn't realize he knew of our arrangement, although I should have known she would ask his advice and permission before our first meeting. For the first time, I understood my father's dalliances. Mama Runtu was my teacher, not a replacement for Kaya, just as Mama Oclla, my grandmother, and all the others couldn't replace Chaska for my father.

My father dropped his head to his hands and whispered, "Your reign will be the last. May Inti always guide you."

At last, I finally knew the truth, or at least their truth. My panic was quickly replaced by a calculating resolve to find another solution. Kaya was scheduled to die in eight months and the northern invasion would follow shortly thereafter. There must be alternatives. I stood and walked away from my mourning father. Alone, and without destination, I left the palace and walked upstream along the river. For three days and nights, I wandered in the mountains, eating nothing, sleeping where I fell. A radically different plan flickered and then gradually developed into a self-sustained flame.

Pacas met me in front of Quispiguanca when I returned. "I was worried about you. Are you all right?" He checked me front to back.

"I'm fine, hungry, but fine. And you?" Pacas was part of my reforms and I needed his trust.

"I can't decide what to do. I want to marry Tinkha, but she would be safer in Cusco," he said as he pounded his fist in his palm.

I faced him and replied in a somber tone even I didn't recognize, "Pacas, I have a plan. Can I trust you to keep it a secret?" Our friendship was strained by my resolve to marry Kaya, and now faced with an unknown plan, he nodded slowly. "Good." I said immediately and briskly walked back to the palace, Pacas hurrying to fall in stride. "Are we still leaving for Cusco tomorrow?"

"Yes, most of the preparations are already completed."

"Then I'll tell you tomorrow as we walk." The conversation reverted to the commonplace as we entered the palace, and I ate a hearty dinner.

The overcast sky suited Huayna Capac's mood. He barked orders as the servants scuttled back and forth packing the team of llamas bound for Cusco. Pacas and I started ahead of the group. The early start allowed more privacy, and I laid out my strategies to alter the empire. As we saw in Tomebamba and Cacha, our system of rule was flawed. I explained my plans to reverse Viracocha's judgment, while Pacas listened intently, asked questions, and made excellent suggestions as we refined the changes. He also suggested we learn my mother's secret when we got back to Cusco, since it might be as important as the men's secret. Pacas fully endorsed my ideas, until I mentioned Kaya. Then we argued continuously. I just couldn't convince him that marrying her was in the best interest of the empire. By the time we reached Cusco three days later, we were barely speaking to one another. I missed his companionship, but I remained resolved to marry Kaya.

We arrived in Cusco the evening before the final event of Homa Raymi, the spring festival. Per Huayna Capac's decree, thousands of men traveled from Cacha to Cusco each winter for military training where everyone learned the strategies of the historic battles. The Hanan members, led by Checa, improved their skills with various weapons. Each squadron of five hundred men learned to scout enemy territory and competed in mock battles. Hurin groups, led by Pusani, learned to identify the bushes of the north that were suitable for bows and arrows. They calculated the number of llamas needed to transport the provisional needs of the soldiers, and to replenish the storehouses as the troops moved north. This competitive event was a perfect opportunity to judge the progress of the soldiers and evaluate what advanced training was still needed before the northern invasion.

Waiting for the competition to begin, most of noblemen from Cusco stood on the towering walls at Sacsahuaman, the massive fortress on the edge of the city. Men drank beer and placed bets on the contestants practicing in the plaza below them. The women spun wool as they gossiped among themselves, and occasionally noticed their children scrambling along the walls trying to find the best view. Checa and Pusani, the Curacas from

Cacha, stood with my father and Sinchi Roca. Pacas preferred to stand with his father and I stood beside Checa. The competition continued all afternoon as archers and soldiers armed with slings competed for accuracy at various distances. Across the field, the hurlers competed with maces, bolas, and their newly designed spear throwers that enhanced their range and delighted everyone. In simultaneous competitions the boys and men demonstrated their skill as the best of both groups advanced to the finals. The prizes stood at my father's feet: a gold statue of a soldier for the best man and boy in each event, and a smaller one for second place. The warm afternoon passed pleasantly with beer, friendly talk, and considerably improved competition compared to the previous year. Of course I was particularly interested in the archery contest in progress, and overheard the conversation beside me.

"That's my eldest son." Checa pointed him out to my father. "This is his third year in Cusco. He's an expert with the bow and arrow, thanks to your men's excellent training."

"He looks like a fine young man. You must be proud of him," Huayna Capac ignored the compliment and answered sincerely.

"Indeed, he is a comfort in these troubling times."

My father apparently didn't care to hear his woes, since he watched the mace throwers and added. "And how are your other children?"

"Happily, my eldest daughter married well and is with child. My two younger boys grow strong working in the fields." Concentrating on a particularly good toss, the Inca said nothing, so Checa continued, "And of course my wife and I, while grateful for the honor, still mourn the loss of our precious young daughter."

"Was she taken by an illness?" my father asked, still distracted.

"No, she was one of the hundred children that Cacha sent to Cusco this year for sacrifice. She was given to Inti just last month as part of the ritual after the sun's disappearance." His voice trailed off.

"Oh, yes, of course. Then she sits with Inti. Rejoice!" The Inca slapped him on the back and simultaneously cheered for a particularly good archer on the field below. Checa stared blankly at the field. Pusani leaned over and whispered something to him. Checa nodded and tried to smile.

I hadn't noticed the group of boys standing behind me until Atahualpa spoke. "They certainly are expert archers, but of course, they're not as skilled as you." He stood beside Tito, while little Huascar, picking his nose, trailed behind. Atahualpa generally avoided me, although I often saw several of my other half brothers.

I ignored his ingenuous flattery and replied, "Hello, Atahualpa. I see you are getting strong yourself. Your archery has no doubt improved as well.

Are you enjoying the games?" He held his bow with a familiarity unusual for a ten-year-old boy. Pacas glanced over and rolled his eyes. He thoroughly disliked Atahualpa.

"Yes, Tito and I were on the plaza earlier helping the men prepare. They look small from way up here, but on the field they're really tall, probably even taller than you."

Tito fingered the stones he planned to use with his sling. He too had grown and was still more muscular than Atahualpa. Several years younger, little Huascar transferred his find from his nose to his mouth. With a sweet, girlish face and carrying panpipes, he looked like a young priest in his perfectly clean tunic and fancy headband. I wanted all my half brothers to go away so I could watch the final match between the two best archers. I tried to direct Atahualpa to the match. "Did you meet either of the finalists?"

"Yes, actually I watched both men practice."

"And which do you think is better?" I asked, indifferent to his assessment.

"The one on the left is stronger, but the one on the right, Curaca Checa's son, is more accurate. I think he will win," he replied calmly. They each had three arrows to shoot at a circle on the ground. The center was marked with a short, wooden stump no wider than the span of my hand. The judge called the shot as the archers lifted and drew their bows. At the judge's command the arrows arced up and then fell to the ground, piercing the wooden stumps. The crowd cheered the excellent marksmanship, but quickly fell silent for the second shot. Again the arrows sailed through the sky and again both arrows squarely found their marks. Remarkable to have seen it once, the second round sent the crowd into a frenzied roar. From the other end of the group, Pacas eyed Atahualpa suspiciously when he edged in beside me to get a better view. "Do you think you could do that?" Atahualpa asked.

I considered the distance and wind conditions. "Yes, I could do that."

"Three times in a row?"

"No, I think I could put two in the stump, with the third in the circle."

"Too bad you're not competing. I'd like to cheer for my brother."

I ignored him and watched the third set of arrows fly through the air. Checa's son looked confident, and his arrow again landed in the wood. Unfortunately his competitor's hit the edge and skittered along the ground. Both contestants lifted their bows and arrows over their heads and approached the wall below us. To the shouting and whistling crowd, the Inca descended the stairs to present the awards to all the competitors. Beside me Checa cheered the loudest for his son, the champion.

"Congratulations!" I added my praise to Checa's own accolades of his son. "You must be very proud. He's a fine archer."

"Thank you. He's a wonderful son and a joy to his mother and me." His back straight and chin high, he watched his son receive the gold statue from my father. Satisfaction poured out of him as he joined the crowd's adulation. After equal pomp for the other winners, the cheering died out and the audience gradually dispersed. We stood on the wall watching the contestants, including Checa's son, collect their belongings. Still jubilant, Checa pointed out his son's friends and other important people from Cacha.

Although Tito and Huascar had wandered away, Atahualpa stood beside us. "My brother told me earlier that he can shoot as well as your son," he said during a lull in our conversation. "Wouldn't it be wonderful to see those two compete?"

Checa faced me with a quizzical expression, "Oh?" he said as he waited for my reply.

"What I said was that on a very good day, I might be able to hit the target from that distance." I knew I was a very good marksman, but I had no interest in challenging his son.

"Ninan is too modest. He is the best archer in the empire," Atahualpa boasted. "I'm sure he could shoot at least as well as your son." I glared at the little monster, unable to find a way clear of the brewing conflict.

Pacas came to my rescue and spoke to Checa. "Your son proved he is an excellent archer today. Atahualpa is just a boy bragging about his brother. I'm Ninan's best friend and I can assure you, he's had plenty of days he couldn't even hit the circle. He's no competition for your son."

Grateful for Pacas' attempt, even if his divergence did come at my expense, I too tried to redirect the conversation. "There's your son now," I pointed down to the field. "He looks like a very noble warrior."

Checa scratched his chin as he considered Atahualpa's remark and then replied. "You would greatly honor my son if you would agree to shoot with him."

Win or lose, his son could tell the story of the day he won the gold prize and challenged the heir apparent, but I didn't want to compete. "Perhaps another day, I don't have my bow with me," I said as I held up my empty hands.

"Ninan, you can use mine, "Atahualpa quickly volunteered. "It's the same size as yours." A smile stretched across his face.

I glanced at Checa, and then at Pacas behind him who shrugged his shoulders. Cornered, I was forced to compete with his son or lose face. "All right then, if your son is interested, I'll compete with him."

"I'm sure he would be honored." Checa started toward the steps to the plaza, and we followed. "Ninan, let's make a small wager to make it more interesting?"

"What did you have in mind?" I asked casually.

"If you win, my son will give the gold award to you. You know how proud he is to have it, but it would rightfully belong to you." He paused before suggesting the other half of the bet. "If my son wins, next year Cacha will be relieved of our duty to provide one hundred children for sacrifice."

Just leaving the field, my father was surrounded by the crowd as they headed back to town. I turned to Checa and said, "That was my father's command. I have no right to reverse his decision."

"Come, come. You are his eldest son. You can convince him to change his mind. Besides, according to Atahualpa, you'll win anyway." He was right. I would likely win. Besides, I thought my father's edict was too harsh. I agreed. Checa hurried down the stair shouting to his son who quickly accepted the challenge. We decided that Pacas would call the competition while Checa would judge the targets. His son and I were nearly identical in height, so I could expect no advantage in strength. Atahualpa handed me his bow and the first arrow.

With no practice or conversation, the competition began. I heard Pacas call, "Nock your arrows." We adjusted the arrows to the bowstrings. "Draw." Together we lifted the bows and pulled the string back. Perfectly timed Pacas called, "Release." The arrows followed parallel arcs, dropped gracefully and plunged into the wooden stumps. We both relaxed and collected the second arrow. Pacas called again, and the arrows followed identical flights to the mark. Checa confirmed the results. The wager would be settled on the final attempt. Atahualpa handed me his third arrow while my competitor carefully selected his. Pacas called the shoot exactly as he had the others. Both arrows followed the same perfect arch up, but my arrow pulled to the right. As it passed the apex it followed the same arc and veered even farther to the right. The distance was correct but it landed fully three paces beyond the edge of the circle. Checa and his son were elated. I was shocked. I sprinted to the target to retrieve the errant arrow. All the others followed at a trot.

"Too bad," Checa consoled me. "You must have had a bad arrow."

I picked it up and immediately saw the problem. One set of feathers had nearly fallen out, pulling the arrow to the side. "This arrow was poorly made, but of course your son wins the competition." I responded to Checa as he arrived with Pacas and Atahualpa. Addressing his son, I added, "Congratulations. You're a fine archer, and I would be pleased to face any enemy with you at my side."

"Thank you, you are very skilled as well," He respectfully replied. While we collected our gear, we talked about the wood and feathers we preferred for arrows. Even Pacas joined in although his expertise was the sling. As we started back to the city, I invited them to Casana for refreshments, an honor no one ever refused. Our friendly conversation helped to divert my thoughts from the trouble that I would soon face with my father. Atahualpa followed behind, but gradually fell back even further. At first I ignored his giggling, but finally a loud guffaw brought us to a halt. Annoyed, I walked back to see what was so funny.

He gasped for air, pointed at me and heckled. "You lost! Now you're the one in trouble with father."

I didn't think that was quite so funny. Then in a flash I understood. "You maneuvered me into a competition and intentionally spoiled the arrow."

Still laughing he held his stomach with one hand and pointed at me with the other. "You deserved it, you miserable toad. Now father will punish you."

I heard the crack when my fist crossed his face. Blood poured from his nose, and I returned to the others. Checa and his son heard everything and stared at my brother while I carefully restated the obvious, "The wager stands. I will address the matter with my father."

They nodded. Pacas suggested we help Atahualpa, but I refused. We continued toward town with Atahualpa shouting obscenities behind us.

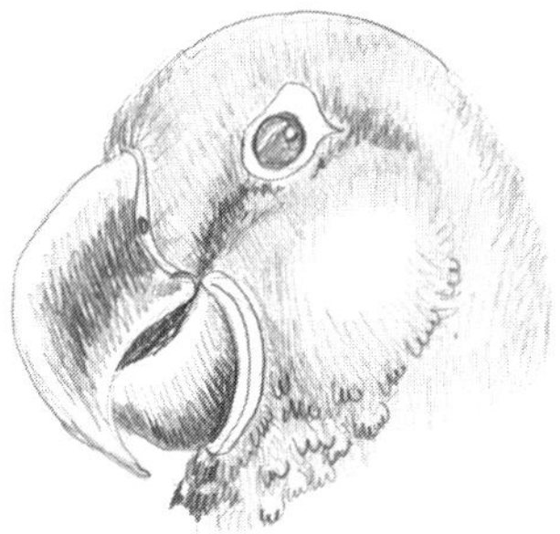

Children

Kaya

"Riku, please let me go with you. I can help you examine the work that's been completed." I pleaded with him as he escorted me back to my garden after the morning lessons.

"You really wouldn't be interested. All I'm doing is inspecting a first statue for the Capac Raymi offerings." A regular occurrence for him, he dismissed the short walk across the main plaza to the artisan section as trivial.

"I don't care. I really need to go somewhere besides the sacred plaza." Riku had little patience for whining, and I tried not to complain. For two days my head throbbed, and again the dull ache settled into my lower back and stomach. I hoped the walk would distract me from the inconveniences of being a woman.

When we stopped on the stairs beside the terrace leading to my garden, he asked, "Are you sure? You look pale. Perhaps you should rest."

"I rest too much. The walk will revive me. You'll see." I smiled through the nagging cramps. Now that the date was fixed for my execution, he allowed more liberties. A year earlier, I never would have even asked to go.

He paused for a moment. "Perhaps you're right. We haven't walked much lately. Wait here while I tell Iska we'll be gone for the afternoon." He disappeared between the buildings, and I sat on the steps, bending over my folded arms to relieve the pain momentarily. The heady scent of new grass tinged with llama droppings saturated the moist air revealing the timeless hope of a new growing season. As I looked down the stairs, I saw an occasional woman with a load of wood or water, and overhead, puffy white clouds suggesting a late afternoon shower. I searched for details to recall, since the low-hanging fog of the rainy season would soon obscure my view. Riku appeared suddenly to find me sitting on the stairs. "Are you sure you want to go?"

"Absolutely!" I replied more energetically than I felt. On my feet, we headed toward the main plaza, walked across the soggy grass field and ascended the stairs to the artisan section.

"You've seen this area from the sacred plaza, but you've never been inside. Perhaps you'll find this more enjoyable than I imagined." Riku echoed my thoughts. "The craftsmen and their families live here. Of course there are weavers and metal artisans, but there are also men who work with gems for ceremonial finery. Even a few potters live in Machu Picchu. Unfortunately there is very little clay around here, so they haul it from Cusco. Still, it's easier to transport clay than fragile plates, bowls, and household jars. We can visit the potters on our way back if you like. I haven't seen them for a long time."

"Yes, please. I'd like to see that," I replied earnestly.

We walked along the terrace above the main plaza, and then turned into a narrow alley with high walls and mud underfoot. A passing cloud cast a cool, deep shadow across the corridor, as Riku stepped through a doorway into a fully enclosed yard. Focused on his work, a man hunched over a bench that stood beside a small fire. Riku stopped by the doorway and began to hum one of my favorite songs about a hummingbird. Before he finished the first verse, the workman lifted his head and greeted us with an inviting wave. "Come. Come, closer. I didn't hear you enter."

"You were so absorbed in your work. I didn't want to startle you," Riku responded as we approached. "Where's your family? They usually announce my arrival."

He put his work on the bench and straightened to greet us. "My children went with my wife to get water and then play with their friends while she weaves with her sister. She's making special clothes for all of us. Everyone is busy preparing for Capac Raymi." He curiously glanced at me, but spoke to Riku. "And who is your companion?"

"My name is Kaya. I'm one of Riku's students." I preferred to answer for myself, and Riku nodded his approval at my vague response.

"Well, you are both welcome. Please, come and have some *chicha*. I'd enjoy your company, and the rest." He quickly assembled the cups and poured while he enthusiastically continued, "I have nearly finished the first statue. I hope you like it." He handed each of us a cup and reached for the statue. "I did the boy first. It's always the most difficult. I'll do the farmer and plow next, and then finish with the eight llamas. That's what we agreed to as I remember." With obvious pride, he carefully handed the gold figure to Riku.

"Yes, your memory is excellent." Riku glanced quickly at the statue and added, "As is your artistry." Setting down his beer, Riku rolled the statue around in his palm as he studied it. "The face is exquisite. I see you're even detailing the strands of hair."

"I think it looks better that way." He smiled. Average in every way, the craftsman could blend into any crowd if he wore a different tunic, but black burns from stray sparks and hot metal covered his dirty work clothes and identified him as a prestigious metal worker.

Riku handed me the figure, which seemed remarkably heavy, considering its size. The boy's face was beautiful. The long forehead and high cheekbones emphasized his lifelike eyes that were trying to escape the statue. His prominent nose dropped to his thin lips and narrow chin. In his hand he held his first pair of earplugs, the most pronounced indication of an Inca boy passing to manhood during Capac Raymi. "Your work is very artistic. I look forward to seeing the other pieces." I said as I handed him the statue, and he accepted the compliment with a smile.

"I too am pleased with the work but sadly, it will be flawed. Only the gods are capable of perfection."

Riku nodded his acceptance and queried, "And the others. Do you have all the gold you need for the other figures?"

"I think so. When I've completed the farmer and one llama, I'll know if I have enough. Would you prefer that I make the llamas smaller, or ask for more gold if I need to?"

"We are expecting to receive more very shortly. Let's discuss it again when you have finished the farmer and the llama." Riku picked up his beer and asked, "Now tell me about your son. Will he go to Cusco for his training next year?"

A proud father, his voice softened as he explained that his son was still two years away from manhood and would leave for Cusco to live with his uncle as soon as the rainy season was over. Feeling better, I happily listened to the two men exchange stories. We were nearly ready to leave when Riku remembered the bag he carried over his shoulder. "Oh, yes, these are for you. I hope you enjoy them."

He looked quickly, and then buried his nose in the bag to take a deep breath before lifting his smiling face. "Dried fish! What a special treat. We rarely find time to catch the ones in the river. My wife will be very pleased. Thank you."

We were back in the alley and heading out of the artisan section when I reminded Riku we planned to pass the potters on our return. Being among people was such a rare occurrence, I wanted to prolong our visit. Halfway down the stairs leading to the main plaza he turned off again and passed a group of women who exchanged greetings with him by name. This area was more open with three descending terraces on our right and a high wall flanking our left. Riku followed the wall until he turned to enter a small yard surrounded by houses.

Two boys laughed and called each other names as they ran back and forth kicking a small gourd between them, intentionally keeping it away from the other children. Without interrupting, Riku skirted the group and approached a man working at the far end.

"Riku, hello. What brings you to this side of the city?"

"Kaya and I are just checking on the preparations for Capac Raymi. She's never seen a potter at work and asked to stop on the way back."

"She must be one of your students." He turned to me and added, "You really should insist he let you get out more."

Surprised he would criticize Riku's methods, I defended him, "Yes, I agree, but Riku has many rules, and he says we'll learn more quickly if we follow them."

He raised one eyebrow as though he doubted the need for rules, but before he could comment further, Riku asked, "What are you working on?"

"I need to paint the design on these jars. During the festival, we'll fill one with our offering. The rest are for our neighbors. My wife is delivering some now, but I have several more to finish." He waved at the neatly shelved jars of various sizes and shapes. "I'll decorate them according to the petitioner's request and then fire them."

"May I watch you work?" I asked.

"Of course, but I'll ask you not to speak. I need to concentrate."

I agreed, and he fell into his project. Riku strolled around the courtyard while I memorized every motion the potter made. The round jar he was decorating had a flared rim and a single flat handle attached at the neck and near the bottom. He carefully balanced the soft jar in his palm and with his finger he painted six vertical stripes evenly spaced around the jar. Next he used a hollow reed to outline the red stripes with black paint. Moving to the handle he striped each edge and then made horizontal lines and crosses along its full length. On the main body he drew vertical stems with branches reaching toward the red stripes. At the end of each branch he painted a small circle by dipping a berry into the paint and dabbing the jar. As a finishing touch, he fingered the flared top with red and accented the edge with a heavy black line. With practiced skill he transformed a simple ochre jar into a container worthy of a sacred gift. Satisfied, he set the jar carefully on the shelf and brought another to his workbench. "You see, it's really very simple. I'll decorate all of these before the evening meal." He rearranged his paints as he spoke.

Riku strolled back to us and noted, "Your work is beautiful, and yet you were able to complete the design very quickly. Inti gave you a great talent."

"Yes, and with years of practice mixing paints and selecting the best tools, I am grateful that my jars are worthy of their purpose." He glanced toward the courtyard entrance and added, "Ah, my wife has returned with our children."

Riku saw her approach and quickly turned to the potter. "Thank you for allowing Kaya to watch you, but we must go now. We'll watch for your jars during the celebration." He motioned to me as he started to leave, intentionally staying as far away from the approaching family as possible.

The potter called out behind us. "Thanks for stopping. Come back whenever you like."

His wife carried a baby on her back as her son raced across the yard to his father. Watching us leave, she joyfully shouted, "Praise be to Inti! It's wonderful to see you again."

Riku stopped and allowed an anguished sigh to escape before responding cheerily, "Well, hello." Trapped, he started toward her, and I followed at a distance.

"When I look at my children, I think of you often." She led Riku to her husband, who looked as perplexed as I felt. "My dear, this is the man who saved my life when I was giving birth to our first child." Suddenly I understood why Riku was avoiding her. This was the woman whose baby died at the hot springs. I was dressed as a boy then, but what if she recognized me as that boy? I was absolutely not allowed to leave Machu Picchu, and if our trip to the hot springs were ever discovered, Riku and I would both be disgraced. Without being conspicuous, I tried to hide my face.

"Oh, yes, I remember you. Your baby was breach." Riku added. "The healer needed my help to turn the baby. A young boy from the north and I were of some small assistance to the healer." He paused and added sincerely, "I'm sorry we couldn't save your child."

"The loss of our first child was painful, but as you can see, we're blessed with a fine young son and a new little daughter." She removed the carrying cradle from her back and set it on the ground. Her husband clasped his hands together and looked at Riku with a renewed appreciation. Together the three of them reviewed the details of the distressing event.

I'd often wondered about this woman; she was so frail. Riku told me she would live to bear other children, but I thought he said that just to comfort me. Now in front of me was the miracle baby I didn't think could possibly exist. I knelt over the cradle, and a beautiful, innocent child smiled and cooed. Without thinking, I asked, "May I hold her?"

Riku frowned, and the mother, noticing me for the first time, replied immediately, "Of course. As a Mamacona, I don't suppose you see many babies." She untied the child and supported her head as she lifted her. When she handed the baby to me she paused for a moment to say, "You look familiar."

I avoided her eyes as I accepted the child. "Perhaps you've seen me during one of the celebrations. I often help the priests."

"Mmm, yes that must be it. Still, it seems like I know you better."

"So, how old is your son now?" Riku interrupted her. "He certainly seems able to care for himself." The child had joined the other children playing in the yard.

His mother laughed and added, "At five he is an active child, but well-behaved. He carried one of the jars we delivered this morning, in spite of his father's protest."

The conversation centered on their son while I held the precious bundle. Her little hands waved randomly until one caught the edge of my shawl and the other wrapped around my finger. Her attentive brown eyes filled her tiny face as she looked from me to the shiny pin holding my shawl. Wriggling in my arms she embodied the innocence and energetic promise that belongs only to the very young. She gurgled contentedly while a tear rolled from my cheek onto her blanket. I wanted children. I wanted to be Ninan's wife and the queen.

Riku pulled the child from my arms as he hurriedly concluded, "We must be going now. I'm so glad you were blessed with other children. Thanks for letting us watch you paint the jar." He handed the baby to her mother and kept talking so neither parent was able to speak. "Good-bye now," he said abruptly as he took my arm and led me away. Barely dry-eyed and as fragile as the baby, I left the sounds of children playing behind.

Holding my arm, Riku steered me back to the stairs leading away from the artisan section, but then turned left again and walked the short distance to the summer solstice shrine. Alone and out of the public eye he settled me on the bench against the wall and waited. I expected him to scold me, but he said nothing. I watched his feet as he tapped his foot on the stone floor and shifted his weight from one leg to the other. His eyes burned through my head. I defiantly glared at him and demanded, "I want to have children and be Ninan's wife even though I know I'm supposed to die. You've explained how important that is, and Pule convinced me it's a sacred and noble honor, but it's not what I want." Choking sobs overtook my voice, and I dropped my head, staring at my blurry hands.

Riku stepped closer to me, spread his feet and crossed his arms over his chest. Apparently ignoring my outburst he calmly asked, "Who's Pule?"

Had I mentioned Pule? Had I betrayed my secret? "Who?" I whispered, hoping he'd drop it.

"Pule. You said Pule convinced you it was your sacred duty." He waited. I knew he'd wait through the night and the next day, if that's what it took to get an answer.

I forced myself to forget about Ninan and babies. That single word was an immediate threat to my life. If I lied and told him Pule was a friend, my lost innocence would be assumed, and I would be killed in disgrace. If I told him I traveled with Pule, I'd be confessing to violating his most important rule, never travel alone. Very carefully I replied, "Pule is my imaginary friend. She's a beautiful blue macaw."

"And when did you first 'imagine' this friend?" He enunciated each word, not believing my explanation.

I should have known I couldn't deceive Riku. Pule wasn't an imaginary friend. She found me; I didn't invent her. "Pule came to me first when you visited the Inca and I was entirely alone for a month. I was in the garden, and the birds brought her to me. I remember her first visit as if it were yesterday. She taught me to fly!" The joy of that first illicit escape still inspired me. I knew that the ability to leave my confinement was vitally important to tolerating my isolation, even if I left only on rare occasions.

"Was that just before you got sick?" His voice softened, and he sat down beside me.

I nodded and added, "She was the one who told me that I am Huayna Capac's daughter and that I was to be sacrificed. I wanted to kill her, but she was too fast for me. I think I fell asleep and lay in the rain all day before Iska found me."

"So a talking bird told you the secret. Iska swore she didn't tell you, and no one else would admit to it." He sounded relieved to finally understand the mystery. "Perhaps you should tell me everything about Pule."

"You're not angry with me?" I asked timidly.

"Why should I be angry?" He honestly looked puzzled.

"You've said many times we should never travel alone."

"Oh, yes, I see." He thought a moment and finished, "But you didn't travel alone. Pule was your guide."

I didn't think an imaginary bird qualified as a guide, but at least Riku was satisfied. "But she is no more real than a melody I sing without making a sound."

"Perhaps, but maybe she's a visitor from another world. How do you explain that she was able to tell you who your parents are? Do you think you knew that?" Confused, I just stared at him. "Why not tell me everything about Pule. Perhaps I can help."

There was no reason to hide anymore, so I told him about her first visit. He intently listened as I spoke about flying to the city gate and finally having a friend. I tried to tell him how hurt I was when my new friend told me I was to be killed. Riku put his arm on my shoulder and offered some sympathy, but he rarely asked a question or interrupted me. Next I told him about her most recent visit just a few months earlier when we went to the mountaintop and glided down to the sea. I even told him about flying toward the horizon and returning to the unknown coast. Riku shook his head and reminded me how dangerous it was to travel alone. When I talked about the silver man he wanted every detail I could remember.

"Was he alone?"

"I didn't see anyone else, but . . ." I stopped to think. Why did I think there were others? "Now I remember. He was shouting to someone, but I couldn't understand what he was saying."

Riku rubbed his arms as he always did when he was thinking. "And you say he was entirely shiny, even his head?"

"Yes, his pointy head reflected the firelight. Most of his face was even covered."

"Are you sure it was a man, not a woman or a wild beast?"

I'd never given it much thought, and he was asking me details I hadn't considered. "Well, the voice was a man's timbre, so I'm certain it wasn't a woman. He wasn't dressed like a man, but he had a man's shape and walked on two legs. I'm fairly sure it was not a wild beast."

"Can you tell me more about the beach? Rocky or sandy? Did you recognize any of the trees or other plants? Were there any buildings nearby?"

"Let's see. The shore was sandy. I remember seeing the waves roll onto a light-colored, flat beach. It was too dark to distinguish plants, but the trees were tall and lined the entire beach, practically covering the mountains behind us. If there were any buildings, they were hidden by the forest, and I saw no lights and heard nothing."

Riku didn't respond. We sat quietly as a spitting shower added more gloom to the gray afternoon beyond the doorway. My stomach started to ache again, and I wanted to go back.

Finally he asked, "Didn't you say Pule convinced you to accept your father's command?"

I nodded, wishing I could curl up in a blanket and sleep. I knew he'd want to hear about Pule's other visit. "Will you tell me how she convinced you?"

I suggested I tell him as we walked back, but he didn't want to be distracted from my journey, so I resigned myself to staying until I finished the story. "Like the first visit, I was in my garden weaving when Pule chose to visit. At first she ignored me and ate the two nuts she carried with her." I told Riku about the starving family and the gruesome funeral pyre.

"I know this place." Riku said. "These unfortunate people lived along the coast south of Tumbes. There was a terrible drought, and our ancestors in the mountains suffered terribly as well. It was soon after that . . ." He caught himself pulling away from my story. "Did your travels continue?"

"Yes, we followed the pathways in the sky to a huge tree along the river that Viracocha traveled when he left." I retold the story, and, to my surprise, Riku didn't ask for more details. Finally I told him about the farmer's family in the Urubamba River valley and our final stop at the Coricancha in Cusco. He asked me to describe the temple in as much detail as I could remember. I knew he had been there many times and didn't understand why he was so interested.

When I finished, Riku calmly asked, "Is there more?" I shook my head. Riku closed his eyes and sat perfectly still. The drizzle grew to a downpour, and a small rivulet ran under my feet. I pulled them onto the bench and wrapped my arms and shawl around my knees. The pressure of the wall on my back and my legs pressing on my front eased the discomfort. My head dropped to my knees, and I slept. When I woke, it was already dark, except for a small torch. Riku paced in and out of the small room and then stared out the doorway at the overcast sky. I shifted my shawl and scuffed my sandals along the bench.

He turned toward me. "Are you feeling better?"

"Yes, the pain is gone, and I'm hungry."

"Good. I thought the rest might help." I stood, expecting Riku to start back home, but he stayed in the doorway facing me. "Kaya, we're not quite ready to leave." I retreated to the bench, and he followed. "When we came here, you wanted to marry Ninan and bear his children. Is that still your wish?"

I was so surprised by his question, I could hardly answer. "Yes, I think so. I want to do what is expected of me here at Machu Picchu, and I want to marry Ninan."

"You know it's impossible to do both. I thought it was imperative that you were sacrificed to Inti. How else could we appease Viracocha? How could we explain an alternative to the people? How could we finish the bridge to the Upper World?"

Those obstacles still remained. "Riku, what has changed?"

"Three times you were visited by a spirit from the Upper World, and you probably saw Viracocha returning. If you can reach across while you're in this world, why should we hasten your death? Your remarkable gift may be better used advising Ninan, the Inca."

I could hardly believe what I was hearing. It sounded more fantastic than talking with birds. "But what about the bridge?"

"I don't know. I'm truly sorry you were unable to tell me this earlier. Huayna Capac has already announced your sacrifice across the entire empire. It may be too late to change."

When Ninan said he would find a way to spare me, I humored him with little hope of his success, but Riku's attempting to change the plan was more than I could have hoped for. "I never thought of Pule as a visitor from the Upper World," I said quietly. "She rescued me from the terror of being alone. Even though I always found her feathers in my garden, I never really believed she visited me."

Riku turned to stare at me with incredulous eyes, "You have her feathers?"

"Yes, I have seven feathers of various sizes," I replied simply.

"Then Pule can't be imaginary. Not only has a spirit visited you three times, she has left behind reminders of your travels with her." He put his hands on my shoulders, his face fixed with conviction. "I don't know if it's possible or even desirable for you to become Ninan's wife. From the visits, Pule seemed convinced you should be sacrificed. Why else would she so elaborately show you the reasons for your sacrifice? But perhaps she came only to teach you how to speak to the spirits from the Upper World and told you what you expected to hear. I'll try to find the true intention of the gods."

With a pounding, hopeful heart I answered, "What more could I ask?"

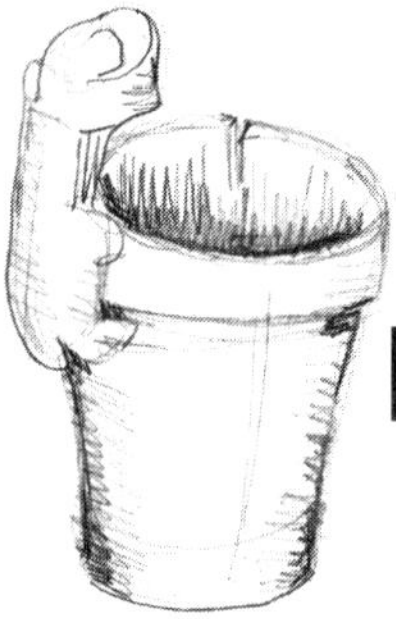

Decrees

Ninan

Acting as host, Pacas stayed in the palace courtyard with Curacas Checa and Pusani while I excused myself to find my father. A passing servant said he was headed for the main entrance, and I hurried to catch him. "Father, may I speak with you before you join the celebration?" I asked, interrupting his conversation with Sinchi Roca.

"Hello, son, we wondered where you and Pacas were. I need to join the people. Can't it wait?" With the festivities, Huayna Capac was cheerful and relaxed.

"Please, father. It's important that we talk before you hear about it in public. That conniving child caused trouble again. I'd rather you heard the story from me."

My father and Sinchi Roca exchanged a glance before my uncle proceeded to the plaza alone. As I led my father toward an unoccupied room, our casual conversation reviewed the competition. Alone, I faced him and blurted out the story. "That insolent Atahualpa tricked me into competing with Checa's son. He tampered with an arrow, and I lost a bet that reversed one of your decrees."

"What? Start over and tell me everything." His expression teetered between surprise and anger. I told him how Atahualpa trapped me into competing in the first place and then loosened the feather in the arrow. I even told him about breaking his nose. He started pacing the room when I told him what Checa and I had bet. "Please, father, discipline Atahualpa before he turns into an uncontrolled menace."

"Atahualpa is the least of your problems. You allowed a child to manipulate you into a situation where you would either lose face or directly contradict the Inca. Your credulity is appalling! How can you possibly expect to be the Inca when you are so easily duped? You've known for years that he hates you. Why did you trust him?"

I expected him to be furious about the bet, but his accurate assessment of my behavior stung bitterly. "On the other hand, Atahualpa's guile and cunning is remarkable for one so young. One day he'll be a formidable warrior. You could have denied Atahualpa's claim that you could beat Checa's son." He continued his diatribe while I cursed my innocence. "You could have refused to compete, excusing yourself as not his equal, or not wishing to tarnish his victory. As the Inca's son you could have flatly refused without explanation. You must learn to control every situation, or someone else will. If I were as gullible as you, I'd be dead by now. The first assassination attempt would have been the last."

He was absolutely correct. I wasn't fit to be Inca, and yet there was so much I wanted to accomplish when I was. There was no point trying to defend myself. I stood staring at the floor while he ranted. "Father, you're right, I am too trusting. I was so sure I could win. My pride blinded me to the danger. I must learn to recognize my enemies, even among family and friends." The Inca stopped pacing. Dreading his response, I continued, "Father, there is still the matter of the bet. Will you spare Cacha's children next year?"

This time I expected his anger, but he controlled his voice to a low growl. "Not only have you compromised your own authority, you have called mine into question. Accepting the bet was entirely your error. How do you explain your stupidity?"

This was not the time to relate my opinion on the excessive harshness of his decree. Without looking up I replied, "I never expected to lose. You know I'm an excellent archer."

"You can't control a situation with a child, and yet you expect to control the vagaries of shooting. Do you always hit your target? Of course not. You've never done anything so unbelievably idiotic." He paced and pounded his fist into his palm as he considered the options. Finally he stopped. "Look at me." I lifted my head to hear his judgment. He face was flushed and his hands clenched. Closed to slits, his eyes felt like spears splitting my head. "The Inca cannot have his commands ignored by anyone, including his son. How can I maintain order, if you're allowed to defy me?"

I would expect equal power when I was Inca. There was no good excuse. "Please forgive me. It will never happen again." I spoke with heartfelt honesty and added, "My actions embarrassed both of us. Can there be no honorable compromise?"

Exasperated, he threw up his arms, allowed them to drop, and resumed pacing. "To spare the children unconditionally is impossible."

Carefully avoiding another confrontation I queried, "Is there something they can do that you would accept instead of the children?"

He stared at me with slightly less disdain and walked fitfully as he considered the situation. "You may be gullible, but you're an excellent peacemaker." Finally he offered a compromise. "Either the children will be given to Inti, as I decreed, or the soldiers who are scheduled for duty will serve for two years instead of one. Since *you* were the one who agreed to the bet, *you* will explain the options and *you* will insure their continued loyalty to Inti and me. Furthermore, *you* will work with the Umu Pilaca and find a way to meet his needs for sacrifices. Is that clear?"

"I will do as you command, and learn from my mistakes. Please forgive me for the trouble I have caused."

The Inca shook his head, still angry. "I pray that Inti protects you until you are wise enough to take care of yourself. Now go, before I change my mind."

I left immediately, ducking into a nearby room to wait for him to leave. Out of sight, I heard him muttering my name as he passed. Alone, I tried to collect my thoughts. As my head cleared, I realized he was very fair with me, and I still had much to learn. Starting with Atahualpa, I resolved he would never again gain my trust nor manipulate me.

When I had recovered, I slowly strolled back to the palace courtyard where I knew Pacas would be entertaining our guests. Pacas was a congenial host, and the three men laughed and told stories while they enjoyed refreshments in the lingering light. I quickly joined their merriment and relaxed after the intense conversation with my father. I knew I needed to address the wager, but waited for an opportunity to arise. In the plaza beyond the palace walls, a popular dance tune mingled with the sunset. Checa commented, "That's my son's favorite song. I'm sure he's dancing and celebrating his victories."

"To his good health and continuing success!" I offered a toast and was quickly joined by the others. "Speaking of victories, I was able to speak with my father about our wager."

Checa responded with a toast. "Long live Huayna Capac. May Inti bless his house and his family!" Of course we all toasted the Inca. "He is a fair man, and I'm sure he has honored the wager."

Pacas noticed my expressionless face and replied, "Perhaps we should hear what Ninan has to say."

Checa and Pusani listened attentively when I said as cheerfully as possible, "Huayna Capac is not willing simply to reverse his decree. However, he has authorized me to offer an alternative."

Checca confronted me directly, "You accepted the bet and now you refuse to honor it. You may be a good archer, but I question your character."

With a steady voice I responded, "We both knew it was my father's decree, and we both thought I could change his mind. I have, but not exactly as I'd hoped."

Checa was about to protest, but Pusani grabbed his elbow and commented in his nasal voice, "Let him speak. You said yourself the Inca is fair."

I nodded my appreciation. "Huayna Capac is willing to spare your children next year on one condition. The men who trained here are scheduled for duty starting in three months. They will travel north where they will fight and share in the plunder."

"And some will be injured and killed," Checa was quick to add. "They are all courageous men and will honor their calling, but how is this tied to our children?"

"Rather than call your children to Inti, the Inca is prepared to spare them, if you agree that your men serve for two years instead of one."

"Instead of one hundred children, the Inca feels that thousands of men are a fair exchange? It's a hardship for the entire area to be without so many men for a year, and now you propose two years?" Checa looked to Pusani for support.

"Giving your children will absolutely result in their death. Fighting for the glory of the gods is an honor, and most will return as wealthy heroes. Surely, if the valley can manage for a year without the men, they can survive for two," I replied.

"Besides, the first soldiers going north will prepare for those who follow," Pacas jumped to my defense. "They'll repair roads, build storehouses and deliver provisions. Your men will likely see no fighting at all until the second year, leaving just enough time for them to become wealthy. Checa, I think this is an excellent alternative."

Looking for support Checa turned to Pusani, who responded, "I too would prefer the conditions of the wager, but we know that's impossible. The men are strong and will bravely follow the Inca. They'll endure and return as decorated heroes. I think we should accept his offer."

"Men instead of children. May Inti keep them safe." Checa turned to me, his face saddened with the decision. "We accept your proposal as an honorable settlement."

Greatly relieved I lifted my cup. "To the men, children and wise leaders of Cacha. Surely Inti will grant his favor to such honorable people." We drank in silence. The servants brought our evening meal, and we drank together well into the night. For the first time, I drank beyond my capacity.

Checa and Pusani were our constant companions through the feasts, drinking and dancing for several days. We even attended the animal sacrifices to Ilyapa and Pachamama praying for their benevolence throughout the growing season. Checa openly mourned for his lost daughter, but I overheard his quiet prayer, thanking Inti for sparing the other children. By the time the men were returning to Cacha, Pacas and I had established sound relationships with both men, and the bitter memory of the modified wager had become an exciting opportunity for the soldiers. As we waved to the departing troops from Cacha, Pacas whispered, "So what happened with your father?"

That seemed so long ago, it took a moment for me to understand his question. Still waving, we exchanged glances. "Pacas, my friend, we were together every waking moment, and yet we haven't talked. Let's go for a walk, and I'll tell you the whole story." He nodded, and we stayed in place beside our fathers until the entire procession was out of sight.

Later, I told him about the meeting. When I finished he concluded, "Well, I agree with the Inca. You should have avoided the entire incident. Don't forget to keep his mother on your list of enemies." Pacas summarized his position with little empathy. "When will you approach Umu Pilaca?"

"I hope you'll join me each afternoon next week. It's a good excuse for you to visit with Tinkha while I contend with the Umu Pilaca. Since your intentions are public, you won't need my supervision."

Pacas heartily agreed and flashed his easy smile for the first time since we left Quispiguanca.

Our friendship needed repair, but I warily asked, "Have you thought any more about the plans we discussed on the road to Cusco?"

He kicked a stone down the road for a while. "Ninan, the prophecy says you will see great upheaval while you're Inca, perhaps even more than Pachacuti. I can see from your plans that you'll initiate at least some of that unrest, but the people are fortunate to have such an honest leader during such turmoil. As your loyal friend, I pledge to fully support and assist you when you become Inca." He stared at the road without further explanation.

"And Kaya?" I asked.

He shook his head with his hands clasped behind his back. "I don't agree with your plan to take her as your queen, but I know you sincerely love her." He struggled to continue. "Marrying Tinkha was preordained by the gods, not a decision I made. I believe Inti has a plan for you and Kaya. You believe that plan includes marriage. Maybe it does, and maybe it doesn't. I'll help you and trust that Inti will accomplish his plan."

Relief and gratitude replaced the weight on my shoulders. "Thank you," was all I said, but nothing would have been sufficient. I smiled to myself and walked with a lighter step. Now anything was possible, even dealing with the Umu Pilaca.

With separate duties, Pacas and I rarely saw each other until the following week when we planned to go to the Coricancha in search of Tinkha and Umu Pilaca. Both were in the courtyard when we arrived. "Good luck," Pacas whispered as he headed directly toward his smiling partner.

Umu Pilaca ignored me as he strolled out the main entrance of the temple. I called after him, "Your holiness, could I speak with you?" His hearing and agility suffered with advancing age, so I quickly overtook him. Towering before him, I repeated, "Your holiness, may I have a word with you?"

His completely white hair crowned his wizened face, but his clear brown eyes sparked like a child's. "Hello, Ninan. What can I do for you?" He tipped his staff toward me as a blessing before returning it to its position as a walking stick.

"Is there somewhere we can talk? I have some important information to share with you."

Thin and small, he looked feeble, but his flashing eyes and alert response spoke to the contrary. "I need to watch the boys grooming the llamas in the plaza. We can talk there."

I glanced toward Pacas, who was already preoccupied with Tinkha, and fell in step behind Umu Pilaca. There was no point trying to speak with him as we walked since he understood by watching lips as much as by hearing. We stood with another priest on the wall overlooking the young boys in the plaza below as they tended a herd of pure white aporucos, the llamas to be used in the approaching Capac Raymi celebration. The gentle creatures nibbled the grass or stood erect, their long elegant necks supporting a regal head topped with ears as expressive as any person's face. Well fed and in excellent health, the animals dwarfed the boys who could barely see over their backs. The boys picked the burrs off their legs, combed their fleece, and cleaned their floppy tails and feet. Accustomed to constant handling, the llamas passively allowed the continual grooming. Speaking to the instructor, Umu Pilaca occasionally commented on a llama or a boy. After a while he was dispatched to address the minutia the High Priest had noted. Satisfied that his wishes were being met, he asked, "And what is it you wish to tell me?" He faced me to see my response.

"You received one hundred children from Cacha this winter, and I believe some were sacrificed when the sun disappeared." I needed to know how much he understood before giving him the bad news.

"Yes, they were excellent children: healthy, well-mannered and obedient. In fact, there are still a few remaining. I personally chose five particularly promising boys to tend the aporucos." He identified the boys in the field below.

"And how many children do you receive in a full year?" I never really noticed the constant stream of children coming to Cusco, or considered what happened to them.

"About a thousand. Of course, most are sacrificed to the gods within a year, but some become priests or Mamaconas here in Cusco. Others are sent to the Urubamba River valley where they learn to tend the crops and prepare the goods for sacrifice. A few even find their way into the royal families and care for the mummies of the Incas." His dark wrinkled face rearranged itself. "Why do you ask such questions? I thought you had information for me."

Hundreds of children sacrificed in Cusco alone? There must be a better way. My immediate task was to save one hundred and regain my father's trust. I nodded and continued without hesitating. "It is imperative that we have experienced soldiers in the north, so the men of Cacha will travel for two years, not the customary one year. In return for their extended service, they won't send another hundred children to you next winter. I'm here to help you adjust your sacrifice schedules accordingly."

"Next year is the special Inti Raymi celebration at Machu Picchu. I need the children to help with the preparations."

I buried my thoughts of the impending celebration and replied, "The Cacha children weren't scheduled to arrive until after the ceremony, so your preparations won't be compromised."

"That may be so, but Inti is expecting his tribute. I must appease him to assure prosperity for the empire."

"There must be an alternative. You must have at least one hundred boys on the plaza now, and there are equal numbers of girls in Cusco. Perhaps you can substitute some of these children, or others from the fields in the valley."

With the will of a warrior battling death, Umu Pilaca straightened and spread his arms to protect the children behind him. "These are my children. I have picked them and raised them myself. None of these children will be sacrificed."

"The children of Cacha were all raised by their parents. No one wants to sacrifice his child. Might I remind you, that's why the gift is so precious?"

"That's different. The people of Cacha are ignorant farmers. They breed too many mouths." He smiled benevolently, failing to see the contradiction.

"If your children can't be returned to the gods, and none will come from Cacha, then we'll need to find a suitable sacrifice other than children." He tried to argue it was imperative that the Cacha children be given as promised, and I repeatedly stated that by Huayna Capac's decree, there would be no children offered from Cacha. The boys had finished grooming and cleared the plaza before he finally accepted the absolute authority of the Inca, and we agreed to search for alternatives the next day. I followed him back into the temple and collected Pacas.

Unwittingly, Umu Pilaca had confirmed the first step in my plan for changing the empire when I became Inca. Years earlier, my father began the process by consolidating the number of sacred sites, but much more reduction was needed. Throughout the empire two of every ten bushels of every crop were dedicated to the religion, and most of it was ceremonially burned. In addition, thousands of children and tens of thousands of llamas were also given to the religion for their use or sacrifice. While the religion had a vital role, the cost was too high, and forever increasing.

By the time I became Inca, the bridge would be complete, and the spirits of the Incas would pass to the Upper World. After five generations, the mummies of the Incas could finally be buried, and the extensive network required to care for the mummies could be dismantled. I planned to redirect the work of thousands who currently cared for the mummies, crops, and animals. Through a series of dreams, Inti would instruct me to bury the Incas and gradually reduce the sacrifices and the number of people supported by the religion. No doubt the farmers would welcome the reduction in the tributes. Those noblemen displaced from the current system would need equally prestigious work, and I expected numerous opportunities resulting from the greater Inca presence in the north.

Pacas concluded his visit with the promise to see Tinkha again the following day. As soon as we were away from the temple, I explained that I expected Umu Pilaca to again insist that he needed the Cacha children. Pacas needed to read the *quipus* to find any surplus that we could substitute. He could visit with Tinkha while I haggled out the solution with the Umu Pilaca. His eyes sparkling, he added, "I hope he doesn't agree too easily. I'd like an excuse to visit Tinkha every day."

"If today is any indication, you'll have your wish." Looking for more cheerful conversation, I asked, "Have you two decided when you'll marry?"

He shook his head as we ambled back to Casana. "We would like to marry at the ceremony during this year's harvest, but Coya Cusirimay insists she needs Tinkha until the Inti Raymi ceremony this winter. It may depend on when we leave to go north. I suggested she stay in Cusco until we return, but she wants to accompany me in spite of the hardships."

We considered alternatives, without reaching a conclusion as we walked.

In fact, Pacas got his wish. The discussions with the High Priest were tedious and protracted. Each day's negotiation began with Umu Pilaca presenting yet another reason why he needed the children from Cacha. My rebuttal and increasingly emphatic declaration that they were not available inevitably followed. Next he repeatedly disputed that any sacrifice could replace the significance of the children. Of course I had to agree, but argued we could enhance the ceremonies of the children who would be sacrificed, and we could supplement the other offerings as well. By reviewing the *quipus* for the past three years, Pacas showed that the Umu Pilaca substantially increased the number of religious weavings, maize, gold statues, gems, and coca in storage. Additionally, the llama herd under his control was expanding and required more grazing area than was available.

In spite of his age, the High Priest remembered every detail and argued that his stores were not excessive; they would be depleted substantially during the upcoming Inti Raymi. Very slowly and resisting every attempt to find a solution, we finally agreed there was excess, and it could be sacrificed. Even so, he wasn't satisfied until Pacas and the Quipucamayo found a hidden treasure. By carefully reviewing all of the *quipus* for the stores in the Coricancha, they discovered some long-forgotten, extremely old and rare seashells. We finally located them in the depths of the temple behind a bin of pottery: snail shells too heavy to lift, conical shells longer than my arm span, smaller mollusk shells in every possible color, and even shells with smooth, iridescent interiors. They were all unique and clearly of great value, but since Umu Pilaca had forgotten he had them, he could find no excuse for not including them in the sacrifice. With nine hundred children, the increases in llamas, coca leaves and gold as well as the seashells, he reluctantly agreed that Inti would be satisfied at the approaching Inti Raymi and all the festivals in the following year. Pacas worked with the temple's Quipucamayo to document the intended sacrifices for each of the ceremonies. With the Umu Pilaca mollified, I had completed the task my father demanded. Pacas regretted the conclusion as much as I welcomed it.

"I like seeing Pacas every day. Thank you." Tinkha said with a smile.

"He was a great help, and I'm pleased he was able to visit you." I said good-bye and left them so they could have a few moments alone, but I finally returned to drag him away.

As we walked back to Casana, Pacas incessantly bemoaned his loneliness, and I was getting tired of his constant whining. Instead I turned my thoughts to finding a way to save Kaya.

"Oh, I need to tell you what Tinkha said," Pacas blurted out.

Expecting yet another adoring anecdote, I only partially listened.

"I asked her if she'd ever heard your mother mention a secret. Tinkha said she once overheard her talking to Cepi, but she's never repeated what she learned. Ninan, are you listening? 'Secret' is the name of Kaya's elder twin."

"What?" I shouted, suddenly focused on every word. "So the rumor is true. That's fantastic! Does she know where she is?"

Pacas shook his head. "Not specifically, but she must be close since your mother said she was going to see her."

Elated for the first time in months, I grabbed Pacas and swung him around. "Now anything is possible! How can I ever thank you?"

"You could leave Secret alone and allow Kaya's sacrifice to take place as planned." Pacas was absolutely serious.

"You know I can't do that!" I joyfully replied.

"I know you *won't* do that. I said I'd help you and I have. Now it's in Inti's hands."

I tried to control my enthusiasm for the sake of our friendship, but I couldn't hide my untamed smile or lighter step. Pacas just shook his head and we walked in silence.

When we reached the palace, our fathers were amusing themselves with a game of chance, and Sinchi Roca spotted us as we peeked into the courtyard. "Pacas, Ninan. Come join us!"

Needing to speak to my father, we willingly entered, and I pressed Kaya from my mind. "Hello father, uncle, we have just returned from the Coricancha, and I'm happy to announce that the Umu Pilaca agreed to sacrifice some magnificent shells, gold, coca, and llamas from his existing stock in place of the children of Cacha."

My father's laughter filled the courtyard. "Congratulations! In only a week you managed to change his mind. Did you get your agreement recorded?" he asked.

"Pacas verified that all the changes to the *quipu* were correct, and you know his work with numbers is always meticulous."

Still chortling, he added, "I expected it would take you at least two weeks to convince the wizard. In fact, you've done so well, I'll plan to use you more often when I need to deal with him." His lilting voice and enthusiastic smile was a pleasant change from our last encounter. "And did you learn anything from this unfortunate incident?"

"Yes, indeed, several things related to my half brother, power, and negotiating," I replied truthfully. Pacas chuckled beside me.

"Good, then we'll put the recent events to rest. Now that your afternoons are free, you two can help us plan the northern campaign. We have preliminary plans, but there are many details to work out. For now let's enjoy the evening. Here, have a cup of *chicha*." My father extended gold cups to each of us before the waiting servant could respond. "To our fine young sons."

We drank to his toast, and I was greatly relieved to be back in his favor.

The next morning began like the others, settling disputes between neighbors in the plaza. Pacas visited Topa Inca's Quipucamayo and continued his studies to memorize every detail of his history, having already memorized Pachacuti's history. In the afternoon, we met at Casana and joined our fathers and a trusted recorder. "You two are just in time. We just finished deciding how many soldiers will come from each region and when each group will arrive in Cusco," my father summarized.

After an extensive review, we learned that five thousand men from Cacha were to arrive in Cusco in just two months. Sinchi Roca would lead these men north soon thereafter. He planned to station groups of about one hundred soldiers at strategic intervals as he moved north, where they would begin constructing storehouses for supplies in front of the advancing troops. Sinchi Roca's final destination was Tomebamba, where he would design the new city with Socso before returning to Cusco.

The main force, one hundred thousand soldiers, would begin to arrive in Cusco in eight months, a month after the winter solstice celebration at Machu Picchu. Concluding the review, my father said, "After gathering in Cusco, the soldiers will head north. With groups of two thousand leaving each day, it will take two months for the last group to leave. By then, Sinchi Roca will have returned from Tomebamba, and I will leave. Since they will stop to complete the building projects, I will pass most of them and reach Tomebamba with the front line."

There were many details to be finalized including how much food and other supplies would be taken from each of the Inca's major storehouses scattered across the south and west. Pacas enthusiastically grasped the complex problem of balancing available supplies with the number of soldiers and llamas conscripted from each region that could carry the goods. "Actually, we have a much larger concern." Sinchi Roca tempered Pacas' eagerness to attack the problem.

My father cleared his throat and began thoughtfully. "As you know we're committed to expanding Tomebamba into the major Inca city in the north. In fact, the plans are to duplicate Cusco in grandeur and size." My memory of the sleepy village set in an idyllic mountain bowl was to be replaced with the bustling and bickering of Cusco. Regretting the loss of a childhood adventure, I listened carefully. "Our Quito allies, Apu Tacana and Masi, presented a convincing argument for a much more substantial Inca presence in the north. We are contemplating whether the empire should be split with an Inca in Cusco and his equal in Tomebamba." Huayna Capac paused and Sinchi Roca continued the discussion.

"The land is much different in the north. As you saw, drought is possible, but generally the warmer climate and abundant rainfall are more conducive to agriculture than the high plains of this area. In fact, with access to the ocean and the plentiful forests, many eat with little need to farm. Perhaps even more important, their gods and leaders are different. Inti is important to them, but their religion places equal importance on the gods of the seas and the volcanic mountains. Unfortunately, where we haven't imposed our order on them, the military leaders consider themselves gods, and as gods, they extract enormous gifts and sacrifices from the people for their own benefit."

"These leaders simply take what they want, and in return, give their own people the right to live on the land they stole from them, and little else," my father said as he shook his head in disgust. "Each city or river valley is independent. Often a military leader forces men to raid nearby cities to capture their wealth of emeralds, gold, salt, or anything else he might deem valuable. This wealth is hoarded by the leaders and traded for personal extravagances."

Pacas squirmed on the bench as he said, "But I've memorized most of Topa Inca's conquests. He established our system throughout the region. You must be speaking about the north before the he arrived."

"Sadly, our values overlay the old system and disputes arise periodically," his father responded.

"But the Quitoans were so supportive of the Inca. Can they be trusted to ally with us as they have declared?" I asked, alarmed by this state of near chaos.

"Yes, Quito, Tomebamba and Cajamarca are strong Inca cities in the mountains," my father answered immediately. "The rest are Inca, but they are loyal to the most powerful. Alliances could change if an alternative presented itself. During his visit, Apu Tacana implied that the coastal city of Tumbes could become that alternative."

I saw the same disquieting surprise on Pacas' face as I felt myself. "I think I understand why Apu Tacana was so insistent on expanding Tomebamba. It becomes the first defense for Quito. His desire for our stronger presence reinforces his military position. Still, why are you considering splitting the empire and having two ruling Incas?"

Huayna Capac fingered his cup and answered calmly, "Essentially we already do that. When I am away from Cusco, Sinchi Roca has the full authority to act as Inca. I have spent less time in the north than I'd like and this instability is the result. There needs to be a leader who lives in the north and can spontaneously act with the absolute authority of the Inca."

"And what happens if Viracocha does return as predicted?" I asked. "How will he judge an empire ruled by two men? Does he judge both Incas? What if one is pardoned and the other destroyed? How could the surviving Inca possibly rebuild?" Neither Sinchi Roca nor Huayna Capac could find a satisfactory answer. We considered other alternatives to ruling the empire such as a single Inca in Cajamarca with two leaders below him, one in Tomebamba and the other in Cusco. After several hours of discussion and no resolution, we agreed to leave it unanswered and called for beer. The question ruminated for weeks. Pacas and I occasionally talked about increasingly more complicated systems, but no solution emerged. The dilemma was still unresolved when a runner arrived late one morning from Quito.

I was in Haucaypata delivering another verdict in a civil dispute when I noticed the exhausted messenger cross the plaza and enter Casana. It was soon after that I recognized my father's bellowing voice from the interior. After finishing the morning's work, I hurried inside. Still ranting, my father wielded a mace at the splintery remains of a wooden platform. His hair flew across his purplish, sweat-drenched face, while his murderous eyes rivaled the hatred spewing from his mouth. "Traitors! Ungrateful brutes. Tumbes will be destroyed. Savages! In the name of Inti and by my hand, they will suffer. They will beg for death before they die."

He didn't notice my arrival, so I quickly walked to Sinchi Roca who stood in the corner with his chin resting on his hand. He told me the rebel leaders in Tumbes assassinated the Inca leaders and their entire families. In his coded message, Apu Tacana reported that all other Incas were immediately exiled from Tumbes and were traveling on foot to Quito. He begged my father to accelerate his plans.

Over the next few days, my father's hatred hardened into calculating, seething rage, and our carefully laid campaign was abruptly modified. Immediately following Capac Raymi, in roughly three weeks, Sinchi Roca would travel north with only one hundred soldiers and extra litter carriers. Moving quickly in a small group, a single man would be stationed at each building site along the route. The rest of the Cacha soldiers were to follow as quickly as possible, divide themselves per the instructions left with the sentinel, and begin the construction at each site. Sinchi Roca would plan the expansion of Tomebamba and return as quickly a possible, enabling Huayna Capac to leave with the first troops immediately following Inti Raymi. With the new strategy defined, Huayna Capac decided to publicly declare war on Tumbes at the final ceremony of Capac Raymi.

With the arrival of the troops from Cacha and Capac Raymi already in progress, the three weeks passed quickly. On the final day of the celebration, my father presided over the naming ceremony of the new men from the golden platform in Haucaypata Plaza, while Pacas and I stood at its base. Wearing a new cloak made of bat wool and decorated with yellow hummingbird feathers in the shape of the Punchau, Huayna Capac stood above the entire plaza filled with nobles dressed in their finest, brilliantly-colored costumes. In the ambience of celebration, my father oversaw the ceremony as each new man went to the podium to be named. At the very end, when everyone expected him to congratulate the men and invite them to the feast, the Inca Huayna Capac delivered his crucial address.

"In the name of Inti, welcome to this glorious and final event of this year's Capac Raymi. Through their military training and month of trials, your sons distinguished themselves with strength, honor, and courage. As Inca, I extend my personal congratulations to each of you and welcome you to manhood."

The jubilant crowd roared its approval and expected the Inca to immediately initiate the feast.

My father waited for them to fall silent before continuing. "Not only does being a nobleman endow a certain honor and privilege, it also carries the responsibility of selfless service to your families, our loyal subjects, and to Inti. Some of you may oversee the construction of our magnificent buildings, while others may have an aptitude for managing the storehouses. Most of you will distinguish yourselves as warriors in that noblest cause, protecting the children of Inti." He paused and surveyed the unsettled crowd. "A messenger recently brought word that the Inca leaders in the north were attacked by traitors."

Waves of shock passed through the crowd in gasps of disbelief, whispered prayers and occasional obscenities. The Inca again waited for the complete attention of the crowd.

"While the soldiers were on a detail in the mountains, the people in the northern coastal city of Tumbes viciously attacked their leaders."

A few keened for their loved ones as others shouted for revenge, but the Inca raised his scepter to call for quiet. "After suffering the indignities of public humiliation, the two leaders were bound and dragged to the center plaza while other rebels gathered all of the local Incas. At high noon, local militia tortured every member of the families. Starting with the youngest, the rebels slit a child's throat and watched the wailing parents grieve for their dying child. While all twelve children lay in pools of blood, the monsters publicly raped, mutilated and finally strangled the four wives. At the end, the two Curacas themselves were burned alive. Not even their spirits were allowed to survive."

Women wept openly while the men shouted so loudly, I could only distinguish a few of them. "Kill the rebels." "Vanquish the evil." Fed by its own hysteria, the crowd gradually shifted to a unison chant, "Tumbes traitors. Tumbes traitors. Tumbes traitors."

After a while, my father raised his scepter with both hands over his head and stood motionless on the platform. Gradually the mob settled into an agitated hush, and he lowered his arms.

"I too am furious at their barbarity. For two generations, we maintained peace in the Tumbes region. We expanded their irrigation system." He lifted his arms to entice a cheer from the crowd and again dropped them for silence. "We built a holding pond to stabilize their water supply. During a drought my father supplied food for nearly two years." Again they cheered their accomplishments. "We built a temple to Inti, and the people participate in the festivals. Now they demonstrate their thanks by terrorizing and killing their benefactors!" My father stamped his foot and pounded his scepter into the platform.

"Ingrates!" "Barbarians!" The crowd shouted their insults at the people of Tumbes, and again my father calmed their indignation before he lost control.

"Soon your young men will marry, have children, and be dispersed throughout the empire. Disrespect and mayhem places them all in danger. Disobedience will not be tolerated. For the security of your children and our loyal subjects, these heinous acts must be punished. It is our sacred duty to civilize these heathens. In the name of all that is good, Tumbes will be crushed."

A spontaneous cheer reverberated through the plaza, and as it died the Inca bellowed, "We will destroy these savages. We will eliminate the scourge they brought to the empire." He lifted his arms and eyes to the sun and waited for the echoing to diminish. "They prospered under our leadership. Now they shall suffer our retribution. They mercilessly tortured and murdered your families. So too they will be annihilated."

The plaza roared its approval. "Our enemies will know the wrath of the gods. But Inti protects our warriors."

The Inca pointed to the corner of the plaza and everyone stretched to see. "Sinchi Roca leaves immediately with his scouts. Thousands more will follow. In the name of Inti, revenge shall be ours!!" With conch shells blaring and the entire crowd repeating my father's call for revenge, Sinchi Roca led his men across the plaza toward the road heading north.

Messages

Kaya

The Temple of Ilyapa was blacker than any night. The four of us sat absolutely still in the eerie darkness, aware of each other only as soft breath seeping through the void. Finally Riku spoke. "Our task is unprecedented. We must determine whether the gods wish for Kaya to sit with Inti, or whether she will become Ninan's wife and queen." The echo of his voice blended with simultaneous gasps from Atuk and Tumbes. Neither expected any role for me other than being sacrificed. "Kaya's visions of Pule demonstrate her gift for speaking with the spirit world. As the queen, she could vastly improve the Inca's ability to interpret the messages from the Upper World, which, as you know, are often unclear."

"Who's Pule?" Tumbes asked. Even though he sat immediately to my left, his position was entirely masked by the echoes off the temple walls.

"Kaya will share her adventures with Pule. When she finishes, we'll have a special drink and ask the gods to clarify their intent." I felt his gentle smile reach across the circle, but it wasn't enough to relieve my anxiety.

To minimize the magic of the temple, Atuk whispered from my right, "Can we ask questions as Kaya tells us?"

"Yes, but let the spirits guide you. Remember, we must answer one specific question," Riku responded. "Kaya, please tell them everything you remember about your visions."

The group waited patiently for me to begin while I tried to ignore my rumbling stomach. In preparation, Riku insisted we abstain from meat and salt for two days, and we'd been in the temple without food since well before dawn. The sun must have risen over the mountains by now, but the carefully sealed thatch roof completely blocked the light. Finally ready, I retold my tales of Pule exactly as I had told Riku. Speaking in the dark and listening to my echo, it seemed like someone else's dreams. I wondered if I'd completely fabricated her, but I clung to her feathers as my validation of her visits. As I spoke they asked only occasional questions. Tumbes wanted to know every detail about Pule, and Atuk asked about the pathways in the sky. Unlike Riku, neither one asked about the silver man or the deserted beach. I finished the story, disoriented and acutely aware of the consequences. My life now rested entirely with them.

Silence again settled over the group until Atuk finally said, "I've always thought of you as my younger sister. Protecting your innocence and helping you prepare for your life beside Inti is a privilege. Now I see that you're worldly beyond your experience, and you're equally suited to be queen." I was touched by his kindness but knew it would take more than his friendship to alter my future. I thanked him without getting overly sentimental or revealing the terror building within me.

"Kaya, since we first met I've felt guilty," Tumbes confessed. "I'm just an orphan from the city of Tumbes, and yet I have been shown every kindness by the Incas. Every need was met from the day I arrived, and being part of this group is a remarkable honor. You, the daughter of the most powerful man in the empire, are restricted, isolated, and destined for sacrifice. I'm relieved that there may be an alternative."

We met nearly every week for years, and I had no idea that Tumbes or Atuk thought of me as anything other than the youngest student. How could I possibly have contact with the Upper World when I was so oblivious to those around me?

I clumsily expressed my appreciation, and was relieved when Riku interrupted. "I think we can all agree that Kaya's visions are remarkable. If Pule will come, we can pose our question to her. There is little doubt that Kaya can help Ninan as Inca, but the dilemma remains. Does the benefit surpass Huayna Capac's obligation to Inti? That is what we must ask to be shown." There was shuffling along the dirt floor that sounded like Riku collecting the bundle he brought with him. "Years ago when the healers visited the hot springs, I asked them to share their medicine with me. There is a tall, straight cactus growing along the coastal deserts that can be used as a painkiller, or, mixed with other plants, it can aid us in our search. Another time I'll show you how to prepare the tea, but since we needed complete darkness, I already prepared the drink for today's traveling."

A metal cup clanked against a ceramic jar as he opened the bundle and continued his instructions, "During our travels I will hum and whistle various songs. Listen for the sound reverberating through the temple. Let it carry you to the spirits and guide you back. Unlike *ayahuasca*, this drink will take each of you in a separate direction, but you must remain aware of the group."

Without warning, Riku whistled a high pitched, piercing tone. My hands involuntarily covered my ears while someone climbed across the roof, and the temple immediately sparkled with rainbows. After sitting in darkness so long, the enchanting colors delighted each of us. I giggled and Atuk scanned the vibrant patches. When our surprise settled into an amused contentment, Riku explained. "My helper has uncovered the quartz crystal on the roof. Inti releases these colors from a single ray of light. Each color will help you see different things, and you are free to move about the temple while we travel. If you are drawn to a particular color, place yourself so its light washes your face, but close your eyes or the bright light could be the last you see. Even with your eyes closed, you will feel the color and benefit from Inti's blessing. The miracle feathers that Kaya holds were given to her for her safety. Please allow each of us to use a feather to direct us toward Pule."

I gladly handed them each a feather as Tumbes asked, "Pule is entirely this color?" I nodded and he added, "She's the magnificent color of the ice in the mountains."

"She reminds me of the zenith just before sunrise. Sometimes I imagine her flying above me in the early morning," I replied, pleased that Tumbes also appreciated her beauty.

As we talked, Riku poured the first drink in the silver cup and handed it to Atuk. "Drink in good health. May Inti guide your visions." Atuk emptied the cup and returned it to Riku who refilled it and handed it to Tumbes. "Drink in truth. May Inti keep you safe." He too downed the contents and returned the cup. He offered the cup to me. "Drink with the grace of Inti. May Pule answer your call." Never had I so desperately wanted his prayer to be answered. I emptied my cup, and Riku immediately drank his before he began to repeat a deep resonating chant.

I twirled the feather through various stripes of light and watched as it changed from drab grey to luminescent blue, just like the sunlight glistening on Pule's wings as we flew through the mountains. I held back the tears as I softly whispered, "Pule. Pule. I beg you. Please come to me. Please answer Riku's question." I vaguely noticed Tumbes and Atuk wandering around the temple while Riku, still stationary, whistled short monotonic blasts that gradually melted into Pule's caw. Dust danced in the rainbow streaming across my feather, and I blinked several times to alleviate the spinning in my head.

Instinctively, I moved my hands in the tingling warmth of the indigo light. Even though the point of light shone only on a small patch, I gradually collapsed into that spot and basked in its soothing brilliance.

The feather fluttered out my hand and then rose toward the sun where it joined the others in the beating wing of a passing macaw. "Pule, is that you?"

She didn't answer, and my feather dropped back to me as the bird disappeared into the jungle. Again I sat with the feather in the intensely purple glow. Always questioning, I asked, "Pule, where are you? How can I find you?"

She had always found me, so I didn't know where to search. A breeze ruffled the finest veins of the feather as macaws called in the distance. The tip turned toward the sound and then flapped as if it were still on the wing. I held the end and lifted off as the single magnificent feather carried me to the clouds. As gently as a butterfly alights on a flower, I landed in the fluffy white cloud with a full rainbow splashing over me.

My feather fluttered away, dipped its quill into the rainbow, and painted a nearby cloud with exactly the same plant design the potter at Machu Picchu used on his jars. Shining more brilliantly than gold, each color blended with the others, and yet held the vitality and intensity of its unique identity. Having finished the first cloud, the painting feather moved to another and mimicked the symbols of the gods that I'd woven so often. As naturally as a bird in flight, the magical feather painted every cloud with exact replicas of the fuchsia in my garden, a llama, the Intihuatana at Machu Picchu and the Coricancha in Cusco. Hundreds of clouds expanded around me as my soft white throne, still flooded with the rainbow, drifted behind the painting feather. "Paint a picture of Pule I called."

My feather stopped to listen, but seemed to hear only the sounds of the distant macaws. Painting faster, the figures became more abstract. The flowers blended into a blur of color surrounded by snowcapped mountains. Still identifiable, the unique patterns sprawled across the clouds. Brilliant purple and gold swirls suggested trees floating over the rolling ocean waves in a green sunset. Orange rain swept across a small village flooding the streams with puffs of wool. Chinchillas jumped from cloud to cloud, chasing the feather and each other as they changed color to blend into their surroundings. Hundreds of images appeared spontaneously, each more fantastic than the previous.

The pictures degenerated into scrawling, twisting lines without any recognizable feature. I knew my time was short and begged the feather. "Where's Pule? We must find Pule!" The feather stopped painting and stood upright as though it tried to understand my question. Again it drew the precise replication of the plant on the potter's jar, and scrawled a black line below it. The quill stopped, bowed to me and drew an elaborate, curving design and followed it with a precise drawing of an orchid. It stood erect, paused and began again. This time a symbolic line preceded my guava tree. Next it drew a short jagged line followed by the Coricancha.

"No, I don't need more symbols, take me to Pule. I must find Pule." The feather ignored my requests and continued faster and faster until the haunting melody, spinning colors, and frenetic feather blurred together in an endless jumble as disorienting as a dense fog. Exhausted, brokenhearted and alone in the confusion, I heard the macaws fade into the distance as I fell into a desperate sleep.

When I woke a sense of doom hung over the temple. By the light of a small torch, I could see the others quietly waiting for me to join them. Surprised to find the feather still in my hand, I sat up and tried to shake off the slow spinning in my head. Riku must have known from my expression, but he asked anyway, "Did you find Pule?" Too devastated to even cry, I shook my head without looking at him. "Well, take heart. Together we may have learned something. I've already asked Kinsa to bring our dinner. We'll stay here for the night and review our traveling in the morning." As if she were waiting for his command, Kinsa entered the temple carrying a steaming pot of rich, earthy bean soup. The spicy dinner tasted better than I expected, and like the others, I slowly and silently finished my bowl. Remembering Riku's words of hope, I tucked my blanket around me and fell asleep.

Again I was the last to awake and found myself alone in the temple. Sunlight streamed through the open door and the hole in the roof where the crystal had been. I stood on wobbling legs, stumbled through the doorway, and squinted at a few wispy clouds in a remarkably clear sky. The others enjoyed the morning sun in the sacred plaza beyond the Temple of Ilyapa. "Good morning!" Riku cheerfully greeted me even though he looked exhausted. "Are you feeling better?"

I smiled weakly, keenly aware of my aching head and eyes.

"Good. Have some tea and maize. We've already eaten." He handed me a cup of tea and bent over a pot to serve the porridge. "When you've revived a little we'll gather here in the sunlight and review what we've learned."

Atuk and Tumbes rested on opposite sides of the plaza. Each acknowledged my arrival and then returned to his thoughts. I chose a spot overlooking the river curling around the mountain as it rolled downstream, and I wondered how far it went before reaching the ocean. Perhaps I'd ask Pule to take me there, if I ever saw her again. Yesterday's disappointment welled up in me, and I tried to swallow it along with my tea. This wasn't the typical breakfast tea. Riku must have a special brew to counteract the cactus mixture. I was recovering faster than I expected and had just noticed that the sense of doom was gone when Riku called us together.

"You all know that our purpose was to ask Pule about Kaya's future role. None of us found Pule, but it is possible the gods have answered our question in another way. If you ask questions during the telling, be sure they are limited to clarifying the vision. Since this journey most directly affects Kaya, I would like you to begin."

I started with the intensely comfortable feeling of the indigo light and the feather flying away to rejoin a macaw. Next I recounted as many of the images I could remember, including the vitality of the early ones and the soothing blur of the later ones. I finished with my desperate attempts to find the distant macaws and being answered with alternating precise pictures of familiar objects and an ornate, abstract line. Everyone asked about the designs, and I even drew a few that I remembered. "I think the feather was trying to show me some new symbols, but they were much too difficult to weave. Perhaps a potter could paint them, but I see no advantage to them. Everyone recognizes the current symbols." I stared at my drawings to hide my disappointment. "Pule didn't come when I called her, and for some reason I was shown these instead."

Riku had little to add and he turned to Atuk.

"It was very exciting!" he began. "I held the feather in my hand, and a small yellow finch landed on my arm and asked if the feather belonged to the wise and beautiful Pule. Surprised that I could understand the bird, I immediately answered yes. It asked why I had her feather, and I replied that I needed to find her and asked for the bird's help. The finch said he knew that Pule recently left the mountains, but a friend might know where she went. She told me to follow her. I flew behind her!" he sputtered his amazement. "With no effort or fear, I simply lifted off the ground and floated behind my tiny guide. I thought flying would be like falling off a cliff, but it's not the same at all. It's like walking on clouds."

Remembering my first flight, I smiled at this delight. Riku let him ramble for a while, before reminding him to tell us the rest of his vision. With a sigh of satisfaction Atuk continued. "We found the finch's friend who told us Pule just left to go to the jungle, so we dropped out of the mountains and asked every bird we passed. There were large birds that couldn't fly who reported having seen her pass. We met slender birds with remarkably long sweeping tails that directed us deeper into the jungle. Finally we saw an eagle soaring high above the river and asked him to look for Pule, but he couldn't see her. Everywhere we went, the birds knew of Pule and many had recently seen her, but we couldn't quite catch her."

Atuk turned to me, his voice still excited, but his eyes filled with remorse, "I'm so sorry, Kaya. I really tried to find her."

"You have done very well," Riku quickly replied saving me the embarrassment of not knowing what to say. "Not only did you discover the wonders of flying, you confirmed that Pule is well known in the spirit world." Atuk found some satisfaction. I was relieved, and disappointed that someone else was discovering my friend's illusive habits. Riku asked Tumbes to relate his story.

Tumbes furrowed his brow and finally threw his hands in the air. "I can't understand this journey, and I hope you can explain it to me when I finish. Like Kaya, I was fascinated with the colored lights and began by moving from one color to the next. I preferred the green light and marveled in its expansive, pervasive vitality. While I was enjoying the light, a perfect double rainbow appeared beside me. Remembering Kaya's sky pathways, I decided to follow the arch. The other end plunged into the ocean, and I found a place to watch from shore, while several terns swooped and glided over the water. The intricate cavorting looked like fun, so I became a tern. Soon I discovered they weren't playing, but trying to outwit one another to gain advantage in capturing the fish swimming just below the surface. The first to dive was more likely to catch a fish than those who dove into a disturbed school. I tried to keep pace, but soon found I couldn't match their speed or skill. Instead I learned another of their tricks. Rather than try to be the first to dive, I allowed another to retrieve the fish, then pestered the laden bird until he dropped it, so I could catch it before it hit the water." Unknowingly, Tumbes swayed about dropping one shoulder and then the other as he reenacted his story.

With worried eyes he continued, "Pleased that I now had a fish for my growing family, I returned to the nest and began to tear away pieces of the flesh for my brood. Perched on the edge of the nest with the fish firmly held under my feet, I had a piece of the flesh in my beak. As I looked down at the insistent chirping, I found a single, featherless macaw. Thinking I had landed on the wrong nest, I looked at my enormous feet to find they now held a palm nut, and that I too was a macaw. Without further hesitation I fed the grateful chick and then flew back as a tern to steal another fish which again became a nut when I reached the nest." Tumbes was puzzled and disappointed. "I asked the tiny macaw if her name was Pule. She said no and begged for food. Kaya, I didn't find her either." He sighed deeply and concluded, "That's all I remember."

"It's interesting that you fed the macaw with stolen, magical food," Riku said. "Perhaps Inti is reminding us that offerings to the gods must be given with a pure heart, unblemished by our actions."

We talked about the baby macaw and wondered if it might represent something else, perhaps a new spirit to the Upper World. We also wondered why Tumbes appeared as a tern and then became a macaw. Was the vision telling him that he was to become a different person, or pretend to be a different person? Although he was a comic actor, Tumbes was not a deceitful man.

Ready to continue, Atuk asked Riku to tell us about his journey. It was a mystery to me that he could maintain the whistling, monitor the three of us, and remember his own journey. He studied us and decided we were still alert, so he began. "The whistling and humming quickly carried me to the jungle where a group of red and green macaws were noisily returning to their favorite stand of palms for the night. I asked if they knew where I could find the home of the blue macaws, and the gregarious flock all offered advice. Finally I learned to listen to only one bird at a time, in spite of the continual ruckus, and was told that the blue macaws lived in drier land farther away. Apparently, they occasionally passed this roost, but I needed to fly directly into the morning sun to find their home. Unable to decline their invitation, I stayed with them through the night and left at first light. By noon I found a few entirely blue macaws and asked if they knew Pule. Like your journey, Atuk, they respected and honored Pule, but didn't know where she was. After some prodding, they suggested I travel a short distance to the place where the mother of all macaws roosted each night. They were sure she would know where to find Pule." Riku shifted his legs, frowned slightly and continued, "I found the roost in an ancient forest and waited until sunset when the macaws returned. Finally I was able to ask the mother of all macaws if she knew Pule. She wanted to know why I sought her, and I told her our question. Finally she agreed to carry our message to her." He shook his head.

Assuming he was finished Atuk said, "You told us you only see places. Today you spoke with the birds and were able to get our message to Pule. Perhaps she'll come to Kaya again."

"Yes, there is a strong possibility Pule will come to us soon." His voice trailed off as he stared at the Temple of Viracocha behind me before continuing. "She said one more thing, and I remember her words exactly. She said 'I expect you'll find Pule when you see Ixiamas.'"

Wary of Riku's answer, I asked if he was expecting Ixiamas.

His brown eyes gently settled on me as he replied, "When we said good-bye, we both expected it would be for the last time, in this world. Even if he does visit Machu Picchu, we can't expect to see him until the end of the wet season. By then it will be . . ." He didn't continue, but we all knew it would be too late at the end of the wet season to change Huayna Capac's decree.

Riku took a deep breath, exhaled slowly and said, "We asked to know whether Kaya is to sit with Inti, or whether she will be Ninan's wife. In return we were shown a new assortment of symbols that Kaya feels are very important, but we don't understand their significance to the original question. We also saw a bird and food modified into forms that were suitable for a baby macaw that we interpreted to be a new spirit in the Upper World. And finally, we learned that Pule is a well-known, highly respected entity who will return to Machu Picchu during Ixiamas' visit." Riku lifted his hands and let them drop to his lap as he dropped his head and concluded, "As usual, the answer to our question was no doubt given to us. Now we must wait to understand it."

He looked tired, and old. His shoulders sagged, and his head jutted forward instead of balancing on his shoulders. Most disturbing to me, his eyes lacked their lively sparkle, and the skin beneath them hung down his cheeks like dried potato peels. Strangely, his demise worried me more than my own. There was still a flicker of hope that I could live a long life as Ninan's wife. Riku was getting old, and there was no hope of postponing his journey to the Upper World. Without Riku, who would Huayna Capac use as his advisor? Consumed by his thoughts, Riku seemed to forget we were there. We all remained silent, waiting for our dear teacher to return to us.

"You're a welcome surprise." Sitting on my right, Atuk cheerfully greeted a visitor behind me. Riku was immediately alert, and Tumbes and I turned to see Ninan covered with mud, approaching us from the path beside the temple that led to the main plaza.

"It's a pleasure to be back, even if traveling in the wet season is difficult."

In the past six months Ninan had shed his remaining youth and stood before us as a confident, robust man. Even caked in filth, his charming smile, muscular strut and winning manner touched my heart. Atuk and Tumbes rose quickly to greet him while I helped Riku to his feet.

"Atuk, Tumbes, hello."

Still ailing from the cactus drink, Riku partially leaned on me as he shuffled forward. With a bow close to reverence, Ninan focused entirely on our leader. "Umu Riku, the priest who searches, it is my honor to be with you again."

"Ninan Cuyohi, the man who carries fire, and soon to be leader of the empire, welcome to Machu Picchu," he replied. Unlike most formal greetings, there was a warmth and genuine friendship between the men. "Tell us, what brings you to Machu Picchu at this time of year."

Ninan finally looked at me, and for an instant, his eyes softened to the familiar yearning before he answered Riku. Addressing us as a group, he said, "Huayna Capac asked me to bring you the news from Cusco, but I have interrupted you. Perhaps I can clean up while you finish your work, and we can share the evening meal."

"Yes, we just finished a strenuous lesson. I would be grateful for some rest before eating. Ninan, are you alone? Where's Pacas?" Riku asked.

"Pacas happily remained in Cusco."

With the dinner plans in place, Riku, not Ninan walked me back to my garden. He claimed he needed to speak with Iska about the evening meal, but I knew he wanted to minimize my contact with Ninan. The three younger men bounded down the stairs before us as they headed toward the living quarters. Riku asked Iska for Ninan's favorite dinner of fish and vegetables before leaving to take a nap.

For me, the afternoon passed slowly as I drifted between restless sleep, images from our visions, and the excitement of Ninan's unexpected arrival. I settled into my garden shelter and haphazardly played the flute between naps. It was dark when Riku woke me as he called from the top of the ladder. "Kaya, are you there? It's time for the evening meal. Kaya, are you ready?"

"I'm coming," I answered, rising quickly. I splashed water on my face to revive myself, quickly straightened my dress and hair, and climbed the ladder to meet Riku. Together we walked to the Inca's quarters where we could enjoy the courtyard, or step into the house if it rained, as it was prone to do in the wet season. The evening was warm, and my excitement mounted as we descended toward the waiting party.

Atuk, Tumbes, and Ninan were already laughing and enjoying the *chicha* under the light of the torches surrounding the courtyard. The yellow light softened the vibrant colors gushing from every bush and flowering plant. Even without a breeze, the flowers danced in step with the flickering light as they filled the courtyard with a sweet perfume. Clean and rested, Ninan commanded the party by his presence; his stately composure blended with his simple honesty created a powerful appeal. Ninan complimented Iska on the meal, while we all satisfied ourselves without restraint. The light and friendly conversation during the meal included the mishaps of his trip and the recent construction along the Urubamba River. After the dishes were cleared and we were comfortably settled with a drink, Riku asked Ninan directly, "What's the news from Cusco that brought you so suddenly to Machu Picchu?"

He immediately dropped his jovial character and donned the somber manner of a man at work. "Let me begin by saying how much I've enjoyed this evening in the company of friends away from the frenzy of Cusco. I cherish my memories with you more than you can know." He gave each of us a genuine smile before continuing, "I carry wonderful news. Pacas will marry Tinkha during the harvest festival!"

"No wonder he stayed in Cusco!" "Congratulations to him." "He must be very pleased." The other three answered together as I murmured, "Lucky woman." Ninan acknowledged all their well wishes with assurances to pass them on to Pacas. "One of my messages comes from Pacas. He would be very pleased if you could all attend."

"Oh, but Ninan," Riku responded immediately, "We are making final preparations. I'm not sure any of us can attend."

"You need to hear the message from Huayna Capac before you make a final decision," he replied in a serious baritone I didn't associate with him. "The natives of the city of Tumbes have butchered their Inca leaders and their families. All other Incas in the region were exiled and by now should be in Quito."

Atuk and Riku took the news calmly, but Tumbes fidgeted and wrung his hands. "Sinchi Roca already left for Tomebamba with a hundred men from Cacha. He will define additional building projects on the way, plan the expansion of Tomebamba, and return to Cusco as quickly as possible. Unfortunately, he will miss his son's wedding. Riku, Pacas would like you to represent his father in the ceremony." Ninan continued with detached objectivity. "Immediately after Inti Raymi, Huayna Capac will lead one hundred thousand troops north."

Tumbes jumped up unable to control himself. "The Incas are generous, benevolent people. Why did it have to be my people?"

I wanted to comfort him, but my fear held me motionless.

"No one blames you, Tumbes," Ninan assured him.

"A hundred thousand men! There has never been such a large force. Where will they all come from?" Atuk sounded incredulous. I couldn't even imagine that many people, much less all soldiers. A repulsive foreboding settled into the courtyard, like a nightmare I couldn't quite remember.

"Riku, Huayna Capac needs you to come to Cusco," Ninan pressed on. "He wants to consult with you about this offensive to be sure Inti favors his plans."

Riku nodded and asked, "Ninan, are you sure your information is correct? That's a staggering army."

"I'm sure. Pacas and I helped our fathers plan the logistics. Huayna Capac declared war at the Capac Raymi ceremony, and the noblemen from across the empire support him. The assassinations must be avenged, or others might face a similar demise."

Who was this man before us? I didn't recognize this matter-of-fact general who calmly spoke of armies and killing. What happened to the gentle, innocent brother that I had grown to love? How was it possible I wanted to marry a man who ordered others to kill? If the shock of the savage attack and planned revenge wasn't enough, the change in my brother compounded my grief and terror. Even worse, Pule had shown me that the Incas would fight in the north. If she was right about that, then perhaps my sacrifice was inevitable.

Lost in my own concerns, I nearly missed Ninan's remark. "When we leave Machu Picchu after Inti Raymi, Pacas and I will go directly north without returning to Cusco. That's why he's marrying Tinkha at the harvest festival. Against my father's will, I still plan to marry Kaya and travel north with her as my wife."

Stolen food was my first thought.

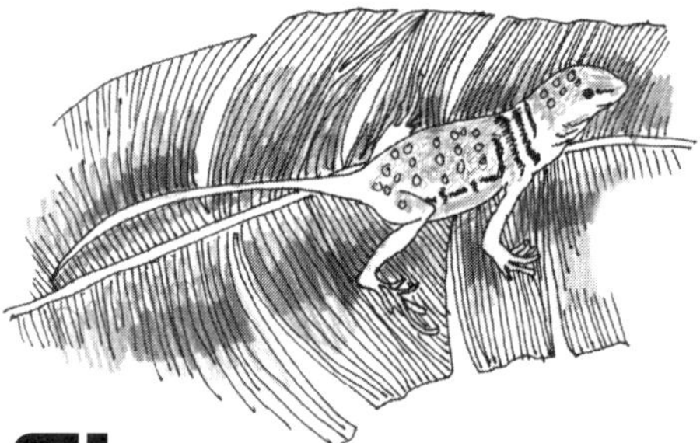

Second Chances

Ninan

The warm rain dug a muddy channel at the drip line of the thatched roof as Riku looked out the temple doorway. "I know Kaya is like a daughter to you, and I should have conferred with you first. I didn't realize how upsetting the attack at Tumbes would be." I crossed the room to lean against the window as I berated my behavior the previous evening. Riku had dismissed the group immediately after I announced my intent to marry Kaya. "I can only stay for a day or two. Huayna Capac needs my help now that Sinchi Roca is gone."

Frustrated with his silence, but unwilling to rush him, I changed my approach and spoke more softly. "I'm nearly prepared to be Inca. I'm fully committed to serving the people and to keeping the order. Already I've become an impartial judge and an able negotiator. In the north the soldiers will witness my courage, and I'll earn their respect as a military leader, but I'll still be deficient. I must have a spiritual tie to the Upper World and since I have no skill, I must depend on someone I can trust. When I asked for your help four months ago, I didn't know Viracocha was to return during my reign. Now I must have Kaya to guide me." I paused to emphasize each word. "Will you support my plan to marry Kaya? You know I love her and will care for her."

I saw his silhouette across the dimly lit room as he turned to face me. His arms hung at his sides, but his face was a mystery as he floated noiselessly toward me. "You think that's an easy question to answer." He shook his head as he approached. "You ask me to betray Inti, the Inca, and possibly Kaya, and yet you expect an immediate response. Last night you announced that the last great battle is about to begin and in the next breath you ask me to ignore the ancient wisdom and support a life of danger and disgrace for Kaya. Your impatience reveals your youth and your inexperience."

I refused to let him see me flinch. The furrows across his forehead and down his cheeks accented his prominent eyebrows and dark, deep-set eyes. "You should know I've been considering the question for the past month, and it was the subject of our discussion when you arrived. Unfortunately, the answer is still unclear."

Startled that he had consulted the entire group, I asked, "What initiated a study of such a personal and controversial nature?"

Riku sighed and headed toward the window beside me. "The rain will continue all day. There is much to discuss, so we might as well be comfortable." He placed two benches opposite one another, and chose the one that allowed him to lean against the wall. Still impatient to return to Cusco, only my respect for the man kept me seated. "Has Kaya ever told you about Pule?"

I shook my head.

The droning rain masked any sound or motion in the temple and beyond. The colorful images of Kaya's visions held my attention as Riku carefully and systematically retold all three visitations: Pule disclosing Kaya's identity, comparing the city ruined by overuse to the Urubamba River Valley as well as viewing the jungle battle and the Coricancha, and finally their journey from the snowcapped mountains to the ocean including Kaya's sighting of the metal man. Occasionally he walked to relieve his stiffness, while I followed to offer a supporting arm. I didn't pester him with questions, but concentrated on remembering the details of her remarkable adventures.

"So you see, Kaya was visited by a spirit from the Upper World who shared vital bits of information. As a seer assisting the Inca, her gifts are invaluable and yet . . ." Riku lapsed into thought. When he began again, he asked, "Do you remember the silver man on the beach?"

I nodded.

"I think Kaya's seen Viracocha returning, confirming the prophecy."

His interpretation hadn't occurred to me, and he moved on before I understood its implications. "Remember, the battles in the northwest were fought in the river jungle, a very difficult location for soldiers trained on open mountain plains. There are no histories to learn from, no elders to teach you. You must prepare for a different type of warfare. Ninan, how will you lead your men?"

"That's why Pacas and I will travel first to Quito and consult with our allies. They've said they know little, but, being so close, they surely know more than we do."

"And do you expect Tinkha and Kaya to follow you into the jungle, or stay among strangers in Quito?"

I hadn't considered their plight and didn't answer.

Noting my hesitation he continued, "Most important, regardless of the war in the north, Cusco and specifically the Coricancha will remain the center of the empire. Why else would Pule choose this place to teach Kaya her most important lesson?"

Riku's conclusion that Cusco would prevail suggested that Huayna Capac's plan to divide the empire would fail. I wondered why. Still, my single purpose was to win Kaya as my wife, and I pressed these troubling issues into the background. I clung to his indecision, hoping to persuade him and save Kaya. "Riku, I deeply, passionately love my sister. Her gifts are a blessing beyond my imagination. If the prophecies are true, surely Viracocha should be met by the Inca and his queen, the intermediary between this world and the Upper World."

"But if we don't complete the bridge, how will he return?" Riku asked as he again stood to pace the temple.

Exasperated, I threw my hands into the air. "He created the entire world. Surely he doesn't need our help to find his way back into the empire. He returns to destroy us all, but he can't get here without our bridge?" I immediately regretted having voiced my opinion about this preposterous notion.

To my surprise, Riku wasn't angry. He simply faced me and asked, "And what of the passage of the Incas to the Upper World? Do you contend that a bridge isn't needed for the Incas to cross? Have you rejected all connections between this world and the Upper World? Are you willing to risk the immediate annihilation of the empire because of your personal lack of faith?"

Miserable that I had ventured into matters better left to the priests, I evaded his question, but he insisted I answer, so I finally offered, "I'm not sure. To me, the ancient vision induced the Incas to build the bridges at an enormous cost. How do we know that the bridge isn't already completed to the gods' satisfaction? Is it necessary to perpetuate this ritual forever?" I'd never dared to speak such blasphemy in Cusco, or even to Pacas. Even now I couldn't be sure whether my motives were sincere or selfish. I stared out the window into the fog that obscured the entire city below and the sky above. Our conversation seemed as constructive as trying to sculpt the fog into gold statues.

I heard Riku at the window beside me. "Can you imagine the relief of definitively answering such a question? That is the power of Kaya's talent. We have tried to contact Pule and ask her whether Kaya is needed for the bridge or whether she should remain as your wife. Unfortunately, all we know is that Pule is a well-known spirit who will return when my friend from the Amazon comes back to Machu Picchu."

We both gazed into the fog, struggling with the unknowable. I longed for the answers to arrive with the facility and validity that Pacas had repeatedly displayed as he studied the *quipus*. I didn't need to ask Riku again; he couldn't support my plan for Kaya, at least not yet. Speaking softly, almost to myself, I asked, "May I see her?"

"I think you should. However, to protect you both, I will insist on being present. None of us could survive a scandal. Meet me here in the morning."

My only consolation was that he hadn't refused to allow us to marry. He could have exposed my intentions to my father, eliminating my prospects for marrying and becoming the Inca. How could I possibly have a more ideal partner than Kaya? Not only did she grow more beautiful with the fullness of womanhood, but her exceptional talents were invaluable. The warm air filled with the scent of new rain reminded me of her. I turned to Riku with an unexpected urgency. "Let's go see her now."

He wasn't there. In fact, he wasn't even in the temple. Alone in the failing daylight, I returned to the Inca's house for a solitary evening.

The rain stopped some time in the night, and the following morning the fog began to lift. I returned to the Temple of Viracocha where I brooded about what I should tell Kaya until Riku arrived. He looked well rested, but his advancing age hung on him like an oversized cloak. We exchanged greetings and immediately descended to Kaya's terrace.

"You and Kaya have every right to meet as brother and sister, and I expect your actions to be consistent with that relationship. I will keep you in sight but will allow your conversation to be private." Riku clearly stated his expectations before adding, "I'll be forced to end the meeting if you act inappropriately." His authoritative presence assured compliance.

He followed me down the ladder into Kaya's garden and carefully monitored our greeting. "Good morning, my dearest sister." I gently placed my hands on her shoulders and kissed her forehead. Even in the dull light of the overcast sky her vibrant eyes and soft skin sparkled like a mountain stream.

"Good morning, Ninan. I'd hoped to see you before you left." She looked over my right shoulder and continued, "Thank you, Riku, for allowing it." She stepped around me and led Riku to her garden shelter as she addressed him. "Ninan and I have many things to discuss. I hope you'll be comfortable under the shelter."

"I'll be fine." Riku dismissed her attentions as he waved her away.

Kaya watched Riku stroll toward the shelter while I stepped to her side. Finally she turned to me and I directed her toward the guava tree at the opposite end of the terrace. The soggy ground kept us standing so we leaned against the fence overlooking the emerging crops. Once again beside my only love, I struggled to begin even though I had planned every word. "You grow lovelier with each passing day." I gazed into her eyes and desperately wanted to wrap my arms around her.

"And you. In six months your earplugs are much larger, and you have assumed the stature of a commander. Soon you'll be old enough to be Inca. Our father must be proud."

The incident with Atahualpa flashed through my head, but I decided not to divert our conversation. "Since we last met, I've been learning the ways of a commander. Pacas, our fathers, and I were already planning the northern campaign when news of the attack reached us. Father was furious, but after a tantrum, his experience as a military leader became obvious. He is a fine man, and I'm grateful to be at his side."

"Yes, you mentioned the plans last night. It seems to me that if the Inca were so skilled, he would settle this dispute and capture the rebel leaders with a far smaller force. How can he even consider risking the lives of one hundred thousand men?" Her voice had a peevish edge that contradicted her soft mellow disposition.

"At first I questioned him as well, but Huayna Capac reminded me that we need to secure the river north of Quito all the way to the ocean as well as end the rebellion." I explained the strategy with the logic of a military leader.

"But most of these men are farmers. Many will die leaving women and children without a man. The suffering will extend through the entire empire, long after the battles are over. Why can't you find another way? I've seen this tragedy on a small village. I can't imagine the horrors of such massive barbarism." Her sad eyes pleaded for an alternative.

Albeit through a vision, Kaya had more experience with war than I did, and yet I would lead men to their death. "I'm sorry you saw such monstrous acts."

She tipped her head to the side as if to ask how I knew.

"Riku told me about your travels with Pule. He is very impressed with your talent as a seer. In fact, I'm sure that's the only reason he's even considering our marriage."

She stared over my shoulder and said, "I'm not sure I want to marry a man who would drive men to their deaths."

Stunned, I studied her beautiful, tormented face. "Kaya, I love you more than you could know, and I need you as my wife. When I become Inca, my duty is to protect the innocent from the criminal acts of war. There will always be hateful, evil men who will challenge the authority of the gods and the Inca. Huayna Capac and the Incas before him resorted to fighting when all options for a peaceful resolution were fruitless. I expect to follow their example, and would be honored to have you by my side to offer alternatives."

Unconvinced she turned away. "It's still horrible. How can you lead such aggression? How could the gods possibly condone such acts?"

I hadn't anticipated needing to justify myself. "As the last Inca, it will be my ultimate challenge to stand before Viracocha and accept his judgment for all the Incas. Some interpret the prophecy to mean that Viracocha will destroy all Incas when he returns. I prefer to think our benevolent creator will show us a better way. Until he returns, my objective as Inca will be to implement as many improvements as possible, starting with stabilizing the north." I watched her carefully to gauge her reaction, and tried not to notice her alluring eyes and unblemished skin. Like the brown patina on exquisitely polished copper, her skin begged to be caressed. I wanted to touch her face, her arm, or at least her hand.

She answered quietly but with no warmth, "One hundred thousand men should be able to initiate a great deal of improvement. What do you have in mind?"

"Let's see, where shall I start?" At least she was willing to listen, even if she questioned everything. Since her experience was so limited, I was surprised by her interest, but she seemed determined to understand. Kaya and I strolled back toward the shelter where Riku dozed peacefully. "The northern campaign will start very soon. We were told that the people of Tumbes resented the tributes they pay the Inca. They claim they suffer greatly by forfeiting so much and that they receive nothing in return. Sinchi Roca believes they are attempting to overthrow our leadership so they can control the north themselves and appropriate their needs from their neighbors."

Kaya listened, but doubted every word; her eyes closed to slits, just like mine. While I was learning to be a judge, Sinchi Roca taught me to control this response since it exposed my position, but Kaya had no reason to hide.

I continued, "After seeing the corrupt leadership in Tomebamba as a boy, I'm not so sure the leaders didn't get a just punishment. In any case, we need to go there to understand the situation. Huayna Capac was extremely angry when he first learned of their savagery, but he is a skilled diplomat and will try to negotiate with the Tumbes leaders before he begins to fight."

"Then why will he lead so many men north? You don't need an army to negotiate." In spite of her reclusive life, Kaya had an innate talent for asking relevant questions.

"Do you remember that when we last visited, Huayna Capac had left his visitors from Quito at Quispiguanca?"

She nodded and I continued as we completed another circle around the terrace garden. "They were adamant that we needed a more substantial presence in the north. The Inca agreed to transform the town of Tomebamba into a city as magnificent as Cusco. Many thousands will be used to build the city." For the first time since I arrived, the woman I loved finally smiled. I wanted to hold her and never let go.

"So that's why so many will go."

"That's one reason. In addition, a huge armed force will encourage the leaders of Tumbes to negotiate rather than fight."

She nodded and I added, "There still must be a battle for the river as you have seen with Pule. Men will die in the effort to secure the path for Viracocha's return."

"I'm sure that's true, but not as many as the size of the army suggests."

I agreed, but didn't add that I too expected many would die fighting against Tumbes.

She brightened and asked, "So, Inca Ninan, after the north is subdued, how do you propose to prepare the empire for Viracocha's return?"

Heartened by her lighter attitude, I plunged into the reforms that Pacas and I continued to refine. "Most important, I believe the tributes supporting the festivals, temples, and shrines are too high. The religious ceremonies are excessive and expand every year in order to justify and support the growing number of people whose sole responsibility is to organize them. The need for tributes can be reduced in several ways: reduce the number of people supported by the religion by not replacing them as they die, return some of the children to their families, offer smaller sacrifices to the gods, and eliminate human sacrifice entirely."

I confidently presented the plan, but Kaya looked worried again. "Won't the gods be angry? Won't they think we're neglecting them and are ungrateful for their protection?"

We reached the fence again and faced one another in the afternoon sun. "I don't think so. That's what the priests would like us to believe, but I think it simply justifies their authority. This is exactly the type of question I hope you could answer by contacting the Upper World."

"You think I can do that?"

"Riku is an excellent teacher, and I believe any of his students is capable of such a task. Of course, I would trust my future wife more than either Tumbes or Atuk." Begging to be touched, her hair framed her face with a soft elegance. I lifted my hand, but she turned to view the city gate on the mountain pass, forcing me to maintain a brotherly relationship.

"And what other plans do you have, brother?"

Distracted by my desire for her, I tried to recall the progression. "Currently the Hanan stores are enormous, but the northern campaign will greatly reduce the surplus since the soldiers will be fed and paid using those resources. When the north is subdued, Pacas will help determine what needs to be replenished. By reducing the number of soldiers and administrators, we'll be able to maintain the lower tribute level." She was not as familiar with these aspects of the empire and didn't question my plan.

There was no reason to trouble her with my concern about the inevitable increase in children when the soldiers returned to their homes. Like Cacha, several regions were already tilling all arable land. Soon there would be more people than the land could support. Pacas and I had discussed this for days, and ultimately we decided that neither war nor human sacrifice was a good solution for reducing the number of people. We planned to seek guidance from the gods, and again I anticipated Kaya's help.

"Kaya, there is one other change you should understand." I took her hands in mine and leaned toward her until our bodies nearly touched. Unlike any other woman, including Mama Runtu, she completely destroyed my ability to think. I forced myself to regain control. "You know I want to marry you and continue to work with Riku to gain Huayna Capac's approval. What I don't know is where we will live. Huayna Capac speaks of splitting the empire north and south. Although there are valid reasons to do so, there are also significant difficulties. I suspect the empire will remain united and two regional leaders will ultimately be accountable to the Inca. Even so, the Inca will travel between Cusco and Tomebamba regularly." Her eyes didn't waver so I continued. "When the bridge to the Upper World is complete, if it isn't already, I plan to announce that the mummies of our ancestors will be buried in a sacred place."

Kaya stepped back and dropped my hands. "What about the sacred traditions! The Incas descended from Inti. How can you tell the people to abandon the sons of Inti?"

I knew she wouldn't agree, but she had to know. We discussed this for some time, and she steadfastly held to the old traditions while I suggested alternatives. Finally I pointed out the basis for the old ways. "The best lands in the empire were taken from the native people and declared the estate of the reigning Inca. By tradition as Inca, I too must appropriate land, probably around Tomebamba, to support my progeny. I don't wish to take the land from the people who have tended it for generations. I expect to build on vacant land in a more modest fashion than our forefathers. I don't believe that hundreds of people should devote their lives to tending my mummy, so I will not need as much land to support my family after my death."

"But where will I raise our children?" Timid eyes overlaid her serene beauty.

"There are many grand buildings in Cusco, the Urubamba River Valley and soon will be in Tomebamba. We'll likely have homes in all three. Please don't worry about this. You will always be cared for, just not in the same way as our forefathers." I tried to soothe her fears by holding her hand and brushing a wisp of hair from her face. "You and Pacas are the only ones who know of my plans. I know some of them dismiss the traditions, but if the Incas and our subjects are ultimately better served, then I must implement them. Do you understand?"

She relaxed a little, but anxiously tugged at her shawl as she turned away. "No. I need time to understand such massive change. You and Pacas have obviously considered many aspects of these revisions, and I know your motives are honorable. Still, you intend to discard much of our tradition."

Riku rose from the shelter and glided toward us.

"Please, Kaya, trust that I'll care for you, and together we will prepare the empire for Viracocha's return. I love and need you. You said once you wanted to marry me. Do you still, knowing what I've told you today?"

"I don't fully understand the changes you are proposing," she replied immediately. "Still, your plans don't alter my dreams. I will gladly marry you and bear your children, if you have the blessings of Huayna Capac and Riku."

The desire to hold her mysteriously melded with a peace I'd never known. "Thank you. You've made me very happy."

As he approached, Riku calmly said, "Ninan, it's time to go. Are you two finished?" He didn't stop until he stood as close to us as we were to each other. We instantly stepped apart to include him in our conversation.

"Yes, we just finished saying good-bye. Thank you for giving us an entire afternoon." I said formally. "Tomorrow I will leave for Cusco and don't expect see Kaya again until Inti Raymi."

Riku nodded and led us back to the ladder. He proceeded to climb, and I again kissed my love on the forehead, promising her, "Soon we will be together. I'm the one who carries fire, and yet you warm me with the joy of a summer afternoon. This winter I'll return, and we'll begin our new life together."

Her eyes moistened, but with a gentle smile she added, "Then may Inti guide you until we meet again."

I followed Riku up the ladder, turned briefly to wave and steal one more glance at the remarkable woman below. She waved and turned toward the shelter while Riku's hand on my shoulder urged me to leave. "Do you and Kaya still hope to marry?" Riku asked as we strolled along the terrace to the main staircase.

"Yes, but Kaya has agreed only if you and our father will bless the marriage."

"You know I can't do that now, but I will seek guidance from the spirits. Meanwhile, all preparations for Inti Raymi will continue as planned."

I nodded, understanding his situation. "I too will seek an alternative. That's one reason I'm so anxious to return to Cusco."

Having reached the staircase, Riku stopped to ask, "Please join Tumbes, Atuk, and me for dinner. We still need to finalize who will go to Cusco for Pacas' wedding. Atuk volunteered to remain behind, since he traveled with me to Quispiguanca last time. I haven't seen Tumbes to ask if he'd like to go." He started down the stairs as he said, "I'll arrange for our meal at their house."

He waited for me to follow, but instead I said, "The sunset will be beautiful over the mountains. I'd like to watch it from Intihuatana."

"Fine. I'll see you later." He still waited for me to start up the stairs away from Kaya's terrace.

The still mountain air carried the sweet scent of new grass and unfamiliar flowers. I followed the stairs to the sacred plaza, passed the ominous sacrificial table and the temples before ascending the final flight to the open platform surrounding Intihuatana. From this high point I could still see a sliver of the sun as it dropped behind the mountains. I relaxed in the reddish glow satisfied that my trip had been as successful as I could have hoped. My thoughts had drifted back to Kaya's gentle manner when motion on my left caught my attention. I turned quickly to see Tumbes step to the edge of the terrace. "Tumbes! Riku and I were just talking about you," I greeted my friend.

Startled to hear my voice, he jumped back from the edge and faced me. "I didn't hear you come up. Have you been here long?"

"No, I just came to watch the sunset. What are you doing here?" I casually stepped down onto the terrace and stood beside him.

He wiped his cheeks with his cloak and stepped away from me. "Waiting for darkness I guess."

"Riku said he would like you to accompany him to Cusco since Atuk went last time."

He pulled his cloak across his stomach as he recoiled. "I can't go to Cusco. I should have done it when I first came up here." He straightened up, threw back his shoulders, held his chin high and deliberately headed for the edge. His intention was obvious, and with a single bound I grabbed his arm and pulled him away from the sheer drop and certain death on the plaza below. Together we tumbled across the terrace to safety. "Why did you stop me?" he wailed. "I'm better off dead!"

"What are you talking about? We need you. Riku needs you, and I need you."

We sat on the ground, well away from the edge, and he covered his face in disgrace. "I can't go to Cusco. It's the center of the empire. People there will hate me. I hate me. I can't stay here now that the people of Tumbes are the enemies of the Inca. I can't go back to my people in Tumbes because I've lived my whole life as an Inca. There is no place for me. "

"Are you out of your mind? No one blames you for the attack in Tumbes."

"But they are my people. I've always dreamed of returning to Tumbes." He buried his face in his hands. "They'll drive me off too."

"That may be so, but you're always welcome here."

"By our small group, maybe. Others will only tolerate me, or worse. I'll be shunned in Cusco by everyone around me."

If he weren't so terrified, he would have cried. Instead his wild eyes held the haunting expression of the would-be assassin whose flaying I witnessed as a boy. Even many years later, that memory still made me shudder. "The only ones who know you in Cusco are Huayna Capac and Pacas. They bear you no grudge. No one needs to know your forefathers are from Tumbes."

"But my name. Everyone will know."

"I think you are exaggerating." Actually, he was probably right; I hadn't considered his name. As a judge, I'd learned how cruel even honest people could be. I carefully suggested an alternative. "Still, if you would feel better, I'm sure we could help you change your name."

"Even if I did change my name, it's too late. I'm a coward and now you know it too. How can I live with the shame?"

I always liked Tumbes. His lighthearted nature showed me the humor in even the most mundane. Hidden from the world in Machu Picchu, he was betrayed by people he never met, but who he considered his family. A coward? No, just alone. "Tumbes, I know how you can prove you're not a coward. If you can do what I ask, then I'll ask Riku to allow you to go north with us, and you can visit Tumbes after we remove the rebels."

His hopeful eyes glowed in the last light of day. "You would do that for me?"

I smiled and nodded, "Yes, but what I ask will not be easy, or without danger."

"I need to prove my courage to myself, as well as to you. I'll meet your challenge."

His body faded into the dark gravel on the terrace as the short-lived sunset gave way to a moonless night. "Here's my plan. Tonight we choose your new name over the evening meal, and you'll agree to go to Cusco." I stopped to allow him to speak, but there was no response. "You know I plan to marry Kaya. In order to do that, I'll need your help in Cusco and throughout the Inti Raymi ceremony. If everything goes as planned you will travel north with us, but you must be willing to return to Machu Picchu. Atuk will need your help with Riku as he ages, and together you must learn his wisdom."

"I understand and accept your conditions," Tumbes answered immediately. "It is my privilege to aid you in your quest."

We sat in the darkness as the aroma of cooking maize, potato soup, and roasting guinea pig intermingled. "I'm hungry, but let's stay a little longer," I said.

He readily agreed and we sat in the deepening darkness. Still trying to calm himself, I could hear his shallow breathing alternate with an occasional deep sigh. "What is that red star just above the western horizon? It's very bright, but I don't recognize it."

Tumbes sounded genuinely pleased to speak of something else. "That's Aucayoc, the red warrior. He stalks his enemies in the Upper World."

Ambivalence

Kaya

The autumn fog chilled the city and obscured the view from my garden. Potatoes waiting to be unearthed, drying maize, and yellow squash covered the fields when the fog first tumbled over the mountains, but since then I'd heard muffled voices and loads of wood falling to the ground. I didn't remember the farmers carrying wood in other years, and certainly not before the harvest. Day after day I listened to their progress and grew more curious while I worked at my loom.

Since my final *cumbi* weaving must be perfect, Kinsa visited regularly. Even though I painstakingly placed each strand of yarn, checked the design, matched the color of each new bobbin, kept the weave even, executed every step exactly as she had taught me, she still criticized my work. "Kaya, redo that last row. The yarn is too thick. No, use this bobbin. It's better."

I wanted my clothes for Inti Raymi to be perfect too, so I accepted her remarks without complaint, even though her changes were beyond my discernment. More distressing than her nagging, I fretted over each row, knowing it took me one step closer to my death. Riku told me he planned to convince Huayna Capac to reverse his decree while he was in Cusco, but he insisted I keep working on my clothes for the ceremony. He also detailed instructions for the preparations and assured Atuk the laborers would arrive as planned to complete the work. Riku's reluctance to delay the work until his return implied he held little hope of changing my father's decree.

Even my nights were filled with turmoil. Some nights I dreamed I traveled north with Ninan, and other nights I dreamed I faced Riku holding a gold knife. Some mornings I awoke trembling with terror, while other mornings I awoke happy and optimistic. The perplexing aspect was that the fear, and joy, followed the dreams of Ninan as often as those of Riku. The pain of being killed horrified me, and I had no wish to die, but traveling north as Ninan's wife into a war-torn, foreign region, and then facing the judgment of an omnipotent god required more courage than I could imagine of myself. Still, having children and being the queen of the most powerful empire in the world held an undeniable appeal that could bring joy beyond belief. Strangely, being honored by all past and future Incas, sitting beside Inti in the Upper World, and guiding Ninan with wisdom unknown to me in this world, was also alluring. I was very confused and uncertain about what I wanted. While I sat at my loom, alone and befuddled, I considered the alternatives, but I often forced myself to empty my thoughts of both possibilities, since Huayna Capac would make the decision, not I. The only thing I could do was to try to reach Pule and ask for her advice.

Riku and Tumbes, now renamed Tucu, the owl, were already on their way to Cusco for the wedding, and Atuk was exceedingly busy in their absence. Even so, Atuk and I continued our daily studies. He came to my garden late in the afternoon, and we walked together to the sacred plaza above or the main plaza below. "Hello, Kaya, are you ready to walk?" Atuk stood at the top of the ladder and always greeted me the same way, even though I could barely see him through the fog.

I stopped immediately and answered, "Of course. Where are we going today?" Atuk was becoming a trusted companion, and I respected him almost as much as Riku.

"I don't think it really matters where we go. You can't see much beyond your feet anyway. Let's go to the Temple of Viracocha. There's a fire burning and the air feels drier." We climbed the stairs noting the slippery spots and the dreary sound of water dripping off the roofs.

Stepping into the cheery warmth of the temple released my apprehension, turning my thoughts back to the exercise. Did you get my picture?" I asked.

"I think so. You tickled my right ear and then called my name. I saw a magnificent double rainbow arching over the western mountains. All of the colors, even the purple, were vivid. In the arch of the rainbows, a distant cloud still dropped rain on the highest peak in the range. Is that what you sent me?"

"That's right. I think this fog will finally lift tomorrow, and I thought a rainbow was a good picture." Riku wanted us to practice sending information while we slept, since that was when we were closest to the Upper World. It was a challenge for the sender as well as the receiver to conceive the image as well as to remember it in complete detail.

After enjoying the fire for a while, Atuk asked, "Have you been able to call Pule?"

Without taking my eyes off the flickering flames, I shook my head and answered softly. "I've invited her to visit me in the early morning to see the dew still hanging on the flowers. I've offered to give her fresh fruit if she came. I prayed to Inti to send her while I sleep. I've even demanded she show herself to Riku or to you. Still nothing. I've not seen her fly over the garden, heard a distant call, or found any feathers. I think she has deserted me."

"I too have tried to reach her, but I always find the same thing. In my dreams I see a blue macaw that looks like Pule perched on a low branch. A fox slowly stalks it through the grass and pounces on the bird, but it squawks and flies away. I've tried to warn the bird, but it doesn't hear me." He sounded frustrated. "I'll keep trying."

"Perhaps we should try together, from a new location," I suggested. Remembering the vivid images we received with the help of Riku's tea, but dreading the accompanying discomfort, I added, "Maybe we should climb Huayna Picchu and travel with *ayahuasca*."

"I know how to prepare the brew and guide the traveling, but Riku insists that I'm still too inexperienced to lead. Can't we find another way?" We both contemplated alternatives, but neither of us could find a solution. Atuk stood to walk toward the doorway. "How did you find Pule the other times?"

"I didn't. She found me. Even when I desperately begged her to come, it was weeks before she appeared. I guess visions from the Upper World appear when they wish." Except for the crackling fire, silence hung over the temple. "It's like the way we send information; if you are unwilling to receive a picture, there is nothing I can do. I guess Pule just doesn't want to visit right now, but we must keep trying."

Resigned to accept the situation, he extended a hand to help me up. "Let's walk some. You'll feel better." A gentle breeze accentuated the damp chill as we walked across the plaza, but it also thinned the fog enough to see the sun as a circle in an otherwise uniformly gray sky. Atuk passed the Temple of Ilyapa where we had traveled through the colored lights.

"What happened to the roof?" I asked. The temple looked nude without its covering.

"Oh, I forgot you haven't been here since the men removed it. It's part of the preparations." Puzzled, I stared at the open building, and he explained, "Do you remember how our voices echoed in the temple?"

I nodded.

"This Temple was built to honor Ilyapa, the god of thunder. Come inside. I'll show you." Stepping into the small room, I looked at the clouds above me while Atuk carefully selected where he should stand. "Cover your ears."

I did as he asked.

In a loud voice, but without straining he said, "Praise be to Ilyapa." The volume multiplied along the flat stone and rose out of the temple. Again he whispered, "Standing here I can be clearly heard through all of the temples, down to the main plaza, and across the terraces on the other side."

"What a fine tribute to Ilyapa!" Still not understanding, I asked, "What does this have to do with the Inti Raymi ceremonies?"

I saw sympathy in his eyes before he looked away. "Much of the celebration will take place around the Temple of Inti behind us and Intihuatana in front of us. When Huayna Capac addresses the people or Riku prays, their words will be repeated by Tumbes, I mean Tucu, here in the Temple of Ilyapa. Everyone will hear the entire ceremony."

"Surely my family and priests can stand in the sacred plaza." The voice enhancements seemed unnecessary to me.

"Hasn't Riku told you anything about the ceremony?" Atuk asked in disbelief.

I shook my head and Atuk led me out of the temple before he answered. Returning to his normal voice he said, "It's easier when I don't have to whisper. Kaya, this festival is the most important celebration to take place during the entire reign of Huayna Capac. Hundreds of thousands would like to attend, but only about ten thousand highly honored guests will be allowed to come. Machu Picchu simply can't accommodate more. There will be people everywhere. That's why the preparations take so long."

I was too shocked to think, too panicked to scream, and too scared to move. "Atuk, how can I face all those people? What if I stumble or worse, cry? What if I get sick?" The thought of embarrassing the Inca or Riku and humiliating myself before the greatest men of the empire was too much. Without another word I leaned over the edge of the mountain path, and lost my stomach. Atuk quickly grabbed my waist, while I spastically vomited even though my stomach was empty. I finally collapsed in a heap, my head resting on my knees.

Atuk wrapped his cloak around me while he tried to comfort me. "Kaya we're still trying to abort the entire ceremony. You needn't get so upset."

Without a word, I looked at him skeptically, and he capitulated, "All right, it's possible the ceremony will happen as planned. I know you're an honorable woman. You'll willingly do exactly what Riku, your father, and Inti expect of you."

"I wish I were as confident as you are. I'm not sure I'm strong enough to offer myself for sacrifice," I mumbled into his cloak. With Atuk at my side, I curled up in a ball and rocked from side to side until the bumps on my arms and legs disappeared. "Take me back to my garden."

Atuk led me through the sacred plaza past the huge sacrificial table. For the first time, I stopped to study the table where I would die. Resting on the ground and nearly waist high, the white granite slab looked large enough to swallow me whole. The cold, nearly flat stone was wider than the spread of my arms and long enough, that two people lying head to foot wouldn't touch. Watched by thousands, I alone would step onto that stone. Imaging the ceremony, my chest exploded. I gasped for air and fell to the ground.

"Kaya, are you all right?"

"I'm scared. Get me away from that thing."

Atuk lifted me to my feet and guided me down the stairs to my home.

"What have you done to her?" Iska wailed when we arrived.

"I'm fine, Iska," I hurried to answer. "Atuk is my friend. He told me a scary story about the jungle cats."

Grateful for my lie, Atuk added, "I'm sorry I upset her. I'll be more careful."

"You'd better," Iska scolded him. "You know how frail she is."

Atuk lifted an eyebrow as if to ask me for an explanation. I rolled my eyes to confirm his suspicion of her overprotective nature. He turned to leave but stopped to add, "It's my turn to send. Look for an emotion." He left, and, in no mood to be questioned, I descended the ladder to my garden where I sat alone, afraid, and unaware of my surroundings.

The next morning the sun triumphantly rose over the mountain ridge into a vibrantly blue sky. The birds cheered our reprieve from the gloomy fog, and every plant gaily displayed its gaudy bouquet. But the sunny sky signaled the rapidly approaching winter and the turmoil before me. I strolled through the garden, pulled an occasional weed as I passed and tried to deny my gripping fear. My garden. How I'd miss my beautiful retreat. Whether I married or was sacrificed, this was the last season I would enjoy my treasured fuchsia. I'd never know how big my guava tree would grow, or whether my infant orchids would ever bloom. I thought Pule was mad when she nostalgically remembered the garden. Now I stooped to touch an amaryllis blossom and clung to my own reluctance to leave.

At the end of the garden, I gazed across the terraces to see the crops still in the fields, as they were when the fog arrived a week earlier, but along the staircase there were also enormous stacks of wood and thatching reeds. Workers continued to haul and pile even more supplies at the edge of the fields. Now that I could see, I was certain the farmers never did this in the past, so I decided it must be related to the preparations. Atuk would explain everything when he arrived.

I looked back across the garden to the shelter and saw my loom waiting for the attention I so easily gave to my garden. My task was clear; the dress and shawl must be completed, whether I was sacrificed or not. Of course Kinsa visited to inspect my work, but this time she brought her own loom to work beside me for the morning. We both wove the same design, a continual string of yellow points representing the sun that was underlined with the deep blue stripe of the sky. The pattern was reversed and repeated above. In the center, the green stripe representing this world was surrounded by the sun's rays. I wove the yellow points around the bottom of my dress while Kinsa exactly duplicated them in miniature for my waist band. We spoke of nothing except our weaving, and I forced myself to think of nothing except my work.

In the afternoon, I continued alone until I heard Tawan in the distance playing her panpipes as she climbed the stairs to my terrace. Pleased to have an excuse to set my weaving aside, I picked up my flute and accompanied her as she approached. We finished the cheery song standing at opposite ends of the ladder while Iska clapped to the rhythm. We entertained ourselves with slow, sad songs, melodic prayers, and bouncy dance tunes. We exchanged instruments, accompanied each other on small drums and danced to our own music. She played for our mutual pleasure, but I played to forget, at least temporarily. She was singing a haunting melody when I remembered my dream from the previous night. A mother llama and her newborn lingered on a high mountain ledge. Below them a young boy hurriedly led the herd toward a distant shelter. Behind them a snowstorm buried the mountain peak as it approached. The mother stamped her feet, bleated, and nudged the foal, urging it to stand. It straightened its forelegs, but it couldn't lift itself. The young mother started down the mountain but returned to encourage the baby. Again she wailed at her young, begging it to follow as she headed down the path. It fell over once again. She looked at the boy partially obscured by the falling snow and then at her exhausted young curled into a tight ball to stay warm.

"What's wrong?" Tawan asked when the song ended.

"Nothing, the song reminded me of a sad story I heard once." It was difficult to explain our studies and I rarely tried. We played a little longer, but I couldn't rekindle my enthusiasm. Tawan tried to cheer me, but her energetic songs were more annoying than soothing. Finally she finished a song she knew I liked and said, "Let's play again tomorrow afternoon."

Pleased to have her leave, I replied, "That's probably for the best. I need to work on my weaving." Without another word, she packed up her instruments and headed for the ladder as I lumbered back to my loom.

"Hello, Kaya, are you ready to walk?" Atuk waited at the top of the ladder.

"Of course." I was surprised to see how much I had woven since Tawan left. "Let's walk down to the main plaza. I'd like to see the crops on the terraces." We descended the stairs, turned right and walked below my garden terrace toward the croplands beyond.

"Atuk, what are the reeds and all the piles of wood for?" The closer we got, the more enormous each pile became and the greater the mystery.

"They're for the festival. Remember, I told you there would be many visitors." My stomach tightened, but I contained my fear. "Well, there's no place for them to stay. Because of the fog, the farmers are a bit behind in delivering the materials, but the workers haven't arrived from Cusco yet, so it doesn't matter. As soon as the crops are harvested, teams of workers will build shelters for the visitors. I'm told a team of four can build a house for a family in a day, if the supplies are all available."

"In only a day? What will these houses look like?" I couldn't imagine such rapid building.

"Let's go down a bit further. Some of the lower fields are harvested and I think one shelter is already built." We crossed the fields and descended the same staircase that Riku and I took to the river many years earlier. I wondered if we would go as far as the terrace that we saw being built, but as we continued down, I realized they all looked the same. Finally Atuk stopped by a new building, and we stepped inside. "You can see there's a large log standing in each of the four corners with the taller ones next to the terrace wall. First the corner posts are erected and held in the soil. Next the smaller logs used to support the roof are tied to the corner posts and cross beams are added to stabilize the structure. The terrace wall becomes the back wall of the house and the other walls are made of vertical sticks tied together at the top and bottom along supporting rods. The roof is made of bundles of reeds like any other thatched roof. With reed mats on the floor and a blanket for a door, these houses will be perfectly comfortable for our guests."

"It all seems so simple. The difficult work must have been collecting all the materials and carrying them to the terraces."

"The local farmers were paid extra this spring and summer to gather it all," Atuk replied as he surveyed the piles. When the visitors leave, the farmers will reclaim all of the materials. There will be enough thatch for every permanent building to get a new roof. The larger logs will replace rotting ones in existing houses. None of it will be wasted, but it must all be removed before spring so the farmers can plant."

Yearning for the spring in Machu Picchu I would never see, regret brought me close to tears as we wandered among the bundles of wood being delivered by the farmers. "How many houses will be built?" I asked.

"About two hundred shelters on these terraces, another four hundred on the ones below for the subjects, and more on the terraces on the other side of the sacred plaza. There is a lot of building to be completed and the workers are scheduled to arrive from Cusco tomorrow."

"Then I'll watch this new village sprout as quickly as the maize grows in the spring." Everywhere I looked, every sound I heard, and every thing I did was a reminder of the approaching ceremony. When I was a child, I longed to escape from the boredom of Machu Picchu. Now the constant activity gnawed on me like cutter ants attacking a plant. After a nostalgic gaze at the maize drying in the fields, we ambled toward the main plaza in the afternoon sun.

"Did you get the vision I sent last night?" Atuk asked. I relayed what I saw including every detail. "And what emotion did you feel?" he asked, reminding me of the purpose of the image.

"The mother was afraid and guilty, torn between two bad options." I didn't tell him that I felt exactly the same way, even if the choice wasn't mine to make. My heart pounded in my throat, and I wanted to hide where no one could find me. Ninan's plans included radical changes that would surely create turmoil, and yet, I longed to be his queen and bear his children. Alternatively, if I stayed, I faced a painful death, an honorable and perhaps even a revered one, but certainly an inescapable one.

"Isn't it remarkable how much a completely imaginary event can affect how we feel? I've never seen any such drama and yet, I too was captured by its troubling sadness," Atuk said without recognizing the similarities. Undisturbed by our approach, several llamas grazed contentedly in the plaza. I wrapped my arms around the neck of a young white female and then buried my hands and face in her fleece. Her warm, earthy scent carried me back to the first llama I ever touched. I longed for those days of innocence and the years of carding, spinning and weaving her relatives' fleece. I scratched her neck and savored her soft nose as she nibbled grass from my open hand. She watched me with the same brown eyes of the llama I sacrificed at the hot springs, and seemed to know I might soon face the same fate. Would I be killed as I had killed?

Finally, we turned back and followed the wall beneath the artisans' quarters. "Tomorrow it's your turn to send," Atuk reminded me. "This time let's make it difficult. Let's see if I can understand a secret." I stopped abruptly, but he took a few more steps before turning and walking back. "Show me something you know to be true, that I don't know."

"But what could that be? I have no secrets to hide." Actually, several things came to mind, but none that I wished to share.

"You'll think of something. Surprise me." His gentle, earnest voice reminded me that I could trust this tall man standing before me.

"I'll try, but you must promise me that whatever I show you will remain between only us." He nodded. I saw motion beyond him on the cliff below the Temple of Viracocha. "What is that?" I asked, pointing to the enormous pile of rubble at the base.

Atuk glanced over his shoulder and nervously clenched his hands behind his back. "It's just more preparations. I think I should take you back to your garden now."

I decided not to pester him with questions since the purpose of the rubble would soon be clear.

Time passed quickly, and I finally saw substantial progress with my weaving. Thanks to Kinsa's persistence, the dress and shawl were as supple as a new leaf, and by far the finest I'd ever made. The blue stripes along the bottom and up the front of the white shawl perfectly matched the design and color in the dress. Even Kinsa was satisfied.

Tawan visited regularly, and I hungered for the comfort her music inevitably brought. We didn't talk much, but she skillfully selected songs to help me forget my troublesome future, at least temporarily. Everyone, Kinsa, Tawan, and even Iska took special care to comfort me as Inti Raymi approached.

Atuk and I continued to meet daily, exchanging many fantastic images and adventures while we slept. We had progressed from pictures of common things to various actions, through emotions to secrets and on to imaginary creatures and impossible situations and places. For my secret, I told him about the one passionate kiss Ninan and I shared in the garden, a moment I often recalled.

Together we tried to reach Pule by talking to the birds in my garden, but they completely ignored us. Carrying Pule's feathers, we climbed Huayna Picchu, hoping she would find us if we were closer to the sky. We sat in the sacred plaza and asked her to show us the sky pathway that would lead us to her. We followed the light spirals to a distant place with two-legged, jumping deer and enormous flocks of parrots, but Pule was not there, nor any other macaws. We even tried to contact Ixiamas, thinking he might know how to find Pule, since they were to arrive together. We couldn't reach him, but Riku heard us and commended our efforts. With each failure, my death became more tangible, more frightening, and more inevitable, while Ninan's proposal became less significant. Sometimes when I thought about the sacrifice, I had to stop weaving because my hands were shaking so badly I couldn't hold the bobbin of yarn.

Meanwhile, the workers arrived, and new houses appeared as fast as the farmers could clear the fields. The work began on the lowest terraces and gradually climbed up the mountain. Atuk and I watched the houses being built, but he avoided taking me to the sacred plaza or the main plaza for almost two weeks. Finally, I insisted that we go there to watch the sunset.

"There are men working there now," he said refusing to look at me. "We'll be in the way. I'll take you there when the work is done."

Determined to know what he was hiding, I demanded, "I want to go now, and I'll go alone if you don't take me."

He knew I could trick Iska or one of the others and conceded. "All right, but don't blame me if what you see upsets you."

I nodded and ran toward the sacred plaza. To my surprise, the ground was covered with a layer of white, rounded pebbles about the size of nuts. Atuk and I wandered across the stones as two workers emerged from between the Temples of Inti and Viracocha. Noting my confusion he asked, "Are you sure you want to know?" I nodded and he replied, "Then follow me."

We passed the roofless Temple of Ilyapa before ascending part way to Intihuatana. On a small terrace overlooking the main plaza, we could clearly see several men around the sacrificial table on the terrace beside the Temple of Inti. The white stones were so alluring I hadn't even noticed the massive table was missing from its usual position in the sacred plaza. "What are they doing?" I asked, amazed that they had managed to move the enormous stone.

Atuk hesitated, but I goaded him into explaining, "As you have seen from the building on the terraces, there will be thousands here for Inti Raymi. Incas and peasants come from every major city as well as many more from Cusco. The offspring of Pachacuti and Topa Inca, as well as most of Huayna Capac's wives and children will all come." He stopped, hoping I would not persist.

"I don't understand. Why are they moving the table?"

He cleared this throat and tried again, "In its normal position in the sacred plaza, the sacrificial table is hidden from view. They will move the stone to the small terrace just beyond Intihuatana so everyone will be able to see Huayna Capac, the Queen, Riku, and you. The people must witness the event to know that the Inca has done as he promised." Waiting for my outburst Atuk held his breath.

"You've already told me that I'll be executed before an enormous audience. It really doesn't matter where the table is located," I replied and he exhaled. "If I'm to willingly climb onto it, lie down and be killed, the result is the same whether it's in the sacred plaza, or on the terrace above us. I'll be terrified until Riku finally stabs me."

Atuk seemed surprised by my composure, but I was bombarded with evidence of the approaching ceremony every waking moment, and often in my sleep. A numbing dullness had replaced my panic, at least for the moment. The table rested at the edge of the terrace with many ropes tied around both ends and stretching around it. On each side of the table there were two squat tripods made of enormous tree trunks. Rope seemed to be everywhere. "But tell me, how is moving that stone possible?"

"I didn't believe it could be done either, but they've already proven me wrong," Atuk answered slowly. "The white pebbles in the plaza made it easier to move the rock on a level surface. It only took ten men half the morning to move the table to the edge. Now they're ready for the most difficult part. The stone is too large to be moved up the stairs we just used. Instead it must be lowered to a terrace almost at the level of the main plaza, pushed along the flat and lifted four times as high to its final position on the terrace just beyond Intihuatana."

I couldn't comprehend what he was telling me. "They can't just push this table over the edge. Surely even this large a stone would break when it landed." Suddenly a hopeful possibility flicked inside. Perhaps they would cancel the sacrifice if the table were broken.

"That's why the table will be slowly lowered to the terrace below them. The drop is nearly the height of three men." Completely incredulous, I asked how that was possible and secretly hoped it was not. Atuk continued, "It's very dangerous, but the workmen assured me it was done before. Perhaps we can see better from over there." Atuk resumed his explanation when we reached the other side of the plaza, but his words went unheard. Beyond my understanding and imagination, I watched as two huge baskets of stones ascended the cliff as the sacrificial table gradually descended.

"I still can't believe it." Atuk stood beside me fascinated by the process. Finally the cheers rose as the table touched the lower terrace and the two baskets were swung onto the sacred plaza. I fought to hold back my tears. "The rest will be easier. Lifting the stone to each successive terrace will use only a fraction of the rope, and pieces can easily be removed as they wear," Atuk said with renewed confidence.

The stone which embodied the spirit of the mountains and a mystical doorway to the Upper World was being moved to the summit of the holy mountain. Collca and Chaska had already been delivered to the gods on that table. Was its third successful descent yet another message from Inti? The honor to be bestowed on me was a burden as heavy as the table itself, but becoming queen was no less onerous.

Ceremony

Ninan

"It is magnificent! The Upper World can't possibly be more splendid." Tumbes, renamed Tucu, enthusiastically extended his arms to the city below us. "Nothing will ever outshine the brilliance of Cusco." He pointed to a shrine surrounded by silver statues on a nearby hilltop and asked, "Ninan, is that the Coricancha?"

"No, the Coricancha is the round building over there." I was relieved to see Tucu's exuberant eyes flashing innocently across the valley, exemplifying his recovery.

"We'll rest here for a while," Riku said as he stepped off his litter to stretch his legs. "Tucu should see the city at its best."

"How could it possibly be better?" He glanced from Riku to me and back, suspecting that we were teasing him.

"You'll see," Riku replied.

Tucu and Riku had met me at Quispiguanca on their way to Cusco for the wedding. I had gone there to speak with the artist making my wedding gift for Pacas and Tinkha. The afternoon passed quickly as Tucu asked about one edifice after another. Neatly lining the roads, the new stone buildings made me proud of my father's accomplishments and provided a striking contrast to the lush valley. Its wide rivers, bountiful fields, and green pastures were testament to Inti's benevolence, but the view was still incomplete until the sun fell from the zenith. With the delightful anticipation of meeting an old friend, I silently thanked Tucu for reminding me of the splendor I now took for granted.

Tucu clasped his hands and stared. "It's fantastic!" From our mountain view it looked like the sun itself emanated from the temple when the descending sun struck the gold plates lining the temple walls. Tucu muttered to himself, "It's beyond description."

We lingered awhile longer, enjoying the spectacle before we descended the mountain to reach Casana after dark. With heartfelt honesty, Tucu thanked his weary teacher for insisting he accompany him to Cusco.

"Finally, you're back," Pacas whispered to me at the palace doorway and to everyone he announced, "Tinkha will be pleased to hear you've arrived." We slowly headed for the courtyard as the greetings continued. "Riku, we're honored to have you here for our wedding. I'm sure you were very busy with the preparations at Machu Picchu."

Tired but strong, Riku replied, "I've always thought of you and Ninan as my sons, along with Atuk and Tucu of course." He directed his smile to Tucu. "It's my pleasure to act as your father in his absence."

Pacas helped him to a bench as he spoke, while a servant immediately offered Riku a cup of *chicha*. "As you know, we planned to hold the ceremony on the new moon, three days from now. I was beginning to think my mother would be the only parent here. Tinkha's parents were expected to arrive from Lake Titicaca three days ago, but we've heard nothing."

I'd never seen Pacas so nervous. He paced the courtyard, his hands clenched at his sides. "Pacas, we're here now, and I'm sure her parents will come soon." I tried to reassure him.

In Riku's calming way he asked, "Have you met her parents?" Pacas shook his head, his eyes betraying his dread. "Relax, how could they not be pleased? Their daughter chooses to be your wife, and is assured of a happy and comfortable future." It hadn't occurred to me that he was worried about meeting her parents. Pacas rescued her from the potential of sacrifice, or worse, marriage as the second wife to a cruel man.

"But I want them to like me," he whined. "What if they wanted her to marry a farmer or someone who plans to live near them? What if they're unhappy with how Tinkha was treated? What if—"

"Pacas, come, sit beside me," Riku interrupted him in a manner Pacas could not have disobeyed. Like a schoolboy, he sat uncomfortably beside Riku. "They'll be unhappy if she is marrying a man who doesn't know his own mind. You are an honorable man who will marry a lovely, hardworking woman. Be yourself, an honest, optimistic, and personable man, who excels with numbers." He saw the strain in Pacas' face and mockingly added, "And until today, a man who feared nothing."

Well acquainted with Riku's humor, Tucu teased, "Pacas is getting married. Now he's afraid of his shadow."

I burst into laughter, and Pacas finally found a smile. "My dear friend," I said as I handed him beer, "You have loved Tinkha from the day you first saw her. What could be more natural? Now, drink. This could be our last opportunity to celebrate!"

And celebrate we did. Riku stayed with us for a while, but soon left for bed. Pacas and I retold, and exaggerated, every story we could remember about our childhood as we drank the endless supply of *chicha*. With perfect camaraderie and no skill, we sang the songs of warriors and bragged about our untested bravery. Through the night, our trio laughed with carefree innocence, ignoring the looming responsibilities of an uncertain future. This night, more than any other, was purely a tribute to our friendship. After overindulging in beer, we wandered the empty and very dark streets bumping into the walls and fumbling our way to the edge of the city. Sprawled across a partially built rock wall, we watched the sunrise as the first farmers headed for their fields. Content, exhausted and still lightheaded, we stumbled back to the palace and collapsed.

It was mid-afternoon when Tucu shook me from sleep. "Wake up. Tinkha's parents just arrived, and Pacas needs you."

I bolted upright trying to clear my head as I straightened my clothes and hair. "Where's Pacas?"

"He's getting ready to leave for the Coricancha Temple. Her parents are planning to meet Tinkha there. They stopped here on the way to invite Pacas to join them, but Riku told them Pacas was busy. He suggested they continue and assured them Pacas would follow."

"Let's go." I hurried out of my room and nearly collided with Pacas rounding the corner as he came to find us. "Morning, Pacas, how do you feel?" I asked, noting my unsteadiness as we headed for the palace doorway.

"I've been better. What a way to meet her parents." Worry returned to his brow as we approached the courtyard.

"Good afternoon, boys." Only Riku could address us as children. "You must have had a late night, or an early morning. Where are you going in such a hurry?"

"To the Coricancha to meet Tinkha's parents," I replied, knowing full well he already knew. "We were just going to ask you to join us."

"Come. Sit a moment first. I have tea for you."

Annoyed, but unwilling to show any disrespect, we obediently joined him. He handed Pacas a cup of tea. "Drink this. It'll make you feel better."

After tasting it, Pacas puckered his lips, while Riku handed his potion to Tucu and me. "Did you boys enjoy your evening?"

"Yes, Tucu was very kind to listen to our stories, and added a few of his own," I said. We all rushed to finish the tea only to have Riku refill our cups.

"Did you rest well?" Tucu asked him.

"Fairly well, but a rowdy group of men woke me." He maintained a stern face, but his eyes betrayed him.

Preoccupied, Pacas didn't notice. "I'm sorry. I didn't realize we were so loud." We all laughed at Pacas again. Remarkably, the tea cleared my head as if it extracted great balls of cotton.

"This tea is wonderful. What is it?" I asked Riku. "The trying headache is gone, and I'm hungry!"

"It's a secret. How do you think your father is able to drink so much? In his position he is expected to drink to excess, but he can never display the effects. I will show you another time, but now you must eat."

A servant arrived with a platter carrying three bowls of steaming soup that we devoured immediately. Still somewhat unkempt, but clear-headed, the four of us confidently walked to the Coricancha where Tinkha chatted with her proud parents in the main courtyard.

"Ninan, you're back." She nodded to her parents and stepped away to greet us. "And you must be Riku. What an honor to meet you." Riku introduced her to Tucu, and she immediately introduced her parents. It was clear from his dress and bearing that her father was not a struggling farmer as I had imagined. Although not an Inca, he obviously was a man accustomed to wielding authority. His strong nose and flashing eyes suited his vigorous body. His wife stood slightly behind him by custom, but was every bit his equal. Her youthful beauty had faded, but her strength and generous spirit were even more becoming.

Pacas had indeed chosen well. Contrary to his fears, he was immediately accepted by her parents who invited him to call them mother and father. We lingered in the courtyard and introduced Tinkha's parents to everyone who passed, including her friends, the Umu Pilaca and my mother, who suggested we all enjoy our evening meal at the palace. The day between meeting her parents and the wedding passed amicably, and with little commotion, since the plans for the wedding were finalized before we arrived. Tinkha had no family living in Cusco, so my mother arranged for the entire ceremony to take place in the courtyard of the palace.

On his wedding day, Tucu and I had stayed with Pacas as he prepared, but he needed little help and no encouragement. Having overcome the fear of meeting her parents, he was delighted to finally take her as his wife. He would see little of her until we left for Inti Raymi, since my mother insisted that Tinkha stay with the Mamaconas to help complete the festival preparations. The couple didn't care; they were to be husband and wife.

"Pacas, are you ready?" Riku asked as he entered the room.

"Absolutely," Pacas replied with a smile as he joined Riku. Dressed in an entirely white tunic and brilliant red cloak, even I had to admit he was remarkably handsome. As his only adornments, he proudly wore the silver pendant from his mother and the gold earplugs his father gave him before he went north. Attached through his earlobes, they covered his ears entirely and were each decorated with an ornate likeness of a hawk. His red headband matched his cloak and accented his shiny black hair and tanned face. With a wooden sandal in hand, he turned to Tucu and me with watery eyes. "Thanks for staying with me this morning. You'll always be my best friends."

It never occurred to me that his marriage might change that. We all strolled purposefully to the courtyard where we joined his mother and my parents.

On the opposite side, Tinkha stood between her parents with Umu Pilaca beside her father and several of Tinkha's friends beside her mother and my mother. Her innocent embarrassment as the center of attention made her even more alluring. She wore a white *cumbi* dress covered with a red shawl matching Pacas' cloak. Mamaconas only wore alpaca wool, never *cumbi*, and I was pleased to see her dressed appropriately for her new role. My mother's softened eyes and quivering lip revealed how close she was to Tinkha. I finally realized that Tinkha had replaced the daughter who was taken from her. Small wonder Tinkha couldn't leave the Mamaconas until Inti Raymi. As it stood now, my mother would lose both her daughters this winter. Perhaps my surprise in Machu Picchu would cheer her.

Pacas took his place between his mother and Riku. I stood with my father beside Riku while two of Pacas' aunts stood with his mother. "You need to go now." Riku said quietly to Pacas who stood frozen with his eyes locked on Tinkha.

Riku's comment urged him into motion, and he walked alone across the courtyard to kneel before Tinkha. "I place this wooden sandal on your foot and am honored to have you as my wife. We will work together as partners for as long as we both shall live. May Inti bless our marriage."

With unassuming grace, Tinkha shed her reed sandal and slipped her foot into the one Pacas offered. She answered, "May we walk together in a love as long-lasting as this sandal."

Satisfied that the sandal was secured, he stood to face her, and then walked back across the courtyard to rejoin his family. Tinkha crossed the courtyard alone, her arms obscured by her shawl. Standing before Pacas, she bowed her head and lifted her hands before her. In her right hand she carried a gold medallion on a green and white woven band while in her left she presented a headband in the same pattern. "With these gifts I pledge to faithfully serve as your wife for the rest of my life. May Killa bless our marriage."

Pacas joyfully slipped the medallion over his head and proudly displayed its intricately formed radial design. How appropriate for him to wear it with the pendant from his mother that reminded him to protect all women. Next he removed his headband, handed it to Riku and replaced it with the one Tinkha offered.

Typically the ceremony would be complete, but the Umu Pilaca slipped forward to lead the married couple to the center of the courtyard. He cleared his throat to allow his remarkably strong voice to emanate from his wizened body. "Tinkha, I have known you almost your entire life, and have watched you grow into a hard-working, generous woman. Pacas, you were wise to choose a woman with such character. May you prove worthy of her." He paused and extended his arms toward the sun before praying.

Most powerful Inti, listen to our pleas.
This couple has the blessing of their families and is dedicated to you.
Magnanimous Inti, father of us all, guide their steps in plenty and in want.
Show them your way and protect them from your enemies.
Most holy Inti, bless this union with children to serve your purpose.
Most benevolent Inti, grant them a lifetime of sharing and love.

He dropped his arms and held their hands in his. Just loud enough for us all to hear he added, "May you find joy in your life together."

Riku led the way as both families crowded around the bride and groom in the center of the courtyard. The celebration continued all day with an endless stream of relatives and guests offering unsolicited advice. "Give him a son first, Tinkha. A man always wants a son to call his own." "Don't feed him too much meat. He'll only get lazy." "She's a strong-willed woman, but you shouldn't hit her. She'll do as you ask, if you take care of her." "She doesn't know how to plant the crops. You'll have to teach her." "Don't spoil her in this first year, or you'll be forced to do so for your entire life."

I don't think they heard any of the advice. They looked completely natural together, and I was very happy for them, even while it accentuated the emptiness and uncertainty in my own situation.

Throughout the afternoon, each person presented them with a gift. Her parents provided an enormous ceramic jar filled with the finest maize seed. It was a generous gift, well-suited for their future life together. Even while they traveled north, they were expected to pay tributes to the religion and the state, and the seed planted by a tenant would meet that obligation. Riku gave them a beautifully painted jar filled with coca leaves that he must have brought from Machu Picchu. Tinkha's friends provided enough blankets and clothes to satisfy their needs for a long time. With a touching gentleness I'd never seen in my mother, she gave Tinkha a fine loom that would last for years. My father's gift was very thoughtful, a sturdy litter for Tinkha to use on the trip north. As sad as my mother was to see her leave, she was pleased that at least Tinkha wouldn't travel on foot.

I had struggled to think of a suitable gift for my best friend. After rejecting many ideas, I finally settled on a unique double container. On the outside, the copper pot could easily be carried in one hand, and was decorated with pictures of the sun's rays emanating from his face on the lid and sides. On closer inspection Tinkha noticed the eyes were actually small holes. The tightly-fitting, notched lid could be twisted to remove it, and expose the covered ceramic jar inside. There were holes in the bottom of the ceramic jar as well as much smaller holes in its lid. The venting was just sufficient to allow coals to burn all day long. Tinkha could hold the container on her lap or at her feet to warm her as we traversed the high mountains. If the weather was warm, the container could hang from her litter or a llama's pack, and provide an easy way to start a fire whenever required. Tinkha and Pacas were both pleased with my selection.

Finally Riku spoke for Pacas' father. "Pacas and Tinkha, I know you plan to travel north together after Inti Raymi, but Sinchi Roca has given you a generous gift that you'll enjoy for the next few days and when you return. On the edge of town near the junction of the river, your father built a fine house for you. May you live there in peace."

"Mother, is this true?" Pacas gasped as he gave her the first hug and kiss I'd ever seen. Tears streamed down Tinkha's face as she tried to express her gratitude. Riku stepped aside quietly, while Tinkha's parents genuinely congratulated their daughter and new son on their good fortune.

The newlyweds celebrated with all of the guests through the evening banquet, until the chill of evening settled in. After a short consultation with Riku, Pacas announced, "Thank you for witnessing our wedding and joining the celebration. We are honored to have such good friends and supportive families." He glanced at Tinkha and then concluded, "Tonight we will live as husband and wife in our new home." After happy farewells and promises to meet in the morning, they proudly turned and left hand in hand.

When the last guests departed, I was alone in the courtyard with Tucu and Riku. "He's still your best friend, you know." Riku spoke softly and I nodded slowly. "You should be happy for them. They are ideally suited for each other."

"I know, but it's different," I said under my breath.

"True, but the moment they agreed to marry, you knew this time would come."

"I'm very happy for them, and that's all I want to feel, but I can't. I'm jealous of their marriage . . . and lonely." I slumped onto the bench beside him.

"It's impossible to feel only one emotion, no matter what the circumstance. Not even fear can exclude all others. Try to savor the rich mixture, like a fine soup." He rested his hand on my shoulder. "Pacas isn't lost to you, and one day, maybe soon, you too will have a wife." He paused and added, "Get some sleep. You'll feel better in the morning."

Secret Plans

Ninan

It was late morning before I decided to rise and find Tucu. I needed his help to spare Kaya, an objective that must now have my complete attention. Resolved to devote myself to the task, I purposefully strode to the courtyard expecting to find Tucu relaxing with Riku. Instead I heard my father's voice echoing from the stone walls. "The visions you've told me are remarkable and fascinating, but I don't understand how you think they can influence my decree." I slowed my pace to a noiseless creep and stopped beside the courtyard wall.

"Kaya made contact with the Upper World, and clearly she has found favor with a spirit who is fully knowledgeable of Inca affairs. And she's seen Viracocha returning. Think of the possibilities. You could get Inti's assistance directly rather than depend on our interpretations of the unsolicited messages we occasionally receive," Riku answered.

I heard my father's steps as he stood and paced the courtyard. "Yes, Pule's messages are all very clear. In fact, each distinctly prepared Kaya for her duty to be sacrificed according to tradition and my decree. Sparing her seems exactly contrary to the intent of this spirit from the Upper World."

Riku rose and shuffled one foot as he approached my father and spoke softly. "She's still very young. We're trying to call Pule to us. In a few years her skills will mature, and I'm confident she will guide us through these turbulent times."

"Your Majesty, if you'll allow me to speak," Tucu timidly interjected.

"Of course. What is it?" my father answered.

Tucu also rose, but presumably only to show his respect, since he didn't approach. "Kaya is a very talented seer. Her visions are much clearer and more complete than either Atuk's or mine." He paused. "Forgive me, Riku, you know you have my highest respect."

"Speak your mind. I trust your intentions." Riku replied.

Silence followed, and I expected my father to dismiss him, but finally Tucu began, "Your Majesty, I know you trust Riku above all other advisers, with the possible exception of Sinchi Roca. Over the past several years I was honored to serve as his student and learn the ways of a seeker. Riku is an excellent teacher, and I have become a fair diviner. In that time, I have watched Kaya, who is several years younger, rapidly surpass my abilities." He paused again, but only for a brief moment. "My dearest teacher is aging quickly. His endurance for *ayahuasca* traveling and counseling you diminishes with each adventure. One day, Riku will be unable to continue, and we will carry on without him. Together Atuk and I might be able to equal his ability. Kaya is rapidly approaching his skill already and may well lead us to remarkable new wisdom. Without her and without Riku, we will struggle. Considering the magnitude of your campaign in the north and the uncertainty of the empire during Viracocha's long-awaited return, perhaps Kaya has a more important role as an intermediary rather than as a sacrifice."

My father cleared his throat. "That one is brave to remind us both of our advancing years and discredit his abilities," he said to Riku.

"He sees the situation very clearly and never puts his interest before the truth," Riku replied.

I peeked around the corner to see my father pacing the courtyard, his hands behind his back and his head bent forward. Tucu moved to Riku's side, seeking reassurance.

Huayna Capac faced them, and I pulled away from the corner. "Do you understand my predicament? The witness list was distributed months ago. Those who live at the far ends of the empire are already traveling, and those closer are making final arrangements. Everyone is expecting the most elaborate, most prestigious, most sacred festival ever held. I can't possibly stop them before they arrive. How could I explain the situation through runners? I'm not even certain I could convince them in person, but more important, I'm not certain Kaya should be spared."

I backed into the wall and let my head rest against it while I held my breath.

No one made a sound in the courtyard behind me as they waited for his decision. "The procession to Machu Picchu will continue as planned.

However, your arguments have cast some doubt on the wisdom of the sacrifice, in spite of the incident with the fading sun and the message in Kaya's visions. If you receive a definite sign from the Upper World, or there is a miraculous alternative, I will, as Inca, retract the sacrifice."

If there was a reaction in the courtyard, I missed it in my own jubilant relief. I threw my hands in the air and barely stifled my cheers. This was as close to a reprieve as I could possibly imagine. I very quietly took a long, deep breath and slowly exhaled as every muscle relaxed.

"Thank you," Riku concluded the conversation. "Your generosity again distinguishes you as the greatest Inca. May Inti make his wishes clearly understood."

"Good morning," I said brightly as I whisked across the courtyard. "Wasn't yesterday's wedding a marvelous celebration? Has anyone seen Tinkha's parents this morning?"

Riku must have guessed I'd been listening to their conversation and answered immediately "They were here much earlier and went to visit the newlyweds at their house. You know they only have two days before Tinkha returns to the Mamaconas."

"Yes, it's fortunate that she has the opportunity to visit with her parents." I looked around. "Is there anything to eat? I'm hungry."

"I'll find something," Tucu offered as he scurried away.

I looked at my father and Riku before unapologetically adding, "Excuse me, did I interrupt something?"

My father spoke quietly, "No, son, we just finished, and I have visitors waiting for me." He turned to leave and called back, "Riku, review my decision with him."

Holding my fingers on my lips as a signal for quiet, I waited until his footfalls faded to light tapping. I smiled broadly as Tucu returned with a platter of maize and beer. "Thank you, Riku, and you too, Tucu."

"Ninan, there are no certainties we will be able to halt the sacrifice," Riku warned me, showing no signs of the optimism I now enjoyed.

"I know, but at least her death isn't a certainty." Between bites, I waved an ear of maize around. "I need Tucu's help for the next few days. Can you do without him?"

"Yes, of course. I need to review the plans for the Inti Raymi celebration with the Umu Pilaca. After that, your father wants to review the plans for the northern campaign with me," he replied. He picked up his cloak from the bench and added, "In fact, I'm just leaving for the Coricancha now."

"So you heard the whole conversation?" Tucu whispered to me as Riku crossed the courtyard.

"And you claim to lack courage. You spoke very well. It's not easy for me to disagree with the Inca, and he's my father."

"I was scared, that's for certain, but I think I helped Riku."

"As well as Kaya and me. Huayna Capac won't hear my reasons for sparing her. He thinks I'm just being selfish, and maybe he's right." I hadn't forgotten the acrimonious debates I'd had with my father.

"So what are we going to do for three days?" Tucu asked, still eager to prove his valor to me, and to himself.

"First you must tell me everything you know about the preparations for Inti Raymi and the celebration itself. Don't leave out a thing."

Tucu very systematically reviewed the number of guests, where they were to be housed, where the offerings were to be kept, and what Kaya and Atuk were doing in his absence. Then he explained every part of the ceremony itself, including what Riku, Atuk, Kaya and he would do, and where my family and the rest of the crowd would be. I asked hundreds of questions, and he answered most of them.

It was late afternoon before we finished the review, and I disclosed my plan. "Tomorrow we will meet with Secret, Kaya's elder twin sister. I hope to convince her that she, not Kaya is the appropriate sacrifice."

Tucu was completely surprised, but he agreed with my objective of saving Kaya from certain death.

The next morning Tucu and I walked to the edge of town where we located a pathetic garden by a small house. A young woman straightened from her weeding as we approached. "What do you want?" her grating voice asked.

"That's her!" Tucu whispered to me.

I stopped immediately at the edge of the rock-infested plot to study the shabby creature before me. Yes, she was the same height and build as Kaya, and her narrow nose and thin lips carefully placed on her oval face were nearly identical. The resemblance ended there. "You must be Secret. I've been looking for you for a long time."

"Not that long. I've seen you parading around like a god plenty of times. What gives you the right to pass judgment on people you don't even know?"

"Our father does. I do the best I can." I wanted a civil conversation with my sister, not a war.

Her eyes closed to slits as she studied us. She brushed her stringy hair out of her face with her dirty hand, smearing mud across her cheek and lips.

Trying to find something in common, I added, "It looks like you struggle with your lot as well."

"Don't you compare *your* suffering with *mine*. You don't know what the word means! You live in luxury while I wallow in misery. Even my own mother refuses to visit me in this wretched hole."

Tucu and I walked through the garden and stood immediately in front of her. Her tattered dress, bare feet, and calloused hands all attested to her hard life. "And why won't mother see you?"

"The bitch claims she might be followed. I'd be discovered, and she'd be disgraced." She licked her lips clean and spat the mud back to its rightful place. "She hasn't even sent any food for two years. How am I supposed to live off this poor excuse for a garden? I can't, I tell you, so I steal what I need."

I decided mother abandoned her because Secret was such deplorable person. I glanced at Tucu's slack jaw and allowed her to continue to rant.

"What else can I do? I begged her to acknowledge me, but she wouldn't. And she told me that she would deny my claim if I tried to come forward. Who am I without a family? No man will marry a woman without family. It wasn't so bad when I lived with my guardians, even if they were just dumb farmers. Can you believe it? The very month I became a woman, they disappeared during the night. I might as well be dead. My past isn't worth remembering, and I've been denied a future. I'll probably be dead within a year." She blew her nose into her hand and wiped it on her dress.

"You're right." I heard myself saying. "You've had a difficult life. Perhaps I can help."

"How? By sentencing me to death for stealing? How can you help a person that doesn't exist?" With her hands on her hips and legs straddling a boulder, she dared me to lift her out of her squalor.

"I can, but only with your help. Would you like to regain your title as the eldest daughter of Huayna Capac and Coya Cusirimay?"

Immobile, she said nothing but fixed her hard eyes on me.

"You can be your parents eldest daughter, become the envy of Cusco's elite, travel to the sacred valley and beyond. You could have everything you always wanted: your namesake, wealth, respect, a place of sacred honor, everything. Or you could remain here, alone with your anger and despair for the rest of your life.

Her arms fell to her sides and she quietly asked, "What do I need to do?"

Tucu and I led her into her meager house and carefully laid out the entire plan. Answering every question she asked, Tucu and I spared no details. Even though she knew she would only live for three months, she gladly accepted her fate in return for her rightful title, eldest daughter of the Inca and his queen. We took her to the house of one of Cusco's finest nobles who I'd helped through an ugly legal matter. He and his wife had previously agreed to care for Secret as their own daughter, if I was lucky enough to find her. After living in the manner to which she was entitled, they were to bring her to Machu Picchu for Inti Raymi. Tucu and I had been so successful in finding and convincing her, I was sure we were simply implementing Inti's plan.

We finalized the arrangements on the same day Riku finshed with my father. Not wanting to stay away any longer than necessary, he prepared to leave for Machu Picchu the following morning.

"Are you ready, Tucu?" Riku asked as he climbed on his litter after saying good-bye to my father, while Tucu and I chatted a short distance away.

"Let's go home." Tucu lifted his small parcel and walked to Riku's side.

Riku nodded and told the carriers to lift the litter and start down the road. They had gone only a short distance when he signaled me to join them. I ran to meet them, and Riku asked, "Is there anything you'd like me to tell Kaya?"

"Tell her about Huayna Capac's decision. Tell her I'll see her soon."

"Is that all?" he probed. He wanted to know why I'd asked for Tucu's help.

"Tell her I love her."

Disappointed I wouldn't confide in him, he sighed but knew he'd learn soon enough. "Well then, we'll see you at Machu Picchu."

I stopped at the side of the road and enjoyed the clear, cold morning as the litter drifted across the valley.

There was so much to do and only nine weeks remained before the grand procession. Tinkha returned to her life with the Mamaconas, so Pacas and I were free to prepare for the long journey north. Although most of the people, including my parents and Pacas' mother, would return to Cusco, we planned to travel north over a rugged secondary road immediately following Inti Raymi. We needed to prepare not only for the celebration, but also for the long trek and extended stay in the north. According to my father, we should meet Sinchi Roca about ten days from Cusco. He would tell us where we were needed most urgently.

The first few weeks proceeded without interruption. Pacas arranged for a distant relative to live in his house in exchange for tending Pacas' crops and livestock. My father allocated llamas, herders, supplies, and carriers. Of course, unknown to him, we then spoke to our assigned aides and increased everything to include Kaya's needs.

First a slow trickle, and then a flood of people poured into Cusco. Each morning Pacas and I stood with Huayna Capac as the new arrivals presented themselves and their gifts to the Inca. From over one hundred cities flung across the entire empire, two Caracas, their immediate families, and four handpicked native families arrived to pay tribute to the Inca before proceeding to Machu Picchu to witness the sacrifice. Remarkably, after being introduced, my father immediately remembered everyone's name including the peasants, women, and children. For the entire morning, he asked details about their city, if he had never visited it, the harvest, buildings under construction, and the general welfare of the people. Since the peasants were carefully chosen, all were highly respectful and able to answer the Inca.

My father was a master at learning the truth, whether it was spoken or concealed. In the afternoon we reviewed what we learned, and gradually pieced together the situation we faced in the north. Apu Tacana from Quito had not exaggerated the urgency of our arrival. The entire region was destabilized following the Tumbes massacre. Each evening we shared an informal meal with the group during which we clarified any ambiguities. The next day the process began again with a different group. There were so many new people and such an overwhelming amount of information, I was exhilarated and exhausted at the end of each day.

Finally, after almost an entire year of planning, the ten-day grand procession to Machu Picchu began beneath a brilliant sunrise in the Haucaypata Plaza. Standing with my parents on a platform surrounded by travelers, Umu Pilaca, the High Priest of Cusco, initiated the Inti Raymi ceremony.

Most powerful Inti, hear our prayer. We come together by your command.
Today we begin the final phase of our pilgrimage to Machu Picchu.
Omnipresent Inti, keep us safe so we may properly honor you.
Guide our steps along your path so we may live in harmony.
Grant us forgiveness as we demonstrate our penance through our sacrifice.
Prepare our hearts for your most sacred celebration.
Most benevolent Inti, hear the prayer of your faithful children.

His voice faded across the crowd, and the shell trumpets sounded their mournful reply. People lifted a drum or a rattle over their heads, and beat in unison as my father, the great Inca Huayna Capac, stepped onto his specially built, glittering litter. A fan made entirely of red flowers covered the litter platform, which was decorated with small quartz crystals and silver streamers. He wore a tunic with yellow images of the sun and a cloak made of purple tanager feathers interwoven with gold threads. The drumming continued, and the crowd split as my mother mounted her equally elaborate litter, and the two crossed the plaza, side by side. I nearly burst with pride as they passed me. Immediately following them, Umu Pilaca, dressed entirely in white, rode on his black litter. As prearranged, I followed with Pacas at my side. His mother and Tinkha were immediately behind us. Tinkha looked mortified as people stared at her riding for the first time.

All of my father's wives and their children mounted in an enormous pack behind us. The seductive Miski and Atahualpa, whose nose healed with a conspicuous bump, reveled in their prominent positions. Led by the mummies of the Inca and his queen, who were dressed as they had been when each had led this pilgrimage, selected members of the royal families of Topa Inca and Pachacuti followed. Finally, dressed in their finest costumes, the Caracas and their families from each of the principalities mounted and left the courtyard. The peasant families and various servants filed in behind their leaders at the edge of the city bringing the gear and offerings packed on thousands of llamas.

As we approached the mountain pass separating Cusco from the Urubamba River Valley, the brilliantly colored and elegantly spectacular procession stretched out behind us. Entertained by flutes and pan pipes, the travelers danced as they walked or swayed on their litters, while flashing reflections of gold earplugs and thousands of other ornaments accented the rhythms. Imbued with the opulence and grandeur of the entire empire, the pilgrimage embodied a sacred, unified purpose for an entire generation. I was surrounded by boundless joy, and yet, I was consumed with anxiety. My plans were complete, but saving Kaya was not a certainty.

Cleansing

Kaya

Riku, Tucu, and I descended the stairs of Machu Picchu toward the river and passed the terraces now filled with the guests from the procession that arrived the previous day. Exactly following the route I took with Riku years earlier, we crossed the bridge and walked upstream to the bustling village near the hot springs. We strolled through streets filled with boisterous children and the exotic aromas of foreign cooking, until we reached the forested path at the foot of the mountain where the trees provided a respite from the ever-increasing commotion of Machu Picchu. As we walked, the voices and activities of the village faded with the colors of the day. Tucu led us into the soft glow of the torch-lit clearing with a startling greeting, "Atuk, you're back, and just in time. Did you find Ixiamas?"

Atuk nodded as he gave the fire a final poke. "We got here yesterday afternoon and decided to wait rather than climb to the city only to descend with you today."

Looking much older, Ixiamas hobbled into the clearing from the direction where I knew the llamas were grazing. Riku glided toward him and they again repeated their silent greeting, which ended in an embrace. "Thank you for the litter. It took a long time for me to reach Vilcabamba. I would have missed the ceremony entirely without it. Atuk was a welcome sight," Ixiamas said in his heavy accent.

"I understand. I used a litter the entire distance during my last trip to Cusco, and I was still tired from the journey. Age forces us to slow down and accept the charity of others. Still, we are all grateful you decided to come," Riku replied as we all found a seat on the mats surrounding the fire.

After Atuk offered *chicha* to everyone, Riku asked Ixiamas the critical question. "In your travels, either coming here or in your visions, have you been visited by a large, entirely blue macaw, or any other spirit that calls itself Pule?" I held my breath, still hoping there might be a way to avert my death in less than two days.

"Yes, I think I have. Is it important?"

Riku briefly explained my visions and our quest to call Pule. He ended saying, "So you see, according to my vision, Pule was to return when you came to Machu Picchu. The entire ceremony rests on the information you bring."

"Then I hope my story will help you."

Riku agreed to translate his story as Ixiamas told it. "After a long illness last spring and a slow recovery through the wet season, I decided to come to Machu Picchu this winter for what will surely be the last time. I knew the journey would be very strenuous, but something urged me to make the effort. After only a few days climbing into the lower mountains, I wondered if I should turn back. I was exhausted and often stopped to rest. I'm not sure if I was asleep or awake, but a magnificent blue macaw circled around me several times and called to me. 'Machu Picchu. You must go to Machu Picchu. This way to Machu Picchu.' Well, I stood immediately and, with new resolve, managed to climb to Vilcabamba. The rest you already know."

I hid my disappointment and forced myself to hold back the tears.

"Apparently, you have a vital role in the next few days. We just don't know what it is," Riku concluded. We sat in silence for a while, and I tried to imagine what this near stranger could do that was so important. Finally Riku concluded, "Since we have no certain knowledge of a change in the gods' intentions, we'll continue with the preparations. We're here to bathe and to thank Pachamama for the gifts she gives us so generously. These healing pools will cleanse your entire body and return the silt to Pachamama. Let the warm water pass through your skin and saturate every part of your being. Let it carry away the past and the future."

With torches in hand, we ambled across the clearing to the first pool that Atuk and Tucu were to use. I had the second, while Riku and Ixiamas continued to the third. The smallest of the pools with its drooping vine suspended above the water—it was my favorite. To my delight, Iska stood beside it, waiting for my arrival. She had surrounded the entire pool with bunches of flame-red amaryllis. "Iska, where did you find them at this time of year? They're lovely!"

"It's a secret, but I'm glad you like them. Please, your bath is ready." She extended a hand toward the water where she had draped fresh branches of verbena around one side. The tangy aroma of its leaves mixed with the scent of the damp, musty earth, drew me toward the pool's inviting warmth. My arms and legs floated across the surface. Tingling with a sense of wholeness, every pore breathed in water as easily as the sun warms the heart. A strangely familiar sense of belonging overtook me, and I basked in its comfort without thought or awareness of the world beyond the pool. I dozed off and drifted in this timeless, empty space. Later I heard Iska's voice in the distance. "Kaya, let me help you wash your hair. I have some lovely herbs."

I opened my eyes to see her round face and a pleasant smile. Pleased to see her kind nature, I accepted her offer. As I kneaded the spicy sweet mash on my head, she did the same with the rest. "You know, I always wanted to be your friend," she said softly, "but Riku advised against it. He thought I would have trouble letting you leave when," she paused, "the time came."

"I thought you didn't like me. I thought you resented having to care for me," I responded immediately.

She stopped rubbing my hair. Her eyes opened so wide, I saw the white around the color for the first time. "That's simply not true. I always felt sorry for you being alone all the time. I had to keep still, or you'd see the pity I felt for you. Do you have any idea how worried I was when you got sick? I thought I was going to lose you every day."

"I remember you were always there when I awoke, and you always forced me to drink that horrible tea! Were you trying to poison me?" Mortified she stared at me with her mouth agape, until I smiled. "I knew it was medicine, and I knew you were trying to help me."

She relaxed and slapped my head. "You always had a sly streak in you. I never did anything to harm you."

"I know. I remember when I was young you carried me up and down the ladder on your back. It was like flying, for me, but I'm sure it was hard work for you."

She tipped her head indifferently.

"Thank you for cooking and washing my clothes for me. You've always taken excellent care of me."

"It was an honor I would gladly repeat. I only wish we could have known each other better."

I agreed, and we finished washing my hair before she left to allow me to savor the bath as long as I chose. Unfortunately, instead of returning to the timeless place, my thoughts turned to Ninan. I saw him ride into Machu Picchu very near the front of the procession two days earlier. From a distance, he looked just like the Inca, proud, confident, robust and virile. I thought he'd visit me, even if it were only to say he'd failed to convince our father. Since he hadn't, I decided he was so brokenhearted he couldn't face me. No matter what the reason, the result was the same. I tried to forget the past and the future, determined to enjoy the pool as long as possible. After napping, the heat of the herbs in my skin and my pounding heart finally forced me out.

I was the last to arrive at the fire circle. Iska joined us for our dinner of potatoes and oca lightly flavored with peppers and the juice of a sweet potato. Our conversation about the colors of the flames and the dancing shadows on the overhanging branches was as earthy as the dinner. Since this was my final opportunity to live in the moment and enjoy the richness of Pachamama, there was no mention of the next few days, and I desperately tried not to think about it. Simple food, a fire, and trusted company was all anyone wanted. We slept on the ground wrapped in the warmth of blankets and contentment. Under the new moon, I woke to find Riku humming as he sat bundled in his blanket with his head tilted back, and gazing at the brilliant stars just above the treetops. I returned to a comforting, dreamless sleep.

The next morning, the day before the winter solstice, we rose before dawn, crossed the river and climbed part way to Machu Picchu. We passed no one on our trek, even though there was new housing scattered along the river and across the terraces. After reaching our destination, a place I'd never been, we rested and ate Iska's hot porridge in the red light of the sunrise. In the quiet, we heard footsteps descending from the city, and soon welcomed Kinsa to our gathering. In the awakening city, a baby cried until a woman sung a soothing lullaby. A fire crackled as its smoke wafted down the mountain slope. I clung to every sound, knowing it might be the last time I heard it, and refused to acknowledge the next day.

Riku inspected the pools several times before he finally announced, "We can begin. The hot springs cleansed our bodies and helped us honor Pachamama. Now that the sun is higher, the sun pools are ready. They were built to help us cleanse and purify our spirits as we prepare ourselves to honor Inti. When we are busy with our daily lives, we forget that we are breathing, that our hearts are beating, and that our bodies function without any effort on our part. So it is with your spirit. Enough of your life force remains to keep each of us here, but it is thin and incomplete. When we do our exercises, you become more aware of your body, and your spirit in and around you. These sacred baths, and Inti, will help you remove the distractions that offend him and consolidate what remains." He carefully studied each of us in his special way of seeing the whole person, not just a face or an expression.

Tucu tentatively asked, "How will I know when I'm finished?"

"An excellent question," Riku replied. "You'll feel more complete, more connected with yourself and your surroundings than you have ever felt before, including when we traveled with *ayahuasca*. Ask Inti to tell you, if you're not sure." He looked around expecting more questions, but continued when there were none. "Kinsa, you will help Kaya at the far pool. Atuk and Tumbes you can use the second pool, but only one should be in the pool at a time. Ixiamas and I will use the closest one."

Together Kinsa and I walked across the slope to a dry pool lined with black rocks. "You must remove your clothes before you enter," Kinsa said, knowing exactly what to do. "I've brought some sage as a cleansing aid that I'll burn along the edge after you get in."

While the morning dew still clung to the mountain, I undressed and stepped down into the pool. Facing the sun, the warm stones surrounded me to my waist and extended over my head behind me. Finches twittered in the bromeliads nearby, and the faintly sweet smoke rose to fill my chest. As Riku had instructed, I closed my eyes and asked for Inti's help to remove anything that displeased him. With each breath I felt fuller and taller until I entirely filled the pool and the clearing above it. When I briefly opened my eyes, I saw my hands and body as I had always known them, but now I felt whole, as though I were standing in the center of an invisible cloud.

Again I shut my eyes and time stopped as wonderful memories flooded back to me: the scent of my guava tree in full bloom, Tucu's comic impersonations, Iska washing my hair, the sun rising over the mountains, Atuk watching over me like a big brother, Pule teaching me to fly, and walking beside Riku through the main plaza. Even more images erupted: Ninan kissing me, burying my hands in a llama's back, Kinsa leaning over me as I sat in my loom, tending my orchids and fuchsia, playing my flute with Tawan, sitting on clouds as a feather painted my world, and many others. The sense of well being was so satisfying, that I had no desire to move, and, judging from the number of past reflections, I indulged myself in the sunlight for a very long time. When I reopened my eyes, my surroundings seemed brighter and more colorful than I recalled.

"Kaya, take my hand. I'll help you out," Kinsa offered when I tried to climb onto the wall.

"Thanks, I feel rather large, not heavier, just bigger," I replied as she pulled me out and helped me dress. "It's strange to be so aware of my spirit cloud. I can feel the rocks and trees as I pass them, and I know your cloud is mingling with mine, and yet each remains distinct."

"What are you talking about? Come on, we need to go. I still need to lay out the clothes for tomorrow." She busily picked up the rest of her cleansing herbs and chatted about the mundane tasks she still needed to do. Looking much revived, Riku and Ixiamas approached us from their bath, and together we wound through the forest to the staircase where Iska, Tucu, and Atuk waited for us.

As we ascended the stairs, everyone we passed was busy with preparations. It didn't matter whether they were speaking a foreign language, carrying a heavy load or simply descending to the river, Riku greeted each with a cheerful good morning. We were regarded as a curiosity, but generally unrecognized by the visitors. When we met a local resident known to the group, the passerby stepped to the side and offered a respectful nod as we quickly passed. We crossed the main plaza to the stairs leading to the Torreon, the royal baths, and the home of Atuk and Tucu where Tawan waited for us with *chicha*. After the sun pools, none of us needed the rest, but we enjoyed the drink and talked about the multitude of exotic visitors we had passed. By headdress or language, Riku was able to establish the distant origins of many of the guests.

After a while, Riku asked to inspect the preparations for the rest of the day. Tawan demonstrated three sets of panpipes, a flute, and a small drum. Since Ixiamas didn't feel he could endure the rigors of the dance in these high mountains, he asked to help with the music, and added a rattle to the collection. Kinsa displayed the clothes we were all to wear after our final bath. She even arranged for a suitable outfit for Ixiamas. Finally, Iska described the dinner she was preparing and displayed an ample supply of *chicha* and coca.

Satisfied with the arrangements, Riku reverted to our venerable teacher. "We cleansed our bodies and our spirits in preparation for establishing a common purpose. During our final bath, the four of us will join together with all the elements of this world and the Upper World. When all opposing forces are present and balanced, we will ask to be shown the future of the Inca Empire."

Together we entered the specially prepared, roofless royal bath. In a shallow pool of water, the entire floor was covered with garnets, emeralds, yellow citrines, aquamarines, and even amethysts. We used many sacred stones in our studies, but I'd never seen so many, or seen such large crystals. "Riku, where did they all come from?" Tucu asked.

"The visitors were asked to bring stones with them as part of the offering to Inti. Tomorrow they will travel with Kaya," he answered. Above us, the top of the walls were lined with magnificent quartz displays. Each had a bed of small crystals and a single large quartz crystal projecting directly into the pool. Color bounced off the water and splashed across the walls in a dizzying array. After removing our sandals, we stepped into the ankle-deep pool and carefully ascertained which color patches were sharp-pointed gems and which were perfect reflections. We soon learned that the real stones were all arranged in a rather small circle in the center.

With bright sun overhead, warm water at our feet, and granite walls surrounding us, we held hands around the gems as Tawan played a haunting melody on a flute, and Ixiamas accompanied her with a drum. Riku led the dance as we raised our hands and threw back our heads, then crouched with our hands in front of us. We faced the direction we moved and then the reverse with hands high and hands low. The circle pulled tightly together and then spread as far as we could reach. We knelt and swayed our bodies from side to side, and toward the center and out. We stamped our feet to the rhythm and kicked up our knees, but we never dropped our hands. Panpipes joined the flute, adding a close harmony. Even the colored lights and shadows followed our rhythm as we moved with the music. The dance continued without conscience thought. We were a single unit pulsing as naturally as a flock of birds beats its wings in unison. As the sun dropped behind the mountains, the crystal light beams paled to a muted haze, and the music diminished to high-pitched panpipes.

Still holding hands and following Riku's example, we knelt and closed our eyes. Riku spoke for the first time.

Most gracious Inti, hear our prayer.
Most merciful Inti, we gather together as your loyal servants.
Omnipotent Inti, show us the empire as a yet unborn child will see it.
Most generous Inti, grant this group our final vision.

I felt my cloud touch and then merge with the others, while my hands pulsed with the heat of Tucu and Atuk on either side of me. Without any willful effort, I saw myself in the center of the circle. Fulfilling my dream, I calmed the crying baby in my arms, while a man prepared a place for me to sit. Standing in the doorway and wearing his heavy cloak, Riku stared at the sky which seemed to darken with a passing cloud, and then blackened into night, completely dissolving the colors woven in his cloak. My baby refused to be comforted while the llamas bleated in the pasture and a mountain lion screamed in the distance. Then as quickly as the sun disappeared, it returned to its daytime strength. The sense of normalcy seemed to be restored as our daily lives reverted to the conventional routine. My son was a strong boy when Riku again watched the sun slide away from us. Once again it returned, but an uncertainty and the pall of death weighed heavily on my shoulders. Still, my son was healthy and became a bright young man. Atuk watched the sun with a weary eye as it once again vanished but finally found its way back to us. Three more times we endured the temporary darkness, and between the frightful events, I watched my son marry and have children of his own. Each time the increasingly ominous darkness hung over us, the strength of the sun weakened as though it were diminished by its battles. In spite of my growing alarm, my son flourished in the new light and carried the memories of his childhood.

As abruptly as the vision started, it also stopped. I shivered as I stared at my three companions, and wondered if they saw the same vision. We stayed in our circle and without rushing, Riku again prayed.

> *Most generous Inti, thank you for granting our request.*
> *Wisest Inti, help us to understand your message.*
> *Most judicious Inti, may we use this vision to serve your purpose.*

In silence we stood together for a final farewell. I was in no hurry to break with the people I trusted. Even though I was perplexed by the vision, I finally felt like I belonged somewhere, and I didn't want the unity and acceptance to end. I didn't want to be alone again. I shivered in the night chill, prepared to remain until the sun again rose to warm me, but Riku dropped his hands and by the light of torches said, "We need to find dry clothes. We'll eat and then review our travels."

I hid my tears.

Kinsa and Tawan guided me to the house where a warm fire shone brightly. Wrapped in a blanket and cradling a warm drink, I rested by the fire while my hair dried. I thanked Tawan for the beautiful music and asked who, besides Ixiamas, played with her while we danced. To my surprise, Kinsa was also an accomplished musician. They repeated an earlier melody before beginning a performance a series of riotous favorites. I eagerly fed on the music, savoring each step of my preparation.

When my hair was nearly dry, they began to fashion it as we had agreed. Kinsa wrapped long strands of gold around each lock framing my face and meticulously joined them together with the hair on my crown to form a single, gold braid that extended to my waist. Next Tawan combed the unbraided hair on the back of my head and laid the braid on top. Together they curled the ends of both the straight and braided hair around a serpent-shaped clasp. When they finished, my head appeared to be covered with a cap woven of gold, while the sparkling braid flowed down my back through a sea as black as night. Careful not to mess my hair, Kinsa helped me slip into the ceremonial dress we had designed and made together. Next she proudly draped my shawl over my shoulders and fastened it with a silver fox pin Riku had given me.

I thought I was ready, but Tawan signaled for me to wait, while she carefully uncovered a necklace. "Tawan, it's beautiful! You've strung Pule's feathers into it. And these beads, I've never seen anything like them. Where did you get them?" I looked at the chain of beads to discover they were really golden shells.

"They are from the north, near my home. Do you like them?"

"Very much. I will proudly wear your creation."

She ceremoniously tied it around my neck and adjusted the feathers so the fox pin lay on top. In the center, the longest feather extended almost to my waist, and the shorter ones fanned across my chest to my shoulders. I'd never felt beautiful, but from their expressions, I must have been. "Thank you, both of you," I said with a lump in my throat. I took their hands in mine and tried to express my gratitude, but nothing was sufficient. Instead they spontaneously hummed a lullaby together, as my mothers cradled me with their love and tears flowed down my cheeks.

Finally, they escorted me to the sacred plaza where the effect of our arrival was obvious. The conversation abruptly stopped, and for the first time ever, the men stood to greet me. Amused and embarrassed by their attempts to compliment me, I quickly turned the attention to their ceremonial attire. Covered with a white cloak, Riku wore a tunic elaborately designed with woven patterns in a myriad of colors. Ixiamas had an identical cloak, but his tunic was less ornate. Atuk tried to hide his pride as he stood before me in a *cumbi* tunic and cloak, but his elevated chin and perfectly straight back revealed his delight. Surprisingly, Tucu seemed withdrawn from the group even though he was dressed like Atuk.

After the novelty of our sumptuous costumes diminished, Iska served a delicious dinner featuring succulent dove cooked with potatoes and peanuts, and served with a side dish of squash and guava seasoned with a bit of cinnamon provided by Ixiamas. Fresh pineapple from the north offered a most satisfying finish. Together, all eight of us, enjoyed the food, *mulli chicha*, conversation, and Tawan's music as tears mixed with laughter throughout the evening. Late in the evening, I bid my teary, final farewells to Iska, Kinsa, and Tawan. I would likely see them the following day, but there would be no exchange.

Since before dawn, we were occupied with some aspect of the preparation, and I'd rarely contemplated the coming day. As I sat by the fire with Riku, Ixiamas, Tucu, and Atuk, trembling terror rushed in through every pore. Desperate to forget, I remembered our dance. "Riku, did we all see the same future?"

"I was about to ask. Why don't you start and tell us what you saw," Riku answered. We each complied, and except for fine details, the vision was the same for all of us. Even Ixiamas, who wasn't part of the dance, but an experienced traveler, shared a similar story.

"Since I had a son, does that mean that I won't be sacrificed tomorrow?" I asked, although I already knew the answer.

"Maybe. We still can't be sure. I'd hoped Pule would appear, but without a clear message, we must assume that, as the only woman in our group, your represented all women, not yourself. Because it was your son, your emotions were stronger, and the message more distinct. Didn't you say that each time the sun vanished, your anxiety for your child increased, even though he remained healthy and the sun always returned?"

"Yes. Didn't any of you feel that?" I asked.

They all shook their heads.

"To me, the sun returned, but each time it was dimmer," Atuk replied. "My concern was for the sun."

"Kaya experienced the fears of every mother, while Atuk dreaded the events in the Upper World. Again the earth mirrors the sky. We needed to see both views to confirm that the prediction is correct," Riku concluded as Ixiamas grunted in agreement.

"But what does it mean?" Tucu blurted out. "We already had one fading last winter. Will Inti, I mean the sun, really disappear six times in a single lifetime?"

In his typical calm manner, Riku answered slowly, "I believe the sun, and perhaps Inti, will indeed leave us six more times, and will mark the end of an era. What we don't know is what each fading represents. The death of six Incas in a single lifespan is unthinkable. Perhaps they represent catastrophic losses in battle, or droughts, or some other natural calamity. Great danger is coming and we aren't prepared for Viracocha's return. Perhaps they foretell of his trials or . . ." Riku paused, not wanting to continue but knew he must. "Perhaps they foretell of Viracocha's judgments."

The significance of such a horrific possibility muted everyone. The interpretations of the vision seemed endless. I wondered how such cloudy information could be useful.

"There is a miracle in the story," he continued more cheerfully. "We know that the sun always returned, and that the child continued to live. I believe that is a clear indication that the Incas will endure and survive whatever catastrophe befalls them, although they may not return to the same circumstances."

"What are we to do? How do we know if our interpretations are correct? How can we advise the Inca? How can we survive such chaos?" Tucu asked, visibly shaken.

"That is why our work is so important. Whether Kaya remains in this world or travels to the Upper World, she will provide the most complete visions. At the moment, it appears she will be in the Upper World, and my only remaining tasks will be to establish contact with her, and teach both of you how to do likewise."

Although my panic returned, Riku wasn't intentionally trying to frighten me. He simply needed to clarify everyone's task, including mine, before the night ended.

"Atuk and Tucu, your lifelong task is to interpret the information Kaya gives us. Use your heart and your logic to find the answers, but if they are in conflict, trust your heart to tell you the truth."

Atuk nodded as though he understood, but Tucu's tense body and unsettled eyes suggested only confusion. Riku continued anyway, "Ultimately you two will likely have the most difficult task. In the midst of unprecedented pandemonium, you must find and train your successors. Meanwhile, you will interpret the information you receive and share it with the Inca, who will likely be in the north. It will take both of you."

Neither seemed comfortable with their tasks. Fortunately, Riku still had time to prepare them.

The conversation continued throughout the night, and I realized that after tomorrow, Atuk and Tucu's task would be much more difficult than my own. I didn't want to die, but without a miracle, death was inevitable. Riku's special tea helped me sleep, at least fitfully, and every time I awoke, someone always offered conversation until I slept again.

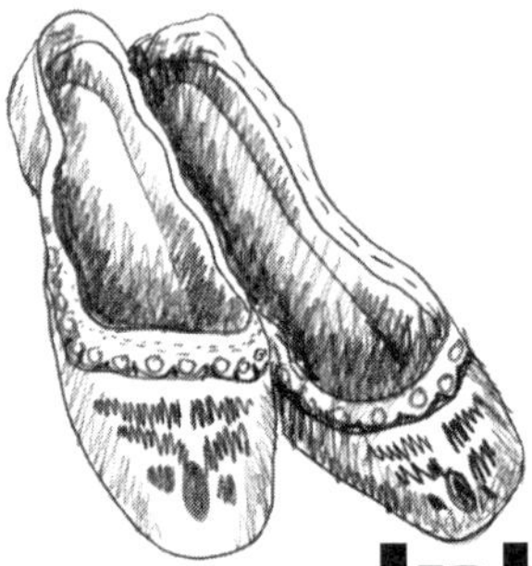

Inti Raymi

Kaya

Riku and I stood in the sacred plaza, bathed in the first rays of sunlight, while, still in shadow, the people below stood like blades of grass swaying in a breeze. Anticipating the sunrise, the elite from across the empire filled the main plaza and the adjacent terraces. His loving eyes encouraging me, Riku asked, "Are you ready?"

I took one deep breath, exhaled very slowly, and nodded. The cool stone underfoot was my only sense of actually moving as we descended the stairs. Touched by the sun rising over the mountains, everyone turned to face us and bowed their heads in unexpected reverence. Temporarily dispelling my fear, the welcoming throng and their outpouring of humble gratitude pulled me toward them.

When we stepped onto the plaza, the unbroken mass of dark heads became a field of individuals. The first Inca I saw wore a tunic with patterns so complicated I could only absorb the colors before we passed him. A tall thin woman with a light complexion carried a basket filled with exotic flowers whose scent lingered with me long after we'd moved beyond her. A small boy stood by his father pointing at my feather necklace. A farmer's wife, bent from years of planting, stood with her hands on the shoulders of two young boys. As we walked, the crowd stepped aside, but immediately closed behind us. Even though their clothes varied from common llama wool to the finest cotton, and their adornments ranged from none at all to sparkling gems set in gold pendants, I felt their solemn purpose and complete unity. I knew none of these people, and yet they showered me with respect and blessings.

For the first time ever, I was proud to be Kaya Chaka, daughter of the Inca. It was impossible to respond to the gratitude with anything but a deep sense of honor and joyful pride. By the time we reached the statue of Pachamama at the center of the plaza, I was floating on the charitable love I received from everyone we passed.

On the platform with the statue, Atuk presented a sheaf of maize that I would carry to the sacred plaza as an offering for Inti. Each harvest-gold stalk had two large, perfectly formed ears, but remarkably, the tassels, stems and leaves were as supple as the fresh greens of spring. Next he presented Riku with a basket overflowing with perfect branches of coca; each carried a full complement of leaves, with none missing, creased or broken. With Atuk immediately behind us, we were about to begin the procession to the sacred plaza when the statue on the platform caught my attention. Pachamama, represented as a detailed woodcarving of a beautiful young woman, watched over the four children at her feet as she tended a llama and her calf.

As I stared at the statue, Riku whispered, "Pachamama and most women experience the joy of children and the bounty of the earth. There are those who wish for your role, as you wish for theirs. You can't have both and we have no message from Pule. Be satisfied with your destiny."

Still, I ached for the tender love of a man and the joy of creating a new life, but since Ninan had vanished, there was no alternative. "Riku, how can I accept the honor of my sacrifice when I'm consumed by Ninan's desertion? Where is he anyway?"

"I don't know. I haven't seen him either. Don't trouble yourself with him. Let the people carry you on their thanksgiving and devotion to Inti."

Riku gently urged me to begin the procession. Again the crowd opened and greeted us with the same respectful blessings, but this time pairs followed behind us. Whether it was an adult and a child, a married couple, or two children, the pair was always a male and a female, and everyone bore a gift for Inti. We circled around Pachamama and spiraled into larger circles as the procession grew. With the exception of a single flute playing in the distance, the only sound was shuffling footsteps. Even the children walked in silence.

Loving warmth pervaded the entire plaza. I savored the wonder and pride I felt for these people, and the unseen multitudes they represented. After discovering the same appreciation on everyone's face, I finally began to understand the significance of the event. I was the messenger to Inti for the entire empire. I was their best hope for a better life for their children. If Inti accepted me as their gift of devotion, then he would continue to bless them with plentiful crops, many healthy children and a peaceful life. Unknown to the masses, I would also act as an intermediary and, most important, I would complete the bridge that Viracocha, in human form, would use to return to this world. Was it possible that I could meet their expectations? All of these people, including Riku, had the faith to believe I could. Even if I controlled my panic, I didn't think I was strong enough, or pure enough to be accepted by Inti. Still, their trust supported me as we continued to pass through the crowd and the spiral widened to fill the plaza.

The flutist repeated the simple melody so long, I started singing it in my head as we greeted a man wearing an embroidered skullcap and another with a headband covered with tiny red feathers. Near the path to Huayna Picchu at the far end of the plaza, we finally reached the flute player. He was playing the tune I modified years earlier. This was the musician I wished would carry me away from my solitude, and so he had. The very old farmer cradled his flute and performed with the lightness of a child's heart. I stopped to listen as the hollow sadness from years of confinement and desperate loneliness flowed away with the tears that streamed down my face. As he continued to play, I bent to kiss him on the forehead. At my request, he joined the procession walking with Atuk behind Riku and me while we made our last, triumphant circle before our ascent.

Just in front of us, young girls scampered up the steps, dropping flower petals as they went. I stood at the base of the staircase, knowing it was the last time I would climb it, knowing each step brought me closer to my death, knowing my heavy feet and ice-cold hands were only the outward symptoms of my deep, overwhelming terror. With Riku's help, I took the first three steps before I stopped, turned around and overlooked the slow-moving spiral.

"Kaya, they're waiting for you," Riku coaxed me. "You can't disappoint them. They're depending on you for their very survival."

I knew he was right, but how could I continue? His hand on my shoulder gently turned me around, and I stared at my feet as I climbed until I reached the terrace path leading to my garden. For all the times I dreaded reaching that point and returning to isolation, now I stopped and yearned for its peaceful sanctuary. Again Riku urged me, "Your path leads this way now. Come with me."

My stomach heaving and my shoulders shaking with grief, Riku lifted my arm and forced my rooting feet to again step toward the sacred plaza. From the top step, I turned for the last time and watched the parade. Like a coiled serpent of the earth, the paired procession spiraled around the plaza and up the stairs as it transformed into a river of life ascending toward the sky.

Together Riku and I crossed the sacred plaza to the shining gold walls of the Temple of Inti where Tucu stood beside the massive altar. I carefully placed the sheaf of maize on the altar while Riku deposited his basket of coca beside the sumptuous gifts already placed there by my family. Tucu prayed with us, "Most generous Inti, accept our gifts as a token of our thanks."

Behind us the procession began to flow past the temple where Atuk and Tucu stayed to bless everyone's offerings. The lowlanders carried the finest fruit and coca. Fabric woven with the best wool in brilliant colors graced the arms of the highlanders as well as jars filled with maize, beans, dried peppers, and every other crop. Those from the coast carried shell jewelry, dried fish, embroidered cotton, and occasionally a conch shell. Baskets of *cumbi*, *chuno*, and quinoa demonstrated the plenty of the highest locales. Even sacrificial llamas led by their owners made the trek to the sacred plaza before descending to the holding pasture.

Riku and I stood by the Temple of Viracocha and greeted everyone in the procession. Although most were strangers to me, everyone I had ever met, except my family, flowed by us. Carrying their best work, Iska, Kinsa, and Tawan all hugged me as they passed. Every pair left their gifts and continued past the Temple of Ilyapa, up the winding stairs to the terrace preceding Intihuatana where they were greeted by Huayna Capac, Coya Cusirimay, Ixiamas and other high noblemen before they descended the opposite side to the main plaza.

As the sun rose higher, the piles of gifts entirely filled the Temple of Inti and stretched across the sacred plaza. Interspersed with the strangers, the gold worker and his family, the potter with his wife and children, farmers and their wives that I recognized from my walks with Riku, and children I had watched from my garden, all offered their thanks as they paraded by us. The diversity of people and their continued goodwill sustained me for a long time, but as the morning dragged on, Riku noticed my trembling and mounting fear. He tried to keep me occupied with the parade of lavish gifts and unique clothing: an elaborate hat from Cajamarca, a tunic from Tomebamba, feathers from Quito and ceramic jars from the southern coast, but they all blurred into a chaotic profusion of color. Honor and sacrifice are gracious ideals, but the certainty of facing the pain of death, and, more important, forfeiting my life without remorse or disgrace became more terrifying with each new supplicant.

When the last of the procession finally left the sacred plaza, Riku led me into the Temple of Viracocha so we could be alone. Out of public view, I collapsed on a bench. "They ask too much. I don't know if I can do this," I wailed, finally resigned to my imminent death.

"I know, but you must," Riku said as he gave me a drink of hot tea. "This will warm and soothe you. There's no hurry. Enjoy it and drink it slowly." The honey-sweetened, vaguely familiar taste was remarkably pleasant. I gradually relaxed enough to stop shaking and regain control of my now blunted fear. I tried to prepare myself for the final step, but all I could do was cry. I knew this was my last chance to talk with Riku, and there was so much I wanted to tell him. I was so grateful for the lifelong, unfailing encouragement and understanding he had so freely given me. Riku sat beside me, took my hands into his and said, "You can't know how much I will miss you. You are a gifted student, and we have shared many adventures. I do expect we will connect again, but it won't be the same." He paused and continued, "Please forgive any pain I may cause you. It is my fervent desire to do this without hurting you." As he straightened my feathered necklace he added, "I'm sorry we didn't find Pule. I tried every way I know. Please try to find the beauty of your deeds."

I didn't know how to respond. I quietly finished my tea and eventually the words tumbled out. "Thanks to you, I have come to love the world that I once so desperately despised. I hope we can build the bridge since that's the only way I can be a part of this world." We sat together in silence a long time before I added, "My only regret is not saying good-bye to Ninan."

He caressed my hands and face, calming and preparing me for the task ahead.

Intihuatana

Ninan

Worried that the evening celebration in the main plaza might continue until dawn, I excused myself from Huayna Capac and the festivities to develop an alternative plan in case the torches were never extinguished. Finally, after the last inebriated man stumbled toward his bed and the plaza was entirely dark, Secret and I started to climb the northern stairs to Intihuatana by starlight.

"How much farther is it?" she asked in her grating voice as we approached the summit.

"Be quiet! And lift your feet when you walk" I hissed. "We're almost there. Remember, if anyone finds us, you'll be killed in disgrace." I probably would be too, but she didn't care about that.

After a short rest, we sneaked down the winding stairs toward the sacred plaza, knowing that Riku and the others were to hold a vigil in front of the Temple of Inti. A clumsy woman, Secret continued to shuffle her feet on the stones and nearly tripped twice, but somehow we managed to get to the Temple of Ilyapa undetected. I held my breath while I slowly opened the temple door, and she stepped inside without her normal clatter. With equal care, I closed the door behind us. After a few deep, silent breaths I finally relaxed in the small building, relieved that we hadn't interrupted Riku's group.

My plan couldn't fail now. The roof of the temple had been removed for the celebration, but the thick stone walls rising to more than twice my height towered over us. Tucu had already confirmed that if we stayed close to the north end of the temple, the high walls would obscure us from the nobles, including my parents, when they stood above us in the morning. I heard Riku talking quietly with Kaya. They were so close, but I wouldn't dare interfere.

Secret stretched out on the bench by the north wall and slept instantly. She had been drinking *chicha* with her temporary mother before we began our climb. Now I wondered if my friend had mixed her drink with something else. It was a good idea if she had; at least Secret was quiet when she slept.

According to her hosts, Secret thoroughly enjoyed her three months in Cusco. It took the entire first day and several changes of bath water for Secret to scrub off the dirt, wash her hair and meticulously clean her finger and toe nails. When she reappeared in a new dress, she was allowed to eat whatever she wished, and quickly acquired a taste for roasted dove and fresh pineapple. Although she was not allowed in public alone, she visited Sacsahuaman, the Coricancha, and several other elite locations with an escort. Since few people had ever seen Kaya, and Secret had stepped beyond her squalid past, there was no fear of her being recognized. I did visit her once shortly before the procession to Machu Picchu. She was happy and still satisfied with her bargain.

While she lay sleeping, I paced the temple in the clear, crisp air of early morning. According to Tucu's description, my parents accompanied by Umu Pilaca, Tucu, and about fifty of the Incas' friends and family would start the day at the Torreon to confirm the obvious; today was the winter solstice. Meanwhile, Riku and Kaya would descend to the main plaza and initiate the procession. A short while later I heard the clamor of the nobles passing our hideout as they walked to the terraces above me to watch the procession. "Where's Ninan?" I heard my father bellow.

"I don't know. I haven't seen him since the celebration last night," my mother responded.

"Miski, have you seen Ninan?"

"No, why don't you ask Pacas or Mama Runtu? They might know."

I wondered if everyone knew Mama Runtu was my teacher. The voices passed, but I could still hear my father calling for Pacas.

A short while later the temple door opened and closed quickly, startling Secret awake. Pacas stood before me. Looking remarkably composed, he whispered. "Good, you got here all right. I told your father you drank too much last night and will join them soon. If I see you from the terrace above, I'll return and knock twice on the door without entering." He glanced at Secret, but made no comment before leaving abruptly. I reassured her that he was a friend and part of the plan.

Tucu was in and out of the temple several times during the procession in the main plaza. With each arrival he stared at Secret, shook his head and commented on how much she looked like Kaya. He claimed he was nervous about his first event as a repeater, but I thought he was worried about her changing her mind and exposing him as an accomplice. One trait Secret had in common with Kaya was her commitment. Once she had agreed to my plan, she never wavered. As the morning slowly unfolded, Tucu's growing restlessness made me jumpy. On one visit he quietly said, "The procession is starting up the stairs now. I need to bless all the offerings. Do you need anything?"

I shook my head. "Did you see Kaya? How does she look?" I asked in a muted voice, anything louder creating an echo.

"She's beautiful, scared, but beautiful." He left to attend to his duties.

Again we waited as the interminable procession passed us on its way to greet the Inca before returning to the main plaza. Generally respectful, the crowd spoke in hushed voices. "Did you see the size of that emerald?" "Yes, but that conch shell, that's what I'd like." "I've lived near Machu Picchu my whole live, and I've never been close to Intihuatana. I can hardly wait." "What should I say when I meet the Inca?" We waited while thousands passed us within arm's length. As the sun approached its apex, the parade ended, but the lack of activity was even more distressing. To her credit, Secret sat motionless on the bench with her eyes tightly closed. After a while Tucu joined us, and I asked about Kaya.

"She's terrified. She's shaking, and she looks like she's about to faint. Actually, if you didn't know her as well as we do, you'd think she looked very solemn and brave. The shaking doesn't show unless you notice her hands, which she hides under her shawl," he whispered. Secret tucked her feet up to her chest and tightly wrapped her shawl around them. I was sympathetic to Secret's suffering, but she agreed to the plan. I was more concerned about the woman I loved.

"My poor sister! I wish we could have told her my intent, but pretending to be scared would be even more difficult," I replied, hoping he would confirm my decision.

"They'll be coming soon. Are you ready?" I turned to Secret who nodded. It seemed like days before we heard them approach.

Tucu threw open the door, and we stood on the path directly in front of Kaya and Riku. Kaya flew into my arms and buried her face in my chest. Riku was surprised but didn't interfere. Lifting her head and wearing a radiant smile, Kaya said, "I didn't think we'd get to say goodbye."

"I'm not here to say goodbye," I replied. "Please stay with me. I need you by my side when I become the Inca." She backed away as she tried to understand, and I continued, "Kaya, this is our mother's secret. She is your elder twin, and is named Secret. Our mother hid her from our father fearing he would insist that you were both sacrificed. She has lived modestly in Cusco her entire life. Secret looks exactly like you, and since she is the elder, she wishes to reclaim her heritage and take her rightful place on the altar. Her hair is arranged just like yours. All we need to do is exchange clothes, but we don't have much time. Change in here."

The two women studied each other carefully. "Secret, is this true? You choose to die?"

"I was deprived my entire life, but Ninan offered me a way to reclaim my honor. I will gladly take your place on the altar." She smiled weakly, and I noticed her hands were shaking.

Kaya looked to Riku, "What should I do?"

Without being rushed he replied, "The decision must be yours."

She stood there, frozen in place, so I tried to explain. "Riku, you remember. At Casana, Huayna Capac said he'd spare Kaya if there was a miracle."

"Yes, that's true," Riku confirmed.

"Well, Secret is that miracle. Huayna Capac will accept her as Kaya's replacement."

Looking very confused, Kaya stepped toward Riku. "Oh, Ninan, you mean you haven't told our father about this? What will he say? I'll die before I disgrace you. You must become the Inca. You are the only hope for the empire."

"When we meet father in the north, we'll tell him that I met you, Secret, just after Pacas' wedding. Now please hurry and change."

"But I'd be living in deceit for the rest of my life! What if we're discovered?"

"Then we'd tell our parents that Secret was the older and the proper sacrifice. Father would have met his obligation, mother would still have a daughter, and I'd have you as my wife." I guided Secret into the temple with one hand and took Kaya's hand with the other. "Come on, they're waiting, we have to go."

Before Kaya could respond, the Inca's voice roared down the stairs behind us. "Riku, what's the meaning of this? We're waiting for you and Kaya." He continued to descend with Ixiamas on his heels. "Ninan, where have you been? Come on, Kaya, its time."

"Wait!" Ixiamas exclaimed. "Wisest Inca, which one is Kaya? Have they already exchanged clothes?"

My father noticed Secret for the first time and motioned her to stand beside Kaya. He looked from one to the other several times while both frightened women stood shaking. "They are identical. Ninan, can I assume you found Kaya's twin and plan to exchange them so you can marry Kaya?"

"Yes, I am entirely responsible for this. This is Secret, Kaya's *elder* sister."

"You intended to exchange the two knowing that I could refuse to name you as my successor, banish you, or have you killed?"

"Yes. I would gladly forfeit everything to have Kaya as my wife." I stood bravely beside Kaya, feeling the fear of death that she'd known for years.

"Riku, come here." He complied, joining my father and Ixiamas above us. All three men participated in the discussion, but of course, Huayna Capac would make the decision. While they debated, I comforted both women and tried to ignore my own anxiety. In the background, Tucu desperately attempted to control his fidgeting, which for some reason struck me as funny. Standing on the stairs above us, the sages of the empire finished, and the Inca said, "Ninan, in the face of extreme personal danger, you demonstrated remarkable bravery. My greatest reluctance to appointing you as Inca is your lack of experience maintaining control in the face of death. I expected to judge your fortitude in the north, but you're first trial was today."

He glanced at one woman and then the other before continuing. "The queen so despised the tradition, I can readily believe she hid Secret. I too heard Coya and Cepi whisper about 'their secret,' but I assumed it was trivial women's talk, not the name of my daughter."

Inside I was elated beyond imagining, but I solemnly waited for him to finish.

"I have loved and yearned for Chaska my entire life. In her memory, I will allow Secret to take Kaya's place on the altar since she is the elder, and your intended deception will go unpunished. Ninan, your fitness to become Inca will still be decided in the north, but you may take Kaya as your wife, if she agrees." He turned to follow Ixiamas up the stairs.

"It's a miracle! Now we can be together for a lifetime. I'll be Inca, and you can raise the children you've always wanted." I threw my arms around her and passionately kissed her in front of everyone, but even in the midst of my joy, her entire body was quaking in my arms. Reluctantly, I loosened my embrace, hoping to see her crying with joy.

"Ninan, I can't marry you. Secret has no training. She may look like me, but she cannot act as an intermediary. We understand very little of our visions. I'm meant to change that, and I can only do that from the Upper World. Inti is expecting me, not Secret. You need me more in the Upper World than you do here, and I couldn't live with myself if I stayed." She took my hands in hers and softly added, "Ever since we met, I sustained myself with the possibility of being your wife and having your children, but now I'm bewildered." Her watery eyes melted my heart as she spoke. "I must decline your offer." In spite of her trembling lips, she tried to smile.

"But how can you refuse your own life?"

She gently covered my mouth with her hand. "Return Secret to Cusco. Let her live openly with our mother, or as your wife. Secret, it was very brave of you to offer to take my place, but now that father knows, you can still reclaim your honor."

Shaking from head to foot, Secret grinned broadly even as she sobbed. "How can I thank you?" she gasped.

Kaya embraced her sister and replied, "Live a good life and forgive those who have wronged you. Now, you'd better remove the gold from your hair and leave this place before there's any confusion."

Turning to me, our eyes met, and she gently whispered, "I will miss you, and I will love you, always." Stunned, I couldn't respond. Riku stepped forward to take her hand, and in a tranquil voice she said, "Now I am ready to die."

Rejected and with no recourse, I finally followed them as they filed up the petal-caked steps, wound past the waiting royalty, and continued to Intihuatana. Gleaming in the sun, the base of the gold-covered statue rose to my chest, and overhead, its pinnacle reached into the sky. Below us in the main plaza and strewn across every terrace on both sides of the pinnacle, the grateful masses shouted their delight.

Riku led the way past my father's favored wives and children, Pacas, his mother, Tinkha, and finally my parents. Kaya nodded to each member of the family she never knew. Reluctantly, but with no alternative, I took my place beside my father. My mother stood straight, her eyes red and swollen, and answered Kaya's respectful greeting with tears. Even the Inca's eyes were moist as he presented his final gift to Kaya. On both hands he offered a red-feathered pillow carrying a long slender knife with a cold, gray blade. "This sacred knife will deliver my precious daughter to Inti. Travel in peace, Kaya Chaka." From the Temple of Ilyapa, Tucu repeated the Inca's words.

When she accepted the pillow, she answered, "It is a great honor to leave this world. May Inti find me worthy." Tucu's duplication echoed around us as though her words carried their own life. She bowed to my father and proudly displayed the pillow as she joined Riku at Intihuatana. At noon on the winter solstice, the tall pillar cast a shadow that pointed directly toward Salcantay Mountain where Kaya would soon rest beside Chaska and Collca. From their perch, they touched both this world and the Upper World, while remaining in full sight of Riku's retreat on Huayna Picchu. Waiting for Tucu's repeat, Riku slowly offered a prayer.

Most benevolent Inti, hear our prayer.
Most powerful Inti, your servants are gathered before you.
Most generous Inti, we celebrate the beauty and abundance of this world.
Most merciful Inti, we offer our precious gift, Kaya Chaka.
Most benevolent Inti, hear our prayer.

Completely numb, I watched as Umu Riku and Kaya Chaka stepped down to the small terrace with its monstrous sacrificial table. Following my family, I helplessly watched my dreams disappear. Umu Riku accepted the pillow with a slow bow, and offered Kaya his hand as she stepped onto the stone altar. Standing above him, she raised her arms toward the sun. Still searching for inclusion, she slowly turned to see the main plaza overflowing with grateful people. Continuing to rotate, she once again acknowledged her parents before she looked directly at me with her head tipped to the side and said she was sorry. Still shocked by her refusal, I couldn't speak. She gazed beyond me toward her garden, her eyes filled with longing. Turning again, she stopped to bow toward Salcantay Mountain, and the crowds accepted her gesture as a signal to cheer. Answering her bow, a loud caw echoed through the river valley. Kaya straightened immediately and faced the sound just as a magnificent blue macaw sailed up the mountain.

"Pule, you've come for me!" Kaya's voice sparkled as the bird squawked and gracefully landed on her outstretched arm. "And you've brought a friend?" Another identical bird arrived and landed on her other arm. Together they seemed to comfort Kaya with cooing and head bobbing.

Riku and my entire family stood in silence, awestruck by the beautiful creatures as they brightened Kaya in ways I couldn't comprehend. After nuzzling both birds, Kaya calmly said, "Riku, they've come to tell me that Inti is waiting for me. Chaska and Collca are ready to show me the way. Will you help me?"

Riku's shoulders shuddered and tears streamed down his face as Kaya extended her arm, and Pule hopped to Riku's hand. The bird cawed again, a signal Riku must have understood, since he stooped to place the bird at the foot of the sacrificial table. Likewise, he turned to Kaya and accepted the other macaw which he placed beside Pule.

"I'm ready now." Kaya announced as easily as if she were going to dinner.

Wiping his eyes, Riku tried to compose himself before he accepted the pin and shawl she removed. He meticulously spread the shawl across the altar and fastened the pin in the corner before she knelt on the supple wool. She gathered her flowing hair and draped it over her shoulder as she lay down. Riku fastidiously adjusted her shawl, her dress, her hair, and her necklace. Everything must be perfect, and the birds patiently watched every step.

My stomach tightened into a knot as he retrieved the knife from the pillow between the macaws. Again he dabbed his eyes, and prepared us with a prayer.

Most charitable Inti, may Kaya Chaka be worthy of your eternal care.
Most honorable Inti, may she bring us all closer to the Upper World.

With both hands, Riku raised the knife over her and looked directly into the sun, no doubt privately seeking Inti's strength. As the birds took flight, Riku struck with the knife, but he hit a rib before plunging too close to the center of her chest. Riku gasped at his blunder. I may have shouted her name. Kaya smiled as she watched both macaws swoop down close to her and then turn toward the sun. Recovering quickly, Riku landed the knife squarely in her heart. Kaya exhaled slowly as her eyes closed. The happiness she struggled to find in life stayed with her now as she lay blissfully still.

Everyone in the plaza burst into joyous singing, even as the drums thundered and conch shells bellowed. Riku didn't seem to notice the din rising from below us. Instead, we followed the aerial display overhead. The brilliantly blue macaws hovered over Kaya and Intihuatana, and then shot straight into the sun. During the next dive, they twirled and cavorted around us before skimming over her again. Unable to accept what I'd just seen, I gazed at my love sleeping peacefully on the sacred table. Suddenly a bird brushed my shoulder as it raced past. Jolted from my stupor, I realized there were now three macaws darting among us. As if by silent command, they converged, circled around Riku one more time, and then gracefully floated on a rising current. Together, sliding from side to side, perfectly following each other, they spiraled upward in a stream of light until they dissappeared into Inti.

Apparently the people in the plaza couldn't see what we witnessed. Umu Riku approached Huayna Capac for a short conversation. The Inca raised his scepter and waited until the crowd was quiet. In his booming voice he declared, "By tradition and the obligations placed on me as Inca, my precious daughter was given to Inti. You all witnessed this act. Everyone, elders and children, you must remember our sacred offering. Tell your children's children about this day. The miracles we have seen today affirm Kaya's acceptance into the Upper World. In return for this sacrifice, and in keeping with his promise, he will bring peace and plenty to all his faithful children."

Everyone jubilantly resumed the festivities. I alone mourned for Kaya, the only woman I ever loved.

Salcantay Mountain

Ninan

All the planning. All the promises. Wasted and rejected. How could she do this to me? Kaya lay on the altar shrouded in the loving acceptance she had only just found. Led by my parents, each noble approached her, paused momentarily, and then quickly proceeded down the stairs to join the celebration. To my surprise, Atahualpa, now nearly a man, lingered by the altar for a respectful interval, but I realized he did so only in ghoulish curiosity. No one knew her the way I did, and no one grieved for her. I stood in foggy disbelief even though I had just witnessed the entire sacrifice. When Pacas led me to her side, I stooped to take her warm hand in mine. Soft as a new leaf and filled with Inti's grace, her hand found my lips while I memorized her sweet scent and radiant face. As if sleeping peacefully, Kaya lay before me, and yet I knew she was gone. I don't know how long I stayed with her, but it seemed like only an instant before Pacas and Atuk guided me down the stairs.

We crossed the plaza and climbed Huayna Picchu to escape the curious crowds. "Riku asked me to make this for you. It will help you rest," Tinkha said as I absently took the cup of hot tea, sat alone to drink it, and without intention, fell asleep immediately. When I woke in the early evening, the music rose from the celebration below, while Pacas, Atuk, and Tinkha chatted quietly a short distance away.

Pacas joined me, but waited for me to shake off the effects of Riku's sedative. I asked, "How did you know she wouldn't marry me?"

Without looking at me, he replied. "Perhaps better than you, she understood the importance of her position in the Upper World, and . . ." He glanced at me as if he didn't want to continued. "Her remarkable courage carried the strength of her spirit, but her isolation in this world left her very fragile. Even protected by your love, she was afraid to leave her garden. You were honest with her and told her about the turmoil she would experience in the north. She couldn't endure that."

"But no one could be a better queen. If she had lived a normal life, she would have happily gone north as my wife. How could my father condemn her to a life of incurable loneliness and pain? How could Riku do that to her?"

"They had no choice, and you must forgive both of them. The isolation that you reject was likely the largest contributor to her ability to receive information from the Upper World. That was her training and her destiny. Besides, in the end, she chose her death," he calmly reminded me.

I knew he was right, but I was still unwilling to accept it.

In the night chill, we stayed together in silence until he jarred me from my memories and suggested we join the others by the fire. Together, our small group watched the skies turn above us just like any other night. Nothing had changed, and yet everything was different. No one spoke, not of the day, not of the moment, not of tomorrow. Gradually the continual noise of the multiple groups playing simultaneously in the plaza diminished to a single haunting flute. Sad and yet hopeful, the melody's charm grew more familiar with each repetition. Finally, as soothing as an old blanket, the tune permanently settled in my heart, and I took refuge in its warmth.

Content to remain in our aerie for a few days, the others carefully avoided intruding on my private grief, but each willingly mourned with me if I initiated the exchange. Through their kindness, I gradually accepted her death as her own choice, not the failing of my father, Riku or me. Even so, losing her consumed me.

I knew the animal sacrifices and gluttonous feasting would continue for at least a week. With thousands of visitors enjoying the celebration of a lifetime, our small group wouldn't be missed. Obviously, Riku had prearranged our retreat since everything we needed had been carefully stored.

"When will Kaya be buried?" I asked Atuk early one morning.

"I'll lead the procession as soon as we return to the city. Riku, Ixiamas, and Tucu are preparing her for the journey."

"May I come with you?"

"If you wish. You understand it will be very cold, and dangerous. It's possible none of us will return from the mountain."

"I know." I replied before adding, "I think we should go back to the city."

"If you're ready, we'll leave this morning." Pacas stood in the background shaking his head.

As we descended, I wondered which of the gods had protected our earlier ascent. I remembered nothing of the climb, and yet somehow we had arrived safely on the mountaintop. I walked beside Pacas and dodged the celebrants as we crossed the plaza. "You don't approve of my trip to Salcantay, do you?"

"No. Our journey north will be risky and the campaign even more dangerous. You're tempting the gods with your recklessness."

"And yet, you know I must go."

"She's gone. Let her go. What do you hope to accomplish?"

"An end, and a beginning."

"Then go, and return with the conviction of an Inca." We were both weary of our constant disagreement on anything regarding Kaya.

"Very soon, my friend, very soon." I said as we parted. They joined the festivities as Atuk and I headed for the sacred plaza.

Tucu was the first to a notice our approach. "Good, you've returned."

"Hello, Tucu. Was Secret returned to Cusco?" I asked, and he nodded. "Was Riku angry with you?"

"No, I think he knew when we left Cusco. He really did try to save her, you know. When he and Ixiamas spoke with the Inca on the stairs, he successfully argued that Kaya would be very helpful in the northern campaign."

"I know. Where is he?"

"In there." He tipped his head toward the Temple of Viracocha. "He and Ixiamas are performing the final rites. None of us are allowed to attend."

"So, we can leave tomorrow?" Atuk asked.

"Yes. The men will pack the llamas this afternoon. Riku has been watching the mountain carefully and thinks you should have an easy climb, but he's worried about a storm during your return."

Only Riku, Ixiamas, and Tucu watched us leave for Salcantay Mountain before dawn the following morning. Atuk and I led the six strong men and eight packed llamas toward the snowy mountain. Easily carried by two men, Kaya was encapsulated in a round bundle and securely tied above two poles. Riku placed us under Inti's care, and we started across the southern slope, following the Urubamba River downstream until we reached the first junction and then turned upstream along the Aobamba River. All the others knew the trail from the trip months earlier when they placed the supplies, built shelters, and prepared the gravesite.

For the first few days, our travel was a steady climb through the warm forest along the river, and we camped where they had stashed supplies. As we walked in single file along the narrow trail, I thought about traveling north and living without Kaya. For two years, every plan I made included her gentle guidance and exceptional visions. Now I struggled to devise alternatives. I felt hollow, as though a part of me had been ripped away. With each footstep, I pulled her memory closer to me, and yet somehow she was drifting away.

Above the forest, we crossed a barren rocky stretch and camped just below a white embankment. The following day, the blinding sun reflected off the snow, but offered little heat to ward off the frigid cold that numbed my carefully wrapped feet and legs. Across snowfields and around icy crevasses, every step proved more difficult than the preceding one, and my chest burned with the effort. Without complaint, the men took turns lifting, carrying, dragging and pushing our precious cargo while Kaya rode comfortably above the snow. The llamas faithfully plodded along, seemingly unaffected. At night, the snowfields were even colder, deadly without shelter and supplies.

Atuk masterfully led the expedition, certain of his role and our final destination. For as much as I wanted to stay close to Kaya, I was relieved when he said we would complete our mission the following day. In late afternoon, we retrieved our supplies from the crude shelter and camped with the comfort of a fire, hot food, and surrounded by llamas.

In the morning Atuk pointed to the mountain ridge above us while the men dug in the snow nearby. "Ninan, do you see the three jagged peaks jutting out of the snow up there?"

"Yes. Is that where we're going?"

"No, those cliffs are too steep. They're never covered with snow, so they're excellent markers for the burial ground before us."

I looked across the snowfield that seemed only slightly flatter than the ones we had already crossed. "Before us you see a single peak that resembles Huayna Picchu. The base of that peak marks the elevation of the graves and the cliffs above mark the position. Weather permitting, all of these sacred sentinels are visible from Huayna Picchu." He looked back toward the city, but everything was still hidden in the morning fog. "The men are digging out her gravesite. Most of the work was done during our last trip, but they need to clear the snow that has accumulated since." Atuk shifted his feet in the icy snow and scanned the entire area. "Can you imagine a more perfect place? Collca, Chaska, and Kaya will rest on one of the highest mountains, as close to Inti as you can be in this world."

I had to admit it was beautiful.

Once the hole was cleared, I noticed that the deepest of the icy walls in Kaya's new home shown with the same translucent blue of Pule's feathers.

I wondered if Pule and the others were able to fly through the snow. Still pondering the miracles I had witnessed, I helped the men untie Kaya from the poles and gently lower her into her grave. Around her feet we carefully placed jars of maize, coca leaves, and mullu seashell, gifts from Pachamama and Cochamama. We packed snow around these gifts and then surrounded her with a row of silver llamas to help her carry her treasures to the Upper World. Around her shoulders we wrapped an intricately woven cloth displaying brilliantly colored birds, a gift from the Mamaconas who cared for her. Again we added snow, carefully keeping the statues upright. Next we surrounded her with fist-sized emeralds from Riku and Ixiamas to protect her from evil spirits, positioning them exactly as Atuk was instructed. Again we packed the snow in place to permanently fix their position. Around her head we placed four gold statues, a perfect replica of Kaya dressed as she was the day she was given to Inti, and others representing our parents and Riku.

"Atuk, may I leave something for Kaya?" I asked, suddenly realizing she carried nothing from me. Except for the top of the bundle surrounding her head, Kaya was already encased in snow.

He nodded.

I removed my silver pendant with the Puma design that my mother had given me at Capac Raymi. Gently placing it over her head, I asked the spirit of the puma to protect her. I stood over her grave mourning my loss, comforted only by the certainty that she was finally happy. Images of her flooded back to me with a vitality as hopeful as the sunrise: the unassuming grace she embodied in every motion, the way she tilted her head when she listened, her shiny black hair begging to be stroked, and her placid face intensified by her searching eyes and inviting lips. A cool breeze lifted her flowery scent to me, and with a heavy heart, I repeated her final words to me, "I will love you always." When I finally stepped back, the men carefully covered the statues with snow, hurriedly filled the hole completely, and stamped the snow into place. Together we huddled on the mountain for Atuk's prayer.

Most gracious Inti, hear our prayer.
Today we returned to you the most miraculous gift you
eternally give your servants, the gift of life.
Innocent and faithful, this woman chose to join you so that
we, your children, can live in your abundance.
Help us to be worthy of her sacrifice and grateful for your
benevolence.

Most mysterious Inti, accept our offering.
Speak to us through Kaya that we may be closer to you.

Most powerful Inti, bless our work.
Today we complete the bridge broken by your enemies.
Grant us passage to the Upper World so we may serve you
in the life that follows.

Most holy Inti, hear our prayer.

The snow swirled around our feet as Atuk said, "She'll be safe here, forever undisturbed, forever surrounded by pristine beauty, forever at Inti's feet. Be happy for her."

"I wanted her as my wife, but she chose to sit with the gods. Who could fault her?" I closed my eyes and a shiver passed through my feet. "A part of her will always be with me. I'll be a better ruler for knowing her." In spite of the penetrating cold, I didn't want to leave and held my ground as the men led the llamas back along our path.

"We must go. A storm is coming, and we must get off the snowfields before dark." Atuk tugged on my arm. "Her destiny is complete. Yours is in another place."

I faced the mountain peak rising over Kaya, inhaled the beauty of her resting place and very slowly exhaled until I was empty. After a long pause filled with sorrow, but not regret, I drew in the breath of my new life.

The descent was faster but more dangerous—just warm enough to melt the snow and leave an icy film underfoot. I leaned into the mountain and tested every step before transferring my weight. Several times the men lost their footing and fell into the icy cold. When the sun slid behind the gathering clouds, the crisp black shadows in each footprint faded into an undistinguishable white blur. We traveled as quickly as we could. In spite of our heavy leggings and extra cloaks, we were cold, exhausted and hungry when we reached our camp and supplies just beyond the last snowfields. The fading sunlight disappeared into gently falling snow.

"Build a large fire and keep the llamas tethered. Pile all the supplies along this slope in the shelter of the cliffs." Atuk was calm, but his urgency demanded attention.

The men immediately did as he ordered, while he and I cooked the evening meal. The wind gathered strength, and the flames leaped out of the fire with equal vigor. After the meal, we huddled around the fire in the open shelter, and even though the llamas were close, they were often obscured by the falling snow. The gale howled through the night depriving us of restful sleep.

The storm blew over by morning, leaving us in snow up to our knees. We ate a cold breakfast and again urgently descended through the snow. Perhaps because of fatigue or the thin air, we all suffered from a shivering stiffness that slowed our progress. Still, we steadily slogged toward the luxuriant green below us.

By late afternoon, Atuk was satisfied we were beyond the reach of another storm, and we stopped to camp on a flat area just below some sheer cliffs. We had only just started to unpack when we heard a single, deep boom followed by the faint, high-pitched cry of an eagle soaring over the mountain well behind us. When I searched for the bird, I saw only a white cloud billowing away from the mountain near the peak. In an instant it grew into a giant white wall that roared down the mountain faster than anything I'd ever seen. Some of the cascading snow entombed the rocks on a ledge while even more slammed into the forest, uprooting full grown trees before it halted.

When it finally stopped, Atuk examined the slope and then leaned toward me to say, "Inti must have accepted Kaya as the last offering. With the snow that deep, it would be impossible to place another."

I searched the mountain in the waning light and found the three peaks above the graves, but I could barely see the tip of the cliff that stood beside them. "The graves must be covered with snow deeper than the tallest tree!" I replied, astonished by the power and speed of the snow. "I always thought of snow as cold, light, and fluffy, not something capable of divine destruction."

"Nothing is exactly as it seems. A day later and we all would have stayed at Kaya's side."

"As you said, I'll die in another place. I have much to do before I return to the Upper World." I was certain Inti had other plans for me.

Suddenly thunder rumbled around the mountain. At least I thought it was thunder, until I realized the shivering beneath my feet was the mountain, not the numbing cold.

"Hurry! Take the llamas over there. Don't stop until you get out of this boulder field!" Atuk shouted to the men who looked up at the mountain to see a few pebbles tumbling down. The terrified animals squealed and thrashed their heads but refused to move. Until then, I'd never seen a man strike a llama, but the hard swats on the rump so startled them, they bolted down the path. We raced behind them sliding, falling and lifting each other. The angry mountain shook beneath us. Boulders the size of a house bounced down the slope behind us like a spilled basket of potatoes. I couldn't hear anything over the pounding rampage.

A fist-sized rock slammed into Atuk. He reeled as he clutched a shoulder, dropped to his knees and rolled on the path. I helped him up and supported his uninjured side as we scrambled down the mountain together. The ground stopped shaking as quickly as it started, and behind us the river of rock diminished to a trickle. Finally, the tranquil silence of our ascent returned to the mountain. Even though he was in pain, Atuk insisted we continue until we were further away from sheer cliffs and snowfields. Flooded with images of the power of the gods, we trudged on until dark.

The rest of the return trip was uneventful, but, even with help, Atuk slowed our pace. Still, we made steady progress through the forest, back to the Urubamba River Valley and then safely arrived at the sacred plaza where we were met by my parents, Riku, Ixiamas, as well as Tucu, Pacas, and Tinkha.

"Riku, Atuk is hurt. Can you help him?" I left Atuk with him and continued to Huayna Capac and my mother.

"That was a foolish thing to do. You're needed in the north." My father complained. "You delayed our departure, as well as your own. Now Sinchi Roca will have to wait for you." He displayed no interest in Kaya's burial or our safety. I glanced at my silent mother who looked ill with grief and worry.

"I'm sorry to have inconvenienced you. Please accept my apology." With Kaya gone, I had no desire to provoke my father, or to explain my decision. "When will you leave for Cusco?"

Apparently satisfied with my contrition, he replied, "Now that you've returned, we'll leave in the morning. You should have celebrated with the visitors instead of disappearing. This was your last opportunity to socialize with the distant people." He was right, of course. It was unfortunate, but it was better to be absent than to publicly display my grief for a forbidden woman.

"I'll have to gain their trust individually as we encounter them in the north." The circumstances might require me to command them in battle without having earned their respect, but at least I wouldn't have lost it. "Will I see you before you leave?"

"We are concluding Inti Raymi this evening with the final feast. Rest until then and join us after sunset." Huayna Capac turned and headed toward the staircase leading to the palace. Trying to conceal her sorrow, my mother glanced at Tinkha standing beside Pacas before following my father.

I crossed the sacred plaza to the crowd surrounding Atuk as Riku examined the angry bruise on his shoulder. He gently probed the injury and asked Atuk to lift his arm in various ways. "You were very lucky. No bones are broken. You'll be sore, but with exercise, you'll recover completely. Take him back to your house and make him comfortable." Riku signaled Tucu while Ixiamas and Riku helped Atuk to his feet. With Tucu supporting him, Atuk hobbled toward the staircase.

I stood beside Pacas, noting the piles of offerings still filling the Temple of Inti and the sacrificial fire before it. "Why weren't these all burned?"

"They've burned from first light until sunset since . . ." he paused, "the winter solstice. They're just not finished yet." He turned to face me, his eyes filled with relief. "I'm glad you're back. Salcantay is a formidable mountain."

I nodded. "And yet, it was so peaceful on the snowfields. It's truly a sacred resting place worthy of three remarkable women." My vivid memory of Kaya's burial site seemed close enough to touch. Shaking off the image, I added, "Inti must have been protecting us during the disaster. We all could have been killed."

"I think Riku helped you too. He and Ixiamas both started chanting before the earth began to move and kept it up all day."

It hadn't occurred to me that they felt it too. I saw no damage and asked what happened. "People started running everywhere, and a few suffered minor injuries. A few of the temporary buildings fell, but there is a serious problem. The water in the city flows from deep within the mountains. Now it only trickles through the channels. There isn't enough to support the city, much less irrigate the crops during a dry season." He tipped his head toward Riku and Ixiamas. "They asked Inti to return the water, and others are searching for alternative sources."

Pacas and I considered various solutions, but nothing arose they hadn't already discussed.

The evening celebration was spectacular. Adding light and warmth for the jubilant guests, great fires surrounded the plaza, while *chicha* flowed abundantly, and delicacies from across the empire created an exotic table. A genuine gratitude and generous spirit infected every conversation, and I soon found myself laughing and enjoying the company of the empire's elite. Apu Tacana from Quito knew of our plans to travel north and invited us to join them. Curaca Checa expected to march with my father to Tomebamba and asked me to describe the city. Pacas described the road to the north to several men from Lake Titicaca and the western coast. By the end of the evening, I too enthusiastically anticipated our departure. Although no less painful, Kaya's sacrifice and the trek to Mount Salcantay seemed slightly remote, as though it were a bad dream.

My parents and most of the remaining guests left late the following morning. Still regal, but without the flamboyance of the procession to Machu Picchu, my father was the last to mount his litter. I stayed with Pacas, Tinkha, and the priests of Machu Picchu while Huayna Capac stood on his litter and faced the parade behind him. He lifted his scepter, and after silence drifted across the crowded plaza, he concluded the festival. "Inti is pleased with his children's offerings, and your commitment to follow his path. Never forget this celebration. Praise Inti forever."

"Praise Inti!" "Praise Inti!" The chant rose and echoed through the crowd.

The Inca sat on the chair of his litter and leaned forward to call me. "Perhaps now you realize how important it was for Inti Raymi to take place as planned."

I nodded and he continued, "I'll see you next year in Tomebamba after you and Apu Tacana scout the river north of Quito. Go with Inti, my son."

"Thank you, father." To my surprise, I replied without anger.

On his signal, his carriers started toward the city gate. Behind him, my mother sat on her litter with Tinkha's hand in hers. "Take care of Pacas. He's a good man, worthy of your devotion." She paused, and I again I saw the tender love for Tinkha I first noticed at her wedding. "You did excellent work as a Mamacona, I'll miss you."

Tinkha blushed, still unaccustomed to her new position. "Thank you for being such a good teacher. Your lessons will always guide me." My mother, the queen who only speaks of happiness, sighed deeply as a tear ran down her cheek, and she signaled her carriers to lift her. Rigidly seated in her chair, she followed my father to Cusco without looking back. She obviously hadn't been told that my father knew about Secret. I smiled to think how pleased she would be to claim Secret openly as her daughter.

Since the men of Quito planned to leave in the morning, we spent the day arranging for our departure. In the evening, Pacas, Tinkha, Tucu, and I were invited to eat with Atuk, Riku, and Ixiamas. Instead of the noisy celebration of the previous evening, we quietly dined in the comfort of friendship. I held no resentment for Riku; in fact I only regretted his advancing age. Tucu and Atuk sat next to each other and entertained us with stories of growing up in the shadow of the empire's greatest diviner. Some funny, some sad, all were retold with the simplicity and innocence of childhood. Riku and Ixiamas sat together, satisfied with the meal, the students, and their friendship. The evening passed quickly, and it was late before we parted company.

I rose before dawn and climbed the stairs to Intihuatana for the last time. While I sat in darkness, I imagined the high peaks of Salcantay Mountain emerging from the emerald sky with their dazzling white silhouette. No place could better cradle my lovely Kaya. I could almost see her walking across the mountain snow, her long black hair drifting in the breeze behind her. She was happy now, content to roam the mountains and the skies. As if to affirm my thoughts, the sun peaked over the mountains and ignited the gold Intihuatana. I was sure Inti was telling me he was pleased with his children. Finally the sun climbed entirely above the mountains and exposed the most remarkable sunrise ever. A streak of yellow light flanked each side of the brilliant sun and as it rose higher, the reflections drew closer to the sun as if Inti was drawing his women, my Kaya, closer to him.

"Machu Picchu is filled with ancient magic," Riku whispered.

I hadn't heard him approach, but in this mystical place his appearance didn't startle me. "Yes, indeed. I understand why Kaya chose to stay."

"But you must leave," he completed my thoughts. "Your empire is beyond everything you can see from here." He put his hand on my shoulder as we faced the sun. "Go with the strength of an Inca, but carry the wonder of this place in your heart."

We stood silently together as the sun rose and its reflections faded. "Will you leave too?" I asked.

"No, I am an old man with modest needs. Even if the water doesn't return, there is enough for a small group. Your father has agreed to support Atuk and me, so we can stay until I die. It was fortunate that Atuk wasn't hurt more seriously, or I would have been forced to leave."

A cool breeze rose out of the valley below. "And Kaya. Will you try to make contact?"

"Yes, we'll continue. Atuk and Kaya greatly expanded their skills during the last few months. I'm confident he'll be successful, even without me. Ask Tucu. He'll be able to follow our progress."

We stood together and listened to the city welcome the morning. "We're almost ready to leave," Tucu enthusiastically pronounced as he bounded toward us. "The entire Quito delegation is in the main plaza. Tinkha even has our breakfast waiting. Are you ready?"

I looked around one last time, and together we descended to the main plaza to share our last meal. Even before we finished eating, the inevitable parting began. Like flames lifting off a burning log, our thoughts turned to the journey ahead. Finally ready to leave, I approached Riku standing between Ixiamas and Atuk. His gentle, deep eyes were filled with the wisdom of age and the innocent hope of youth. No words could adequately express my affection for this man who had helped me so many times, and ultimately was forced to take my sister. He spoke easily with the kindness that always surrounded him. "If you trust Inti to send you friends to help you, you'll be a great ruler. Remember, a true friend can stand before you, or in your heart. You're never really alone."

Riku's unfailing ability to recognize a quintessential mystery still amazed me. I knew he'd exposed my ultimate fear. "We will soon endure a bloody war and the return of our creator. In the face of extreme uncertainty, I am resolved to be a great Inca, and I'm certain my trusted friends, and Kaya, will guide me. Even so, I must face this world and the Upper World alone, as does everyone."

Understanding the paradox, he smiled and placed his hand on my shoulder. "Until we meet again, my friend, go in peace."

Glossary

Alpaca Domesticated relative to the camel standing five feet (1.5 m) to the top of its head with excellent fleece. Well adapted to high altitude mountains.

Amauta Historian, singer and actor, responsible for exactly remembering and reciting or singing the official history, usually a book-length verse.

Antisuyu The eastern quarter of the Inca Empire with boundaries extending roughly northeast and southeast from Cusco, including Machu Picchu. Except for the Urubamba River valley, this region, primarily the eastern slope of the Andes, had little arable land. It was prized for the tropical crops, most notably cotton, tropical fruits, and coca, which could not be grown at higher elevations. Also a source of gold and feathers. The Incas had minimal influence in the jungle below about 4000 feet (1500 m).

Aporucos Sacred white llamas, specially bred, fed and groomed before being used in the most important religious ceremonies.

Ayahuasca Hallucinogen used for divining. Made primarily from the Amazonian vine, Banisteriopsis Caapi. Three or four other ingredients allowed digestion and enhanced hallucinogenic potency.

Ayllu An extended family related by paternal lineage, used here exclusively to refer to the lineage of the Incas.

Canari(s) The People of the Tomebamba area who peacefully joined the Inca Empire under the reign of Topa Inca.

Capac Raymi Royal Festival held for an entire month (December) around the summer solstice during which boys became men through a series of trials and celebrations.

Casana Thing which freezes, Huayna Capac's palace in Cusco located on northwest side of Haucaypata. It was called Casana because it was so beautiful, people stood and stared at the building. Home to Huayna Capac, Coya Cusirimay, his second wife, Cepi Chimpu and Ninan. Sinchi Roca, his wives Pilpintu and Huarmi, and Pacas also lived in the palace. A large complex of buildings with room for entertaining and housing large numbers of guests, and reputed to have encompassed a small lake.

Chanca The people and place where they lived. Located west and northwest of Cusco.

Chaska The planet Venus. Revered by the Incas as one of five stars that move. That is, the five planets visible to the naked eye, including Mercury, Mars, Jupiter and Saturn. Particularly important because Venus is seen close to the sun as the morning star and the evening star.

Chicha Beer made by fermenting maize in combination or separately from a variety of other grains or fruits. Consumed regularly by the Incas and in great quantities at festivals by everyone.

Chinchasuyu The northern quarter of the Inca Empire, with boundaries running roughly northwest and northeast from Cusco, including Peru north of approximately Lima from the Pacific coast to the eastern slope of the Andes and all of Ecuador from coast to eastern slope. Agriculturally based cities existed in the southern coastal desert along the river valleys descending from the Andes. In Ecuador, the coast becomes swampy mangroves. In the highlands, agriculture varies with altitude and latitude, and is centered in the wide river valleys. Population is dispersed along the arable stretches, with llama grazing extending the useable land. A source of copper, emeralds, and quartz.

Chuno A small potato grown at high elevations. After being dug, the potato is left in the field to dry in the desiccating cold. When dried, it can be stored for long periods. Chuno retains a chewy texture after cooking.

Coca Erythoxylon Coca- The shrub was considered sacred and was cultivated at low altitudes. The leaves were chewed to relieve fatigue caused by high altitude. This is the same plant used to make cocaine. In its unrefined state, the physical effects are mild.

Cochamama Goddess of the ocean. Life giver and guardian of sea creatures.

Collasuyu The south quarter of the Inca Empire with boundaries extending roughly southeast and southwest from Cusco, including Lake Titicaca, Cochabamba, Bolivia, and Santiago, Chile. It extended from the Pacific Ocean to the eastern slopes of the Andes, including parts of Peru, Bolivia, Chile and Argentina. Because it offered a permanent water source and a moderating effect on the weather, the Lake Titicaca region was inhabited very early and was a heavily populated agricultural area during Inca rule. Along the coast heading south, the river valleys were also ancient centers for cultivation.

This region includes the Atacama Desert and other sources of Lapis Lazuli, a gem stone.

Collca The constellation Pleiades or commonly called the seven sisters, is a tight cluster of seven stars. Known to the Incas as the mother of all stars. It first appears at predawn in the southern hemisphere in early June.

Coricancha The primary temple in Cusco with gold-covered walls. Contained massive gold and silver statues, such as life-size likenesses of stalks of maize decorated with jewels. Inside the structure there were individual temples dedicated to each of the gods and decorated appropriately.

Coya Queen. Wife to the Inca and in some cases his sister. The queen was responsible for the Mamaconas.

Cumbi Supple and lightweight like silk, and yet a very warm cloth made from vicuna wool. Worn by the Inca and on very special occasions by other high-ranking Incas. Also burned as an offering.

Cuntisuyu The western quarter of the Inca Empire with boundaries extending roughly northwest and southwest from Cusco, including the current city of Arequipa, Peru. The smallest of the four quarters, it includes high sierra and coastal deserts crossed by rivers extending to the Pacific. Agriculture centered in the river basins and occasional fog moistened upland slopes. In the mountains, there was some agriculture and herding along the rivers. Silver and other minerals were also available in this area. Ocean resources were used extensively.

Curaca(s) Leader(s). Usually Inca or at least trained by the Incas to rule a city-state within the empire.

Cusco Navel. The center of the Inca Empire. Located in a river valley at 10,500 feet (3,200 m), it housed at least the last five Incas before the arrival of the Spaniards, as well as the Inca noblemen. It was also the religious center. The city was fabulously rich with architecturally beautiful palaces, gardens with fountains, stone streets, solid gold and silver statues, and gold-plated platforms and religious buildings. One of the first eye- witnesses briefly describes the lavish use of precious metals and jewels, and then refrains from continuing claiming no one would believe him if he described every detail.

Cuyo(s) Inhabitants in the area of Pisac in the Sacred Valley defeated by Pachacuti.

Earplugs When an Inca boy became a man, his earlobes were pierced. In time the holes stretched to hold ever-larger gold plugs. Eventually, the plug supported a decorated plate that entirely covered each ear. To help support the weight, there was often a band that fit over the ear like present day glasses. All Inca men wore earplugs in public as a statement of their status.

Guancabelica A mountain people originally from an area approximately 200 miles (300 km) northwest of Cusco.

Hanan One of two governing groups of the Inca people responsible for maintaining order in the empire. They had civil judicial authority, as well as military force for waging war within and outside the empire. Also responsible for assessing and collecting all taxes needed to support the military according to the Inca's demands. Commanded by the Inca through a hierarchy similar to the modern military.

Haucaypata The central plaza in Cusco estimated to be a half mile on a side with the stone-lined channels of the Huatanay River running through it. Some sources claim the entire area was covered with hard-packed white sand from the ocean. It was the site of many religious festivals as well as an area for public gathering. The Incas' palaces surrounded the plaza. Currently, the Plaza de Armas stands on roughly half of the original plaza.

Huayna Picchu Young Mountain- creates the northern barrier to the city of Machu Picchu, forcing the Urubamba River to bend around the mountain and the city situated on the saddle 500 feet (150 m) below its peak.

Hurin One of two governing groups of the Inca people- responsible for all religious ceremonies whose primary function was to regulate the agrarian year and assure the blessings of the gods. Also responsible for assessing and collecting all taxes needed to support the religion according to the Inca's demands. Ruled by the Inca through a structure similar to the Roman Catholic Church.

Ilyapa God of Thunder, and indirectly rain. Created by Viracocha, highly important to an agrarian society that is subject to el Niño related floods and droughts.

Inca The Emperor and a direct descendent of Inti, the god of the sun. Absolute ruler of the empire. Also, anyone of the small tribe of agrarian people located in the Cusco valley before the rise of the empire. In the time of Huayna Capac, they were the elite in the Hurin and Hanan groups, with an estimated population of 40,000.

Inca Empire During Huayna Capac's reign, the empire stretched from the present day northern border of Ecuador to Santiago, Chile, a distance of over 3,400 miles (5500 km), and extended from the Pacific Ocean to the eastern slopes of the Andes. The population of the empire was estimated at ten million, with the Inca people accounting for a mere 40,000. Within the empire there were 18,000 to 25,000 miles (30,000 to 40,000 km) of stone-paved roads that were wide enough for six people to walk abreast even at mountain passes. Along the arterial roads, a series of runners were said to be able to carry a message 155 miles (250 km) per day. In the arid climate, irrigation systems extended to a large proportion of the cropland, including the stonewall terraces on mountain slopes. By a sophisticated system of reciprocity, the ruling class extracted a tax in both goods and labor. In return, it provided food and other necessities during times of want, most commonly droughts caused by El

Niño, as well as protection from invaders or insurgents. While the sun was central to the Inca religion, other religious beliefs were tolerated and sometimes incorporated into the primary religion.

Inti Sun God. He lived in the sun and was the benefactor of the Inca people. Inti interceded for them with Viracocha, in a manner similar to Jesus Christ interceding with God for Roman Catholics.

Inti Raymi Sun Festival. Held on the winter solstice (June), this festival is a plea to Inti to return from the north so the crops will flourish.

Intihuatana Believed to be a point of contact for Inti on earth. This massive monument is carved in the native stone at the highest point in the city of Machu Picchu. The base is large enough for the Inca to sit, and at its center, a roughly square pinnacle rises approximately six feet. The pinnacle and base were thought to be covered with sheets of gold. There were similar monuments in other cities that were destroyed by the Spaniards.

Intipuku Gate of Inti—The main gate to the city of Machu Picchu, set in a high pass about two miles (3 km) from the city through which the sun sets during the winter solstice.

Killa Goddess of the Moon and Inti's wife—protectorate of women and fertility.

Litter A platform with a chair or bench built on long poles and carried by four or eight men. Used only by the Inca or Inca people, unadorned litters were used for daily activities. For festivals and special occasions, the litters were elaborately decorated with a canopy, wood carvings, paint, gold, feathers, shells and other items of importance to the individual or region.

Llama A mild mannered, domesticated relative to the camel standing six feet (1.8 m) tall to its head with coarse fleece used for blankets and everyday clothing. The only beast of burden in the Inca Empire besides its people, a llama is capable of carrying 80 pounds (36 kg) in mountainous terrain and will refuse to carry more. Also used for food, its meat is dried to make charqui (jerky).

Machu Picchu Ancient Mountain. The white granite mountain southeast of the city of the same name. The city is thought to be founded by Pachacuti for multiple purposes: escape from the cold winters of Cusco, fort to defend against invasion from the jungle, religious sanctuary, and oversight of crops of semitropical plants like coca. The city rests on a mountain saddle at about 8,000 ft (2,400 m) and is surrounded on three sides by the Urubamba River 2,000 ft (600 m) below it. Population of the city at the time of Huayna Capac is estimated at 1,000-2,000.

Mamacona(s) The chaste girl(s) and women of the religion who are responsible for making ceremonial beer, weaving cloth for sacrifice, and other endeavors for the religion.

Mayu River. Can refer to a river on earth. More commonly, the river of stars in the sky, that is, the Milky Way.

Mita The labor tax placed on every family. The tax could require a certain amount of cloth to be woven by women, or the inscription of the men as soldiers or laborers on civil projects for three months to two years.

Mitima(s) People who were moved from their homeland and resettled in another area. This could happen by choice, but more typically it refers to conquered people who were divided into smaller groups, isolated from one another, and therefore could more easily be controlled.

Mullu A pink shell or beads made from it. Most likely, the shell was from a bivalve mollusk that lives in the relatively warm waters near Tumbes, Peru.

Pachamama Goddess of the Earth. Provides the riches of the land necessary for abundant crops and was very sacred to the farmers.

Pisac(s) Place or the people who live there. Located in the Sacred Valley, a section of the Urubamba River valley approximately 35 miles (56 km) northeast of Cusco.

Punchau A highly revered icon in the Coricancha representing Inti. The design was believed to be a large solid gold circle with a face on it and gold rays emanating from the face. The piece was elaborately decorated with jewels.

Quechua The language of the Inca. Although there were many local languages, Quechua expanded with the empire and became the official language, spoken and understood by most of the people.

Quinoa A common but highly valued grain grown in the high Andes to 12,500 ft (3,800 m). It is one of a very limited number of plants in the world that contain all the amino acids, the building blocks of proteins, needed by man.

Quipu A long rope with many smaller strings tied to it. Based on the decimal system, numbers were recorded by the number and types of knots tied in the string. Different colored strings designated different types of information. Each quipu recorded a specific event, for example, the number of men involved in a military campaign, or the tributes paid by various members of a city. Roughly equivalent in function to accounting ledgers.

Quipucamayo An accountant, the person who kept the quipu up to date. Many types of data were maintained including a census for the empire, contents of all storehouses, due and collected taxes, military goods and soldiers, religious and agrarian calendars and associated astronomical events, historical war data, and trade agreements.

Quispiguanca Huayna Capac's country palace located in the Sacred Valley, approximately halfway between Cusco and Machu Picchu.

Quito(s) The people and city where they lived. Located at the current site of Quito, Ecuador.

Sacred Valley The river valley of the Vilcanota River which descends from the rugged mountains between Cusco and Lake Titicaca to become the more temperate Urubamba River situated in a wide, fertile valley north of Cusco. The

Incas each built country palaces along the Urubamba River.

Sacsahuaman A massive fort and temple on the edge of Cusco built during Huayna Capac's reign in the shape of a puma's head. The Spaniards disassembled much of it to build houses and cathedrals in Cusco. Today, a twenty five foot tall, fitted-stone wall remains. A single stone in the wall is estimated to weigh 300 tons. The zigzag wall is said to be the puma's teeth.

Tiwantisuyu The Inca Empire, literately, the four quarters of the empire. The boundaries of the four quarters roughly mirror the position of the Milky Way at the solstices.

Tomebamba The city of Huayna Capac's birth. Topa Inca brought this region into the empire. At and altitude of 7,755 feet (2350 m) and just 220 miles (350 km) from the equator, the climate is pleasant year round. It did not see major growth until near the end of Huayna Capac's reign. Currently known as Cuenca, Ecuador.

Torreon A nearly circular fitted-stone temple in Machu Picchu used for astronomical measurements, most notably the winter solstice.

Tumbe(s) The people and city where they live. Located on the ocean and extending into the mountains in Northern Peru.

Urubamba River The primary river of the Sacred Valley. It flows northwest from the mountains south of Cusco to beyond Machu Picchu. It joins the Ucayali River at the eastern base of the Andes, passes Iquitos, Peru and eventually flows into the Amazon River.

Vicuna Undomesticated relative to the camel standing four feet (1.2 m) tall to the head with exceptionally fine fleece. Fiber diameter is roughly one third the diameter of human hair. Herds were captured, sheared and released at altitudes ranging from 10,000 to 20,000 feet (3,050 to 6100 m), yielding eleven ounces (320 g) of wool per animal per year.

Vilca(s) The mountain source of the Vilcanota River which becomes the Urubamba River and the people who live there. Vilca also lived in the range of mountains west of Cusco.

Viracocha The supreme god and creator of the sky and world. He created all life while he walked on earth as a man and then returned to the Upper World by following a river in the northwest out to sea. There was a closely held prophecy that he would return to earth and destroy the Inca Empire during the reign following Huayna Capac. According to Spanish historians, Huayna Capac repeated the prophecy on his death bed.

About the Author

K.L. Smith is an adventurer, spiritualist, gardener, time traveler, music lover, and a published scientist. Fascinated by the Incas and Machu Picchu since childhood, she has traveled in several South American countries while doing research for *Bound for Inca Snows* and its sequel. She recently abandoned corporate America to pursue a career as a writer and an MFA in creative writing. Currently living in the Midwest, she and her cherished husband have explored remote corners on every continent.